W9-BAA-583

"A riveting tale of consummate evil. A complex, imaginative plot, strong imagery and well developed characters that will delight the horror fan looking for a fine chiller."
—*VOYA* on *The Burning*

The Chosen Child

Graham Masterton

TOR®

A TOM DOHERTY ASSOCIATES BOOK
NEW YORK

This is a work of fiction. All the characters and events portrayed in this book are either products of the author's imagination or are used fictitiously.

THE CHOSEN CHILD

Copyright © 1997 by Graham Masterton

First published in the United Kingdom in 1997 by Mandarin Paperbacks.

A Tor Book
Published by Tom Doherty Associates, LLC
175 Fifth Avenue
New York, NY 10010

www.tor.com

Tor® is a registered trademark of Tom Doherty Associates, LLC.

ISBN: 0-812-54533-8
Library of Congress Catalog Card Number: 00-031685

First Tor edition: December 2000
First mass market edition: January 2002

Printed in the United States of America

0 9 8 7 6 5 4 3 2 1

AUTHOR'S NOTE

By 29 July 1944, the Red Army had reached Praga, on the eastern bank of the Vistula, in sight of the German-occupied city of Warsaw. Radio messages were sent from Moscow to the Polish Home Army: "People of Warsaw! To arms! Help the Red Army ... show the way! The hour of action has struck ... by fighting in the streets of Warsaw we shall bring nearer the moment of ultimate liberation!"

On 1 August, at five o'clock in the afternoon, in response to these messages, and to orders from the Polish government in exile in London, the Home Army rose up against the Germans, and managed to seize more than two thirds of the city in three days. There were nearly 40,000 of them, with 210,000 unarmed helpers, but they were short of weapons and supplies, and the Russians stayed where they were, on the eastern bank of the river, so that the Home Army found themselves fighting alone against overwhelming odds.

Molotov denied that any calls to arms had ever been broadcast from Moscow, although the Russians' motives in hanging back were obvious. Stalin regarded the Home Army as "power-seeking criminals," and he wanted to see them broken by the Germans before taking Warsaw and installing his own communist regime.

The price that was paid was terrible beyond belief. German reinforcements poured into the city, under the command of SS Lieutenant-General Erich von Bach-Zelewski, whose forces included the Dirlewanger penal brigade and 6,000 Russian defectors, who enthusiastically obeyed Himmler's instructions to destroy "tens of thousands."

Gradually, the Poles were forced back into shrinking pockets of territory. They had no food, little water, and dysentery was rife. Young children crawled miles through the city's slimy sewers carrying messages; and on 24 September, the 2,500 insurgents left alive in the Old Town had to escape to the northern suburbs by the same route.

The German advance was relentless and sadistic. Rape and looting were widespread. Doctors and nurses in hospitals were all shot on the spot. Thousands were herded into Warsaw's parks and executed.

After the Home Army surrendered, however, the Germans recognized them as prisoners of war, and more than 15,000 of them were marched away to prison camps. People knelt as they passed, which shocked even the insurgents themselves. "In Poland, you knelt only for the Holy Sacrament."

1

Her bus came grinding to a halt at the bus stop and he said, "One last kiss," not knowing that it really would be.

She laughed and gave him a flurried little peck on the cheek. He took hold of her hand as she started to climb the stairs of the bus and tried to pull her back.

"Come on, I don't have all night!" the bus driver snapped at her.

The doors shut with a sharp pneumatic hiss, and Jan was left at the kerbside while the bus bellowed away to Mokotow in a thick cloud of diesel smoke. He briefly glimpsed Hanna waving at him, but then the bus was lost in the traffic, and she was gone.

A small fat woman in a headscarf came hurrying up to him, puffing and sweating. "Was that the 131?" she demanded, as if it were his fault that it had left without her.

"Don't worry. There'll be another one in five or ten minutes."

"That's what you say!" she protested. "It's worse than the old days!"

He laid a hand on her shoulder and gave her a wide, movie-idol grin. "Where are you going?" he asked her.

"Czerniakowska. What's it to you?"

He turned his back to her, crouched down, and extended his hands behind him. "Hop on. I'll carry you there myself."

This enraged her even more. *"Idiota!"* she spat at him. "What do you take me for? I'll give you 'hop on!' " But he was in such a good mood this evening that he didn't care. He left her at the bus stop and started making his way north on Marszalkowska with the confident, unhurried stroll of a man for whom everything is going right.

It was just past nine o'clock on a warm and windy August night, and the center of Warsaw was brightly lit and busy. Taxis banged and jolted past him on worn-out suspensions, and half-empty buses blared diesel into the air as they headed out for the suburbs of Zoliborz and Wola and east across the river to Praga. Newspapers were tossed by the wind and tangled around the legs of the people walking past the brightly-lit shops on Jerozolimskie Avenue.

That afternoon. Jan's producer Zbigniew Debski had told him that his idea for a new weekly satirical program had been approved, and that Radio Syrena was going to increase his salary to 950 zlotys a month. Jan was going to have enough money to save up for a car, and the chance to do what he did best, which was waspish, irreverent investigations into political scandals. Zbigniew had celebrated by bringing out vodka and platefuls of chocolate biscuits. At least he hadn't hugged him and kissed him, which he was occasionally inclined to do. Zbigniew had a mustache like a bramble-bush and boar-like body odor.

Best of all, though, Hanna had at last agreed to move in with him (her eyes shyly shining because she thought it was so daring). On Saturday he would borrow his friend Henryk's van and transport all of her belongings from her parents' apartment on Goworka to his own new apartment overlooking the river at the Slasko-Dubrowski bridge. He knew that Hanna's mother would complain, but mostly because the family would now be deprived of Hanna's income. Although she had graduated as a doctor of microbiology she worked as a fashion buyer at Sawa department store, and made almost as much money as Jan did, 650 zlotys a month.

Hanna's mother might miss the money, but she couldn't deny that he and Hanna were suited. They were both twenty-five years old; they both liked Blur and REM; they both enjoyed dancing and nightclubbing and pizzas and staying up most of the night talking about what they would do when Jan was famous. They could both collapse into helpless laughter at the slightest provocation. Their only difference was their complexion and their looks: Hanna was blond and round-faced and a little plump. Jan was thin as a rail, with dark cropped hair and eyebrows that looked like children's drawings of two rooks flying over a potato field. At least, that was his own description of them.

High over Marszalkowska towered the Palace of Culture and Science, over 230 meters high, with 3,000 rooms, a gigantic monument to Stalinist architecture, as if a baker of impossibly grandiose wedding cakes had been commissioned to design a rocket ship. By day it was gray: by night it was luridly lit with amber lights.

Jan reached the corner of Krowleska and waited to cross. A group of teenagers were larking about, passing around a bottle of vodka and cans of 7-Up. One of them was playing air guitar and singing "Born in the USA" in a thin breathless whine.

Most of this corner was boarded up with high, red-painted hoardings. A huge sign on the Marszalkowska side showed an artist's impression of a twelve-story hotel, a tall column of glass and stainless steel—*"Warsaw Senate Hotel, A Joint Development of Senate International Hotels and Vistula Bank Kreditowy."* Up until a month ago, the old Zaluski-Orbis Hotel had stood here, a relic of the worst that the Communist years had offered in the way of dingy accommodation, poor food and surly service. Jan had described it on his radio show as "Heartbreak Hotel." But now the whole of the center of Warsaw was being regenerated with glossy new stores and shiny new offices. Sheraton had just completed a new hotel on Plac Trzech Kryzyzy, and the Senate Hotel would be the next.

The lights changed and Jan was about to step off the kerb when he heard a faint but very high-pitched scream. He stopped, and turned, and listened. The teenagers were all crossing the street, laughing and looning around. He called out, "Hey! Did you hear—?" but it was obvious that they hadn't heard him, let alone a distant scream.

He waited, and then he was sure that he could hear another scream, and then another, although a bus roared past him and blotted it out. He was sure that the screams had come from somewhere behind the red hoardings. They had sounded like a woman, or a child, although he couldn't be sure.

He walked back along the hoardings, peering between the cracks. There were one or two knotholes which he might have been able to see through, but they were too high up. All he could make out was a single arc lamp, which presumably had been left shining for security.

At the very end of the hoardings he came to a crude door. It must have been padlocked at one time, but now it was fastened only with a twisted length of wire. Jan stood looking at it and wondered what to do. If somebody was hurt or needed help, he really ought to take a look. Or maybe not. Maybe he ought to call 997 and leave it to the police.

As usual, there were no police on the streets, although a stocky man in a blue uniform and a peaked cap was approaching him, carrying a briefcase.

"Excuse me," Jan said. "I think there's something going on in here. I heard somebody screaming."

The man stopped and doubtfully stuck out his bottom lip. You would have thought that he didn't understand plain Polish.

"Two or three screams," Jan insisted. "It sounded like a child."

The man cupped one hand to his ear, then shook his head. "I can't hear anything."

"I wasn't sure what to do. You're wearing a uniform."

"I work at the Palace of Culture. Doorman."

The man waited for a while, then shrugged and started to walk away.

"Listen!" Jan called after him. "I'll go in—you call the police!"

He didn't know whether the man heard him or not: he kept on walking and turned the corner into Krowleska. Shit, Jan thought. Thanks for your help.

He tried untwisting the wire. It was stiff, heavy-duty stuff, and whoever had twisted it up had obviously used a pair of pliers. He gashed his thumb, but he wrapped a handkerchief around it and continued trying to pull the wire free. A few people stopped for a moment and stared at him while he was doing it, although nobody intervened, except a thin youth with spiky hair and the beginnings of a silky black mustache. He stood close to Jan in his jeans and his denim jacket, and lit a Marlboro.

"You're wasting your time, man," he said. "That site was stripped weeks ago."

Jan glanced at him. "I thought I heard somebody inside. There were screams, two or three of them."

"Cats, probably."

"Well, I just want to make sure."

"I thought you were scrounging for salvage. I found a bronze fireplace in there. I got 400 zlotys for it."

Jan pulled at the lapels of his bottle-green suede jacket. "Do I look like I'm scavenging for salvage?"

"I don't know. It takes all sorts. Do you want a hand?"

The youth took a Swiss Army knife out of his jacket, inserted one of the blades between the twisted wires, and slowly levered them apart.

"Thanks," said Jan. "I'll give you a mention on the radio for that."

The youth looked perplexed.

Jan held out his hand and said, "Jan Kaminski, Radio Syrena."

"Really? That's cool. I'm Marek: but most of my friends call me Kurt—you know, after Kurt Cobain."

Jan tugged open the door in the hoarding, and stepped into the demolition site. The Zaluski-Orbis had been knocked down to ground level, and all that was left were its dark cavernous basements, like entrances to the underworld. The arc lamp gave the site the brilliant, artifical appearance of a deserted movie-set. Weeds and nettles rustled in the wind.

Over to their left-hand side, a Russian-built crane and a caterpillar excavator were parked, silent mechanical dinosaurs. On the right-hand side were two temporary wooden huts with tarpaper roofs, and a stack of drainage pipes. A latrine stood at a dangerous tilt, and somebody had scrawled on the side "The Leaning Tower of Pisa." There was a strong smell of building-dust, and damp, and something else, too. Something sweet and ripe that clung in the nostrils.

"Sewers," sniffed Marek.

Jan stood still and listened. He thought he could hear somebody crying. A thin, pathetic wailing cry—the way that children cry when they're utterly exhausted, or women cry when they feel that everything is absolutely hopeless. The traffic noise was slightly less deafening inside the hoarding, but all the same it was difficult to tell if it was really somebody crying, or whether it was nothing more than the wind blowing across the hollow piping.

"Can you hear that?" he asked Marek.

Marek sucked the last hot smoke from his cigarette and flicked it away. "I don't know. Maybe there's something."

Cautiously, they approached the brink of the excavated basements, and peered down into the darkness. It was so black down there that they couldn't see anything at all, but they could feel a soft, rotten draft blowing into their faces. And yes, they could hear crying, although now it was even fainter.

"You're right," said Marek. "There is something down there. But it sounds more like a cat to me."

"I wish we had a flashlight."

"There's probably one in those huts."

"Oh, yes, and how do you propose to get it? They're both padlocked."

Marek looked around and then picked up a heavy chunk of broken brick. He went right up to the door of the nearest hut, and bashed the padlock with it, three or four times. The padlock sprang open and dropped off.

"My grandfather showed me how to do that. He used to break into German food stores during the war."

"Sounds a handy kind of character to have around."

"Oh, he was, when he wasn't pissed. The trouble was, he was pissed twenty-three hours a day, and the rest of the time he had a hangover."

They swung open the door of the hut. Inside, the atmosphere was solid with sweat and stale tobacco smoke and the rank smell of demolition and disturbed soil. The light that shone through the dust-encrusted windows picked out a table crowded with dirty coffee mugs, coffee- stained newspapers and tin lids overflowing with cigarette butts. The walls were stuck with pinups. One huge-breasted girl sported a felt-tip mustache just like Lech Walesa and the caption "Miss Poland."

In the far corner, beside a scarred collection of hard

hats, Marek found a big canvas holdall. He rummaged through hammers, drill bits, crowbars and screwdrivers, and at last produced a flashlight. He shone it up into his own face, so that he looked like a thin grinning ghoul.

They walked back to the brink of the basement and shone the flashlight into the darkness. They saw cascades of rubble, and an overturned chair, but there was no sign of anything alive.

"Nothing," said Marek. "Just the wind, probably."

But as they were about to leave, they heard it again, the same crying, but much more distinctly this time.

"Are you sure it's a cat?" Jan asked. "Maybe we should call the police."

"Why don't we take a quick look? Here—we can climb down this brickwork."

"Well, I'll go down first," Jan volunteered. "You point the flashlight so that I can see where I'm going."

Jan knelt down on the concrete-strewn edge of the basement, and carefully felt behind him for toeholds. He found one, and then another, and the rubble seemed quite firm. He slid a little way, but he was able to snatch at a large chunk of brick and stop himself from slipping any further.

He swung his left foot from side to side, trying to find another toehold. His shoe caught on a protruding timber, partly wrapped in chicken wire. He tried his weight on it, and it seemed to hold, so he lowered himself a few feet further. He rested for a moment, clinging to the rubble, breathing heavily.

"Hey, are you all right?" called Marek.

"Fine. Just out of condition, that's all."

He thought he heard a whimpering sound; and then another. But after that, he could hear nothing but his own harsh panting, and—beyond the hoardings—the weary grinding of home-going traffic. He was beginning to think he was mad, climbing down here to look for a child who was probably a cat. Up above him,

Marek lit another cigarette and blew smoke into the evening breeze.

"Come on, now," he urged himself, under his breath. He swung his right foot around, but he couldn't feel another toehold anywhere. He would have to try sliding down the rubble a short way, in the hope that he would find one farther down.

His heart thumped and he could hear his blood pumping in his ears. He let himself slip half a meter, then a little further, his fingernails digging into the dust and the disintegrated mortar, trying to stop himself from sliding too far. Two or three meters down, he found another toehold, and then another. It couldn't be much further now. In fact, he was congratulating himself when a heavy lump of concrete gave way beneath his right foot and he found himself sliding uncontrollably down the rest of the rubble, clawing at anything he could.

He hit the basement floor so hard that he was convinced for a moment that he had broken his back. He lay there for a while, too jolted by his fall even to grunt.

"Hey—are you all right?" Marek called.

Jan managed to lift himself up onto one elbow, and then roll himself over into a kneeling position. "I don't think anything's broken," he called back. "Just winded."

He stood up and banged dust from the sleeves of his jacket. "I'm okay. I'm just going to take a look around."

He made a slow circuit of the basement, peering into crevices and alcoves and dust-filled ventilation shafts. On one wall, a torn sheet of wallpaper still fluttered. On another, there was a faded red scrawl "Basi," whatever that meant. Marek followed him from above, walking around the rim of the basement, shining the flashlight down from one side of the room to the other.

"See anything?" asked Marek.

"Not yet. But these basements are all joined together. I'm going to try the next one."

All of the basement doors had been torn off, so that he could see into the next room, where there were stacks of broken packing cases and collapsed wine racks.

He crunched across a thick carpet of brick dust and pulverized glass. Marek kept on flicking the flashlight around, but there was no sign of anything moving.

Jan looked upward, and began to wonder how he was going to climb out of here. Maybe there was a ladder in one of the other rooms, or a heap of rubble that was easier to scale. He walked through to the next room, and then turned right into the next, and it was then that he heard the crying again, much more clearly than he had before. It sounded as if it were coming from the opposite side of the room, so he whistled to Marek and called, "Over here! I can hear it again!"

Marek swept the flashlight beam across the basement floor and illuminated the opposite wall. It was still filled with shelves, some of them stacked with dusty jugs and empty pickle jars and rusted colanders. But right in the very corner of the room, there was a triangular hole in the floor, a little less than two meters across, and it was out of this hole that the crying was echoing.

Jan approached it, and peered down it, but it was too dark to see anything. The sewage-smelling breeze was coming from here, too; and he could hear water gurgling.

"It's here!" he called. "It's definitely here!"

"Is it a child, or what?"

"I don't know. Why don't you throw down the flashlight?"

"Do you want me to call the *gliniarze*?"

"Let me take a look first."

Marek came right to the edge of the basement and tossed down the flashlight. "Just be careful," he said.

Jan went back to the hole in the floor and shone the flashlight into it. He could see curved concrete piping, thick with whitish slime, and some broken rubble which must have fallen into the sewer when the excavator broke into it. He could also see a small knitted doll, with a serious, frowning face. She must have been wearing a maroon dress once, but now it was greasy and gray.

"Hallo!" he shouted. "Can you hear me? If you're trapped in there, I can go for help! Don't panic! I can find somebody to get you out!"

He paused. The crying went on, although it sounded further away now. The smell from the sewer was almost overwhelming, but he knelt down beside it and leaned over as far as he could.

"Hallo!" he shouted. "Hallo, down there! Can you hear me?"

There was another scream—high-pitched and drawn out. The sewer pipe distorted it so that it sounded like a slide whistle.

"Jesus," said Marek. "What the hell's happening down there?"

"I think I'd better find out," Jan told him. "You call the police, and the ambulance, too."

"You're not going down there?"

"I've got the flashlight."

"Yes, but supposing—"

"Supposing what?"

"I don't know. Supposing there's somebody down there?"

"Like who? It's only a kid. She's probably stuck, that's all."

Marek hesitated for a while. Then he said, "Okay. I'll call the *gliniarze*."

Jan took a deep breath, and then retched because of the smell. But he gripped the flashlight tighter, and made his way right to the very edge of the broken sewer. He knelt down, and cautiously backed his way

toward the hole, until he was able to swing his legs
down into it. The first thing he felt when he reached
the bottom of the pipe was cold sewage filling his
shoes: he hadn't realized it was going to be so deep.

"Shit," he said, under his breath.

The pipe was a little over one and three quarter meters in diameter, which gave him just enough room to
crouch his way along it. He took out his handkerchief
and tied it around his face like a bandit. He wished he
had some aftershave. Anything had to be better than
the smell of greasy human excrement. He couldn't
imagine how the Resistance had tolerated spending so
much time in the sewers during the war.

"Hallo!" he called. "Can you hear me! I'm coming
to rescue you! Just stay where you are! Don't move,
and keep on calling out to me!"

He listened, but there was no reply. Still—the child
hadn't sounded as if it were very far away, and how
complicated could the sewers be? They followed the
pattern of the streets, so they must be straightforward,
and there were dozens of manholes, in case he needed
to climb out of them somewhere else. With his head
bowed, he made his way along the pipe, his shoes
plashing in the sewage. The flashlight threw curved
patterns of light against curved concrete, and gremlin-
like shadows that hopped and danced with every step
he took.

"Hallo!" he kept on calling, and his voice boomed
back to him, filling his ears.

He turned awkwardly around to see how far he had
come. The arc lamp faintly illuminated the broken pipe
where he had entered. He felt as if he had been hunch-
ing his way along the sewer for at least five minutes,
but he had probably gone no further than crossing
Krowleska. His eyes were watering and his nose was
running, but he was beginning to grow accustomed to
the stench. It was worse when his uncle Henryk came
to stay, and spent twenty minutes perched on the toilet

every morning, reading *Gazeta Wyborcza* from cover to cover and filling the room with the stink of beer and yesterday's sauerkraut.

He carried on, grunting with effort. Every now and then he stopped to rest, and to call out, "I'm coming! Can you hear me? I'm coming!" His voice echoed and re-echoed until it was so distorted that it sounded as if somebody else were in the sewers, calling *him*.

After two hundred meters, the noise of running water began to grow louder. He crouched along a little further, and then abruptly the narrow pipe in which he had made his way from the demolition site opened out into a huge echoing concrete chamber, nearly twelve meters deep, with a curving channel of thick sewage gushing through the middle of it. Waste poured into here from all the main streets around here, and flowed off rapidly south-eastward toward the River Vistula.

Jan stood above the chamber, shining his flashlight into each of the arches. If he wanted to explore the sewers any further, he was going to have to wade knee-deep, and he wasn't going to attempt that without boots. He called out. "I'm here! I can't go any further! If you can hear me, tell me where you are!"

He waited, and listened, but all he could hear was the endless rushing of water. He didn't want to be cowardly, but he had come this far without finding anything, and only a saint or a madman would have carried on.

If there had been a child down here, he decided, it had obviously found its own way out.

He was about to turn back, however, when the sewage–filled channel below him suddenly churned. There was a moment's thrashing, and then a figure burst out of the water—a small figure plastered in gray—a figure that opened its mouth and screamed at him *aaaaaaaaahhhhhhhhh!*

Jan jerked back in terror, and jarred his shoulder against the sewer pipe. The figure was so thickly cov-

ered in sewage that it was impossible for him to tell
whether it was a boy or a girl. But there was one thing
he could tell: it had no arms. It had raised itself out of
the water on its knees, and now it was wagging itself
backward and forward and letting out bubble-filled
screams of unimaginable agony.

Jan screamed back at it, "Wait! Wait! I'm coming
to get you out! Wait!"

There was a flight of deeply-rusted rungs which led
down from his own sewer pipe to the bottom of the
chamber. He turned himself around and started to climb
down them. The figure kept on screaming and screaming; but before he was halfway down, the pipes let out
a huge gurgling gush, and hundreds of litres of fresh
sewage cascaded into the chamber, and swept the figure
into the channel, and under the nearest arch.

Jan clung onto the rungs while the chilly sewage
swallowed his feet and rushed around his knees. He
saw soggy rafts of toilet paper and swirls of every
imaginable shade of brown. He saw a drowned rat, too,
but no further sign of the figure that had risen up out
of the channel and screamed at him.

As quickly as he could, he climbed back up the ladder and into the pipe. He still couldn't really understand what he had seen. A child, with no arms; or a
dog, with no legs; or even a seal, maybe, that had found
its way into the sewers, from the river.

Coughing, he started to make his way back along the
sewer. All he wanted to do now was to get out of here.
His back was aching from bending over for so long.
His head was thumping. He felt a rising sense of panic,
as if the figure in the sewer had managed to wriggle
its way up the rusty rungs like the caterpillar man from
Freaks to follow him. He hopped, and crouched, and
hit his head again and again; and he kept thinking that
he must be nearly there, he must be nearly there. But
the sewer pipe seemed to have mysteriously length-

ened. He couldn't even see the hazy aura of the arc lamp.

After two or three minutes he had to stop, and bend over, his hands on his knees, trying to catch his breath. His stomach kept on tightening and he retched a long string of chocolate-streaked saliva, but that was all.

He dragged out his handkerchief and wiped his face. He told himself to calm down. That couldn't have been a child, back in the sewage chamber. It was a dog, most likely, that had accidentally strayed into a ventilation shaft or an outlet. How could a child get deep down into the sewers?

Whatever it was, it couldn't possibly be following him. It was mutilated, drowned, and washed away. All he had to do now was find his way out of this pipe and get himself cleaned up.

He started to crouch his way along again, sweeping the flashlight from side to side. He was worried that in his panic to escape he might have taken a wrong turning, a turning that had no way out. It was a nightmarish thought that he could spend weeks desperately trying to find his way out of an ever-narrowing labyrinth of sewers. He imagined being trapped in a narrow pipe right beneath the massive weight of the Palace of Culture and Science, his flashlight battery failing, and darkness closing in.

But it was only a few more minutes before he saw the dim light coming from the place where the pipe was broken, and he said his first prayer since his mother had died. "Holy Mother thank you for delivering me from harm. I beg your protection from despair, and from all evil things."

It was then that he heard the noise.

He stopped, and listened. At first, he couldn't make out anything but the trickling of water, and the soft, melancholy booming of air as huge drafts blew along the main sewers. They sounded like massive beasts, calling to each other.

But then he heard it again. A thick, leathery *shuffling* noise, as if somebody were dragging a soft but heavy bag along the sewer pipe.

He turned around, and shone his flashlight back the way he had come. It was difficult to see if there was anything there, because of all the shadows, and the scimitar-shaped reflections. But the odd thing was that the reflections seemed to stop, about fifty meters from where he was standing, and the sewage that flowed in herringbone patterns along the bottom gully no longer glittered. It looked as if something was actually blocking the tunnel. Something very big, and dark, that deadened all reflections and allowed no light to pass.

Something that made a shuffling noise, because it was coming his way.

Jan began to back away. He didn't like this at all. Maybe that small screaming figure in the sewage-chamber couldn't have come after him. But what was *this*?

He kept on backing and backing, shining the flashlight toward the shadowy shape that was following him. He tripped once or twice on uneven pipe joints, and he had to trail one hand along the wall of the sewer to guide himself even though he could feel that it was coated in excreted fat.

Anything big enough to block up the whole pipe couldn't move fast. That's what he reassured himself. But with a hundred meters still to go to reach the break in the pipe, he began to have the unnerving feeling that this thing was gaining on him. It might be heavy, but it moved with remarkable speed. He could hear the shuffling coming nearer and nearer, and it was almost like a train bearing down on him.

He stopped, one hand balancing him against the side of the pipe, and said "No!"—and then "No!" again, as if he could make this all stop happening simply by not believing in it.

It couldn't be true. He had heard all kinds of stories

about pets being flushed down toilets into the sewers, and growing to giant size on a rich diet of human excrement—alligators and turtles and even Christmas carp that nobody in the family could bear to kill. But they were stories, right? They were legends.

If this was anything, this was a man; and Jan could stand up to any man.

The shuffling slowed; but still it came nearer.

"Who are you?" Jan called. "Why are you following me?"

The shuffling was slower and slower; but still it came nearer.

"Can't you speak?" Jan demanded. "Who are you? Listen—you don't have to be frightened."

The shadowy thing was only a few meters away now, but Jan's flashlight was dimming, the bulb was little more than an orange wink, and the thing was so dark that it seemed to absorb light rather than reflect it.

Jan said, "What do you want? I'm not afraid of you."

He thought he could hear breathing, of a kind. Tuneless, patient breathing. Then he heard another shuffle, and a sound like an old, musty velvet curtain being slowly dragged down. There was a smell, too, which he could distinguish even above the cloying smell of sewage.

It was a smell like very bad meat; like rabbit that had been left hanging for too long.

"You're not frightening me," said Jan. "You're just a man."

All the same, he started to back away again, glancing quickly behind him to see how far he had to go. If he bent his head down and really made a run for it, he was sure that he could reach the opening in the pipe before the shadowy thing, or man, or whatever it was, caught up with him. In any case, maybe it, or he, was harmless. Maybe it had followed him along the pipe for no other reason than curiosity. Maybe it, or he, was

just a tramp, who used the sewers as a shelter. Maybe
he was deaf, or dumb, and that was why he didn't
speak.

Or maybe not.

Jan took one step back, and then another. His pace
quickened, but he was still too scared to turn his back
on the shadowy thing and make a run for it. The shuffling and the sliding noises quickened, too, and Jan had
the impression not just of one heavy sack being
dragged through the pipe, but many. Many, heavy, and
horribly soft, as if they held things that you wouldn't
like to touch. As if they were *sodden*, too.

The shadowy thing was advancing so fast now that
Jan stumbled. He went down on one knee, but he managed to pull himself up, and twist around, and that was
when he started running. His head bowed, his hands
outstretched to guide him through the suffocating pipe,
his feet making a *chop-chop-chop* noise as he ran
through the water.

He reached the broken opening. The arc lamp blazed
directly in his eyes and dazzled him. Gasping, he
gripped the shattered edges of the pipe and tried to
heave himself up into the fresh air. He was charged
with adrenaline, but he was panicking, too, and he lost
his grip and fell heavily back into the pipe. Soil and
fragments of concrete showered down on him, half-
blinding him, and filling his mouth.

Whether it was man or beast, the shadowy thing
didn't give him a second chance. He was trying to get
a grip on the greasy concrete when he was hit with the
force of a speeding car. He was knocked three or four
meters further along the sewer, out of reach of the
opening.

He tried to get up. He was so dazed that he slipped
over; and then slipped again. He coughed, as if he were
going to say something.

But instantly, his neck was seized, and he was
thrown against the side of the sewer so violently that

he heard his skull crack. Something huge and impossibly heavy climbed on top of him, and kept him pinned against the curving floor, with sewer water gushing against the side of his face. There was a momentary tussle, and then his whole head was dragged into what felt like a wet leather bag. He breathed in, trying to shout out, but his nose and mouth filled up with thick, curdled mucus. The stench of rotten meat was overwhelming, but he couldn't breathe and he couldn't speak. All he could do was wrestle and struggle and try to kick out at whatever it was that had taken hold of him. But it was just like kicking at curtains. The thing seemed to be nothing but fabric, and completely empty underneath.

He choked for air. He wanted to cry out for his mother, to tell her what was happening to him, but he couldn't. He kicked at his assailant again, but that was all he could manage.

I'm dying I'm dying I'm dying don't let me die.

But then he felt a sharp, painful blow to the side of his throat; and then another; and then another.

And his very last thought was: Oh Mary, Mother of God. He's cutting my head off.

2

Sarah was blowdrying her hair when Piotr knocked on the door of her room. He knocked so timidly the first time that she couldn't hear him, and when he did pluck up the courage to bang really loudly she pulled open the door and demanded, "What? Hotel's on fire? What?"

Piotr stood in the doorway twisting his fingers together like a small boy who has to report to the principal. "I'm afraid worse."

"Worse? What do you mean, worse? Come on in, somebody might see me looking like this and think I'm Ivana Trump."

"You're not dressed, Ms. Leonard."

"Not dressed for the street, Mr. Gogiel, but perfectly decent. Besides, I don't know what to wear for something that's worse than the hotel being on fire."

Piotr edged his way into the room, and stood awkwardly next to the window, as far away from Sarah as he could manage. Sarah sat down in front of the mirror and started to brush out her full, blond bob as if she had borne a grudge against it since childhood.

"The police called me at home this morning," said Piotr. "They said that somebody was killed on the construction site."

Sarah put down her brush. "Killed? Oh, my God, I'm sorry. How did it happen?"

"They don't know yet."

"I always said that Brzezicki's safety standards were shit. Didn't I say that? Half of those guys were walking around without hard hats. I saw one guy knocking down a wall and all he had on his feet were goddamned plastic sandals. I mean, what a bozo. You'd think they were spending the day on the beach, not demolishing a six-story building."

Piotr swallowed. He was a big, gentle young man with a huge round head and very little hair, although he couldn't have been older than thirty-one or thirty-two. He had the brightest blue eyes that Sarah had ever seen. She liked him a lot, and what was more, she trusted him, which was more than she could say for some of the natty, slick-haired new managers who worked for Vistula Kredytowy. They'd all watched *Wall Street* too many times, and thought it was true.

"It wasn't an accident, I'm afraid. Somebody was murdered."

"Are you kidding me? Not one of Brzezicki's men?"

"No, no. It was somebody called Jan Kaminski. He's a radio announcer—quite famous in Warsaw. They found him in a sewer. They said it was totally horrific."

"Oh, God. It's not going to hold things up, is it?"

"I don't know. You'll have to talk to the police about that."

"I intend to."

She sat down in front of the dressing table and put on her eye make-up. Piotr didn't know whether to watch her or to stare out of the window at the stylized trees painted on the blank brick wall of the opposite building. She was worth watching, however. She was a very smart, highly-groomed thirty-year-old with a strikingly pale face. Although she spoke with a brisk Chicago accent, she looked distinctively Polish, which was part of the reason she was here. She had inherited

her mother's high cheekbones and translucent aquamarine eyes, as well as her short upturned nose.

She dressed behind the closet door, still talking,
while Piotr fidgeted in embarrassment. She was wide-
shouldered and big-breasted, but the perfectly-cut dove
gray suit which she put on made her look leaner and
taller than she really was.

"This Jan Kaminski. Should I know who he is?"

"Not really. He does a news show for Radio Syrena
. . . well, a sort of investigative news show with satirical comments, you know? He's quite popular these
days. Well, he *was*."

"Are the police still on site?"

"They said they'd talk to you later."

"Crap. I need to talk to them now."

"Well . . . I don't like to criticize, Ms. Leonard, but
I don't think that you can treat the police in the same
way as the Wydzial Gospodarki Przestrzennej."

He was talking about the planning department which
had opposed the original plans for the Senate Hotel.
Sarah had gone to meet them and reduced two of the
senior officials to tears. The same afternoon the plans
were approved with only one minor alteration to the
façade. There is no exact Polish word for "ballbreaker,"
but that was the day that the men in charge of Warsaw's architectural planning discovered what it meant.

Sarah laughed, and gave Piotr a reassuring pat on
the shoulder. "I don't intend to make them cry, if that's
what you mean."

Piotr followed her apprehensively out of the automatic doors of the Holiday Inn. It was a warm, bright
morning, and the streets were crowded. They made
their way through the parking lot opposite the hotel,
between dilapidated Polonez estates and dented Volk-
swagens, as well as a few lovingly-waxed Volvos and
Mercedes. She walked so quickly that he had difficulty
keeping up.

"They said he was killed late last night. Some teen-ager found him."

"What was he doing on the site?"

"They wouldn't say."

"Why didn't they tell me earlier?"

They crossed Marszalkowska and were almost run down by a roaring, relentless bus. It didn't take more than another two minutes of power-walking before they reached the demolition site. Five or six police cars were parked outside, and the whole of the sidewalk was cordoned off with red-and-white tapes. Sarah pushed her way through the crowds of bystanders with a series of clear, commanding *"proszes."* When she reached the tape she ducked straight underneath it.

A policeman immediately came up to her with his hand raised. "You can't come in here."

"Of course I can. My company owns the damn place."

"Madam, it doesn't matter if your company owns half of Warsaw. Nobody's—"

"Who's in charge here?" she cut in.

"You're not allowed in. You'll have to go back behind the tape."

"Excuse me? I thought we'd finished with that part of the conversation. I want to speak to the officer in charge."

The policeman appealed to Piotr, but all Piotr could do was shrug. "She doesn't understand what 'can't' means."

At that moment three detectives came out of the door in the hoarding, followed by a photographer and a man carrying a large aluminium briefcase. One of the detectives stopped when he saw Sarah, and walked over to her. He was a stocky man with white, short-cropped hair. His head was too big for his body, but he was handsome in a craggy, pitted kind of way. He wore a crumpled tan suit and a jazzy red-and-yellow necktie with lightning flashes on it.

"What's the problem?" he wanted to know.

"This lady wants to come in, komisarz. She says her company owns this site."

"There's no 'says' about it," Sarah retorted. "Are you in charge here?"

"That's right," the detective told her. He took out a Camel and lit it one-handed with a heavy stainless steel lighter. "There's been a murder, I'm afraid. You can't come in."

"Can you tell me what happened?"

"No, I'm afraid I can't."

"Well, can you at least tell me how long it's going to be before my contractors can get back to work?"

"I can't tell you that, either. My forensic people haven't finished yet."

"What are we talking about? Hours? Days?"

"I'm afraid that I really don't know." His eyes were unblinking and amused.

"What's your name?" Sarah demanded.

"Komisarz Stefan Rej, from the Wydzial Zabojstsw— homicide division."

"Well, Komisarz Rej, do you realize how much it costs per day to keep this site idle?"

"I expect it's a lot of money."

"You're damn right it's a lot of money. If you worked it out in zlotys, it would have so many damn zeros they would stretch from here to Poznan. And back by the scenic route."

"Please, madam—" Rej began, patiently.

"Sarah Leonard. I'm vice-president of Eastern European development, Senate Hotels."

"You'll have to forgive me, Ms. Leonard. My colleagues and I are very busy at the moment. I'd like to talk to you later, though. Could you tell me how I can contact you?"

"I'm staying at the Holiday Inn, at least until Thursday."

"And then? You're not leaving the country, are you?"

"What do you mean? You're going to talk to me before Thursday, aren't you?"

"It depends."

"Depends on what, komisarz? Listen, I happen to be good friends with Inspektor Grabowski."

"I'm very pleased for you. I wish I was."

With that, he turned and rejoined the other detectives.

Sarah said, "Damn it, this is all we need. We're three weeks behind schedule already."

Piotr shrugged. "I warned you about the police. The harder you push them, the more uncooperative they are. Also, you're a woman."

"What the hell difference does that make?"

"Pph! To a man like Rej, it makes all the difference in the world. He thinks that women are for sex and cooking, that's all. Look at him. People died to get rid of bastards like him, but they're still here, all of them."

Sarah looked at her watch. "Well . . . there's nothing else we can do here. We have a meeting with the development people at eleven, don't we?"

"It's because you're American, too," said Piotr, as they crossed back toward the Holiday Inn. "The police don't think much of Westerners. The chief of police told them to be polite to Westerners, and of course that put their backs up."

"You know something, Mr. Gogiel? You're a cynic."

"In Poland, Ms. Leonard, we don't call ourselves cynics. We call ourselves realists."

o Sarah's surprise, Komisarz Rej was waiting for her outside the development office after she had finished her meeting. He was sitting on the wall in the pale yellow sunshine smoking a cigarette.

"Ms. Leonard? Perhaps we could have that talk now."

"You're very prompt," she said. "You didn't have to worry that I was going to leave the country."

"I know. You're moving out of the Holiday Inn and into an apartment on Jerozolimskie Avenue. A very fine apartment too. More than I could afford."

"How did you know that."

"I'm a detective," he said, blowing out a thin stream of smoke.

Sarah said, "I suppose I can spare you a half-hour. But I have to be at the airport by one o'clock. I'm meeting someone."

"I'll drive you. We can talk on the way."

Piotr came up to them, closely followed by Jacek Studnicki, one of the slick-haired young turks from Vistula Kredytowy.

"Is there a problem?" asked Jacek, putting an unwelcome arm around Sarah's shoulders. He was slightly shorter than her when she wore heels, which didn't help.

Sarah unwound herself. "Mr. Studnicki, this is Komisarz Stefan Rej, from the Wydzial Zabojstw. He's investigating our murder."

"Well, well," said Jacek. "I hope you catch your man, whoever he is."

Rej gave him a bright, hard look and smiled. "We'll catch him. We don't have anything better to do."

He walked with Sarah to his car, a ten-year-old Volkswagen Passat with its back seat filled with newspapers and paper bags and other assorted rubbish, including a broken umbrella and a Barbie doll without a head.

"You have kids?" asked Sarah, noting the doll.

"A girl. I don't get to see her very much."

Sarah climbed in. The vinyl seats were unpleasantly sticky, and the glovebox was hanging open so that it kept knocking against her knees. Komisarz Rej started up the engine, and they pulled away in a cloud of blue smoke.

"I suppose you didn't know Jan Kaminski?"

"Never heard of him, not until now. He was on the radio, wasn't he?"

"That's right. He did a news commentary programme. Quite funny, some of it. He used to take the mickey out of the government, and the TV stations, and LOT airlines, and the Polish football team. Once he even took the mickey out of Senate Hotels."

"I didn't know that."

"He was quite insulting about you, as a matter of fact. He said that from his experience of Senate Hotels, they might just as well have left the Zaluski-Orbis standing. All we could look forward to was a better class of rudeness."

"Oh, really?" said Sarah. "And precisely what was Mr. Kaminski's experience of Senate Hotels, did he say?"

"I think he stayed at the Senate Belgrade."

"Well, yes, we did have some teething troubles in Belgrade. It's a hell of a job finding the staff. The chambermaids looked like orangutans."

"Not good publicity, though?" Rej suggested, as they turned into Oczki Street. "There was something else he said, too. He suggested that some of the officials who approved of the Senate Hotel had been given holidays in Florida, and a little help with their bank balances."

"That's ridiculous! That's not only ridiculous, that's libellous!"

"You're quite right. But is it true?"

"What kind of question is that? Of course it's not true."

"It wouldn't be unusual."

"For Senate it would. We don't do business that way."

Rej took out a Camel, tucked it between his lips and pushed in the cigarette lighter. "Everybody has to oil the wheels, Ms. Leonard."

"I don't oil the wheels, komisarz. If they won't

move, I push them until they do. And I'd like to know what you're trying to suggest. *And* I'd really prefer it if you didn't smoke."

They had almost reached the end of Oczki Street. "You see there?" said Rej, nodding toward a group of drab buildings with ivy fluttering on them. "That's the old Akademia Medyczna, the medical academy. That's where Mr. Kaminski is now, in the morgue. And you see there? Right next door, Number 1, that's the Zaklad Medycyny Sadowej, the department of forensic medicine. That's where they're going to be doing the autopsy, to find out what happened to him. We could stop and see him, if you like."

"I don't like," Sarah retorted. "And what I like even less is your insinuation that Senate had something to do with this man Kaminski's death."

"You're angry now, aren't you?" said Rej, as he turned toward the airport. "I suppose you're going to make a complaint about me to your pal Inspektor Grabowski."

"Any reason why I shouldn't?"

The cigarette lighter popped out of the dash and fell on the floor. Rej leaned forward and tried to find it, but it rolled under his seat. Sarah shook her head in disbelief, and made a point of looking the other way. In the end, Rej threw the cigarette on the floor, too.

"Let me tell you something," he said. "This is the seventh murder in the center of Warsaw in three months. Every time it's the same ... the victim is found in the street, or on a plot of waste ground, always in the open. We don't know who we're looking for, a man or a woman. But the TV news has started calling the murderer the Executioner, because every time, the victim's head has been missing."

Sarah turned and stared at him. "You mean Jan Kaminski's head was cut off?"

Rej nodded, and sniffed. "They found him in the

sewer pipe, down at the bottom of your demolition site."

"What on earth was he doing down there?"

"Looking for a lost child, apparently. We have a witness who was helping him to search. He left Kaminski to call an ambulance, and when he came back Kaminski was dead."

"Dead, with no head?"

"That's right. The same as all the others."

"What about the child?"

Rej shrugged, and took out another Camel. "I've had the sewers searched half a mile in all directions. No child. But thousands of condoms."

"What are you trying to tell me? That Polish men are extra-specially virile?"

"I'm just telling you what we found, Ms. Leonard."

"Maybe. But you haven't told me what you're looking for."

"Evidence, Ms. Leonard. That's all."

"Evidence that Senate Hotels took out a contract on Jan Kaminski because he said rude things about us on a radio show?"

"That's not what I said."

"You didn't need to say it. God, and I thought *American* police were stupid."

Rej hunched over in his seat and started groping for his lighter again. "In America, Ms. Leonard, the situation is different. Here, we have quite a few years of catching up to do. And there is also the problem of predators. When there's blood in the sea, what do you get, sharks."

"Very poetic. You're talking about gangsters?"

"Gangsters, yes. Only last week we found another headless body in the Vistula. He was involved in pirated software. You see we have the very latest vices, as well as the oldest."

"Well, I can you assure that Senate isn't involved in any vices, modern or not."

"I don't mean that, Ms. Leonard. I mean that there are people in this city who want to have control of everything . . . from selling drugs to running hotels. If you stand in their way, they will kill you, as quickly as a killing a pig. You're Polish, I know that. But you were brought up in the United States. You don't understand the mentality. We're survivors. We have prosperity now. A market economy." He tapped his forehead with his finger. "In here, though, it's still war-time. You should remember that. Every man for himself."

Sarah said, "I'm going to tell you this just once, komisarz. Senate Hotels had nothing to do with the murder of Jan Kaminski, and I'll sue your ass from here to the Baltic and back if you even *mime* such a suggestion."

"What about your friends at Vistula Kredytowy?"

"They wear red braces and they all think they're Wall Street tycoons. But they wouldn't be party to murder."

Rej had at last located his lighter. He held it up triumphantly. "See? Now I can smoke."

Sarah snatched it out of his hand and threw it out of the window. "See? Now you can't."

Rej dropped Sarah outside the new airport terminal. The sun was momentarily reflected on her face from a low-flying 727.

"I'll probably have to talk to you again," he said, trying to sound grave, but smiling.

"What for? I can't tell you anything more."

"Of course you can't tell me anything more. So far you haven't told me anything."

Sarah gave him a testy little sigh. "Komisarz Rej, if Senate Hotels were going to be stupid enough to take out a contract on some small-time commentator from some ditsy Warsaw radio station, don't you think they would have had more sense than to leave his body on the site of their own hotel?"

"Who am I to say how stupid anybody is? I'm not a judge. I'm just looking for the truth."

"The truth? I thought you were looking for a murderer. Only a hopeless optimist looks for the truth."

"Are you as tough as you pretend to be?"

"Pretending? Who said I was pretending?" She smiled at him platinum-bright, her pale eyes shining with a greater challenge than he was prepared to face—just for now, anyhow. "Now I really have to go—my friend will be wondering where I am. Good afternoon, comrade."

Rej stuck another cigarette in his mouth and sat in his battered old car watching her walk into the airport entrance. He was only thirty-eight, but for the first time in his life he began to feel old. Not just old, but redundant, like a man in a vast moving throng of people who suddenly stops, and looks around him, so that everybody else jostles past him, leaving him behind.

Sarah had stung him, calling him "comrade." She meant that he was still showing signs of a pre-1987 mentality: and it was true that he didn't believe in God and that he still missed the certainties of communism, as many other people did. More than half of the electorate had voted-in Aleksander Kwasniewski, a former member of the Communist party, in place of Lech Walesa. Rej had, too. That didn't mean that he was any kind of dinosaur. Life in Warsaw was more colorful and open and there was much more to buy, if you could afford it. Crime had changed, too, becoming far more international and at the same time far more violent. These days the casinos of the city center hotels weren't crowded only with Polish gangsters, but Russians and Bosnians and Turks and men of indeterminate nationality in circus-tent Armani suits and new BMWs and with rolls of zlotys as thick as small joints of meat. They were secretive and quick-talking, all doing business in computers and automobiles and wood-pulp and probably drugs too; and guns; and although Rej was especially skilled at making contacts and winkling out possible informers, he was finding it increasingly difficult to gain any kind of entrée into the inner circles of organized crime.

Most of the time, the best he could do was pick up the casualties—five Romanians, burned alive in their VW camper on Kasprzaka Street in the western district of Wola; three Russians, shot dead in their room at the Sobieski Hotel on Tarczynska Street; and, worst of all, the seven headless bodies that had been found in the city center in the past three months.

None of the seven seemed to be remotely related to each other. Two were female, the rest were male. Jan Kaminski, the seventh, had been a radio commentator, and his remarks about Senate Hotels might have made him some enemies. But the first six had been a mailman, a doctor, an assistant from a food store, a taxi driver, a music student, a tourist guide and a pharmacist. What the hell had *they* ever done to anybody?

Rej reached instinctively toward the dash, and then remembered that he didn't have a lighter anymore. He didn't believe in spirits, or messages from beyond the grave, but lately he had repeatedly felt as if somebody were trying to warn him that his life was in danger. Perhaps it was time for him to change his life: to give up police work and do what his father and his grandfather had done, and tend a small plot of land, and keep bees, and watch the sun coming up and the sun going down, until he died. It would make more sense than searching for a random madman who cut off people's heads and took them away with him.

His radio crackled. "Komisarz Rej? Can I have your location, please?"

"Okecie. Why?"

"Nadkomisarz Dembek wants to see you at 1500 hours this afternoon."

"Tell him to—No, don't tell him that. Tell him I'd be delighted."

On the way back to the city center he stopped off at Oczki Street, parking his car at an odd angle on the kerb. The day had suddenly turned to the color of mother-of-pearl, the way that it could in Warsaw, and the buildings and the lime trees turned gray, too. He walked across the cobbled sidewalk and up the steps of the Department of Forensic Medicine. The swing doors grunted like discontented pigs.

Inside, it was cool and dark and smelled strongly of disinfectant. On the wall in front of him was a huge stern portrait of the great Polish surgeon Johannes von Mikulicz-Radecki, the first surgeon to wear a face mask during operations, and the first surgeon to be arrested by the police in Breslau for racing teams of horses through the streets. The corridors echoed.

A sharp-faced woman in a dark suit was sitting at the reception desk, peering at the screen of a word processor as if she expected it to speak to her.

"Is Dr. Wojniakowski still here?" asked Rej.

"Upstairs. Room Three."

Rej waited. The woman knew perfectly well who he was. Her phone started to ring but the look on his face told her not to answer it and that he was still waiting.

"Sir," she added, after one of the longest pauses in the world history of pauses. Nadkomisarz Rej inclined his head in acknowledgment and climbed the concrete staircase to the second story. Here there were more portraits: the Pomeranian surgeon Rudolf Zirchow, who discovered how blood clots are formed, and who fiercely fought for the sanitary conditions of Polish peasants in Silesia. And right at the end of the corridor, by the door to Room Three, a dark portrait of Marie Sklodowska, the Warsaw scientist who became world famous as Marie Curie.

Rej pushed open the doors of Room Three. The

lighting was harsh and blue. There were three stainless steel autopsy tables positioned side by side. Two of them were empty and gleaming. On the third one, on the far side of the room, a naked body was lying, white-skinned and ribby, its arms politely crossed over its chest, with thin hairy legs and a little dark tuft of pubic hair.

God, thought Rej, how irrelevant our cocks and our balls look when we're dead. No more sexy than dead fledglings fallen from the nest.

Even less sexy when we're headless, as this body was. Nobody could even kiss Jan Kaminski goodbye.

He approached the body as if he were trying not to alert it, walking circuitously around the other autopsy tables. Dr. Wojniakowski was bent over it, a bony, angular figure in a long white coat, his white hair sticking up in a cotton-candy frizz. He was carefully scraping debris from underneath the headless cadaver's finger-nails and dropping the debris into little numbered polythene bags. As usual, he was smoking Extra Mocne, a particularly pungent brand of untipped cigarettes.

"That you, Rej?" he asked, without turning around.

"That's right, Teofil. How's it going?"

"Slow but sure. It looks like the other six, superficially, but don't quote me on that."

"Head cut off with a cleaver?"

"All the signs of it. I haven't tested the skin for steel fragments yet. Lots of bruising, though. This one put up quite a fight. He may even have managed to snag some fibers from his assailant's clothing. That's the best we've had so far."

Rej approached the end of the autopsy table and couldn't help looking into the corpse's neck. His head had been taken off at a sharp angle, so that the flesh on the left-hand side went almost up to ear level, while the right-hand side had been cut right down to the collar bone. It was horribly interesting to see all the parts of his larynx and his trachea, a thick collection of tubes and pipes, reds and darker reds and gruesome beige colors. Unconsciously, Rej placed his own hand over his Adam's apple.

"There's a lot of sewage contamination, of course," said Dr. Wojniakowski, looking up through clouds of smoke. He had an enormous pitted nose but a pasty, triangular face that seemed to be much too small for it, and a straggly white beard that grew right out of his undervest, like a bramble bush in a fairy tale. "Judging from the condition of his clothes, I'd say that he'd been standing almost up to his waist in it."

"But in that part of the sewer the water was only six or seven centimeters deep."

"So perhaps you can conjecture that he had visited other parts of the sewer, where the waste matter was much deeper."

"Well . . ." said Rej, "our witness did say that Kaminski had gone down into the pipe to look for a child. We found him by the opening, but I suppose he could have wandered around anywhere. We searched the sewers but we didn't find anything." He coughed. "Apart from what you'd expect to find in a sewer."

Dr. Wojniakowski stood back from the table and peeled off his plastic gloves with a theatrical snap. "I suppose the only difference between this killing and the previous six is that the assailant took three strokes to cut off his head instead of one."

"Maybe the killer—I don't know—maybe he hesitated."

"Oh, no. Each of these three strokes was equally powerful. Look . . . you can see how the first penetrated through to the larynx, and the second cut through the spinal column, and the third finished the job off by taking the head clear off. In my opinion, the only reason it took three strokes instead of one is because of the limited amount of space in the sewer pipe. He was killed inside the sewer rather than outside and then being dropped into it. The assailant couldn't swing his arm back far enough."

"Shit," said Rej.

"I'll let you have a fiber analysis as soon as I can," said Dr. Wojniakowski. "The DNA's going to take longer. Meanwhile, there is one oddity you could be thinking about."

"What's that?"

"From the lacerations on Kaminski's hands and inner wrists, and the amount of builder's debris under his fingernails, it looks as if he was desperately trying to climb out of the sewer pipe."

"You mean—?"

"I mean the probability is that his assailant didn't follow him into the pipe. His assailant was down there already."

Rej looked at him hard, expecting him to come to some further conclusion. But Dr. Wojniakowski simply made a dismissive face, and lit another Extra Mocne from the glowing butt of the first.

Rej drove back to the demolition site. It was still cordoned off, although there was only a handful of onlookers. However, a television crew had just arrived, and as Rej made his way to the door a determined young woman bustled up to him, carrying a clipboard.

"Komisarz Rej! Anna Pronaszka, from *Panorama*, TVP 2. "Can we ask you some questions?"

"Not at the moment, Ms. Pronaszka. I'm a little busy."

"We just want to know if the murder of Jan Kaminski is connected with the other six headless murders."

Rej sighed. "There's no conclusive evidence that any of the six other headless murders were connected with each other, let alone with this one."

"Do you have any new leads, komisarz?"

"I have a new body, and every new body provides valuable new evidence."

"How many bodies do you need before you have enough evidence to catch the Executioner and lock him up?"

"No further comments," said Rej and began to walk away.

"Wouldn't you say that the Executioner is beginning to make you look like clowns, komisarz?"

Rej stopped, and turned around. His face was transfigured. He walked the three or four paces back, and then he said, "The police are doing everything they conceivably can to find a violent and determined murderer. Yes, it's a difficult case. Like I said, it may even be seven totally separate and unconnected cases. But we're using all of our resources to find who committed these crimes and eventually we will. The only clowns I see around here are those people who try to turn a series of particularly horrible killings into a public circus."

Anna Pronaszka gave him a sweet but glacial smile. "We'd still like to know why you can't catch him."

Rej took a deep breath to control himself. Less than seven years ago nobody could have spoken to him like that. "You want to know why, Ms. Pronaszka? Because nobody has ever seen him; and nobody has the slightest idea who he could be: and he leaves almost no physical evidence. Also, he seems to kill people at random, with no discernible motive whatsoever."

"What about Jan Kaminski? He was investigating Senate Hotels, wasn't he?"

"He made a couple of critical remarks about the Senate Belgrade on his radio show, that's all."

"We heard that he was looking into their finances, too."

"Who did you hear that from?"

"That's privileged, I'm afraid."

"*What?*" Rej barked at Anna Pronaszka with such

fury that she took an involuntary step back. "There are seven people dead and you have the brass neck to quote *privilege* at me?"

At that moment, Rej's deputy, Jerzy Matejko, came out of the demolition site. He was a tall young man with protruding ears and a gangly, marionette-like way of walking, which was emphasized by his cheap, flappy brown suits. In spite of his physical awkwardness, however, he was one of the cleverest young detectives in the homicide squad.

"Komisarz! Can I—ah?"

Rej gave Anna Pronaszka one last glare, and followed Matejko through the partition onto the site. The site was crowded with idle demolition workers, uniformed police and sewage workers in waterproof overalls and high boots. Everybody was smoking and drinking and laughing and nobody seemed to be doing any work.

"What the hell's this?" Rej demanded. "A garden party?"

"We've found something," Matejko told him, soothingly. He took him by the arm and led him across to the excavated basements. "By the way, I'd be careful what you say to the media, sir. Nadkomisarz Dembek has been getting a lot of flak from the inspektor about these murders. There was a story on CNN this morning, and he's spitting nails."

"What did they say?"

"They're calling them 'The Pole Axe Murders.' "

Rej shook his head. "These TV people can make a joke out of anything, can't they?"

"With all due respect, sir, I don't think they're going to make much of a joke out of that remark you just made about new bodies and new evidence."

"So what? It's true. I just went to see Wojniakowski. He's managed to dig some clothing fibers out of Kaminski's fingernails."

"Well, maybe he can make something of this, too."

Six or seven aluminium ladders had been propped up against the walls of the basement, and Rej and Matejko climbed down. They were met by two young uniformed officers and a balding forensic investigator with staggeringly deep bags under his eyes, as if he hadn't slept for three years.

"What have we got, then?" asked Rej.

One of the young officers held up a large plastic evidence bag. Inside it was a small greasy-gray doll, its smile almost obliterated. Rej took it, and turned it over and over.

"Where did you find it?" he asked. "I thought we'd searched these sewers already."

"It was underwater, komisarz, trapped against a grating, about seventy-five meters north of here. We missed it the first time, that's all. Anybody could've."

"Well . . . it may not mean anything," said Rej. "But Kaminski *was* looking for a child, or so that Marek lad said. Take it over to Oczki Street and have it tested."

"There's something else," said Matejko. He nodded to the second officer, who produced another bag, this one filled with a lump of wet, grayish fabric, with a single metal button on it.

"What's this?" asked Rej, holding it out. Even in a plastic bag, it felt disgustingly cold and squishy.

"That we found fifteen meters south of the hole, in the other direction. Again, it was very easy to overlook. It's a piece of old velvet by the look of it."

The baggy-eyed forensic investigator stepped forward. "It looks as if it was torn, forcibly."

"What is it?" asked Rej. "Part of a coat, or what?"

"I can't tell. Not until we look at it properly."

"All right," said Rej. "Is that everything?"

"I wish we had more," said Matejko.

Rej gripped his shoulder. "You look tired, Jerzy. That new baby of yours isn't keeping you awake?"

"Of course she is. That's what babies do for a living."

"How's Helena coping?"

"Helena's fine. She can't wait to get back to work."

"What's the matter? We're not paying you enough?"

"Some overtime would help."

"Okay then, finish up here, and then go around to Radio Syrena. That ginger-haired bitch from TVP 2 said that Kaminski was working on some kind of investigation into Senate Hotels, and maybe Vistula Kredytowy, too. See if he left any research material, any notes. You two!" he snapped at the uniforms. "What the hell are you doing? You should be around at Oczki Street by now!"

The two officers clambered up the aluminium ladders as if their trousers were on fire. Rej watched them go, and then he lit a cigarette and tiredly pushed his hand through his hair.

"There's no obvious logic to this, Matejko. The media are all trying to make out that it's some kind of contract killing. But who kills a mailman and an ear-nose-and-throat doctor and a piano student and a girl who cuts kielbasa at a neighborhood food store?"

"I was thinking about that," said Matejko, as they walked back to the ladders. "I was thinking, well, if they seem to be killing for no reason at all, perhaps we ought to stop worrying about it. Perhaps they're killing for no reason at all. I mean, sometimes you have to accept that people do terrible things, murders and God knows what, and even *they* don't know why."

Rej put his foot on the first rung of the ladder. "Let me tell you something, Mr. Psychiatrist," he said, his head wreathed in cigarette smoke. "Everything happens for a reason. All of these people were beheaded for a reason. Don't you ever forget that. You might think the reason is illogical, or irrelevant, or stupid. But that's not the point. To the person who did it, at the time that they did it, it made perfect sense. It seemed like the only course of action open to them. You understand me? And if you and I can understand what that sense was, then we might begin to understand why it was done—and, more than that, who did it."

A muscle pulled in Matejko's cheek. "Yes, sir," he said. "I understand."

Rej reached out and gripped his shoulder again. "I want you to understand something else. I don't ever want to give you that crappy speech again."

3

$\mathfrak{B}$en looked so different when he came through the gate at Okecie airport that she scarcely recognized him. He was thirty pounds heavier; his curly hair had turned lavender-gray; and he was wearing a monstrous powder-blue suit and a necktie with explosive pink chrysanthemums on it.

When she first caught sight of him, she smiled at him, and waved: but as he came nearer her smile disassembled itself and her wave collapsed. The next thing she knew he was kissing her with cheeks that reeked of Davidoff Blue Waters aftershave (travel-size).

"Sarah, you look gorgeous!" he brayed. "Poland sure suits you! What did I always say? A flower always flourishes in its native soil!"

"Did you always say that?" Sarah asked him. "I don't remember."

"Don't start ribbing me, Sarah. It's been a *very* long day."

"Let's find a taxi," she said.

"Didn't the office give you the limo?"

"No . . . I was driven out here in *very* great style, by Komisarz Rej. He's the detective who's been trying to solve our murder. Not very adeptly, I'm afraid. I think he needs to go back to remedial detective class."

Ben said, "I don't think I like you calling it 'our' murder. Senate wants to distance itself from this kind of thing. You remember what happened in Moscow. We do like our business associates to keep their manhood connected to the rest of their body."

They reached the entrance and Sarah whistled two-fingered for a taxi. A creaking yellow Polonez drew up alongside her, driven by an unshaven man in a Romany bandana who looked as if he was taking a day off from sharpening cutlery and mending pots. They climbed into the back seat, which was covered with a thick woven shawl. "Holiday Inn," said Sarah. "And don't try going via Gdansk."

Ben sat with his knees tucked up under his chin. "We're trying to get Citibank involved in the Tatra Mountain Resort. We don't want them to get the idea that there's any kind of mobsterism involved in what we're doing here."

"Well, there isn't, is there? Although Komisarz Rej has some *ridiculous* idea that we had this man murdered because he made rude remarks about us on the radio."

Ben shook his head in disbelief. "And they wonder where Polish jokes come from."

He hefted his briefcase onto his knees and snapped it open. "Here . . . here's that book on hotel management structure that you asked Jenny to get for you. And here are those stockings you wanted from Bloomingdales. And here's a little commemorative gift from me."

He handed her a flat, square jewelry box.

"What's this?" she asked, defensively.

"I guess it's a way of saying 'forgive me.' And, well, maybe we could start over."

They were driving along the broad dual carriageway of Zwirki i Wigury Avenue, named for the two 1920s Polish pilots who flew around the world. The sun had come out again, and it shone in Sarah's eyes so that they turned amber instead of green. "It's a little too late for starting over," she said. *Besides which, the Ben Saunders I used to love was lean and hip-looking ... not this overfed corporate heavyweight.*

"Hey, I'm not talking romance," Ben protested. "I'm talking pals. We're going to be working pretty damn close together, after all."

"We're pals already. I don't need jewelry."

"Just open the damn box, will you? Christ, you don't change much. The titanium fist in the iron glove."

Sarah laughed. She opened up the box, and inside it, resting on dark blue silk, was a diamond brooch in the shape of two Ps, back-to-back, the symbol of the Plaza Hotel in New York.

"What's this supposed to mean?" she asked him.

"What do you think it's supposed to mean? That's where we started it, and that's where we agreed to end it."

"'Agreed to end it?' We had a stand-up screaming contest. I tipped a dish of hickory-smoked almonds over your head."

"Two dishes of hickory-smoked almonds. And half a glass of chardonnay."

"Well, excuse me. You don't remember what vineyard it was, do you?"

They were rippling over cobbles now as they traversed Zawiszy Square. Light and shade flickered through the taxi like a sunlit river. Ben turned to Sarah and said, "Listen ... don't start giving me a hard time, Sarah. It's all water under the bridge. I want you and me to be friends, genuine friends."

Sarah lifted the Plaza symbol out of its box. "How much did this cost you?"

"Not very much."

"It's Tiffany, for God's sake. It's 18 carat gold, and diamonds. How much did it cost you?"

"It didn't cost me a penny more than I wanted to pay."

"You're incredible, Ben, do you know that? If I accept it, then I'm submissive. If I don't, then I'm some kind of unforgiving hardass."

"You don't understand, do you?" said Ben. "The most attractive women are the hardest to get."

"Oh God," said Sarah. "What have I done to deserve you?"

They reached the Holiday Inn on Zlota Street, and Ben stood patiently by while Sarah argued with the driver about the fare, because he had multiplied the figure that showed on the meter by three. In the end, she reached into the back seat, dragged out the shawl on which they had been sitting, and refused to give it back until he had dropped the price.

"Hey, come on!" the driver protested. "That was my mother's!"

"Your mother would turn over in her grave if she knew what a thief her son was!" Sarah shouted back.

"My mother's still alive!"

"Well, give her the shawl back, then!"

At that, Sarah started laughing, and couldn't stop. She stuffed the shawl back into the taxi, and gave the driver fifteen zlotys, which was half what he had asked for. He pulled away with a screech of tyres, and almost collided with a huge gasoline truck.

"You're incredible," said Ben, putting his arm around her shoulders. At least he was taller than Jacek Studnicki.

"Come on," said Sarah. "Let's get you settled; then let's go to the office for a progress report."

As they waited by the check-in desk, Ben took hold of her hands. "You don't know how good it is to see you, Sarah. It's been too long. I've changed, you know. I've really changed a whole lot."

"Well, five years. I guess we all have."

"You'll accept the brooch?"

"I suppose so—just so long as there are no conditions."

"Just one. You'll let me buy you dinner."

"Dinner?" she said, patting his stomach. "You don't need dinner."

"Thanks, sweetheart. I'll say one thing about you. You always giveth with one hand and taketh away with the other, don't you?"

"Mister, I had expert tuition."

ej was late for his three o'clock meeting with Nad-komisarz Dembek. For that reason, Dembek kept him waiting for more than twenty minutes on a hard varnished bench outside his office. Through the wired-glass windows, the sun sank behind the next-door building.

At last Dembek appeared, wearing a new blue suit that he had bought in Germany. It was two shades too bright to be serious. He was small, bald, with five strands of hair carefully arranged over his scalp in a sunray pattern. He had first joined the Wydzial Za-bojstw as one of Rej's trainees; but he had always been meticulously political, and when Rej had tried to show allegiance to his old boss, Nadkomisarz Grzyswacz, Dembek had been careful to distance himself from any of the old regime.

Rej had kept his job because he was both dogged and inventive; and his conviction rate was better than anybody else's; and there was nobody else. But he knew that he had lost any chance of serious promotion, and that Dembek would probably end up as inspektor, with a weekend cottage in the Tatra mountains and an invitation to every champagne reception that was ever held for visiting dignitaries. Sometimes he didn't care, but occasionally it hurt him so badly that it made him wince, like indigestion.

He believed that the collapse of communism had not only undermined his career, but destroyed his relationship with his wife Maria. He had never been much of a party member, but his life had been structured. In those days, you knew where you were, even with your enemies. He just couldn't believe how many of his colleagues had suddenly reinvented themselves, as if they had never even heard of communism. Maria, too. One day she had been calm and collected and their marriage had seemed completely ordered. The next day she wanted everything. A job, and a Zanussi washing machine. Not only a job and a Zanussi washing machine, but God, too. She had turned to the church, and Rej couldn't stick the church. All those effigies, and all that incense. All those holy relics. He had seen too many dead bodies to believe in any of that. A priest had come to their door one morning and Rej had told him to go screw himself, him and John Paul II, too.

Dembek beckoned him into his office. Out of the window, there was a view of Wileza Street, and the sun sparkling from the buildings opposite. Rej sat down in a tubular steel chair without being asked, and took out a pack of Camels. On the wall hung an inept oil painting of Morskie Oko, a mountain in the High Tatras (obviously painted by Mrs. Dembek), and a photograph of Mr. and Mrs. Dembek meeting President Walesa.

Dembek closed the door. Then he said, "This latest Executioner business."

"You mean Kaminski. We're making some progress, yes."

"Oh, really? How much progress?"

"We've found some cloth in Kaminski's fingernails, and another piece of cloth in the sewer."

"Do they match?"

"We don't know that yet."

"What else?" asked Dembek, with exaggerated patience.

"We've found a child's doll. We're circulating a picture of it to see if anybody can identify it."

"What about Kaminski's investigation into Senate Hotels?"

Rej's eyes narrowed. "You've been talking to that Pronaszka woman."

"She called, yes. And I'd prefer it if you didn't smoke."

Rej snapped his lighter shut but kept his unlit cigarette between his lips. "Kaminski made some sarcastic comments on the radio about the Senate Belgrade. Anna Pronazska said that he was also looking into their finances. It could have been a motive for somebody to get rid of him."

"Why didn't they just shoot him?"

"I don't know. Maybe they wanted his death to look like all of the others. Random, you know. The work of some psychopath."

"Maybe it *was* some psychopath. Maybe it was the Executioner."

"I'm keeping an open mind, nadkomisarz."

"That's the trouble. Stefan. Seven people have had their heads cut off and you're keeping an open mind. I've had two phone calls from Inspektor Grabowski that practically burned the hair out of my ears, and another call from the city president's office. This business is making Warsaw look like the murder capital of Eastern Europe."

Rej said, "I just need to find a connection, that's all."

"That's what you said after the first one. That's what you said after the second and the third and the fourth and the fifth and the sixth."

"Yes, nadkomisarz. And I'll go on saying it until I find it."

Dembek drummed his fingers on his blotter. Then he said, "I'm sorry. I want a result by the end of the week. Otherwise I'm going to replace you."

"Replace me? What are you talking about?" Rej demanded. "Replace me with who? I know more about this case than anybody!"

"You mean you know as *little* about this case as anybody."

"You can't do this, Artur."

"Stefan, I don't have any choice. If you can't find this murderer, I've got to hand this over to somebody who can."

"What you mean is you have to look as if you're doing something, even if it's totally misguided. You always were the perfect bureaucrat, weren't you?"

"I can replace you right now, if that's what you want!" Dembek snapped at him.

Rej stood up. "You'll get your Executioner, nadkomisarz. Don't worry about it. You'll get his head on a plate."

"I wish I could believe you."

Rej went out and closed the door behind him with the care and quietness of absolute rage. He stood for a long time in the corridor outside, breathing deeply to steady his temper. That was what you got when the world was turned upside-down: the fools and the crooks all rose to the top and the wise and the good were buried underneath.

A pretty young secretary came past, her blond hair tied up, a red file clasped self-consciously to her bosom. "Is everything all right, komisarz?" she asked him. "You're looking so *pale*."

"I'm—" Rej began. But he didn't know what he was. He gave her a quick, ill-assembled smile and then he walked back along the corridor to the windowless office he shared with Matejko.

While Ben went upstairs to unpack and freshen up, Sarah waited in the bar on the mezzanine floor of the Holiday Inn, reading up on promotional reports. She drank orange juice although she could have murdered a vodka. She had been feeling tense about Ben's arrival ever since Senate had appointed him president in charge of Eastern European operations, just after 4 July. She knew that she didn't love him anymore. She had been through two intense relationships since the night of the hickory-smoked almonds—the first with a deeply sophisticated forty-eight-year-old Frenchman called Patrice who had shown her some of the stranger sights of Paris, and then shown her how he could eat a freshly-shucked oyster from between her widely-parted thighs, an experience which still made her shudder when she thought about it, with glee and disgust. Patrice had disappeared one day as if he had never existed, and she often wondered what had happened to him.

Two months later, however—and very much to her own surprise—Sarah became entangled with Nat, a young American rock singer who had been trying to make it in Prague. He was three years younger than her, thin-faced, beautiful and dreamy, with long flowing hair, and for two months she had remembered what it was like to have stars and moons and suns in your eyes and dance barefooted down the street. But nobody can do that forever; and Sarah's time for doing that had already passed, and now it was back to business.

She remembered what her father had told her when she was thirteen: "Everything happens just the once. You can't relive it. If you spend all your time trying to relive it, you'll miss whatever happens next."

Ben . . . well. Ben at first had been brilliant. He had seemed knowledgeable, witty, highly *together*—the perfect companion for the late 1980s. He freely taught her everything he knew about hotel development, and helped her to rise from assistant projects manager to junior vice-president in charge of development, all within the space of six months. But in return, he wanted everything. Her body, her affection, her undivided attention. He liked Bruce Springsteen, so she had to like Bruce Springsteen. He loved Tex-Mex food, so she had to love Tex-Mex food. He had appeared to be so generous, but in fact he was leaching all of her individuality out of her. Towards the end, she had nothing left to give, and she was so dependent on him that she wouldn't even speak unless he invited her to.

She couldn't believe now that she had ever allowed anyone to control her like that. She still couldn't think *why*. But she had learned a painful lesson. She had recognized that even a woman as focused and as motivated as she was could have deep emotional weaknesses. That realization had made her stronger, more complete. She had sworn that no man would ever dominate her like that again.

Especially Ben. Especially this new, smooth, bigger Ben, whose well-shaved skin seemed to be too tight for his face.

Eventually, he appeared out of the elevator, wearing a navy sports coat with brass buttons and tight gray slacks. "All righty, I'm refreshed. How about telling me what's been going down?"

He popped his fingers to attract the attention of the cocktail waitress. When she came over, he ordered himself a Canadian Club on the rocks. Before she could go back to the bar, however, he took hold of her wrist and looked her straight in the eyes. "You know what I think?" he told her. "Polish women are the most beautiful women in the world, bar none."

The waitress smiled nervously, and managed to twist her hand free.

Sarah said, "You've embarrassed her, Ben. This isn't New York."

"What? I was only paying her a compliment. And I was paying *you* a compliment, too."

"Oh, sure. I know your compliments. You pay compliments the way some men open their trousers and waggle their dicks at people."

Ben leaned forward. "Listen," he said, in an aggressive undertone, "if you don't want that brooch—"

"I don't. There you were, talking about a new beginning, and what did you do? Give me a ludicrously expensive memento to something I'd rather forget."

"That was all it was. A memento."

"Thank God we didn't have an affair at a Best Western."

"Jesus, Sarah. What is it with you?"

"Nothing. I'm busy, that's all, and I don't have time for any mawkish saunters down memory lane."

Ben said nothing, but hunched in his chair and pulled the kind of face that men pull when they think that women are being impossible.

Sarah opened her briefcase and took out a sheaf of ground plans and computer-generated architectural impressions. "I just want to go over the completion schedules first. There may be some delay with the conference floor because of the way the ceiling's suspended. The building regs people have raised about seven pages of technical queries."

"In Polish, I suppose."

"No, in double-Dutch. What do you think?"

"Have you talked to them about it? Do they know what kind of money is involved, if they ask for any alterations?"

"You might say that I've made it more than abundantly clear."

"Well, make it clearer. You're good at that kind of thing."

"I don't think they're going to budge. Not on safety."

"What you mean is, you've chickened out of trying to budge them?"

"Ben—we're talking about a 400-ton concrete ceiling suspended above an area where 1,800 people are going to be congregating."

"And you don't think that our architects have thought about that? This building is so over-engineered it's going to last for two hundred years. Who's in charge of building regulations?"

"A man called Gawlak. But I don't think—"

Ben raised a hand to stop her. "Leave it to me, okay? I'll show him the full structural analysis."

"I've already done that."

"No offense meant, but I always think that technical assessments are a whole lot more convincing when they come from a man. A *guy*, rather. Guys don't worry about petty nuisances like building regulations."

Sarah was about to give him a scathing answer when her mobile phone rang.

"What is it?" she demanded, still staring at Ben, her eyes saying what her mouth couldn't.

"It's Jozef Brzezicki here. I have a problem. The police say we can continue with the work, but the men won't do it."

"What are you talking about?"

"They refuse. They say there's a devil."

Sarah momentarily closed her eyes in exasperation. "A devil? Are you serious?"

"They say that Kaminski was killed by a devil, and they won't go near the site."

"All right. I'll be right across. Don't let any of your men leave."

"What is it?" asked Ben.

"Just a little labor relations problem. Are you coming?"

Ben glanced across the bar at the waitress, who was bending over to pick up a fallen table mat. "I don't know. Let me finish this drink first. I'll be over in a while."

At the demolition site, Jozef Brzezicki and his thirty-five workers were standing outside the huts, arguing with each other. Brzezicki was a huge grizzled man with a face like a dried-up swede. He wore a battered red hard hat and a pair of baggy blue overalls, with every conceivable kind of wrench, screwdriver, ruler and spanner crammed into his pockets.

Sarah walked right into the center of the crowd of men and looked around at them with obvious annoyance. One or two of them coughed and looked away.

Only a short, weatherbeaten man in a checkered shirt and blue jeans, returned her stare.

"All right, then, what's the problem?" she demanded.

"It's too dangerous," said the man in the check shirt. "We can't carry on until somebody gets rid of it."

"What's your name?" Sarah asked him.

"Tadek will do."

"So what it is that you're afraid of, Tadek?"

"That poor bastard Kaminski had his head cut off."

"Yes, I know. But the police have searched the sewers and whoever did it has gone. You don't seriously think that he's still going to be hanging around here, do you? And besides, there are two dozen of you and only one of him."

"Except that it's not a 'him,' " Tadek retorted. He spat onto the ground.

"You mean it could be a 'her?' "

There was a burst of derisory laughter. Brzezicki's men liked Sarah, but they had a very ambivalent attitude to being bossed around by a young woman. Behind her back, they called her "the Ayatollah."

"He means it's an 'it,' " said an older man standing close beside Tadek. "He means it's a devil."

"You really believe that?" asked Sarah. "Come on, Mr. Brzezicki. This is almost the twenty-first century."

"This isn't superstition. It's true. You can ask anybody."

"I'm not asking anybody. I'm asking you. Exactly what is this devil, and where does it come from?"

"On the TV, they call it the Executioner," said Brzezicki. "That's just a name. It doesn't really have a name. It was supposed to live in people's cellars, places like that. They found one living in a cellar in the Old Town once, before the war, that's what my mother told me. It would come out at night and cut off people's heads."

"Tadek, there is no such thing."

"Oh, yes? Tell that to Jan Kaminski. You tell that to all those other people who got themselves killed."

Sarah turned to Brzezicki, who was standing with his arms folded, placidly smoking. "I'm sorry about this, but you'll have to get them back to work. We've lost a day already."

Brzezicki shrugged. "They won't do it, Ms. Leonard. Don't you think I've tried?"

"All they have to is replace the broken sewer pipe . . . then it won't matter if there are fifty devils down there, they won't be able to get out."

"Sorry, they won't go near it."

"In that case I'll find somebody who will, and you and all your gang of girls can consider yourselves sacked."

Brzezicki shook his head. "That won't do any good, Ms. Leonard. You can ask as many other demolition companies as you like. They won't do the work, either, once they find out what's happened here. I told you: this isn't superstition. If we refused to stick our fingers into an electric point, you wouldn't call that superstitious, would you? And you wouldn't call us girls."

"I don't *believe* this! These are grown men and this is the middle of the most modern city in eastern Europe. And they're afraid of a *devil*?"

Brzezicki said, "You don't think it's strange that they believe in God, do you? Why should you think it's strange that they believe in devils?"

"Oh, spare me," said Sarah.

At that moment, Ben came walking across the site with his hands in his pockets. "What's going on?" he asked. "Are we having a union meeting here?"

"They won't carry on working," Sarah explained. "They think that there's a devil down in that sewer and they won't go near it."

"A devil? You mean, like a demon-type devil? With horns and a tail and a pitchfork?"

"That's what they say."

"So what did you say?"

"I threatened to sack them. But they say there's no chance of us finding any replacement labor."

"And why is that, may I ask?"

"Because, apparently, *all* Polish workmen believe in this devil."

Ben turned around, and approached Brzezicki. "You in charge here?" he asked him.

"Jozef Brzezicki, yes."

"And do *you* believe in this devil?"

Brzezicki pulled a non-committal shrug.

"What you're saying is, Mr. Brzezicki, that we wouldn't be able to find any Polish workmen who didn't believe in this devil?"

Brzezicki pulled another, different, face.

"In that case," said Ben, "I'll just have to find myself some Romanian workmen, won't I? Or maybe some Albanians, or Bulgarians, or Russians?"

"You're welcome to try, sir," said Brzezicki, patiently. "But everybody knows this devil. Romanians, Russians, everybody. It's a fact, not a story." He crossed himself, and all his spanners jingled. "Apart from that, you'll run into some pretty big trouble with the trade union."

"You're going to strike, is that it?"

"No," said Brzezicki. "These men are not on strike. This job is a good one and they don't want to lose it."

"In that case tell them to get their asses back to work."

"They won't . . . not until they know for sure that the devil is gone."

Ben turned back to Sarah. "Well, little Ms. Genghis Khan, what are you going to do now?"

"Brzezicki gave you the answer himself. They won't work until they're certain there's no risk. So what we have to do is show them that we've chased their devil away."

"Did I miss a class on this at business college?"

"Probably. It's called getting your own way by appearing to make concessions."

"That's funny. I thought it was called surrendering your common sense to supernatural claptrap."

Sarah beckoned to Brzezicki and said, "What if I offer your men a special bonus to seal off the sewer pipe?"

Brzezicki talked to Tadek for a moment and then came back and shook his head. "This isn't about money, Ms. Leonard. The men are happy with their pay. But they're afraid that the devil will find out who sealed it in the sewer, and hunt them down in their own homes."

"Jesus," Ben breathed.

"What *will* it take, then?" asked Sarah. "Another search of the sewers? An exorcism?"

"Somebody has to find this thing and kill it and bring its body to the surface."

"Have you lost your marbles?" Ben shouted at him, in English. "You're holding up work on a multimillion dollar project because you're afraid of some imaginary bogeyman; and now you're telling me that you won't start up again until you see this imaginary bogeyman's body! What are you . . . kids?"

"Ben," said Sarah, taking hold of his sleeve. "Yelling won't do any good. Especially non-Polish yelling."

"Then what?"

Sarah said, "These men may be afraid of an imaginary bogeyman, but somebody killed that guy last night and *that* somebody wasn't imaginary. So let's see what we can do to help Komisarz Rej to find his man."

"Oh, yes? How?"

"We have to bring in our own detective, that's how, and give him all the facilities he needs to find this homicidal fruitcake and hand him over to Komisarz Rej."

"And meanwhile this site stands idle?" Ben demanded.

"What do you take me for?" said Sarah, under her breath. "We can bring in some German laborers until this is sorted out. They may be three times more expensive, but at least we'll keep the project on schedule."

"What about the unions?"

"I think I can handle the unions, thank you. They're only men."

Ben looked around him, and then nodded. "Okay. But let's get right on it, shall we? If this hotel opens one day late, these guys are going to wish their devil got to them first."

4

Rej and Matejko met at the Pizza Hut on Widok. They sat at a corner table next to a twittering party of Italian nuns, and ordered a large meat feast pizza to share between them. If he expected to work late, Rej usually cut a big stack of salami sandwiches and ate them at his desk, but yesterday he had forgotten to buy himself any fresh bread.

"So—how did you make out at Radio Syrena?" Rej wanted to know.

Matejko shook his head. "I didn't get much. Kaminski's boss knew that he was following up a couple of leads about the way in which foreign businesses have been bribing Polish government ministers, but that was all. He let me look through Kaminski's desk, but there was nothing there. Only a few magazines and a couple of chocolate bars. But I found his address book. There could be something useful in that."

He produced a small, worn, green vinyl book, and passed it across the table. Rej flicked through it with a nicotine-stained thumb. "Check these out. See if any of these people were helping Kaminski prepare his report."

"I've had a quick look already, and there are three

or four possibles. Especially this one . . . Antoni Dlubak. He works for Vistula Kredytowy."

"That's worth looking into. Vistula Kredytowy are
jointly financing the Senate Hotel, aren't they? Go talk
to this Dlubak first. But be subtle, you know. I don't
want any doors to start slamming shut before we can
find out what's behind them. Who's this—Hanna
Peszka? Her name's underlined about fifty times."

"That's Kaminski's girlfriend."

"Oh, right. The one who's under sedation. When can
we get to talk to her?"

"Tomorrow morning should be okay. But I don't
think she can tell us anything. Kaminski put her on the
131 bus and that was the last time she saw him. We've
found an old woman who saw him at the bus stop, too.
She says that he was making stupid jokes. In fact she
said that he was acting like a *kretyn*. She was the last
person to speak to him before young Marek Maslowski
found him trying to open the door into the demolition
site."

Rej picked up a slice of pizza and unenthusiastically
bit off the point. "There has to be a pattern somewhere.
I just can't believe that these people are being murdered for no logical reason at all."

He opened his worn-out briefcase and took out a
folded map of the center of the city. "I've been trying
to work out if there's any kind of geographical pattern.
The furthest north, that was the taxi driver, he was
killed at the junction of Wislostrada and Solidarnosei
Avenue. The furthest south was the music student,
found at Zelazna and Jerozolimskie Avenue. The doctor was the furthest west and the shop assistant was the
furthest east. Just out of interest I drew intersecting
lines between them and I ended up with one central
location: the parking lot just beside the Central Station.
It could be that our killer doesn't actually live in the
center of Warsaw, but always arrives by train from one
of the suburbs . . . or even from another town. But that

would give him the problem of going home in the middle of the night with his clothing heavily stained in blood."

"He could have brought a suitcase with a change of clothes," Matejko suggested.

"I don't know . . . shit, it's possible, but it doesn't seem likely. Is anybody really going to go hunting for murder victims, carrying a suitcase? And where's he going to change and wash, without ever being seen?"

Rej swallowed more beer, and wiped his mouth with the back of his hand. "Next I tried to see if there was any kind of pattern to the time of night that these people were killed. Apart from the fact that they were all killed during the hours of darkness, there isn't—well, none that I can see, anyhow. I've tried to draw connections between their ages, their professions, their school backgrounds, their places of work, their leisure interests, their part-time work activities, their religion, their banks, their medical history, their family trees . . . everything. So far, it still looks as if they were killed totally at random."

"You mean we're looking for a psycho?" asked Matejko.

Rej continued to stare down at his map, his finger tracing lines between the seven red crosses which marked the place where each body had been found.

"Even if he's a psycho, he'll still have a motive. You remember that headcase who murdered his wife and children in Zoliborz last year. He seriously believed that his real family had been taken away in a flying saucer and replaced by Martians? But I don't think the Executioner is a psycho. I really have such a strong instinct about this one. There has to be a logical reason why these particular people were killed, even if we can't see it. Even if it's just some kind of disgusting ritual, you know?"

"Maybe we should talk to a psychiatrist," Matejko suggested.

Rej finished off his beer and lit another cigarette. "Maybe we should wonder what he was doing in the sewer pipe when Kaminski went down there."

"Well, Kaminski was supposed to be looking for a crying child, wasn't he? Maybe he was doing something to the child."

"But we searched that section of the sewers and we didn't find any child."

"You found a doll."

"Oh, sure. But that could have come from anywhere. Some kid might have flushed it down the toilet. You know, sending it off on a big adventure. They do things like that, kids."

"Maybe he killed Kaminski and then took the child away with him."

"That's conceivable. But we haven't had any reports of a child going missing in that area, and it really doesn't answer the main question, does it? What the hell was he doing down in the sewer in the first place?"

"Hiding, I suppose." Matejko shrugged. "The same way the Resistance used to hide from the Nazis. You can go all the way across town without ever coming to the surface." He paused, and then he said, "Maybe he's *always* in the sewers."

Rej looked down at his map again, his finger tapping thoughtfully on the table. "That's a very interesting idea, Matejko. I mean, nobody has ever witnessed this man murdering anybody, have they? And more to the point, we've had seven murders, seven beheadings with litres of blood pumping out everywhere, right in the city center, and yet nobody has ever reported seeing a man in heavily bloodstained clothing anywhere near any of the crime scenes. He wouldn't need to carry a change of clothing, would he, if he simply escaped down the sewers?"

Matejko said, "I'll see if I can get hold of somebody from the sewage department. We're going to need a map, aren't we, to see if there's access to the main sewers at each of the crime scenes."

"That's right. And then we're going to have to do some extremely disgusting searching."

They looked down at the remains of their meat feast pizza. Usually, they would have eaten all of it, even if they weren't particularly hungry, because it cost so much. But they both pushed their plates away, and Rej raised his hand to the waitress and said, "Check, please, miss."

"Something wrong with your pizza?" she asked him.

He shook his head. "It's fine. It's just that I don't relish the idea of meeting it again later."

Later the same evening, at two minutes after eleven, a young dark-haired woman alighted from the H bus at Grojecka and crossed the street toward a huge gray 1950s apartment block. Although Grojecka was a main road, it was almost deserted at this time of the evening, apart from two or three taxis and a huge tractor-trailer bellowing past with a load of rusty steel pipes.

The ground floor of the apartment block was taken up by shops—all of them closed now, and shuttered with steel gates: the Biblios bookstore, the Kepliez delicatessen, and a furniture store which sold nylon-covered sofas in all kinds of hideous colors, such as raspberry and bronze and turquoise. The entrance to the apartments over the shops was down a narrow alley on the left-hand side of the building. The young woman took her keys out of her purse in readiness and jingled them as she entered the alley. She was late and she was tired, but she wasn't frightened of coming home late at night.

A single unshaded light-bulb shone under the curved concrete canopy above the entrance. It threw intense shadows along the alley and across the walls of the adjacent building, shadows like winged gargoyles and stretched-out monks and hunched-up dogs. It was so bright that it left dancing after-images on the young girl's eyes.

She climbed the steps, opened one of the double doors, and let herself in. Inside, the hallway was gloomy and smelled of dust and disinfectant. She reached across and pressed the light-switch, but the bulb had gone, and all she could hear was the ticking of the timer, which allowed residents just eleven seconds to reach the second story and press the next switch.

But over the ticking, she thought she heard something else. A deep, soft dragging sound, from the alley outside, as if somebody were pulling a hessian sack full of heavy, wet things from one end of the alley to the other. She stood by the door, holding it less than two centimeters open, listening and wondering what it was.

She was curious, but still she wasn't frightened. She opened the door, and cautiously stuck her head out. She peered up the alley toward Grojecka, but there was nothing there, only a passing bus, and a girl arguing with her boyfriend. She looked back the other way, which was a deadend. There was nothing there either, only garbage bins. She waited, and listened. Nothing. She closed the door behind her, and made sure that it was locked.

She climbed the stairs in darkness. She lived on the second floor, all on her own since Leon had left her. Her apartment was very small, but it still cost more than she could afford, which was why she had been taking evening classes at the College of Music, teaching piano for "junior and senior beginners." She sat on her stool for four hours every evening and tried not to think that Chopin would have cut his wrists if he had heard what she was doing. She closed her ears to the sullen plonking of eleven-year-olds: and the rapturous discords of arthritic old age pensioners.

She let herself into her apartment and her tortoise-shell cat Kaska came jumping off the sofa to greet her. "Come on, I know you're hungry," she said. "Give me a chance to put my bags down."

She switched on the lights and drew the thin olive-green curtains. The apartment was painted cheese-colored and sparsely furnished. She had just managed to buy a new armchair and a coffee table. The walls were decorated with posters for the Royal Castle Concert Hall and the Teatr Wielki, the opera theater. In one corner stood an upright piano with a bust of Chopin on it.

She took a paper napkin out of her bag and went into the kitchenette with it, hotly pursued by Kaska. She unwrapped the napkin and dropped a large lump of minced meat onto Kaska's dish.

"Pork zrazy tonight, madam," she said, but Kaska was too busy devouring it.

She plugged in the electric kettle. Then she went back into the living room to brush her hair in front of the mirror. She was a dark, striking girl with long hair and lambent eyes. She was very thin: she was wearing a sleeveless gray sweater and her arms looked almost breakable. Her father always used to complain that just because she was a musician, she didn't have to look as if she were starving. But during the day, she worked as a waitress at Kuchcik, so she always had more than enough to eat—and so, of course, did Kaska.

Her name was Ewa Zborowska, and she was three days away from her twenty-fourth birthday.

She switched on her portable television. There was a discussion about drug abuse on TVP 1 and the movie Zorro on TVP 2. She switched it off again. She was saving up to buy herself a second-hand grand piano; but after the piano she wanted to buy a satellite receiver.

She heard the kettle boiling, and she was just about

to go back to the kitchenette when she heard something else: a fearsome, persistent banging.

She hesitated, alarmed. It sounded as if somebody were beating with both fists on the doors downstairs. Now and then, one of the tenants would forget their key, and they would knock loudly until another tenant came grumbling down to let them in. But this wasn't somebody knocking. This was somebody pounding the doors so furiously that Ewa could hear them shaking.

She went to her apartment door and opened it. The banging noise echoed up the stairwell, so that it became a thunderous double-banging. It just went on and on, until Ewa could hardly hear herself think.

Mr. Wroblewski came down from the third floor, in a maroon cotton bathrobe and slippers.

"What's going on?" he demanded. "Who's making all of that racket?"

"I don't know," said Ewa. "It can't be anybody who lives here."

"Maybe they're drunk," said Mr. Wroblewski, peering over the banisters.

Mrs. Konopnicka appeared on the landing below, her hair in curlers. "We should call the police."

"I don't know why we just don't tell them to stop," said Ewa.

"Well, you can if you like," said Mr. Wroblewski. "It sounds like a mad person to me."

"We should call the police," Mrs. Konopnicka repeated.

Ewa left her door on the latch and went down the first flight of stairs. The banging continued. The doors had been shaken so violently that the air was filled with dust. Ewa thought that if it went on much longer, it might even bring the doors right down. She went down the last flight into the darkened hall. Through the frosted-glass panels in the doors, she could see a black shadowy shape, violently heaving as it beat on the wooden doorframe.

She approached as close as she dared, and called out, "What do you want? Stop that banging! Stop that banging and tell me what you want!"

There were two or three more deafening bangs and then they stopped; although Ewa could still see the dark shape outside.

"Can you hear me?" she said. "Tell me what you want, and I'll see if I can help you."

"Ewa—you be careful," called Mr. Wroblewski.

From close behind him, his wife snapped, "If you were any kind of man, Kaczimicz, you'd go yourself!"

Ewa glanced up. She could see everybody's pale faces looking down the stairwell.

"Have they gone?" asked Mrs. Konopnicka.

"No, they're still here," said Ewa. "I can see them on the step."

"Ask them again what they want. Disturbing everybody's sleep like that."

Ewa approached the door more closely and strained her eyes to see who was standing outside. But even though the light over the doors was so bright, she could distinguish only darkness, only a shadow, as if a man were standing outside with a black cloak draped over his head.

"Why were you knocking?" she asked, quite quietly.

"Knocking, she calls it," said Mrs. Konopnicka, scornfully. "More like beating the door down. At night, already, when everybody's trying to sleep."

"What do you want?" asked Ewa. "Do you want to see anybody here?"

Still there was no reply.

Ewa said, "I can't help you unless I know what you want."

The dark shadow wavered for a moment. Then it moved away. Ewa found herself staring intently at a locked door, and nothing else.

"They've gone?" asked Mr. Wroblewski.·

Ewa went right up to the door and touched the

frosted glass panels with her fingertips. She had a strange, sad feeling—as if the man who had been banging so relentlessly was somebody who desperately needed friendship and help. He had banged and banged, but nobody had answered, and now he had turned away, and disappeared back into the night, rejected as he had always been rejected.

She waited for a moment, and then she opened the door. She looked out into the alley, frowning a little against the bright, unshaded light.

"Hallo?" she called. "Is anybody there?"

She put her head out further. The night was warm and noisy. In the distance she could hear traffic and music and somebody laughing. She waited for a moment, listening, breathing the city air, and then she went back inside . . . just as something huge and dark rushed toward her out of the alley, one of the gargoyle-shadows come to life.

Ewa screamed, and slammed the door shut. There was an ear-splitting bang as the shape collided with the door, and the whole architrave trembled.

"What's happening?" Mrs. Konopnicka cried out, her voice as shrill as a chicken's.

"It's all right!" said Ewa. She felt bleached and trembly: but she was determined not to be scared. She had never been scared, ever since she had started living on her own. She had refused to be scared. She had been accosted by drunks on her way home from the College of Music; she had been jostled and pickpocketed when she was looking for bargains in Warsaw's bazaars: she had been propositioned by customers when she was serving meals. Whatever *this* was, she could deal with it. She stood with her back to the doors and closed her eyes and said a prayer: God help me and protect me.

"I should call the police!" said Mrs. Konopnicka.

It was then that the mailbox in the right-hand door burst open, and a clawlike hand seized hold of Ewa's wrist. She screamed, and tried to pull away, but her hand was dragged into the mailbox slot, and out of the other side, followed by her forearm. The bronze flap over the mailbox dug into her skin; and her arm was pulled so violently that her flesh was torn away from her bones, and ruffled up all the way to her elbow, like some thick, grotesque glove.

Ewa struggled and pushed and kicked against the door, but whatever was dragging her through the mailbox was strong beyond belief. There was so much flesh bunched up around her elbow that it had to pause; but then it made another huge effort, and wrenched her entire arm outside, stripping all her skin and muscle away from her bones. She couldn't see her arm, it had all been pulled out of the door, but she could feel the evening air on her naked nerves, and the pain was more than she could understand.

She heard running. Mr. and Mrs. Wroblewski were hurrying down the stairs to help her. But she knew that something terrible was going to happen to her and that nobody could stop it. She had been so brave, in her life, but she had always been a victim, and tonight her destiny had come to the door and demanded its due.

She knelt against the door, too shocked even to scream, as her arm was pulled harder and harder through the mailbox. Her face was pressed against the frosted glass. With her other hand, she tried to push herself free. But she didn't have the strength. Her arm was pulled and pulled until she felt the few remaining tendons stretching and the cartilage crackling between the joints. Then her shoulder exploded, and her entire right arm disappeared through the mailbox, in a burst of blood.

Ewa fell backwards onto the hall floor, convulsing in pain and shock. Blood jetted out of her axillary artery all over the mosaic tiles. Mr. Wroblewski came rushing down the stairs, losing one of his slippers on the way. He knelt down beside her, dragged off the belt of his bathrobe, and tried to tie it around her shoulder in a tourniquet.

"Call an ambulance!" he shouted. There was blood spattered all over his face.

He tried to find Ewa's artery so that he could knot it, but her shoulder socket was nothing more than a welter of flesh and gristle. Her entire arm had gone, and so he had nothing to tie his belt around to stop the pumping of blood.

"Ewa!" he begged her. "Ewa, stop bleeding!"

His wife came hurrying down with a bath towel. "Here," she said. "Let me try."

"The ambulance is coming!" called Mrs. Konopnicka, in a wavering voice that was almost a scream. "I told them hurry!"

Mrs. Wroblewski rolled up the towel and pressed it into Ewa's arm socket. But almost as soon as she did so, it began to be darkly and irresistibly flooded with red.

"Please God, don't let them take too long," she said. "This poor girl is dying."

Mr. Wroblewski stood up, his bathrobe belt hanging uselessly in his hand. "Who could do such a thing?" He looked toward the front door. "How can you pull off somebody's whole arm like that? I never saw anything like that before."

Ewa stopped twitching and lay still. The only indication that she was still alive was her fluttering eyelashes. But she didn't have more than a few seconds left.

Mr. Wroblewski took two or three steps toward the door. His one bare foot made a sticky noise on the tiles. He peered through the frosted glass, and then he took hold of the door handle.

"Don't!" warned his wife. "He could be waiting out there for the rest of us!"

"I can't see anything," said Mr. Wroblewski.

"Well, leave it, wait for the ambulance."

Mr. Wroblewski opened the door just an inch. He hesitated, and listened, and then he said, "No, there's nobody here. He's gone."

Mrs. Wroblewski leaned over Ewa and tried to detect if she was still breathing. "I think she's dead, the poor darling."

Up on the landing. Mrs. Konopnicka was twisting her handkerchief between her hands and sobbing loudly. "I said to call the police. Didn't I say to call the police?"

Mr. Wroblewski opened the door a little more.

"Be careful, for goodness' sake," his wife warned him.

"It's all right. There's nobody here. I'll go stand on the corner to wait for the ambulance."

He stuck his head out of the door, looked left and then looked right.

There was nothing. The night was quiet. But then there was a soft rumbling, rushing noise; and a sharp crack like somebody bursting a paper bag. Mr. Wroblewski dropped heavily forward onto the front doorstep, and lay there without moving.

"Kaczimicz?" said Mrs. Wroblewski, turning around.

There was no reply. The door remained half ajar. Mr. Wroblewski lay on the doorstep in his maroon bathrobe, with one slipper and one bare blood-printed foot.

"Kaczimicz, what's happened?" screamed Mrs. Wroblewski. "Mrs. Konopnicka, come down here! Please, help me! Something's happened to Kaczic!"

She glanced frantically down at Ewa. Ewa was lying still now; her face white; her head lolling. Mrs. Wroblewski laid her down quickly and gently, and then stood up.

She was about to open the front door wider, but her hand stopped itself in mid-air, and then slowly came back to cover her mouth. Now that she was standing up she could see what had happened.

Mr. Wroblewski was lying on the doorstep under the glare of the overhead bulb, his arms by his side, as if he had fallen without making any effort to save himself. Above the collar of his bathrobe there was nothing at all. No head. Just a steady river of blood that ran down the step, almost too liquidly bright to be real.

Mrs. Wroblewski tried to close her eyes but she couldn't. In the distance she thought she heard people howling, the way she had heard them howling during the war; but it was only the ambulance, arriving too late to save anybody.

Sarah was looking over her new fourth-floor apartment on Jerozolimskie Avenue when Ben appeared, and knocked loose-wristed at the half-open door.

"Anybody home?"

"I'm in the living room. How did you know I was here?"

He strolled in with his hands in his pockets, wearing his navy sports coat and chinos. His silk necktie had hot-air balloons on it. "I've already made friends with your secretary."

"Irena? Well, don't get too friendly or I might be forced to fire her."

"Don't tell me you're jealous?"

"Where were you when God gave out modesty? I just don't want every move I make to be bush-telegraphed around Warsaw."

Ben looked around the living room and nodded in appreciation. The apartment was in one of the few art nouveau houses left in Warsaw after the destruction of the Second World War. It was airy, bright, with high ceilings and decorative windows, and a balcony over-looking the street. A huge marble fireplace was decorated with twining vines and languid lilies. The sofa and chairs were grandiose and gilded and pompous and completely out of period, but they made the apartment feel luxurious and comfortable.

Sunshine quivered on the carpet, reflected from a huge art nouveau mirror.

"This is wonderful," said Ben. "I'm almost tempted to move in with you."

"Don't even think about it. Did you have your meeting with Gawlak?"

"Sure. Great. Just finished."

"What's the verdict?"

"Well . . . he's going to have to go back to his chums in the building department, and have a little pow-wow. But the general impression that he gave me was that some of his associates had been over-enthusiastic about safety standards."

"How can anybody be over-enthusiastic about safety standards?"

"Very easy. If you construct a suspended ceiling weighing four hundred tons and you hold it up with pinions that are capable of carrying eight hundred tons then that's called over-engineering and it's a waste of money."

"The ceiling wasn't Gawlak's only crib."

"No . . . but you know how it is."

Sarah sat down on the large satin-covered sofa. Today she was wearing a short aquamarine dress that matched her eyes, and a loose white linen jacket. The colors were a shade too pale for her: but in the bright sunlight they gave her an intriguing bleached-out look, as if she were scarcely there.

"I don't know how it is," she said. "You tell me."

Ben sat down next to her. "Sarah, we both work for Senate and whatever Senate wants we have to deliver."

"I never knew that Senate wanted to bribe the building regulations department."

Ben laughed and shook his head. "Sarah—sweetheart—you've done a terrific job for us here. Nobody but you could have got this project so far ahead. When it comes to persuasion, when it comes to bullying, you're the best mover and shaker we've got. But sometimes people just can't be persuaded. Sometimes they say thus far and no further. And when it comes to that situation, you have to forget about Plan A and turn to Plan B."

"Meaning B for bribery?"

Ben laughed. "We're not talking bribery, for God's sake! We're talking business expenses! We're making new friends, that's all! Oiling the wheels!"

Sarah jabbed him with her fingernail in his hot-air balloon tie. "It's bribery, Ben. It's illegal, and it's immoral, and in the long term it's bad for Senate's reputation. When it came to planning permission, all right, I shouted at those poor guys until they would have come around to the Holiday Inn and washed my pantyhose for me. That's business. That's negotiating skill. But it doesn't take any skill to put ten thousand dollars into some poor bastard's bank account so that he doesn't kick up a fuss about inferior concrete mixes or substandard wiring."

"Hey," grinned Ben. "I'll come around and wash your pantyhose any time you like."

Sarah gave him a look that her intimidated male colleagues used to call "the ray." "What happened to you, Ben? You used to be so *acute*. Look at you now. You're coarse, you're crude, and you're corrupt, too."

Ben was still smiling but every muscle in his face was clenched. "Why do you think I gave you that brooch? To show you that things were just the same. You're the one who's changed, Sarah, not me. Just because your parents were Polish, you think you have some God-given right to come to this country and behave like Joan of Fucking Arc."

"Joan of Fucking Arc was French."

"Sarah—for Christ's sake—these people need every Western cent they can lay their hands on. They need

to grow, they need to develop. I know they're proud.
I know they need to have all of their committees and
their departments and their goddamned regulations. But
that's just theater. The reality is that the West is screwing them on one side and the Russians are screwing
them on the other. So what are they going to choose?
Senate Hotels and McDonalds, or some gun-running
crack-dealing bunch of Moscow mafiosi? You can call
it bribery if you like. But from where I'm standing, it
looks like nothing worse than financial encouragement
to make the wiser choice."

Sarah stood up. She was fuming. She couldn't stop
clenching and unclenching her fists. "Mafiosi? Who's
the goddamned mafiosi? Those men at the Wydzial
Gospodarki Przestrzennej, they were scared of me, yes,
but they respected me, and I respected them. I never
once offered them money. Never. How can I go back
now and look them straight in the face?"

Ben admired his fingernails. "All you have to do is
smile. And I didn't offer them money *per se*. All it
took was six new BMW 5-Series and six three-week
family vacations at Disney World. Cheap at twice the
price."

Sarah stalked to the high french windows and
opened them. The noise of traffic suddenly filled the
room. She stepped out onto the balcony and looked
down at Jerzolomiskie Avenue and for the first time
since she had come back to Warsaw she felt insecure.
Ben came up behind her and stood with his hands in
his pockets jingling his loose change.

"This is a great, great city," he remarked, after a
while. "You and me are going to make it even greater."

She turned around and looked at him. *Did I once
really love you?* she thought. *Did I really stroke your
hair and run my fingertips along your jaw and kiss
your lips as if I could drown in them? Can anybody
change so much—or is it me, have I lost my wide-eyed
innocence?*

"We were a terrific couple," he said.

"No, we weren't. We were terrific, but we weren't a couple. We were two yous."

He tried to put his arm around her waist but she side-stepped across the balcony, and sat on the balustrade.

"You know something?" he said. "I never really understood you. I thought I did. But when it came down to it, there was always something that you were holding back."

"People do that. Ben. That 'something,' as you call it, is their own personality."

He ignored that remark. "We were still a terrific couple," he said. "God . . . if you'd given us half a chance."

She looked down at the sidewalk below; at the people walking back and forth. She could tilt herself backwards, over the balustrade, and be dead within six or seven seconds. Or Ben could push her. She stepped back. It was only vertigo. But she wondered what the attraction was. Almost everybody felt it. The fear of falling; and yet the terrible desire to do it.

She was still looking down when she saw a dented red Passat pull up to the kerb directly below, and a white-haired man climb out. He crossed the sidewalk and entered her building.

"Komisarz Rej," she remarked.

"He's coming up here? What the hell does *he* want?"

"I expect he wants to tie me to a chair and beat me with a rubber hose. Most men do."

Ben caught her arm. "Listen, Sarah. I'm serious about you and me. I know things went out of control the last time around. But we're both different people now. We're more mature. More—I don't know—more—"

"Sensible?" Sarah suggested.

"If you like, yes. More sensible."

"Well, in that case, let's hope we're sensible enough to keep our relationship on a business footing only."

"Sarah, quit playing with me, will you?"

She pried his fingers off her arm, one by one. "I wouldn't play with you if I was the last little girl on the planet Earth, and you were the sole surviving Raggedy Andy."

He gave her a look which she didn't like at all. It was a distillation of possessiveness, jealousy, and sexual frustration. She had never been raped, but she could imagine that a rapist might look like Ben just at that moment. He was about to say something to her, but then the doorbell rang, and she pushed past him to answer it.

Rej was standing in the doorway in a brown coat that looked as if it had been fought over by four Dobermanns, and washed-out, tubular trousers. His hair was sticking up at the back and he looked immensely tired.

"Have you heard the news?" he asked her. He spoke English this time.

"What news? I've been working all morning."

"Two more dead. One beheaded. It looks as if it could be the same perpetrator."

"Not at the Senate site?" said Sarah, in alarm.

"No, no. Grojecka, an apartment block. A young girl and an elderly man. I've been there most of the night, and I'm going back there now."

"I'm sorry."

"I'm sorry, too. But I still have to follow up the idea that Jan Kaminski might have been killed because he was being too nosy about your company's finances."

Ben made an explosive, derogatory noise with his lips. "All of these people are being murdered at random, mister. You've got yourself a homicidal maniac out there, that's what you've got. The fact that Jan Kaminski was looking into Western scams is totally irrelevant."

Rej gave him a long, old-fashioned stare. "In a homicide inquiry, we don't rule out anything as irrelevant until we've proved it as irrelevant."

"You want to look at our books, is that it?"

"That would be a good start."

"You'd better get yourself a court order then, hadn't you?"

Rej said, "I was hoping that you would offer them up voluntarily."

Ben smiled and shook his head. "Sorry, mister. Not a snowball's chance in hell."

Rej looked around the apartment. "Fine. Okay, if that's the way you want it. I'll be in touch." He went to the door. "Nice place you've got here, Ms. Leonard," he added, and left.

After he had gone, Sarah said, "You could have been more co-operative. The sooner he catches this killer, the sooner Brzezicki's men can get back to work."

"He's clutching at straws, Sarah, can't you see that? Kaminski just happened to be in the wrong place at the wrong time. Same as all those other victims. Your friend Komisarz Rej doesn't want to admit that he's looking for an out-and-out loony, that's all."

"I like him. He's all kind of battered and defeated and sad."

"Is that what's happened to you? You've gone off winners, and started to feel sorry for losers? You said it yourself. The guy's hopeless."

Sarah checked her watch. "I'd better get back to the office. That German gang should be here by four. By the way, I think I've found us a good private investigator. I called my father last night and he knows a retired detective from the Chicago police department. He's going to ask him if he's interested in flying out here to help us."

"That's great," said Ben. "Anybody has to be better than our little Rej of sunshine."

Sarah said, "One more thing, Ben."

"Oh, yes? What's that?"

"I know you'd like us to get back together again, but it's not going to work. I'm happy on my own. I love my work and I'm not looking for any kind of intimate relationship."

"You're going without *sex?*"

"That's none of your business, Ben. I just want you to stop pushing me, that's all."

Ben came close up to her and leaned against the doorway. "The day I stop pushing you, Sarah, is the day I cut my throat and die."

5

$\mathfrak{J}$t was just after three o'clock in Lazienki Park, southeast of the city center. The breeze was warm and the sky was filled with huge, majestic clouds, full-rigged to cross a continent. They were reflected in the ruffled lake that was Lazienki's centrepiece. On one side of the lake stood a small eighteenth-century palace, built in high romantic style, with urns and pillars and stone balustrades with live peacocks strutting on them. Further around the lake, there was an open-air auditorium, with rising rows of wooden seats, and facing it, on an islet, a stage set with fake ancient ruins.

A Polish military band was playing this afternoon, selections from Karol Szymanowski and Witold Lutoslawski. The music echoed across the water, and the trees on the opposite shoreline shushed and rustled.

On one of the seats in the auditorium sat Jacek Studnicki, Sarah's associate from the Vistula Kredytowy Bank. He was wearing a dark business suit and a striped shirt, and he was perspiring. He was thin-faced, almost hawklike, but too many business lunches and too many late nights were beginning to make him look jowly, and his eyes even more heavily-lidded.

He had been waiting in the auditorium from more than half an hour, but the people he was meeting were rarely on time, and they weren't the kind of people to whom it was wise to express too much irritation. So he kept on waiting, and checking his Rolex wristwatch, and feeling tense and impatient.

The first half of the program finished, and the lake rippled with applause. It was then that three men appeared in the distance, walking across the wide patio in front of the palace, and around the side of the lake toward the theater-on-the-isle. The man in the middle was immensely tall, and built like a prize ox. He wore a wide-brimmed black hat and a long black linen coat. His head was huge. It looked as if it had been carved out of a single block of limestone and then sand-blasted to make it pitted and scarred. He had a wide, flared nose and slitted, Slavic eyes.

The two men beside him were small by comparison, but they still looked hard and well-muscled. One of them wore flappy brown trousers and a short-sleeved shirt; the other wore a black shell-suit. They walked with a threatening self-consciousness, glancing tightly all around them as if they expected to be set upon at any moment. They reached the auditorium and stopped. Jacek stood up, and beckoned them. They climbed up between the seats. The tall man in the black coat made no attempt to shake hands.

"How are you, Roman?" asked Jacek.

"How do you think?" the tall man replied. His voice was so harsh that it almost gave Jacek a sore throat to listen to it. "All this fresh air . . . it's poison."

"I just thought it would be safer if we met here. The Wydzial Zabojstw are showing an interest in our finances, as well as the Wydzial Przestepstw Gopodarczych, the fraud squad."

"Because of this Jan Kaminski character?"

Jacek nodded. "They want to go through Senate's accounts."

"They won't find anything, will they?"

"It depends how hard they look. We still haven't

cleared that last payment through Gdansk."

"Don't they have to have a court order of some sort?"

"Of course. But they'll certainly get it."

Roman Zboinski bit the edge of this thumbnail and slowly tore off a jagged crescent, which he spat out onto the auditorium floor. "Who's investigating all of these murders?"

"Komisarz Rej. Do you know him?"

"Oh, yes," said Zboinski, with a lipless smile. "I know comrade Rej. He and I are very old friends."

"Do you want me to have a word in his ear?"

"There's no point, not unless he's changed. Comrade Rej was never susceptible to—" and he rubbed his finger and thumb together, in the classic gesture for paper money.

The military band returned from their break and started to tune up again. Jacek said, "We'd better sit down."

"No, I can't stand music. It makes me nauseous. Let's walk."

They left the auditorium and started to walk through the woods. The sunlight flickered through the leaves and shone amongst the ferns.

Jacek said, "That last payment should be safely credited to Senate by next Friday. Then Rej can look all he likes."

"There could be another payment by the following Wednesday," Zboinski warned him. "I've already got seven Mercedes from Berlin and three BMWs coming in from Prague."

"What about that shipload from Britain?"

"I'm not sure yet. We're probably bringing them in through Rotterdam. Four Jaguars and seven Range Rovers. Right-hand drive. I want to move them straight through to Japan."

They walked back toward the Lazienki Palace. The peacocks screamed and spread out their tails. The pal-

ace had been built as a bath-house for Marshal Lubom-
irski, and had taken over thirteen years to build. After
the Warsaw Uprising, the Nazis had burned it to the
ground—but, like so much of Warsaw, it had been reconstructed after the war by architects and builders
who could not bear to see their national heritage erased.

Zboinski stood in front of it, his long black coat
flapping in the breeze, and said, "I hate history. What's
the use of it? It only reminds you how hard things used
to be."

Jacek said, "I have to ask you something."

"Nothing that's going to upset me, I hope?"

"It's these Executioner murders . . . all these headless
bodies. You don't have any idea who's doing it, do
you, and why? The trouble is that the workforce on the
Senate site have got it into their heads that it's a devil,
and they've downed tools until somebody catches it.
Which of course makes it even more difficult for us to
doctor our cashflow."

"They think it's a *devil?*" Zboinski grated, then
laughed.

"I wish you'd tell me different. I mean, if you had
any inkling who was doing it, I could tip off Rej, and
then he wouldn't need to look into Senate's accounts,
and the workforce would get back to clearing the site."

Zboinski nibbled his ragged thumbnail into some
semblance of smoothness. "I haven't heard a whisper.
It's not as if this maniac's killing dealers or runners.
Cutting heads off, that's Czvdowski's style, but then
he usually cuts the hands off, too. Anyway, I get your
point. I'll have my people ask around."

"My people" stood a little way away, their hands in
their pockets, looking as if they could get an answer
out of anybody.

They walked back up to the main road, past the sou-
venir stand, where a large black BMW was parked.
"Let me tell you one thing, though," said Zboinski. "If
Rej starts becoming a nuisance, then the Executioner

might very well strike again . . . when he's least expecting it. And if Rej finds any of my money in Vistula Kredytowy's accounts . . . then maybe the Executioner won't just strike once, but twice."

He twisted Jacek's lapels between his nail-bitten fingers and pulled him so close that Jacek could smell the onions on his breath. "I'm a calm man, Jacek. Everybody knows that. I never lose my temper, ever. Do you know why? Because I'm never frustrated. If I want a woman I can have her. If I tell somebody what to do, they do it. If somebody upsets me, I make sure that they don't upset me anymore. Do you know what my father used to say? He said, 'Only the mad dog sleeps undisturbed.' Well, the mad dog is me; and people take care not to wake me up; because if they do, they know very well what will happen to them."

Jacek managed to twist himself free. He looked queasy, and he couldn't look Zboinski straight in the eye. "You don't have to threaten me," he said. "I'll do my bit with the bank. All I'm asking you to do is to keep you ear to the ground . . . see if you can find out who's been doing these killings."

Zboinksi laughed harshly and patted Jacek's cheek. "You're a good fellow, Jacek. I'll see what I can do."

He climbed into the back seat of the BMW and put down the black-tinted window. He grinned at Jacek, and then he growled and said, *"Woof!"*

Jacek stood by the side of the road watching the BMW drive at high speed back toward the city center. There were times when he wished that he had never involved himself with Zboinski; but if he hadn't, then somebody else would have, and the amount of commission that he was paid almost trebled his salary at Vistula Kredytowy. But there was always the fear that his money-laundering operation would be discovered. The prospect of jail didn't frighten him. But the thought of what Zboinski might do to him was enough to make his bowels turn to icewater.

Roman Zboinski's nickname, which he had probably invented himself, was The Hook. It was supposed to date back to his days unloading frozen meat in a warehouse in Gdansk. He still kept his baling hook and he still knew how to use it. A few months ago, Jacek had come across a Yugoslavian trader from Zabowska Street who had tried to take one of Zboinski's cars without paying for it. He had ended up with only one eye and his cheek perforated through to his tongue.

Jacek walked over to his Volvo, unlocked the door, and climbed in. The radio started playing "Only The Lonely." One second the sun was shining, the next everything was shadowy and colorless.

The bodies had been taken away but the scene of the murders was still screened off from the main road with tarpaulin sheets. Rej pushed his way through them and walked to the doorway where Mr. Wroblewski had been beheaded. Matejko was hunkered down by the steps, talking intently to the baggy-eyed man from forensics.

"Oh, you're back," said Matejko, with a hint of disapproval.

"I've checked the records," Rej told him. "We don't have any information on either of the victims. I talked to the people at Senate, too."

"You mean you paid the delicious Ms. Leonard another call?"

"Don't get funny with me, Jerzy. The Senate connection is the only motive we've got for any of these killings."

"But these two didn't have any connections with Senate. Neither did any of the other victims, apart from Jan Kaminski."

Rej ignored him, and circled around the steps, looking at the dried blood which ran like a dark and turgid river from the edge of the second step, across the alleyway, and down the nearest drain. It was divided into dozens of tributaries, like the Amazon seen from the air.

"Any footprints?" Rej wanted to know.

"Nothing distinguishable."

"Any material evidence at all?"

"Nothing."

Rej had already talked to the witnesses, Mrs. Wroblewski and Mrs. Konopnicka. They had both described how Ewa's arm had been dragged through the mailbox, and how Mr. Wroblewski had rushed to help her. After that, they knew nothing. "He opened the door, he fell on his face." Except, of course, that he didn't have a face.

"No sign of the head?" asked Rej.

"Nothing. We've checked for bloodspots and torn-out hairs. We've sent some sweepings off for testing. You never know. They might contain more than concrete dust and dog crap, just for a change."

"Did you find the nearest access to the sewers?"

"Right out in the middle of the street, look."

"And where do they run from here?"

"Northeast along Grojecka until they reach the Plac Narutowicza, then they turn sharp right toward Zoliborz."

Traffic on Grojecka was being diverted while Rej's forensic team were dusting the four-pointed manhole cover. He walked across the road and stood watching them, hands in his pockets.

"Any sign that this was opened last night?"

"It's impossible to say, komisarz. There's so much heavy traffic along here, the cover's always being shaken."

The baggy-eyed forensics officer shone a flashlight down the manhole. Rej could see the sewage sliding by twenty feet below, a glittering yellow-ochre tide. "Let's put it this way," said the forensics officer. "*I* would rather be caught than try to get away down there."

"Wait . . . what's that, caught on the bottom rung?"

The forensics officer directed his flashlight to the opposite side of the manhole. "Nothing. Piece of wet newspaper."

"Bring it up."

"What?"

"I said bring it up. I want to take a look at it."

The forensics officer snapped his fingers at one of his colleagues, a wide-eyed young officer in khaki overalls and rubbers. The young officer climbed cautiously into the manhole, and reappeared a few moments later with an expression of total disgust and a sheet of wet newspaper, dripping sewage. Rej took it and laid it flat on the road.

"Now, look," he said. "It's only really soaked at one corner," he said. "And what do you think these are? Bloodstains?"

"We can test them, of course," said the forensics officer, his patience deeply tinged with skepticism.

"But here, look," Rej pointed out. "Yesterday's date. This paper wasn't carried here by the sewage . . . it fell down here last night." He lifted it up again, and peered at a pattern of three dark brown blotches. "The killer could have used a newspaper to wrap up Kaczimicz Wroblewski's head, so that he wouldn't leave a trail of blood. Unfortunately for him, he lost the outer wrapper on the way down the manhole."

Matejko came up. "There's nothing more we can do here, komisarz. We've interviewed all of the witnesses and we've searched Ewa Zborowska's apartment."

Rej showed him the paper. "You were right," he said. "He escaped down the sewers. Call whoever's in charge of sewage and tell him we don't want to go down the sewers tomorrow, we want to go down now, today. I want a systematic search of all of the sewers within a five-block radius; and if we don't find anything then, I want to set up a search of every damned sewer in the whole city center."

"Do you have any idea how long that could take?" Matejko asked him. "The sewer system . . . it's a labyrinth. There were dozens of Home Army soldiers who went down there in the war and never found their way out again."

"Just get it organized, Jerzy, will you?" Rej retorted. After the last dressing-down from Nadkomisarz Dembek, Matejko was questioning his authority more and more openly. They still worked well together, but Rej had the feeling that Matejko was wriggling his toes in anticipation of stepping into his shoes.

He was walking back to the apartment building when Anna Pronaszka and her cameraman came hurrying across to intercept him. "Komisarz Rej! Is there any truth in the rumor that you are going to be taken off the Executioner case?"

"Where did you hear that? Did you dial 31-91-21?" He was making a sarcastic reference to the Warsaw telephone company's horoscope service.

"I've talked to the city president this morning. He's very unhappy about the way in which you're handling this investigation."

"I'm not happy about the way he's handling the city, but then we're both entitled to our opinions."

"Komisarz Rej, I'm going to have to ask you again: how many more innocent people are going to die before you catch this maniac?"

"We're working on some new leads, Ms. Pronaszka. That's all I can tell you."

"Is it true that you're working on the theory that the killer escapes by using the sewers?"

"That's one possibility, yes."

"Is it also true that you're investigating Senate Hotels?"

"I'm not going to comment on that."

"Have you anything to say to the people of Warsaw, who are now living in constant fear of being attacked and beheaded?"

Rej turned wearily toward the camera. "All I can say is that if anyone has seen anything connected with these killings, no matter how inconsequential it may seem, they should call me at police headquarters."

"Provided you're still on the case, of course?"

"Get stuffed, Ms. Pronaszka."

He went up to Ewa's apartment. Kaska the cat came mewling around his ankles and rubbing her head against his calves. He knew that Matejko had carried out a thorough search, but he still wanted a last look for himself, if only to get some feeling of who Ewa had been.

Although none of the circumstantial evidence supported it, he was still sure that something connected all of the Executioner's victims—whether it was revenge, or numerology, or some kind of ritual sacrifice. He had checked all of the psychiatric hospitals and high-security mental institutions throughout Poland, and none of them had reported an escape. He had checked every prison for escapes and recent releases, and none of them had reported that any murderer had either absconded, finished his sentence, or been let out on license.

He had asked for assistance from Germany, the Czech Republic, Slovakia, Romania, and Russia. There were several terrorists missing; and two dangerous German bank robbers; but nobody whose movements tallied with those of the Executioner.

He stood looking at himself in the mirror on Ewa's wall, as if his image could miraculously give him an answer. Then he went into the kitchen and opened some of the cupboard doors. A jar of instant coffee, a bottle of ketchup, canned peppers, a tin of anchovies. Salt and pepper shakers in the shape of two white mice. He went back to the living room. He picked up Ewa's books, one by one. *The Life of Chopin; Encyclopedia of Music, The Castle* by Franz Kafka; *Chance*, by Joseph Conrad.

Chance fell open in the middle, because somebody had inserted a photograph in it. It was a faded black-and-white picture of two men in berets standing in front of a barricade built of cobblestones. They were both wearing cloth armbands; one of them was holding a rifle. There was a message scribbled in greenish ink across the bottom of the photograph: *"To my friend Janusz Zborowski, from Tadeusz Komorowski, July 31, 1944."*

Some of the lines in the book had been marked in pencil. They read, *"In fact we had nothing to say to each other; but we two, strangers, as we really were to each other, had dealt with the most intimate and final of subjects, the subject of death. It had created a bond between us."*

Rej read the lines twice, and then closed the book. He held up the photograph in his left hand, looking at it sideways, the way that a woman looks in a hand-mirror. Janusz Zborowski, presumably, was Ewa's father. He could soon find that out for sure. And if this picture had been taken in July, 1944, it had been taken a few days before the Warsaw Uprising, when the Home Army had risen up against the occupying Germans, in the expectation that the advancing Soviet Army would come to help them.

Tadeusz Komorowski was none other than "General Bór," the leader of more than 380,000 resistance fighters.

Rej tapped the photograph with his finger. He had the extraordinary feeling that the two smiling men were trying to tell him something, but he simply couldn't understand what it was. He sat in Ewa's chair, staring at it for nearly ten minutes, while the light in the room brightened and faded, brightened and faded, as the clouds sailed across the sun.

Matejko knocked on the door. "You have a visitor,

komisarz, from the sanitation department."

"Good. Tell him I'll be right down."

Matejko looked around the room. "Is everything all right?"

"Sure. You know me. I was just trying to get a feel for my victim."

"Pretty, talented, worked hard. Lived on her own."

"Yes, but she was more than that. She was some-body's friend, somebody's lover, somebody's daughter. She was all kinds of different things to all kinds of people." He stood up. "The only thing I don't under-stand is, what was she to the Executioner? Did he at-tack her because she was young and pretty, or did he attack her because it's the second Tuesday in August and she happened to fit into some stupid occult plan?"

Matejko said, "The director says we can borrow four of his sewage workers, as well as protective clothing and breathing equipment. He will also provide maps."

"That's very cooperative of him."

"Well, the director also has a charge of drunken driv-ing pending in the courts."

"Ah. I understand."

They went downstairs. The director of sanitation was sitting in the back seat of a police Polonez, talking to the baggy-eyed forensics officer. He looked like a man who might make a living out of filtering other people's waste. He was small and greasy with thick glasses and an extraordinary lop-sided snarl on his lips. He wore a shiny bronze suit and sandals; and there were six ball-pens tucked in his breast pocket.

"Mr. Chwistek, how are you?" said Rej.

"They tell me you wish to start searching the sewers right away," said Mr. Chwistek. "Can you tell me what you're looking for?"

"We're not entirely sure. We're looking for some sign that somebody's been down there. There's also a possibility that we may find some human remains."

"You'll have to have experts with you. Some of the

pipes are very narrow, you have to crawl on your elbows. Some are obstructed with gratings, too. That's
to catch the lumps! We don't have any sewage process
works in the center of Warsaw . . . everything runs to
Bielany and flows straight into the Vistula, and we
wouldn't like the same thing to happen to you. It would
be such a waste!"

"The sooner we can get down there, the better," said
Rej.

"Of course. At the moment, it's comparatively dry.
You don't want to go down there when it's raining.
Nothing worse than drowning in a sewer, don't you
think? Bad enough drowning in the sea."

"You know what they say, Mr. Chwistek. An un-
lucky man would drown in a teacup."

They waited for a moment in silence. Rej waited;
Mr. Chwistek waited. Then—from behind Mr. Chwistek's back—Matejko made a tippling gesture with his
hand, and then pretended to be turning a steering
wheel.

"Oh!" said Rej. "My deputy tells me you've been
having a little trouble with the courts lately, Mr. Chwistek. Something to do with drinking and driving."

"It wasn't my fault," Mr. Chwistek protested. "They
had a serious breakdown at the sewage works at Bial-
oleka, in Praga—one of the pumps. I had to leave a
dinner party to supervise the repairs. I'd had a few
schnapps, for sure, but I could drive perfectly well.
You'd think the *gliny* would have something better to
do."

Rej laid a hand on his shiny shoulder. "Don't you
worry, Mr. Chwistek. I'll sort something out. A public-
spirited man like yourself—well, he shouldn't have to
worry about petty rules and regulations, should he?"

"Komisarz Rej, you're a very understanding man.
I'll arrange your search right away."

After he had gone, Matejko said, "What are you going to do? Talk to Traffic?"

"What? Fuck that, I'm not going to do anything. It serves him right for driving when he's drunk. If he runs over a child, what's the difference between him and the Executioner?"

6

Sarah was back on site on Marszalkowska when the Germans arrived in two white buses marked *Osterreisen*. As they disembarked, the Polish workers whistled and catcalled, and three of them tried to block the entrance until they were heaved away by police. In the end, however, the Germans pushed their way through, and the door was locked behind them.

Brzezicki came up to Sarah in a huge pair of Levis and a red-checkered lumberjack shirt. "I'm sorry you chose to do things this way, Ms. Leonard."

"You didn't leave me much choice, did you? It's my job to finish this hotel on time, and that's what I'm going to do."

"Yes—but just because these Germans don't believe in the devil, that doesn't mean it isn't there."

"Mr. Brzezicki, for God's sake. I know that it's a shock when somebody gets killed. But I can't believe in any devil."

"It goes back a long, long way, Ms. Leonard. You should ask my mother about it. It goes right back in history. It was a thing that used to obey whoever fed it. If you asked it to take revenge on somebody you hated, then it would kill that person for you; and that person's parents, and that person's spouse; and every descendant of that person until there was nobody left alive."

"Very Biblical," said Sarah. "Now, if you'll excuse me, I have a site to clear and a hotel to build."

"Ms. Leonard, why don't you talk to my mother? She'll tell you."

Sarah pressed the heel of her hand against her forehead. "Mr. Brzezicki, I don't want to talk to your mother. I don't believe in devils of any kind and I can't understand why you do. You would be doing both of a us a very great favor if you tried to overcome all this superstition and got your men back to work."

Mr. Brzezicki shook his head. "I can't, Ms. Leonard. They won't do it. Not until they see that creature carried out of that sewer, dead."

"In that case, they've got themselves a hell of a long wait."

She stepped inside the door into the site. The Germans were milling around, unpacking and shouting to each other. Sarah found their foreman, a big gingery man with eyes like freshly peeled grapes. "Herr Muller? I'm Ms. Leonard. I want to thank you for bringing your men here at such short notice."

"For what you pay, Ms. Leonard, *kein Problem*."

"The architect and the construction director will be here first thing tomorrow, to tell you what stage we've reached and what needs to be done next. The first thing you have to deal with is a broken sewer pipe. The last crew went through it with a mechanical shovel. You can probably smell it."

Muller said, "How bad is it? Some of those old pipes are pretty difficult to patch. We may have to take out a whole section."

"I'll show you," said Sarah. She went to the nearest ladder and began to climb down. One of the German workers wolf-whistled, and another called out, "Watch out, Muller, she's after your job!"

Muller followed Sarah down the ladder and through

the basements to the huge broken hole in the pipe. He sniffed at the hole. Then he leaned forward a little way and listened to it.

"What are you doing?" Sarah asked him.

"You can tell a whole lot about a sewer pipe by listening to it. Its length; how full it is; whether it needs repairs."

Sarah listened, too; but all she could hear was the trickling of foul water and a distant booming sound—the echo of buses and heavy trucks trundling over manholes.

"It just sounds like echoes to me."

"Well . . . perhaps by the time we've finished we can make you an expert."

Muller crunched his way back to the ladders, and Sarah turned to follow him. As she did so, however, she thought she heard a faint, high-pitched cry. A cry like a child in distress.

She stopped, and listened, and there it was again. Very far away, very distorted, but a child crying all the same.

"Herr Muller!" she called. "Come back here!"

Reluctantly, Muller came back. "What's the matter? We can't do anything now until tomorrow."

"No—listen. I'm sure I can hear a child crying."

They listened, both of them, but all they could hear was the airy booming of traffic and the sickly trickling of sewage.

"They make all kinds of strange noises, these pipes," said Muller. "Think about it, they cover every street in Warsaw, and a few streets that don't exist anymore."

Sarah waited for a long while, but she didn't hear anymore crying. She followed Muller back up the ladder, accompanied by more wolf whistles.

"Are your men happy here?" she asked him. "They can all eat at McDonald's tonight. Senate will pay. There's a food store on Krolewska if they need coffee or bread."

"We'll manage," Muller assured her. "And don't worry about your excavation . . . we'll have your foundations dug before you know it."

Sarah hesitated at the doorway. She thought she could hear the tiniest of cries. But the traffic was far too noisy, and as she stepped outside, Brzezicki's workers began to jeer and shout, *"Krauts out! Krauts out!"* and she wouldn't have been able to hear a distressed child if it had been crying in her ear.

They stood around the open manhole in their khaki waterproof suits, four sewage workers and six police. They talked a lot and smoked a lot but none of them seemed to be particularly anxious to be the first to enter the sewer.

"The main drain along Grojecka is big enough to stand up in," Mr. Chwistek told them, consulting his plastic-covered map. "But if you want to search any of the pipes that lead into the side streets, you will have to crawl on your elbows. You'll soon get the hang of it. You all have your lines . . . don't attempt to search any of the narrow pipes without making sure that it's fastened to the main drain. Some of these pipes keep on branching off, and it isn't difficult to get lost. Besides which, *some* of them are so narrow that it's impossible to turn around."

Rej zipped up his crackly waterproof suit and tugged on his heavy-duty rubber gloves. Mr. Chwistek gave him an ingratiating smile and Rej tried to give him a reassuring nod in return.

"I don't see why we have to do this ourselves," said Matejko. He walked even more like a puppet than ever.

"We have to do it ourselves because we have to show the media that we're prepared to do anything to catch this bastard . . . even crawl through shit."

Matejko looked uneasy. He gave a "hmm," which meant that it might be necessary for Rej to crawl through shit to save his reputation, but why did *he* have to do it, too?

"I **have** to say this, komisarz. I don't want to go down **any** of those really narrow pipes, I'm claustrophobic."

"Twelve-year-old kids did it during the war. Why can't you?"

"This isn't the war, Stefan. This is a homicide investigation. And I'm not a kid."

One of the sewage workers came up and gave them a gaptoothed, maniacal grin. "Are you ready?" he wanted to know. "Just watch out for rats. If they come at you in one of the narrower pipes, just smack them to one side, like this."

"Oh, shit," said Matejko. "Rats."

The sewage worker slapped him cheerfully on the back. "You've got it. That's what this business is all about. Shit and rats."

An officer came across with a mobile phone. "Komisarz Rej . . . Nadkomisarz Dembek wants to talk to you, urgently."

"Tell him I've gone down the sewers."

"He says it's to do with this evening's news bulletin on TVP 2."

"Oh God, it's that bitch Pronaszka. Tell him I've gone down the sewers and I'm not expected back until next week."

He left the officer holding out his mobile phone, and climbed down the manhole. The gap-toothed sewage worker immediately followed him. Matejko went next, followed by two more sewage workers, the rest of the police officers, and a single sewage worker to take up the rear.

Rej eased himself off the lowest rung of the ladder and into the stream of sewage. Fortunately, it was early in the evening and it wasn't too deep or too malodorous. The waste water was mainly from showers and kitchen sinks. He waded a short way northeast, in the same direction as the flow of sewage, flicking his flash-light beam from side to side. The sewage worker came splashing down behind him, followed, very awkwardly, by Matejko.

"Holy Mother of God," said Matejko, as the weight of the sewage pressed his boots against his shins, "I didn't join the police force for this. I thought it was going to be all fresh air and fast cars."

"Don't whine," Rej snapped at him. "And don't blas-pheme, either."

"I thought you were a nonbeliever."

"What does that matter? She was somebody's mother."

They waded fifty or sixty meters along the sewer, until they reached a large domed intersection with an-other main pipe. "This is Wawelska," said the sewage worker, his flashlight darting about. Water and waste matter was pouring in from both sides, filling the cen-tral channel even more deeply. There was another iron ladder here, leading up to a manhole cover directly above their heads.

Matejko said, "How do we know which way the Ex-ecutioner went?"

"We don't," said Rej. "We'll just have to search every sewer until we find some evidence."

The sewage worker grinned, and spat. "Search every sewer? I've been working down here for seventeen years, and I don't think I've seen a tenth of them yet. The trouble is, they were built in 1886. An Englishman built them, did you know that? But they were all changed and modernized in 1939. Then the city was flattened by the Nazis, and rebuilt, and new pipes were laid, and nobody knows where half of the old pipes actually run."

He took hold of Rej's sleeve, and said, "Let me tell you something. We still find skeletons down here, now and again, in some of the disused pipes. Two years ago we found a young girl's skeleton. She couldn't have been older than ten or eleven. She was trapped in a whole mess of rusty barbed wire that the Nazis had crammed into the sewer to stop the Home Army from using it. She was still wearing a little felt coat and little woolly mittens, and she was still carrying a message in her hand. Who knows how many men and women died because she never got where she was supposed to be going?"

Another sewage worker called out, "Let's get on with it. Don't listen to him. He's been down the sewers so long he's full of crap."

They carried on northeastwards, toward Plac Narutowicza. The sewage was much deeper now, and colder, and the air stank of methane gas. They made a *slop, slop, slop* sound as they walked, and they had to be careful that the sewage didn't pour over the top of their boots. "You should see some of the foot infections people get down here. Believe me, you'd rather have leprosy." Rej's eyes began to water, and he cupped his hand over his nose and mouth in an attempt to suppress the smell. He swung his flashlight from one side of the sewer to another, into the dark, dripping subsidiary pipes, looking for any kind of unusual debris, or any scratching or scoring on the filth-caked concrete to indicate that somebody might have crawled that way. So far, they had all been the same: dark, stinking, and dripping. Rej had boldly called for a general search, but now that he was down here, things seemed very different. Even the *thought* of having to shuffle along one of these narrow pipes on his knees and elbows made him hyperventilate, and he began to pray to himself that they wouldn't find anything at all.

He couldn't imagine how children could have made their way through these pipes, with nothing but candles to light their way, under constant threat of gassing or being roasted alive by burning gasoline, or being trapped underground until they died of thirst.

They had just passed the major sewer junction under

Plac Narutowicza when Matejko said, "Look—what's that? Is that newspaper?"

Off to the left, in one of the narrower pipes, a double sheet of yellow paper was stuck to the wall. Rej waded across and peeled it off. It was *Ex Libris*, the book section from yesterday's newspaper, the same paper that they had found on the lowest rung of the manhole. It was heavily stained with blood, but most of it was still dry.

The sewage worker aimed his flashlight up the pipe. "No doubt about it . . . he went this way. You can see the marks on the walls."

"Headed where?" asked Rej.

The man consulted his map. "Right underneath the Church of the Immaculate Conception."

"Don't suppose we'll find many condoms in there," joked Matejko, but was instantly silenced by Rej's stone-hard face.

"Do you want to take a look?" asked the sewage worker. "Put this line around your waist first. If you get stuck, or if you panic, we can always drag you back out again."

Rej said, "Matejko?"

Matejko stepped back, and the sewage slopped into his boot. "I'm sorry, komisarz. I'm really claustrophobic. I can't."

"You'll be tied to a line. What are you worried about?"

"I just can't stand confined spaces, that's all. It's bad enough here, where there's headroom. I mean, even if I did find the Executioner, what could I do?"

"What could *he* do, in a pipe as small as that? Besides, you've got your gun."

Matejko came up close to him—so close that Rej thought for one absurd moment that he was going to kiss him. "Stefan, I can't go up that pipe. Please don't ask me."

"I'm not asking you. I'm ordering you."

Matejko took a deep, quavering breath. "I don't care whether you're asking or ordering. I still can't do it."

"Because you're claustrophobic?"

"Because I'm shit scared, if you want to know the truth."

"I'm sorry, I didn't hear that."

"Because I'm shit scared!"

"What?"

"Because I'm shit scared, all right?"

Matejko's voice echoed and re-echoed through the sewers. All of the other men looked at him, but there was no reading their faces. They were probably just as scared as he was, and were quite relieved that somebody else had come out and said it first.

Rej turned to the sewage worker and said, "Okay, then. It looks as if it has to be me. What will you do, follow up behind?"

The sewage worker nodded. "You'll be all right. The main thing is to keep very calm. People get bigger when they panic, their lungs inflate and their muscles tense up. Panicking always makes things worse."

Rej took off his gloves and reached inside his overalls so that he could extricate his Tokarev automatic from its shoulder holster. Then the sewage worker knotted a line around Rej's waist and another gave him a heavy-duty flashlight. "All right," he said, "Let's do it."

He turned to Matejko and said, "If anything happens to me, Jerzy, you can have my tropical fish. Make sure you clean them every two days."

Matejko said nothing, but with an expression of humiliation and helplessness watched Rej climb up into the narrow pipe. There were times when he found himself wishing that Rej would be injured in the line of duty so that he would have to retire. He liked Rej: he was almost an older brother. But because Rej could never forgive his own weaknesses, he could never tolerate anybody else's weaknesses, either.

Rej found it harder to make progress along the pipe than he had expected. It was too narrow for him to crawl properly, and so he had to shuffle himself along on his elbows and knees. Holding a gun in one hand and a flashlight in the other didn't help, but he wouldn't have been without either of them.

Up ahead of him, the pipe ran in a straight line for fifty to sixty meters, and then curved off to the right. Its sides were thick with grease, and the bottom of it was filled with a gritty beige sludge. Rej had only been crawling a few meters before his overalls were caked in filth.

"In America, you know, they use skateboards to roll themselves along pipes like this," said the sewage worker. "I asked my boss for a skateboard but he said I was down in the sewers to work, not to play."

Rej thought he heard a scuttling, scuffing sound. He stopped for a moment and directed his flashlight further up ahead. He glimpsed something moving, a curved shadow that flickered across the inside of the pipe and then vanished. He listened, but he couldn't hear anything. It must have been a reflection from his own flashlight.

"What's wrong?" asked the sewage worker.

"I don't know. I thought I heard something."

"Rats, more than likely."

"They don't bite, do they?"

"Only if you're trapped, and you can't fight back. But don't drink their piss. That's fatal."

"I wasn't planning on it. I'm a schnapps man myself."

He continued to shuffle himself forward, with the sewage worker following close behind. Too close, most of the time, because he could wriggle through the pipe much faster than Rej, and he kept nudging Rej's shoes.

"Where does this pipe lead?" asked Rej, as they reached the bend.

"The intersection of Niemcewicza and Jerozolim-skie."

"Then where?"

"Wherever you like, komisarz. We could crawl from one side of the city to the other, and never see daylight once."

Rej kept on heaving himself forward. His elbows were beginning to feel sore now, and every time he bent his knees they knocked against the side of the pipe. He tried not to think that he was seventy-five meters along a filthy pipe that was only one meter in diameter. He tried not think that he was deep beneath the foundations of the Church of the Immaculate Conception, under tons of soil and tons of stone. More than anything else, he tried to forget that he was sliding through untreated sewage, and that every breath was thick with the stench of human waste. For a moment, he had to stop, because he was starting to breathe too quickly, and he was very close to the edge of panic.

"Are you all right?" asked the sewage worker.

"I was just listening, that's all."

He was about to carry on when he heard a sharp, scraping sound, somewhere up ahead of him.

"Did you hear that?"

"Rats, that's all. We've disturbed them; and they hate to be disturbed."

But then there was another scraping sound, and something else. Up until now, a faint current of air had been blowing through the pipe—but now, abruptly, the air had become stagnant, as if the pipe had been blocked.

"Do you feel that?" asked Rej.

"Yes. Something's obstructed the airflow."

"A rat couldn't do that, could it?"

"I've seen some monsters . . . but I've never seen one big enough to block a whole pipe. It's a man."

Rej managed to twist his head around and shine his

flashlight on the sewage worker's face. "A man? You're sure about that?"

"It's always the same, when somebody else enters a narrow-diameter pipe. They cut off the airflow."

"Then there *is* somebody down here!"

"It feels like it. But don't start shooting. It could be one of our guys."

Rej turned back and shone his flashlight further up the pipe. "Who's there?" he shouted. His voice didn't echo anymore: it sounded flat and muffled. "Is anybody there?"

They listened, and waited, but there was no reply. "Maybe he's too far away to hear us," Rej suggested.

"He can hear us, all right," said the sewage worker. "In these pipes, you can sing 'Jeszcze Polska nie zginela' in Zoliborz and they can hear you in Mokotow."

"What do we do, then?" asked Rej.

"You tell me. You're the one who's trying to catch him."

Rej listened again. There was no doubt about it, he could hear a slow, thick, dragging sound, and it wasn't retreating along the pipe, it was coming toward him.

"Hallo!" he shouted. "Is anybody there? This is a warning—come out slowly! We're armed police!"

The dragging sound was louder now, but there was still no reply. Rej was shining his torch directly up the pipe but he still couldn't see anything, only darkness.

"Come out and identify yourself!" he demanded. His voice was off key. He cocked his automatic and straightened his arm, so that it was pointing straight down the pipe. He wasn't a very good shot, but if somebody was crawling up the pipe toward him, there wasn't much chance of missing.

Still there was no response. But now Rej could see that there was something dark filling up the pipe, something that seemed to blot out all reflected light. The dragging sound grew louder, like somebody heaving something wet and indescribably filthy. Another sound became audible, too. A regular, labored *scratching*, as if overgrown fingernails were making a terrible effort to claw their way along the grease-lined pipe.

Rej was not a coward. He had been attacked by drunks and petty criminals more times than he could remember. But whatever was approaching him along this sewer pipe filled him with a feeling of dread that he had never experienced before. His gun-hand was shaking uncontrollably, and he couldn't keep the flashlight still, either.

"What is it?" the sewage worker asked him, in a frightened rasp.

"I don't know. But I suggest you start making your way back."

"Can you see it?" the man wanted to know.

"I can and I can't."

"What does that mean, you can and you can't?"

"It's dark, it's totally dark. But I can see something there. I mean I can see it because I can't see anything else."

"Oh, shit," said the sewage worker, and immediately tugged on his rope.

"What? What is it?" Rej asked him.

"You stay and find out, komisarz. I'm not."

He tugged his rope again. There was a moment's pause, and then he was dragged back out of the pipe, feet first. Rej heard him sliding around the bend in the pipe with a sound like somebody riding the toboggan in the winter Olympics, then there was nothing but an echo, and then he was gone.

Rej waited and listened. He was sweating from heat and exertion and nausea. He was also beginning to feel immensely claustrophobic. The pipe was so low that he couldn't even straighten his neck, and his whole body was beginning to judder from keeping himself in a crawling position.

The dragging sound continued; and came closer still. The air, which had temporarily been motionless, began to stir past his face, forced along the pipe by whoever was coming his way.

"You have one last chance!" Rej shouted. "Either you stop, and identify yourself, or else I'm going to shoot!"

He heard a metallic clanking sound. He lifted his flashlight; but then his flashlight began to die. The beam faded to dull yellow and then to orange, and then he was left with no illumination except for the tiny amber filament of the bulb. There was a moment's pause, and then he was plunged into absolute darkness.

He held his breath. The dragging noise slowly came closer. Whoever it was, *whatever* it was, it sounded as if it were no more than four or five meters away. Rej breathed in, and when he breathed in, he smelled not only sewage but a sour, rotten stench, like fish guts. It was so putrid that he retched.

"Hold it!" he yelled, into the blackness. "Hold it right there!"

But then there was another metallic clank, much louder than the first, and another; and sparks flew from the side of the pipe. He glimpsed a shining triangle of steel, and he suddenly realized that somebody was approaching him with a huge knife, which was clattering from one side of the pipe to the other.

What was more, this somebody was dragging himself along the pipe at an unbelievable speed.

Rej fired. The shot deafened him, but all he saw in the muzzle flash was a momentary glint of steel. He couldn't have missed, yet the knife blade continued to rattle against the pipe with increasing fury. He felt a quick, intense pain in his left hand, and then a terrible hacking on his left shoulder.

He yanked wildly at the rope. *"Get me out of here!"* he screamed.

He was hit across the cheek. He felt warm blood pour down the side of his face. In panic, he fired his

gun again. The blast was so close that it scorched his
hand.

*He thought for one instant that he saw a face. A
white bony cheek; a half-closed eye. He thought he saw
a mouth that was stretched open impossibly wide.* But
it could have been nothing more than a fold of fabric,
or a complicated arrangement of shadows.

For a few seconds, though, Rej's attacker hesitated—
and in that moment of hesitation Rej's rope abruptly
tightened, and he was dragged bodily back along the
pipe.

His knees and his elbows were burned by the fric-
tion. His head was knocked against the sides of the
pipe. But all he wanted to do was to get away from his
attacker as fast as he possibly could.

He slid around the curve in the pipe, literally bod-
ysurfing on raw sewage, and now he could see reflections from the sewage workers' flashlights. *Made it*, he
thought.

But then he heard the clatter of his attacker's blade,
and it was coming nearer, and *fast*. The dragging of
fabric sounded like a steam locomotive, and ahead of
it the stench of rotting carcasses came in a nauseating
wave.

"*Faster!*" Rej shouted. "*For God's sake, faster!*"

He felt another sharp blow on his forehead, and he
clamped both his hands on top of his head in case his
attacker tried to split his skull open. In the next instant,
however, an even brighter light shone up the pipe; and
the dragging and clattering suddenly stopped. Rej was
dragged at high speed along the last twenty meters and
pulled out into the main drain. He stumbled, and almost
fell, but he was caught by Matejko and one of the sewage workers.

"I saw him!" he shouted, almost hysterically. "He's
in there! I saw him!"

"Jesus Christ, Stefan," said Matejko. "What did he
do to you?"

"What?" said Rej. He looked around and everybody was staring at him. "He hit me, that's all."

"Yes, but what with?"

Rej looked down at his left hand. It was smothered in blood, like a glistening scarlet glove. He lifted it up, and saw to his horror that the last joint of his little finger was missing.

"He—he cut my finger off!" he shouted, in amazement. "My God, look! He cut my fucking finger off!" He stared at it, unable to believe that it didn't hurt.

"He cut your face, too," said Matejko. "We'd better get you out of here right now. You don't want to get infected."

"My face?" said Rej. He cautiously lifted his right hand to his cheek. He thought that his attacker had dealt him only a glancing blow, but he felt a deep, gaping cut. He touched it with his fingertips and he could actually feel his bare cheekbone.

He stared at Matejko and understood with complete clarity that he was in shock. "Yes," he said. "You'd better get me out of here."

"Do we go after him, komisarz?" asked one of his officers.

Rej shook his head. "Leave him for now. The speed he travels, you'll never catch up with him anyhow. At least we know how he gets around."

Matejko helped him to splash back toward the manhole.

"We know *how* he does it," said Rej. "All we have to work out is why."

"Let's get you to the hospital first," said Matejko.

Rej turned around and looked back toward the entrance to the sewer pipe. "I'll get him, Jerzy, I swear to God that I'll get him."

7

Sarah was just about to leave the office for lunch when her secretary Irena came in. Irena was a tall, wide-shouldered brunette of frightening efficiency. Sarah had hired her because she was capable of intimidating Polish men almost as much as she did herself. Irena had dark brown eyes and a slight but alarmingly attractive squint, for which she wore large glasses to correct. She always wore a crisp white blouse and a slim black skirt. Sarah may have been called "the Ayatollah," but Irena was called "Ayatollah II."

"Mr. Gogiel to see you," she said.

"He doesn't have an appointment, does he?"

"No, but he says that he needs to talk to you urgently."

"All right then. Is the taxi here yet?"

Piotr Gogiel was standing waiting for her, pretending to admire the scale model of the Senate Hotel that stood in a glass case in the middle of the entrance lobby. He looked sweaty, as if he had been walking fast.

"Ms. Leonard, I'm sorry to bother you."

"Listen, Mr. Gogiel, I'm late for a lunch appointment. I'm taking a taxi to the Old Town. Do you mind coming with me, and talking on the way?"

"Not at all."

The morning was humid and the air was tinged yellow with photosynthetic smog. Even with the windows rolled right down, the interior of the taxi was sticky and smelled of other people's perspiration. Sarah leaned forward and said to the driver, "Don't go by Krakowskie Przedmiescie, it's going to be solid."

The driver said something deprecatory about interfering women, his cigarette waggling up and down between his lips. Sarah ignored him.

"What's so urgent?" she asked Piotr.

"This is very embarrassing." he said. "I didn't know whether I ought to tell you or not, because I don't have any real proof, not as yet."

"You don't have any real proof of what?"

"Well . . . there's a chap in the foreign investment department called Antoni Dlubak. I happened to be talking to him about Jan Kaminski—you know, and the way that work was being held up because the demolition workers think he was killed by a devil. *He* said that Kaminski had been in touch with him two or three times, because he was investigating Senate's finance structure."

"I know he was. But I don't know what he expected to find."

"Antoni Dlubak knew what he expected to find, and Antoni Dlubak helped him to find it."

Sarah turned to him with narrowed eyes. "What are you talking about, Mr. Gogiel?"

Piotr lowered his voice. "Dlubak had been curious for two or three months about the irregular way in which large sums of money were moving in and out of Senate's contingency account."

"When you say 'large sums,' how much are you talking about?"

"Two, two and a half. Sometimes less, mostly more."

"Two, two and a half thousand? That's not much."

Piotr shook his head, and Sarah's eyes widened.

"Two and a half *million*?" she said. "I've never authorized expenditure on that scale—and we've never had any receipts on that scale. As far as I know, there's about $750,000 in that account, probably less."

"That's how much there *should* be. But it looks as if somebody's been using Senate's account to launder money. That was what Kaminski was on to."

"And that would easily be a motive for somebody to murder him, wouldn't it?"

"Well, yes. These days, people are being killed for a roll of carpet."

Sarah worriedly sat back in her seat. "Mr. Gogiel—this could be catastrophic. Does your friend Dlubak have any inkling who's behind this laundering?"

"He says he's made an educated guess. But he won't tell me what it is. He says he wouldn't tell Kaminski, either, not until he was sure. Even when he has proof, he says he'll have to be very, very cautious. The kind of men who are laundering ten or eleven million dollars a year are not the kind of men who are going to take kindly to whistle-blowers."

"Do the police know about this yet?"

"They've arranged to talk to Dlubak this afternoon. Two detectives . . . one from the fraud squad and one from the homicide squad. He's not going to tell them anything, but he'll have to show them the records."

Sarah said, "Who has the authority to move money in and out of the Senate contingency account, apart from me?"

"You're the only one . . . and, as you know, even you need a countersignature from Jacek Studnicki. I suppose somebody from Senate's headquarters could authorize transactions directly from New York, but they would always inform you, wouldn't they?"

"Not if they didn't want me to find out about it."

Piotr nodded. They had reached the Old Town Market Place, wide and cobbled, with medieval façades on all four sides, every one of them reconstructed from rubble after the war. The taxi stopped outside the Basilisk Restaurant, and the driver twisted around in his seat and dropped ash onto Piotr's knee.

"Wait a moment—I'll be going back," Piotr instructed him. Then, to Sarah, "Listen, Ms. Leonard, you have to be very careful about this. If somebody has managed to move so much money through Senate's accounts, then you can be sure that they've covered their tracks. You may even find that they've made it look as though *you're* responsible. I don't want to frighten you, but if they were prepared to cut off Jan Kaminski's head . . . well, you shouldn't do anything rash."

"You mean they'll want *my* head, too?"

Piotr flushed. "I didn't want to put it that way, but yes."

"In that case, thanks for the warning. Call me later this afternoon, when the police have finished talking to your friend. This is one time when I need to stay well ahead of the game."

Rej came back from hospital to find Nadkomisarz Dembek in his windowless office, talking to Matejko. He still felt battered and sore. His left arm was in a sling, his cheek and his forehead were bandaged, and he walked with a limp because both knees had been severely bruised when he was pulled out of the pipe. He walked around Dembek as if he were no more significant than a hat-stand, and sat at his desk.

"Have you drawn up that plan for a full-scale search of the sewers?" he asked Matejko, lighting up a Camel and blowing out smoke.

"If he has," said Dembek, "it's no longer any concern of yours."

"Meaning what?"

"Meaning that you don't tell television presenters to get stuffed on the evening news. Especially when they're voicing a genuine public concern about a major series of crimes which *you* can't solve."

"What is it with you and this Anna Pronaszka?" Rej demanded. "Don't tell me there's something going on between you. She may be a bitch but she's a good-looking bitch."

"You're off the case, Stefan. You can't solve it and you can't handle it. You're on suspension until further notice."

Rej said, "This is a joke, right?"

"As you've told me often enough, I don't have a sense of humor. I want you to hand all of your notes and files over to Witold Jarczyk."

"Oh, for God's sake, Arthur! Witold couldn't find an elephant if it was sitting in his lap."

"I'm sorry . . . you haven't left me any choice. Go home, take some leave. When was the last time you went on vacation?"

Rej was about to start shouting at him when Matejko caught his eye and gave him a quick shake of the head. He had every right to be angry, but it wasn't worth it. The more abusive he was, the longer he would be suspended. He might even lose his job altogether, and he certainly couldn't afford to do that.

"Get some rest," Dembek told him. "Go up to the mountains, I always do. It gives you a chance to think."

Rej nodded in resignation.

"We all need to think things over, now and again," said Dembek, trying to be conciliatory. "Our batteries get run down. Who knows, once you've had a rest, maybe you'll think of a way to catch the Executioner."

"Yes," Rej replied, with deep sarcasm. "Maybe it'll come to me in a vision."

"You can laugh, Stefan, but homicide investigation is 90 percent spadework, 10 percent intelligence, and 100 percent inspiration."

Rej blew out a long thin stream of smoke. "You

know who said that? I did, to you, on your very first day on the homicide squad."

He drove back to his apartment block in Ochota, one of six identical blocks built right under the flight path to the airport. He went up in the elevator to the fifth floor, opened his front door, and closed it very quietly behind him. He felt totally drained, as if he had been visited by vampires every night for a week. Apart from that, his left hand was throbbing, because he had taken it out of the sling so that he could drive.

He hadn't taken any kind of vacation since Maria had left him. He hadn't seen the point of it. Two years ago, he had taken a day trip to the picturesque town of Otwock, on the River Swider, and had wandered in the rain through its aromatic pine forests feeling more miserable than he had ever felt in his entire life.

He took off his coat and hung it up on the peg in the hallway. Then he went into the living room, poured himself a glass of vodka, and went out onto the balcony. Below him, on the scrubby grass, some small boys were playing gangsters. One of them had made a model Uzi out of two pieces of wood, and was mowing his friends down with six hundred imaginary rounds a minute.

Rej's apartment was painted white and sparsely furnished with cheap varnished furniture, but there were still feminine touches around. He always kept a bowl of fresh fruit on the sideboard, even if he didn't eat it until it turned brown, and there were lace doilies under the ashtrays. He always tried to remember to buy fresh flowers, at least once a week. An apartment without flowers was too painfully lonely. There were some bronze chrysanthemums on the coffee table, but they had started to drop their petals.

On the wall hung a print of Cracow in winter: snow-covered roofs, and church spires seen dimly through the fog. Maria had been born and raised in Cracow, and that was part of the reason that their relationship had been flawed from the very beginning. Warsaw was a place: gritty and competitive. But Cracow was a state of mind.

Rej sat on the balcony in a rickety green-and-white striped picnic chair that Maria had bought from a street trader. He was trying very hard to feel angry and humiliated that Dembek had taken him off the Executioner case, but after his first vodka he was surprised to find that he was almost relieved. Apart from the physical damage that the Executioner had done him, his finger and his forehead and his shoulder, he was beginning to suffer mentally, too. The Executioner case was like a Rubik's cube. No matter which way he twisted and turned it, he couldn't grasp how it worked, or what he had to do to match one incident to the next. If he was at home, maybe he could think about it more laterally. Maybe, for all of his sarcasm, he might indeed have a vision that would make it all clear.

He sipped vodka, and listened to dogs barking and the *brrrrrrpp-brrrrrrppp* of boys playing with pretend machine-guns. He watched washing idly flapping on makeshift lines, and women coming and going with baby-buggies. He saw all the everyday things that happened around his block of flats, which he had never seen before. The very ordinariness of it all was a revelation to him: the way the sun rose and people walked past and buses came and went.

He sat on his picnic chair and his eyes filled with tears.

Sarah was down at the excavation site on Marszalkowska when her cell phone vibrated in the back pocket of her jeans.

"Sarah Leonard." She was watching the German workmen noisily digging up the broken section of sewer pipe with an excavator. Senate's civil engineers had estimated that they would have to tear up thirty meters of old piping and replace it with new; and Muller, the German foreman, had agreed with them.

"You have to do this job properly. Once you have a hotel standing on this site, it's going to be too late. Do you know how much human waste a twelve-story hotel produces in a day?"

"I do, as a matter of fact. Solid waste, eleven hundred and twelve pounds. Liquid waste, forty-five hundred and four gallons. Paper, four hundred and twelve pounds. Tampons, pantyliners and other material, thirty-seven pounds. Do you want that in metric?"

Muller had stared at her for a long time, and then walked away.

The voice on the end of the phone said, "Sarah? This is Clayton Marsh."

"Mr. Marsh! I'm so glad you called! Did my father tell you what all this was about?"

"He gave me a serious inkling, let's put it that way. In fact I'll tell you how serious it was. I'm here now, at Warsaw airport."

"I can't believe it! Listen—if you can wait there for twenty minutes, I'll have the company limo pick you up."

"That's all right. I'll take a taxi. Just tell me where you are."

"Our office is Grzybowska 12. Ask for Irena, she'll take care of you. She's booked you a room at the Marriott, you should be comfortable there. I'm down on site at the moment. I'll meet you later."

Sarah tossed back her hair. She was feeling better already. Not only had Muller and his men made enormous progress on the demolition site in only a few hours, but now Clayton Marsh had arrived. Clayton was retired now, but his track record in homicide investigation was legendary. He had caught Jay Wakeman, the baseball player who had killed his wife and her lover in a housefire that even fire department investigators had described as "accidental." He had found

Rafaello d'Annunzio, the racketeer, and secured a conviction for first-degree murder, even after nine people had sworn that he was attending a charity concert in Cicero at the time the homicide had taken place. Clayton Marsh had one of the most original minds in criminal investigation, and if he couldn't find the Executioner, then nobody could.

Muller came over and said, "We're just about ready to take out the old sewer pipe and replace it with a new section. Do you want to watch?"

"Sure, why not?"

They climbed down the aluminum ladders into the basement area. Muller's men had excavated all around the broken section of pipe and cut it free at both ends. They had wrapped heavy-duty chains around it, and now they were preparing to lift it out.

Sarah said to Muller, "You know why I called you in, don't you?"

Muller nodded. "Your Mr. Brzezicki made a point of telling me. Well, more fool him, that's what I say. If he wants to miss out on a fat contract like this just because he's scared of some devil . . . I'll tell you what, if any of my men came face to face with this Executioner, devil or not—" He made a neck-wringing gesture with both hands.

The crane's diesel bellowed, the chains jangled and tightened, and the broken section of sewer pipe shifted in the soil. Slowly, dripping sewage, it was raised out of its excavated bed, and lifted over their heads. It was loaded onto the back of a dump truck, and then the chains were lowered back into the basement so that the workmen could hitch up the new section of pipe.

One of the workmen jumped down into the excavation with a sweeping-brush to clear soil away from the severed ends of the piping.

Muller said, "Once we've got this sewer sealed, do you think Brzezicki and his men will want to come back?"

"I don't know. Some of his men were saying that they would only come back if the Executioner was caught and killed and they could see the body for themselves."

Muller tapped his forehead. *"Verrückt,"* he said. "They're mad."

The new pipe was chained up and swung over the hole. They were just about to lower it, however, when one of the workmen whistled and lifted a hand to stop them. "Hey! Where's Hans?" he called out.

"He was down there, sweeping out the pipes."

"Yes, but where is he now?"

The workmen looked around. There was no sign of Hans. Sarah had seen him down at the open mouth of the sewer pipe, but she couldn't recall having seen him climb out. Muller said, "Uwe! Jurgen! Take a look inside the pipe! We don't want to seal him up in there!"

Two workmen jumped down into the trench and peered inside the pipe. "Hans? Hans, are you in there? Come on, Hans, we're closing the pipe!"

Sarah frowned at Muller and approached the edge of the excavation. "Did anybody see him climb out of the hole?" asked Muller. There was general murmuring and head-shaking.

"How could he disappear like that?" asked Sarah.

"He didn't go for a piss, did he?" Muller demanded. "Jakob, go take a look in the john."

"Hans!" yelled one of the workmen down in the hole, his hands cupped around his mouth. "If you're in there, Hans, you'd better come on out quick!"

All they heard was an echo. The man hesitated for a moment, and then ducked his head and entered the pipe. They could hear his footsteps splashing along the watercourse. Then they heard him say, "Christ, it stinks in here."

A few seconds later, though, he came back out again, and he was holding the long-handled broom that Hans had been using to sweep away the loose soil. His face was serious. "I found this," he said. "And it looks as if there's blood in the pipe, too."

Muller gave Sarah a quick, hard glance. "Maybe your Mr. Brzezicki wasn't so stupid after all. Jurgen, go find a couple more flashlights. Go down that sewer as far as you can and take a look. Take a pick-handle with you. Jakob! While you're up there, get on the phone for me and call the police, and an ambulance, too. Who's the detective in charge?" he asked Sarah.

"Komisarz Stefan Rej. I've got his number."

Armed with a pickaxe handle and a crowbar, the two workmen switched on their flashlights and crouched their way into the sewer.

Muller called, "Hey, you two! Any sign of trouble, don't worry about being heroes, just get your asses out of there."

"Try to stop us," came the sardonic, disembodied reply.

Sarah checked her watch. She tried to appear upbeat, but she was beginning to feel anxious and edgy about this project. She had suffered catastrophic setbacks before, and even fatalities: two workmen had been buried alive in concrete when they were building the Senate Sofia. Nine more had been injured when scaffolding collapsed at the Senate Belgrade. But this project was different. This project had the smell of brimstone about it; the feeling of irredeemable ill luck. It wasn't just Jan Kaminski's murder, either, or Jozef Brzezicki's superstitious belief in an underground devil. It was the way that Ben had suddenly appeared to take personal control—Ben, with all his talk of persuading city officials "to take a better decision"—and Piotr Gogiel's allegations of criminal money-laundering.

She knew that she was going to have to take back control of this whole development, otherwise she was going to find herself increasingly pushed to the edge of what was really going on—while still being answerable for the consequences. If she lost her grip any further, her head would be at risk, and not just from the Executioner, either.

"Nothing so far!" came an echoing voice from out of the pipe. "But this definitely looks like blood!"

Muller jumped down into the excavation himself. "How far does that stretch of pipe run?"

"Two hundred meters. Then it runs into a wider chamber."

Sarah heard police sirens in the distance. But she heard something else, too. Deep within the pipe, a throaty, tremulous sound, like a primitive wind instrument, or someone blowing across the neck of a large empty bottle. She frowned at Muller, and he said, "Air . . . moving along the pipe."

"Why should it do that?"

"Could be a surge of water. I don't know."

Then they heard another sound. A slow, insistent chuffing. This was followed almost immediately by an odd, strangled noise, and then a ringing, reverberating clang of metal.

"Jurgen!" shouted Muller. "Uwe!"

There was no answer. Muller looked up at Sarah uneasily. "Maybe they went further."

"Maybe they did, but don't try looking for them. Leave it to the police."

The workmen began to shuffle and murmur. One of them said, "We can't just leave them there, can we? Supposing they're hurt?"

"Let's give them a couple more minutes," Muller suggested. "They've probably gone around a bend in the sewer, and they can't hear us."

At that moment, a fragment of something crimson came flying out of the open mouth of the sewer pipe. It struck Muller's shin, and dropped to the ground just beside his shoe. He reached down to pick it up, and then suddenly stepped away from it, his face contorted with disgust.

"What is it?" Sarah asked him, although his expression said everything.

"It's a—part of—somebody's hand."

Sarah stared down at it. Muller was right. The bloody fragment was somebody's palm, chopped off like a cutlet. No fingers, no thumb, only a squarish bonyjoint.

The sirens were whooping closer now. Sarah pressed her hand over her mouth. She had never seen a dead body before, except for her grandfather, in his casket, with a Bible held in his hands. She didn't want to see one now. Muller said, "There's somebody in there, apart from them. Somebody's killed them, for God's sake!"

Sarah said, "You don't know for sure that they're—" But she was interrupted by a terrible wet bursting noise, and the frantic clashing of steel against the sides of the sewer pipe. The next thing she knew, more pieces of flesh and bone came flying out, a grisly blizzard of arms and feet and curved sections of rib, followed by long stringy streamers of intestine and soggy lumps of lung. Muller, standing right in front of the opening, was inundated in human offal. He stood there, too stunned to move, while half a pelvis hurtled out of the pipe and fell at his feet, and then a shin bone hit him on the right shoulder.

Sarah turned away. Her whole body was stiff with shock. She took two mechanical steps toward the ladders, and then she couldn't move any further. She felt as if her nervous system had shut down; as if her body couldn't understand what her brain wanted her to do.

She stood rigid while police and ambulancemen came hurrying down the ladders, passing her by on either side. She heard them shouting; and the workmen shouting back at them in German. She heard somebody saying, "Oh God, oh God, oh God," over and over again.

*   *   *

he was still there an hour later when Clayton Marsh arrived. He was a tall, heavy, silver-haired man in his early fifties—handsome in the mold of Howard Keel. He was wearing a camel-hair coat and dark brown trousers. An enamel pin in his lapel bore the badge of the Chicago Police Department. He gripped Sarah's hand and said, "Hi. Your secretary told me you were here. Looks like you've got yourself some kind of pig's dinner."

"You're not joking. There were three workmen killed here, less than two hours ago. Not just killed, they were chopped up."

"You saw it happen?"

"I was right here. Whoever did it, he just—God, he just chopped them to pieces."

"Are you all right?" Clayton asked her. "You look like you could use a stiff drink."

"I'm okay, really. I just can't stop shaking."

Clayton looked around. "Listen, I just arrived, there's not very much that I can do now. I don't want to step on anybody's toes. But I wouldn't mind talking to that Komisarz Stefan Rej you mentioned."

"They took him off the case. I don't know why; he seemed to be making some real progress. The new man they've put onto it seems pretty dim to me."

"Oh, well, that's good news," said Clayton, hitching up his belt. "The dimmer the cops, the more chance I've got of solving the case without any interference."

Komisarz Witold Jarczyk came over. He was dark-haired, and thin to the point of emaciation. With his sharp nose and his pointed ears he looked like a court jester, starved of approval and overwhelmed by gloom.

"Thank you for waiting, Ms. Leonard," he said. "We might need to speak to you again later, but you don't mind that, do you?"

"No, komisarz, I don't mind that."

Clayton said, "Pardon me, sir, do you have any idea how these three men died?"

Jarczyk stared at him with bulging eyes. "I'm sorry? Who are you?"

"I'm a friend of Ms. Leonard's, that's all."

"Well . . . we don't know yet. They were cut to pieces with a very sharp instrument. But we'll have to wait for the autopsy to find out how, or why. Quite frankly, we don't know whose fingers belong on whose hand. Now, if you don't mind—"

"Can I go now?" Sarah pleaded.

Jarczyk was fumbling in the pockets of his baggy brown suit. He produced a single unwrapped mint and started sucking it. "Yes, of course. I'll let you know if I need to talk to you anymore."

Clayton shepherded Sarah out of the basement area and helped her up the ladder to street level. There were people milling everywhere—police lights flashing, TV lights glaring. "Let's go someplace quiet," Clayton suggested.

They went to the mezzanine bar in the Marriott Hotel. A pianist was playing a convoluted version of "The Girl from Ipanema." Clayton ordered a Jack Daniel's on the rocks and Sarah joined him. She didn't usually drink hard liquor, but after seeing those men massacred, she needed it. She was still trembling as if she was coming down with a fever, and when she caught sight of herself in the mirror on the other side of the bar, she looked completely bloodless, paler than ever.

Clayton said, "Your pa sends his love. All the same, he's worried about you, what with all these murders."

Sarah sipped her drink and looked away, trying hard not to cry.

"I've read all of the e-mail you sent me," Clayton told her. "But I'm not so sure that Kaminski was killed because he was checking out Senate's financial affairs. I can't see anybody at Senate taking a contract out on anybody, can you, just because he stumbled across a little palm-greasing. These days, even the Mafia prefer to take somebody to court, rather than go to the trouble of whacking them and then disposing of the body."

Sarah said, "It was more than bribery, it was fraud. Piotr Gogiel thinks they could be laundering ten to twelve million dollars a year."

"Jesus H. Priest. Now *that's* a reason for putting someone away. Listen—I'm going to have to see your bank records. It shouldn't take too long to find out who's been using your account."

"Whoever it is, he's been very clever."

"I'm sure he has. But I'm not just some dumb old flatfoot, Sarah. I took a three-year course in accountancy with the FBI. It takes more than clever to hide funny money from me."

Sarah said, "I just can't work out if these murders are connected to Senate International or not. We've had four people killed on our site now, but the Executioner is supposed to have killed at least twelve people altogether, and they don't seem to have anything in common."

"Well, that's what I gathered from your messages. But there are ways and means of finding guys like this, even if there's no obvious connection between any of his victims."

Clayton ordered another drink, and explained to Sarah how he was going to isolate the linking factors between the Executioner's victims. "The cops run through all of the obvious data, and so they should. But if your linking factor isn't immediately apparent, then you have to carry on and start intersecting your non-obvious data, such as star signs and shoe size and speech mannerisms and all kinds of arcane stuff like that. And if you're still drawing a blank, you really have to go right off the map and intersect factors like what age they lost their virginity and where they were on 13 April, 1991, and what's their favorite tropical fish."

He reached across the table and laid a paternal hand on hers. "Let me tell you this, Sarah. I've investigated thirty-seven multiple homicides. I didn't catch all of the perpetrators, but I never once failed to discover what it was that linked all the victims together. Once, it was the fact that they lisped. Can you believe that? The perpetrator couldn't stand anybody who lisped. He had a perforated eardrum and lisping set his teeth on edge."

"It said on the news that the Executioner hides in the sewers. You know, like Harry Lime."

"Sure—and I bet there's a reason for that, too. But it's no use searching the sewers. If this guy knows his way around, they'll never find him down there, not with a hundred cops with tracker dogs. We had a pretty similar case on the South Side once, a guy using the sewers as a getaway route. All we caught was hepatitis. No—the only way to find him is to work out the factor that links all of his victims, and make sure that we're there when he goes for his next victim."

"You mean a trap? An ambush? Wouldn't that be too risky for the victim?"

"Properly worked out, not at all. This guy has a driving force, Sarah. I don't know what it is yet but I intend to find out. It could be revenge, it could be guilt, it could be the fact that his mother was frightened by an aardvark when she was eight months pregnant. Who knows? Nobody knows, as of right now, but we're going to find out."

"How's your Polish?" Sarah asked him.

"I couldn't give the Pilsudski Memorial Lecture, but I can get by. My mother was Polish, and she didn't speak anything else when dad was at work. That's why I grew up calling a doughnut a paczki."

"This could be really dangerous, you know. Whatever happened today, those poor men were chopped up like—God, like something out of an abattoir. They were just *bits*."

"That's part of this Executioner's technique," said Clayton, leaning back in his chair. "He's got this reign of terror going, and the more frightening he is, and the more everybody panics, the more he gets off on it. Taking the heads off, that's part of it. But a killer is a killer is a killer. I mean, sure those guys were just bits. But when somebody kills you it doesn't matter how they do it or what they do with you afterward, does it? You're fucking dead, excuse my language."

"Do you really think you can catch him?"

"Oh, for sure, I'll catch him. He's taking too many risks now . . . killing right out in the open. And he's not expecting *me*."

He tipped back the last of his drink. "By the way . . . I overheard one of the cops saying that your friend Komisarz Rej is pretty damn pissed because he was taken off the case. I'll give him a call tomorrow and see if I can't pick his brains."

"Good luck," said Sarah. "He's good, but he's not what you'd call amenable."

"We'll see." Clayton was silent for a while, staring at a point just west of the Marriott ashtray. Then he looked up and said, "Your pa didn't tell me what a looker you'd grown up to be. Do you want to show me some of the nightlife in this Godforsaken city?"

"I don't know about tonight."

"What are you going to do, sit in your apartment all night and have nightmares? Come on, it'll do you good. It'll do me good, too. I haven't had a pretty woman on my arm since my wife passed on."

8

As soon as the ambulance crew had left, the door swung open and Rej came in. Dr. Wojniakowski looked up from the sink, unsurprised.

"Oh, Rej, I was wondering when you would pop up."

There were three stainless steel autopsy tables and there was a large black plastic bag on each of them. Dr. Wojniakowski dried his hands, took out a cigarette, and lit it with nerveless fingers. Once he had puffed out a satisfactory amount of pungent blue smoke, he approached the first bag and palpated it gently between both hands.

"Pigs' guts," he remarked. "Not literally. That's what it feels like, that's all."

Rej said, "The news report said they were chopped to pieces." He approached the bags cautiously, almost as if he expected them to burst open, and three hideously-disassembled bodies to come jumping out.

"It certainly *feels* as if they were chopped to pieces."

"In just a few minutes? The three of them? How the hell did he manage that?"

Dr Wojniakowski coughed, and cleared his throat. "That's what we have to find out."

He started to untie the first bag. The early afternoon light fell through the wired-glass windows and illumi-

nated Room Three like a chapel, with Dr. Wojniakowski's cigarette smoke for incense. "You shouldn't
be here, you know, Rej. You'll get me into all kinds
of trouble."

Rej approached the autopsy table and smelled that
thick pungency of recent death—blood and fat and di-
gestive acids, as well as excrement. He watched while
Dr. Wojniakowski rolled back the top of the bag and
revealed a heap of bones and flesh. He saw pallid,
sliced-open lungs; dark slippery slices of liver; and
endless bloody coils of intestine.

"I don't know what they expect me to do with all
this," he said. He reached into the bag and took out an
indescribable piece of flesh with another piece dangling
from it. "Do you know what they said? They've done
their best to put all the right pieces in all the right bags,
but there may be some margin of error."

Again, he plunged his hands into the bloody heap in
front of him. This time he came up with two penises,
one with a single testicle attached, and one without any
at all. "Margin of error?" he said, snorting smoke. "Either they don't know anything about anatomy, or this
man had the happiest wife in the whole of the German
Republic."

Rej swallowed, and peered into the glutinous depths
of the bag.

"Do you want some gloves?" asked Dr. Wojniakowski. "Then you could really rummage."

"I can't see a head," said Rej, cautiously; praying
that he wouldn't.

"No, that's right. None of them has a head. Your
colleague Komisarz Jarczyk warned me of that, on the
phone."

"So it could be the Executioner?"

Dr Wojniakowski looked at him steadily. "I don't
know who it is, or what it is. Who do you know who
can chop up three grown men in only two or three
minutes? Or what?" He paused, and smoked, and then

he said, "By the way, you'd left the office before my results were sent round, but your friend Jan Kaminski was definitely beheaded with the same knife that beheaded all previous six victims: and so was Mr. Wroblewski. There were microscopic traces of metal on all of them, and they all matched."

"How about the fabric sample?" asked Rej.

"That was very interesting, too. We'll be testing it again tomorrow, but the fibers under Jan Kaminski's fingernails matched the fabric sample that you found in the sewer . . . so, presumably, the fabric was worn by Kaminski's assailant. The reason we're testing it again, though, is because of its apparent age."

"What are you talking about, 'apparent age?' "

"It's velvet; and it was originally dyed black. Our chromograph tests show that it probably dates back to the mid-seventeenth century, maybe even earlier."

"Seventeenth century? Are you kidding me?"

"There's no mistaking it. The button supports it, too. It's made of solid brass, handmade, and it's embossed with the face of some kind of beast. We took it to our button-making friend on Zabkowska Street, and he confirmed that it had to have been made well before 1700 . . . that was when they stopped using powdered zinc ore to make brass and started using molten zinc. The beast, too, is a very old symbol. We think it's a basilisk—a monster that was supposed to paralyze anybody who looked at it."

Rej said, "What do you think? Do you think that the Executioner was actually wearing this seventeenth-century velvet?"

"That's beyond my competence, I'm afraid."

"Was it rotten? Would it have torn easily, when Kaminski grabbed hold of it?"

"Oh, yes. It was soaked in sewage, of course, and it was just like rotten velvet curtains."

Rej shook his head. "I don't know what I'm dealing with here, Teofil, I really don't."

"Oh? I didn't think you were dealing with anything. I thought you were on suspension."

Rej untangled his bandaged left hand from its sling and defiantly held it up. "See this? I think this gives me an interest in what's going on, don't you? It was sheer luck that *I* didn't end up all jumbled up in a plastic bag, like these three poor bastards." He took a deep breath. The scent of death was beginning to make him feel queasy. "What about the girl, did you find any new evidence on her?"

Dr. Wojniakowski shook his head. "We don't have her arm, so it's impossible to say whether it was pulled through the mailbox manually or mechanically. I'll tell you something, though. It would have taken the force of your average carjack to tear her arm off like that."

"More power than most men could muster?"

"More power than *any* man could muster, in my opinion, except if he'd been on steroids or some kind of drug like the athletes use. Even so . . ."

Rej blinked at him impatiently. "Even so, what? Where does that lead us?"

"I don't know, Rej. You're the detective."

Rej took a last look at the plastic bags. "All right, then. Thanks for everything. I'll leave you to it."

With a thick squelching sound, Dr. Wojniakowski plunged both hands back into the mess of stomachs and intestines. For the first time since Rej had first met him, fifteen years ago, he thought that Teofil looked genuinely happy.

Muller was waiting for Sarah when she returned to the office. He was wearing a cheap beige suit and his face was ashen.

"I'm sorry, Ms. Leonard. The men won't go back to work."

"Somebody's going to have to seal the sewer."

"I know that. But it won't be us."

Sarah sat down at her desk. Her computer screen

said *Welcome! Have A Positive Day!* but she couldn't think of anything positive. All she could think of were bloody lumps of body, flying through the air. All she could think of was legs and hands and pieces of rib-cage.

"You were down there," she said. She still couldn't help quaking when she thought about it. "What do *you* think happened?"

Muller shrugged. "I couldn't tell you. I couldn't see anything at all. First of all I saw their flashlights, then there was nothing but dark. Then—" he raised both hands as if he were still warding off the shower of flesh. "I only once saw anything like that before, and that was when a man walked into an airplane propeller at Tempelhof."

Sarah was quiet for a moment. Then she said, "You wouldn't like another day to consider?"

"I'm sorry, Ms. Leonard. *Es tut mir leid.* But the men all believe that it was some kind of devil, and they won't go back. Perhaps Mr. Brzezicki and his men weren't so mad after all."

There was no point in reminding Muller that he was under contract. Senate International could be liable for millions of dollars of compensation if the dead workers' families decided to sue, which they almost certainly would. Sarah said, "All right, then, if that's the way you feel. I can't say that I blame you."

Muller stood looking at her as if he wanted to say something but couldn't find the words. At last, he said, "It wasn't natural, you know. The way those men were killed. It was—something out of a nightmare."

Sarah gave him the smallest of shrugs. She was supposed to go to a meeting with a Polish advertising agency this afternoon, but she pressed her intercom buzzer for Irena and told her to postpone until next week. Muller waited as if waiting might solve something; as if it proved his sincerity. Sarah started writing in her diary and he stayed where he was, not moving.

She stopped writing and looked up. It was only then that she realized that his eyes were closed, as if he were asleep.

Because it was so warm, Antoni Dlubak took his sandwiches into the Saxon Garden and sat down to eat them on a bench in front of the fountain. He unwrapped the greaseproof paper, and immediately four or five birds came hopping up to him.

He should have eaten his lunch in the office because he still had the Interpress accounts to finish, but he spent most of his days and all of his nights alone, and he enjoyed coming out and mixing with other people. In the nineteenth century, the Saxon Garden had been called "the Warsaw salon" because the cream of society used to meet here. Today the passers-by were less fashionable, but Dlubak usually managed to find somebody interesting to talk to—a bus driver, or an antiques dealer, or a waitress, or an old soldier.

He munched his sandwiches and expectantly looked around. The broad avenue that runs through the center of the garden was crowded with strollers. The sun sparkled through the oak trees, and threw dancing shadows on the statues that lined the avenue on either side—figures representing the seasons, and the arts, and strange mythological creatures—so that they looked almost as if they were alive.

A pretty girl in a tight white T-shirt and a short pink skirt came walking toward him. Dlubak silently willed her to stop and sit on the bench next to him, but of course he had no such luck. She didn't even glance at him as she strutted past. All she gave him was the briefest waft of perfume, and then even that was gone.

Dlubak was twenty-eight years old. He had contracted rickets when he was four, and so his legs had never developed properly. His blond hair was thinning, and he was plumper than he ought to be, but he was oddly good-looking, with a broad, genial face, and a

winning smile. The trouble was, his good-looking face
sat so incongruously on his distorted little body that
women seemed to find him more repellent than they
would have done if he had been out-and-out ugly.

He had only ever had one girlfriend, a very plain girl
called Magda who worked for Mazurkas travel agency.
Magda had no interests in life except her skin condition
and complained about everything. They had made love
three times in Dlubak's room. After the third time, she
complained that he "didn't know how to make a
woman happy" and that was the last he saw of her.

He wasn't altogether sorry. She never stopped
scratching her elbows.

Dlubak had diverted his frustrated sexual energy into
his work. He had already been promoted four times at
Vistula Kredytowy, and now he was the youngest
member of the international loans and finance department. He stayed at the office late every night and
worked on projects which his superiors had never even
asked him to do. Which was how he had come to detect
the unusual movement of millions of dollars through
Senate International's contingency account.

He didn't much like his sandwiches today, mashed
sardines with tomato ketchup. It was close to the end
of the month and he hadn't had enough money for
sausage. But while he was sitting there eating them, a
man in a brown suit came from nowhere at all and sat
down next to him, and said, unnecessarily loudly,
"They look tasty!"

Dlubak blinked at him. The man was very swarthy
and unshaven, with thick dry lips and a bulbous nose.
He smelled of cigarettes and body odor, which he had
unsuccessfully tried to mask with an aftershave that
smelled like Pif-Paf flyspray.

"They're only sardine," said Dlubak. "But you can
have one, if you like."

The man took the proffered sandwich without hesitation and started to eat it. Dlubak was expecting him

to say something, but all he did was wink and nod as if he thought that Dlubak were party to some incredibly funny private joke.

"It's nice here, isn't it?" said Dlubak. "The fountain, the trees. I always sit by the fountain."

The man glanced at the fountain without much interest. It was like a huge champagne glass, made of stone, decorated with dolphins. The water glittered in the sunlight, and the breeze blew trails of spray across the flowerbeds.

"Summer is never long enough, don't you think?" asked Dlubak. "Mind you, that's something to do with age. When I was a boy, summers seemed to last forever."

The man finished his sandwich and brushed crumbs from his lap. "Nothing lasts forever, Mr. Dlubak."

Dlubak stared at him open-mouthed. "How do you know my name?"

"I was given your name, that's how."

"Not by me, you weren't. Not unless we've talked before. And even then, I don't usually—"

The man said, "We haven't talked before, don't worry. Mr. Zboinski sent me. Do you know Mr. Zboinski? Mr. Roman Zboinski. Very powerful businessman."

The name sounded horribly familiar, but Dlubak wasn't sure why.

"Mr. Zboinski wants a little chat with you," the man continued. "He thinks that private affairs ought to stay private, that's why."

"I don't think I understand what you're getting at."

The man grinned at him. "You don't mind if I have another sandwich? I'm quite partial to sardines. But you shouldn't put so much ketchup on them." He dipped into Dlubak's greaseproof wrapper without waiting for an answer. He took a mouthful of sandwich, and then he said. "My car's parked just across the street. This won't take very long."

"You want me to come with you now? I can't do that. I have a meeting in twenty minutes."

The man swallowed and sniffed, and then—almost as an afterthought—he held open his coat to show Dlubak the butt of an automatic pistol stuck in his belt. Dlubak couldn't believe it. He looked quickly left and right, as if one of his colleagues from the office were suddenly going to appear and tell him that it was all a practical joke, and that the rest of the international finance department were smothering their laughter behind the trees. But passers-by came and went, talking and laughing. A mother pushed her baby past him in a buggy with red balloons tied to the handles. The fountain continued to sparkle in the sunshine, and everything was so quiet and normal that Dlubak knew that the man was serious.

"Come on," the man told him. He lifted the packet of sandwiches from Dlubak's lap, took one more, and threw the rest in the nearest waste-basket. "Get walking. This way."

With Dlubak walking slightly ahead, they left the Saxon Gardens and walked past the huge marble slab which commemorates the suffering of the people in Warsaw during the Second World War. They crossed the street and the man took out his keys and unlocked the doors of a dilapidated white Polonez estate. Dlubak glanced quickly around for any sign of a police car, but then the man gave him a sharp nod of the head and said, "Get in."

For the first few minutes they drove in silence. The car felt as if it didn't have any shock absorbers and the tyres were only half inflated, so that they made a flatulent noise on the tarmac. They passed the Centralna Station and headed east, crossing the Vistula over the Poniatowski Bridge. The river gleamed in the sunlight as if it were polished bronze, and Dlubak had to shade his eyes. "You're not taking me far, are you?" he asked. The man turned to him and winked, but said nothing.

They were now in the suburb of Praga South, and Dlubak was growing increasingly anxious. They drove along a crowded, grimy street where most of the 19th-century brick houses had escaped destruction by the Nazis, so that they still had the between-the-wars seediness of one of Warsaw's less prosperous districts. The sidewalks were thronged with cheaply-dressed people and there were battered trucks and cars parked everywhere, even one or two East German Trabants.

Dlubak lived on the northwest side of Warsaw, in a small dull housing development between Wola and Zoliborz, and he had visited this part of Praga only once or twice before. He found it too intimidating: too seedy and down-at-heel. Besides, his wallet had been pickpocketed on his second visit, and he had lost almost a week's wages.

They passed a roadside stall where a dark Mongolian woman in a shaggy goatskin bolero was selling blankets and saddles and offering to tell people's fortunes. She was disturbingly beautiful; and for some reason her eyes caught Dlubak's as he was driven past her, and she fleetingly frowned, as if she could tell that something terrible was about to happen to him.

The man drove to an almost-deserted square. On the corner stood a Byzantine orthodox church, with five onion domes. The man drew up outside it, and parked.

"Where are we?" asked Dlubak.

"You'll see," the man told him.

They climbed out of the car and crossed the street to a tatty block of 1960s apartments. A drunk in a soiled suit was sitting on the low concrete wall outside. When he saw them approaching, he clambered unsteadily to his feet and called out, "Hey! What about some change?" in that thick, vulgar accent that nobody speaks in any other part of Warsaw anymore.

"Fuck off," the man told him. The drunk spun on

one heel as if he had been physically slapped; staggered; and only just managed to regain his balance.

They entered the apartment building. Inside it was echoing and painted diarrhoea-brown. The man pushed Dlubak into a small elevator and pressed the button. They had to stand so close that Dlubak had to breathe in his body odor and his Pif-Paf aftershave. What was worse, he kept silently burping sardines.

When they reached the fourth floor, they left the elevator and walked along a narrow corridor until they came to a reinforced steel door with a spyhole in it. The man grinned at Dlubak and knocked three times. There was an ostentatious unlocking of locks and banging back of bolts, and then the door swung open.

"After you," the man told Dlubak.

Dlubak stepped into a large, almost-empty apartment that smelled strongly of burned cooking-fat. All the floors were covered in cheap, rucked-up carpet in a nasty shade of tan. He passed the open doors of three bedrooms in which blankets were nailed up at the windows, and the bedding was nothing more than soursmelling mattresses. In one of the bedrooms, a bare-breasted woman was sitting on a frayed basketwork chair, her hair dyed violently black, her toenails painted crimson, trying to light a cigarette. There was a huge bruise across her back, as if somebody had hit her with a chair leg.

In the living room, the principal piece of furniture was a massive Toshiba television, badly tuned, with the sound turned down. Sitting in front of it, in a bulky armchair, was a huge man, dressed all in black. He was talking on the telephone, but his eyes were fixed unblinkingly on the television screen. Another man in jeans and a polo shirt was standing close beside him, cleaning his fingernails with a small screwdriver. A third man sat cross-legged on the carpet. He was naked to the waist and his upper body was covered with tattoos. Demons, mermaids, star-signs, and butterflies.

"He's here," said the man who had brought Dlubak. The large man in the armchair didn't take his eyes away from the television, but said, "Good."

Two or three minutes went past. Nobody moved. Nobody said anything. At last Dlubak cleared his throat and said, "I'm late for a meeting, back at the bank. Do you think we could sort this out, whatever it is, and let me get back to work?"

There was another long pause. But then the large man slowly turned his head and stared at Dlubak as if he had trodden something disgusting into his rucked-up tan carpet.

"You have an appointment this afternoon, so I understand?"

"That's right. In fact, I should have been back at the bank five minutes ago."

"Who were you meeting, Mr. Dlubak? Can you tell me that?"

"The police, if you must know. One officer from the Wyzdial Zabojstw, the homicide squad; and another from the Wyzdial Przestepstw Gopodarezych, the fraud squad."

"Well, well," said the large man, in a voice like gravel being churned over in a cement mixer. "The homicide squad and the fraud squad. You must have some pretty big secrets to let out."

Dlubak didn't know what to say. He glanced back at the man who had brought him here, but the man only winked and smiled, as if this was all some tremendous joke.

The large man heaved himself out of his armchair and stood over Dlubak like a building that blots out the sun. "Do you know who I am? I am Roman Zboinski. Do you know what my father did for a living? He used to work on a farm, digging potatoes and picking cherries and rearing pigs. He almost starved. Do you know what I did for a living? I used to unload frozen meat in a warehouse in Gdansk. Can you imagine what

a life that was? We unloaded whole sides of beef, and
yet were paid so little that we couldn't even afford to
buy a piece of tripe. Then what happened? Everything
changed, and we had the chance to make big money.
Now we take cars from people who are so rich that
they don't care what they lose; and we sell them to
people who are so rich that they don't care what they
pay. The people who have lost their cars get new ones,
through insurance; the people who want new cars get
the cars that they want; and I make a profit. This is
social justice, not a crime."

Dlubak flustered, "Of course it's a crime. If you
didn't think it was a crime, why did you go to so much
trouble to launder your money through Vistula Kredytowy? Why are you angry now? If it's not a crime,
you won't mind me telling the police about it, will
you?"

Zboinski looked even more building-like than ever.
"You are the only person who knows, right?"

"Not anymore. My colleague Piotr Gogiel, for instance. I've already told him; and I'll be telling a few
more people, too. Once *everybody* knows, you won't
be able to touch me."

"Senate International won't be very pleased with
you."

"Of course they will! They don't want their bank
accounts used by gangsters."

Zboinski turned his back for a moment. He cracked
his knuckles inside his leather gloves; and his nostrils
began to stretch open.

"You still have a chance, Mr. Dlubak. Even an idiot
like you should know that. If you refuse to talk to the
police, and you refuse to testify in a court of law, then
there is nothing that anybody can do about it, not one
blamed thing."

"I'll have to show them all of Senate's accounts.
And once you know what you're looking for, all of this
money-laundering is obvious. It was obvious to *me*."

Zboinski lowered his head and thought for a moment. Although Dlubak couldn't see his face, the tattooed man was looking up at him, and he mimicked Zboinski's expressions like a mirror. Rage, followed by decision, followed by malicious pleasure.

Dlubak found these echoed expressions even more alarming, because they were performed with such accuracy, and such malevolence.

"You want me to say nothing?" he asked.

Zboinski didn't reply.

"You want me to pretend that none of those payments went in and none of those payments went out?"

Still Zboinski didn't turn around. Still he didn't speak. On the huge blurry screen of the television, Goofy was running and running up a grain-elevator, pursued by angry chickens.

Dlubak saw no signal from Zboinski to his henchmen, but the next thing he knew, the man who had kidnapped him from the Saxon Gardens had taken hold of his right arm, and pressed the muzzle of his automatic behind his right ear. It was very knobbly, and it hurt. The man in the jeans and the T-shirt put away his screwdriver and took hold of Dlubak's other arm. God, they all smelled of recently-soured sweat, these men, and Dlubak was so fastidious.

Zboinski approached him and glared into his face as if he could dissolve him with sheer rage.

"There's nothing I detest more than honesty. Honesty! The only people who embrace honesty are the stupid fuckers who have failed at cheating!"

Dlubak's larynx hurt so much that he could hardly swallow. What was he supposed to do? If he promised Zboinski that he would never say anything to the fraud squad and the homicide squad, he would be lying, because it was his duty to Vistula Kredytowy and Senate International to tell them everything he knew. Not only that, his pride was involved. His status, as a good accountant.

And if he let Zboinski get away with laundering the profits from stolen cars, where was it going to end? What was the point of capitalism if it had no morals? It wasn't capitalism any longer, it was anarchy.

Dlubak was frightened, but he knew what he believed in.

Zboinski said, "Go back to your office, talk to the *gliny*, and tell them you made a mistake."

The tattooed man laughed, and said, "Tell them you were high. Why not?"

"No," said Dlubak.

"*No?*" said Zboinski. "Did I hear you say *no*? This is serious, you know, not a game."

"I'm aware of that."

Zboinski went over to the opposite wall, and then abruptly changed direction and went over to the window. He was obviously agitated, and that alarmed Dlubak even more. But in a situation in which there appeared to be no rules, he had to stick to what he knew was right.

"You see that church?" Zboinski demanded, pointing to the five onion domes. "The Metropolitan Orthodox church of St. Mary Magdalene. St. Mary Magdalene, who sold herself, but was still blessed by Christ! I love that church! Have you ever been inside it? It has two tiers, and two iconstases, and polychromes and icons! She sold herself, don't you understand, but she was still beloved by Christ!"

Dlubak stared at him. He was so frightened that he had slowly wet himself, and a wide dark stain was spreading down the left leg of his beige summer trousers.

Zboinski came up close. "You're not going to change your mind, are you? Not without some extra persuasion."

From nowhere, in his right hand, he produced a large baling-hook. He held it up close to Dlubak's face. He said, "Do you know what damage these can do? More than you even want to think about."

"I can't tell a lie," Dlubak panted. He didn't know whether he felt hot or cold.

"You want this in your *eye*?" Zboinski grated. He lifted the point so that it was less than an inch from Dlubak's wincing eyeball. His eyelids fluttered so wildly that he almost felt as if he were flirting.

"No," said Zboinski. "You wouldn't want this in your *eye*, would you?"

He nodded to his men, and without warning they kicked his legs from under him and toppled him onto the carpet. Winded, Dlubak tried to twist himself over, but the tattooed man knelt on one wrist and the man in the jeans knelt on the other, while the man from the Saxon Gardens held his ankles. Dlubak gasped and struggled like a beached porpoise, but they were all too strong for him.

Zboinski leaned over him, holding up the baling-hook. "I never lose my temper," he said. "That's because I don't ask for much. I want friendship from my friends, submission from my women, and loyalty from the people who work for me. From everybody else, all I ask is live and let live."

He reached down with his left hand, found the zipper of Dlubak's pants, and tugged it down in three distinctive jerks. "You've pissed yourself," he said, in a very matter-of-fact way, as if he expected that from men who tried to betray him. "You're wet."

All the same, he twisted open Dlubak's underpants and produced his shrinking penis. It was so small and wrinkled that he could barely manage to grasp it between finger and thumb: but he did, and stretched it upward so that Dlubak gasped, the same gasp as a man jumping into a cold swimming pool.

"Now," said Zboinski, "I want you to tell me everything you know about my money."

Dlubak wildly shook his head. "I don't know anything about your money! I don't even know who you are!"

"I told you, Roman Zboinski. The Hook, they call me, and now you know why. You were going to talk to the police, yes? To the homicide squad and the fraud squad, and you were going to tell them all about me, weren't you? I wouldn't be surprised if you were going to frame me for that Kaminski murder."

"I don't know what you're talking about!" Dlubak panted. His face was crimson and he could scarcely breathe.

"Oh, I think you do," said Zboinski. "I think you know *exactly* what I'm talking about. Let's see if I can jog your memory."

With that—and with no hesitation at all—Zboinski forced the point of his baling-hook deep into the opening of Dlubak's penis, twisted it around, and pulled it upward as hard as he could. Dlubak let out a falsetto shriek, and tried to wrench himself free, but the other men were far too strong for him. His penis was stretched out like a burst plum on the end of a string.

"I'll tell, I'll tell!" Dlubak screamed.

"Are you sure? I'm just beginning to enjoy myself."

"I'll tell! For God's sake, I'll tell!"

Zboinski gave one last twist of his hook and then let Dlubak free. Dlubak rolled over onto his side, his hands clutched between his legs, sobbing deep asthmatic sobs.

"Well, then," said Zboinski. "Let's get down to business. How about some vodka, Mr. Dlubak? Business is always more pleasant with a little vodka, don't you think?"

9

When Sarah left her apartment just after 9:30 the following morning, she was surprised to find Komisarz Rej waiting for her in the large, mosaic-tiled vestibule. Outside, it was raining, and the day was unseasonably dark. Rej had obviously been waiting for some time, because the vestibule was filled with smoke and there were three crushed cigarette butts around his feet.

"Good morning, comrade," she teased him. "I thought you were off the case."

"I am," he admitted. "But that hasn't stopped me from being curious."

"What are you curious about now?"

"I'm curious that my deputy went to Vistula Kredytowy yesterday afternoon to interview one of the people concerned with Senate's accounts; and that this person didn't show up for the interview, and still hasn't shown up."

Sarah gave him a long, steady look, but didn't say anything. She didn't like the implications of this.

"The person's name was Antoni Dlubak," said Rej. "He was last seen at 12:45 or thereabouts, leaving the bank with a packet of sandwiches. He didn't return to

his apartment last night and so far this morning he
hasn't turned up for work."

"Maybe he's sick."

"People who are sick usually stay at home."

"Maybe he had an accident."

"He hasn't been admitted to any Warsaw hospital."

"Well, how should *I* know what's happened to him?"

Rej gave her a shrug and a smile. "I told you, Ms.
Leonard. I'm just curious."

Sarah glanced at her watch. "I'm sorry I can't help
you, komisarz. I'm running late already."

She pushed her way through the revolving doors
onto the street. There was very little wind but the
clouds were low and the rain was coming down in a
fine, persistent drizzle. Sarah put up her umbrella and
started to walk toward the Central Station and the Marriott Hotel. Traffic drove noisily up and down Jerozolimskie Avenue, taxis with windscreen wipers flapping,
red-and-white buses with steamed-up windows.

Rej caught up with her, his collar turned up. "Listen," he said, "I'm not trying to suggest that anybody
in your company had anything to do with Dlubak's
disappearance, but he's the second person connected
with Senate to go missing in a week."

"You don't know for sure that he's dead."

"I don't know that he's alive, either. And it's the
only connection I've got."

Sarah stopped. "All right," she said. "I'll help you if
you help me. I've brought in a police detective from
Chicago, an old friend of my father's, to try to find the
Executioner."

"You've *what?*"

"What else was I supposed to do? *You* couldn't catch
him, could you? And what have you got to complain
about? You're not supposed to be handling the case
anymore."

Rej raked his hand through his wiry white hair. "Do
you know something, Ms. Leonard? You have the ca-

pacity for making me feel about fifteen years old."

"Don't kid yourself. You look more like fifty. Now—do you want to come and talk to this detective or not? His name's Clayton Marsh and according to my father he's one of the best there is."

"I don't have anything to lose, do I?"

They walked the rest of the way to the Marriott. Sarah didn't offer to share her umbrella with him: she was wearing her new black Armani suit and she didn't want to get it wet. Rej had to hunch his shoulders and clasp his upturned lapels close to his throat, and occasionally duck his head to one side to avoid being jabbed by her umbrella spokes.

"What are you doing now?" Sarah asked him.

"Officially I'm supposed to be sitting at home contemplating my navel. But they've put a guy called Witold Jarczyk on the case, and he's about as much use as a bloodhound with a blocked-up nose. It's all politics in the police these days . . . even worse than it used to be. I used to think that politics didn't matter, that the only important thing was catching criminals. When everything changed, I was out-maneuvered."

"You don't regret the changes, do you?"

"I don't know. Some things are better. But cheeseburgers don't make a revolution. You have to change people's hearts . . . and that can take a whole generation."

They reached the Marriott and went inside. Rej brushed drizzle off his coat and wiped his face with a grayish handkerchief. Clayton was waiting for them in the cocktail bar, drinking coffee. He was dressed in a brown leather jacket, jeans and cowboy boots. He stood up and gave Sarah a hug, and then gave Rej the hardest handshake that he had ever experienced in his life.

"I brought Komisarz Rej along with me," Sarah explained. "He tells me that somebody from the Vistula Kredytowy bank has gone missing . . . the man they were supposed to be interviewing about the money-laundering."

"I don't know," said Rej. "Maybe he'll show up, safe and well. But if he doesn't . . . well, there could be some connection."

Clayton said, "I'll tell you what interests me, my friend, much more than this bank-fraud business, and that is the *strength* of this Executioner character. I've been reading the papers, and you said yourself when he whopped that finger off you that he was traveling so fast along that sewer pipe that you were lucky to get out of there alive . . . even though your colleagues were pulling you with a rope. Now, who can travel at any speed along a narrow pipe like that unless they have phenomenal training and phenomenal strength? And look at that poor Zborowska girl . . . he dragged her whole arm through a mail-slot? Not to mention those German laborers he turned into short ribs."

"Don't," said Sarah.

Clayton laid a hand on her arm. "I'm sorry, Sarah, but I think this is one of the most important lines of investigation. I don't think we're going to establish a connection between any of these murder victims by trying to find out *why* they were killed. First of all we have to find out *what* killed them."

"You don't think it was a man?" asked Rej.

"I'm not saying that. Maybe it was a man and maybe it wasn't a man. If it *was* a man, I'd sure like to know what kind of a man he is; and if he isn't, then I'd sure like to know what kind of a creature he is."

"I don't understand. What do you mean by 'creature?' All of the victims had their heads cut off with a large metal blade . . . a creature wouldn't use a knife."

Clayton turned to Sarah. "Your man Brzezicki thinks that it's a devil, doesn't he?"

"That's just superstition," said Rej.

"You know for a fact that it isn't a devil?"

Rej looked perplexed. "Of course I know for a fact

that it isn't a devil. There are no such things as devils."

"Let me tell you something," said Clayton. "Seventeen years ago there was a fire in a third-story slum apartment on Grand Avenue in Chicago. Nine women were incinerated, six children, and one man. The fire department investigators said that the fire was arson, although there was no trace of any known accelerant. Just one room was burnt: floors, walls, ceiling, furniture . . . everything turned to cinders. But outside of that room you wouldn't have known that there had been a fire in that building at all. Not even the smell of fire.

"I investigated that fire and I spent three days interrogating the landlord. I had three witnesses who said they heard him threatening to evict those people who lived in that apartment. I had one witness who heard him say he was going to kill them all. But he had a watertight alibi—he was playing pool with some friends the night it happened—and there was no forensic evidence whatsoever, even though we searched his apartment on our hands and knees.

"There was only one thing: a book called *Chaldean Magic*. The only book in the apartment of a man who obviously read nothing but the sports pages. I didn't think anything about it at the time. But for some reason the title stuck in my mind. I tried to locate a copy but nobody had ever heard of it. So I talked to Professor Lanormant at the University of Chicago—he's an expert on ancient Middle Eastern religions. He said that Chaldeans had the greatest demonology in all history. He also told me they had rituals for summoning up demons to help them.

"One of these demons had breath that could burn a whole roomful of people to death. Reduce them to carbon. Apparently it could only stay in the real world for a limited time, and when it went back to wherever it had come from, it left its own burned remains behind. Five days after that fire on Grand Avenue, an incinerated body was found on a vacant lot. There wasn't much of it left, but the medical examiner said that he had never seen a bone structure like it before. It wasn't human. It wasn't animal. You could only call it a creature."

"Well, that's a very good horror story," said Rej. "But it doesn't exactly prove that devils exist, does it?"

"Maybe not. But it *does* prove that you don't solve crimes by being narrow minded."

Sarah beckoned the waitress to bring them coffee. Then she said, "There's something else, something I almost forgot. When Muller first took me down to see the sewer pipe, I thought I heard a child crying."

"That's what Kaminski heard," said Rej. "That's why he first went down there."

"Maybe that's worth looking into," Clayton suggested. "How do we know he heard a child crying?"

"He mentioned it to a doorman from the Palace of Culture and Science, who was passing the construction site that evening on his way home. And of course there was the young boy who helped him to open the door of the hoarding and take a flashlight from the builders' hut. He heard the crying, too."

"But you found no child down there?"

Rej shook his head. "There were no children reported missing that night, either. The only thing we did find was a knitted doll, but that could have found its way into the pipe purely by chance. We showed pictures of it on television and in the newspapers, but nobody identified it."

"Do you still have it?"

"Of course. It's together with all the rest of the evidence. Not that there *is* much evidence."

"Could you get hold of it?"

"I could have done, but I'm off the case now."

"I'd really like you to get hold of it, if you can."

Rej looked cautious. "I don't understand. What can you do with a doll?"

Clayton sat back in his seat and pressed his hands together as if he were praying. "The thing is, komisarz, that ever since that fire on Grand Avenue I started to take a much wider view of crime and criminal behavior—particularly when it came to crimes that seemed completely inexplicable. If I encountered a crime that had no discernible motive, no circumstantial evidence, and no logical explanation, I put it into a special dossier. I still carried on trying to solve the crime in the traditional way, but at the same time I experimented by trying to solve it in other ways . . . such as using Tarot cards, or runes, or mediums."

"Did it ever work?" asked Sarah. She felt embarrassed. She knew that her father had called Clayton "the best damn detective that Chicago ever produced," but she had never believed in spiritualism. As far as she was concerned, the dead stayed dead. She hoped that flying Clayton across to Warsaw wasn't going to prove to be an expensive and embarrassing mistake. In any kind of business, women were watched far more critically than men. She was having a difficult enough time convincing Ben and her bosses in New York that she would soon be able to get excavation work restarted. The very last thing she needed was to be criticized for having poor judgment of character.

Clayton said, "Sure it worked. Not always, but then not all of the crimes were susceptible to being solved that way. But on two separate occasions we were able to identify bodies by giving their clothing or possessions to experienced mediums who could visualize the people they used to belong to."

"This isn't possible, is it?" asked Rej, turning from Clayton to Sarah and back again.

"Of course not," Clayton told him. "Not in the world as we usually perceive it. But just because you can't perceive something, that doesn't mean it isn't there. Like high-frequency sound, or infrared light. We accept their existence, we use them every day. Yet they have no 'reality,' do they, in the sense that we can detect them by touch or by smell or by sound or by sight."

Sarah said, "You're still going to carry on a conventional investigation, though, aren't you?"

"Oh for sure," Clayton reassured her. "I'm not a complete wacko, if that's what you're worried about. But it's always worth trying the far-out stuff as well as the good old tried-and-tested legwork. I've seen too many investigations drag on for week after week because *first* they interview all of the witnesses and *then* they interrogate all of the suspects and *then* they try to link the suspects to the evidence, and so on and so on, they're so damned *linear*, do you know what I mean, when they could be trying anything and everything from DNA testing to crystal balls."

Rej thought about that, and then he nodded. "You're right. I like that thinking. All today and all tomorrow, Jerzy Matejko is organizing a search of the sewers. It won't be very systematic, because the sewers aren't very systematic. But it's worth doing and it may turn some thing up."

He lit a cigarette and blew out a long thin stream of smoke. "Jerzy's been itching to step into my job for the past two years, but he's still a good friend. If they find anything, he'll tell me."

"That's just what we need," said Clayton. "Meanwhile, who was the kid who helped Kaminski get into the demolition site? I'd like to talk to him."

"His name's in my notebook," Rej told him. "But all he heard was a sound like a child crying, or maybe a woman."

"And you heard it too?" Clayton asked Sarah.

"That's right," she said. "It was like . . . *sobbing*, more than crying out. You know, somebody who was inconsolably sad."

"Any words? Any distinguishable words?"

"I don't know . . . I don't think so." She tried to remember what the crying was like. There *had* been words, of a kind, but they had been blurry and faraway, like somebody shouting from a boat offshore. "No . . . I think there may have been something, but I don't know what it was."

"Well, if you *did* hear something, it's possible that we may be able to reclaim it by hypnosis."

"Hypnosis!" Rej exclaimed, in open admiration. "He thinks of everything!"

"Don't get too excited," said Clayton. "We don't even know if we've found ourselves a fat lady yet, let alone heard her singing."

Rej frowned; so Sarah translated. "He says it's not over till it's over."

"Okay, fine, I understand. Listen—let me make a call to Matejko, to see how this sewer search is going."

He went off to find a phone while Sarah poured Clayton some more coffee.

"Nice guy," Clayton remarked.

Sarah smiled. "Yes, he is, in a stuffy kind of way. I sometimes think that dad would have been the same if he'd stayed in Poland. He seems to find it hard, all this change. He's very moral. He believes in finding out the truth, as if there ever was such a thing. He thinks that Big Macs are no substitute for *pozytywne myslenie*— you know, positive thinking."

Rej came back. He looked tense and even more bedraggled than before. "I've just talked to Matejko," he said. "They were searching the sewers around Powstancow Warszawy Square. They found a body with no head. All the evidence suggest that it's Antoni Dlubak."

"Well, my friend," said Clayton, in English. "It looks like the game is afoot."

hey found Marek Maslowski sitting on the steps of the Palace of Culture & Science, talking to six or seven of his friends. He was wearing his black leather jacket and a new pair of Levis, and his silky black mustache hadn't grown any longer. At first he didn't recognize Rej in his damp-corrugated coat, and his plastered-back hair, but then he did.

"Hey, the *gliniarze*," he said, and several of his friends stepped away. "To what do I owe this dubious pleasure?"

Rej immediately sat down on the step next to him. "Listen," he said. "No bullshit. This is Clayton Marsh, he's a detective from America. We're trying to find out what it was that killed Jan Kaminski."

Marek blinked at him. "Did I hear that right? Did you say *what?*"

"What do you think?" Clayton asked him. "You heard what Kaminski heard. Crying, or sobbing, or whatever. What do you think it was?"

"Well, how do I know? I didn't see it, and I couldn't hear it too clearly because I was up on ground level. I don't know. It could have been a woman, but it sounded more like a kid."

"Think back," Clayton urged him. "Try to remember *exactly* what it sounded like."

Marek glanced at his friends. "I don't know why I'm helping you people. All you ever do is give us grief."

"You helped Jan Kaminski."

"Jan Kaminski wasn't a pig."

"All the same, you could help us to find out how he died."

Marek hesitated for a moment, then he pressed his fingertips against his forehead and tried to concentrate. "I don't know. There was lots of traffic."

"Did you hear any words?"

"I don't think so. It was just like crying."

"Think harder. Did it sound as if it could have been words, even if you couldn't make out what they were?"

After a long pause, Marek said, "Sure . . . yes, it could have been words."

Several of Marek's friends were growing impatient. A pretty girl in black leggings with a ring through her right nostril said, "Come on, Kurt, these are the *enemy*, for Christ's sake."

Clayton laid a hand on her shoulder. "Listen, miss. I've come all the way from Chicago, Illinois, to talk to this gentleman."

"So, why do I care?" the girl challenged him, in English; although she was plainly impressed.

Clayton answered her in English. "I'm not asking you to care. I'm just asking you to put a sock in it for a couple of minutes."

The girl frowned at Marek, and said, "Sock in it? What does he mean?"

"He means shut up," Marek told her.

The girl gave Clayton the finger; and then she gave Marek the finger, too. "What are you now?" she said. "Kurt the cop lover?"

"Oh, go take a walk, Olga," Marek told her; and she flounced off to join the rest of her friends.

"Kurt?" asked Clayton. "Why did she call you Kurt?"

"I look like Kurt Cobain a little. You know, from Nirvana."

"You mean you look like Kurt Cobain before he blew his face off."

"I've nearly been there, man," said Marek, intensely. "So have some of my friends. You think it's easy, growing up in a shit-heap like this? You wake up every day and all you see is advertisements for BMWs and Ducati motorbikes and Christian Dior aftershave and you know that if you live to be a hundred-and-eight and you work your ass through to your buttock-bones every day of the week, and you steal whatever you can carry away, you will never ever be able to afford any of them. BMW? I couldn't even buy a fucking BMW steering wheel, let alone the rest of it."

"That's a worldwide problem, son," Clayton smiled. "Just be grateful you're not in Ethiopia."

"I might just as well be. Poland? It's just Ethiopia with extra sauerkraut."

Rej put in, "You don't have to help us if you don't want to. Officially, I'm off the case; and officially, this gentleman shouldn't be investigating it, either. But we've got thirteen innocent people dead now. They found another one this morning with his head cut off."

"I'm not sure," said Marek. His friends were whistling to him now, and calling "Come on, Kurt, we're going to Olga's!"

Clayton leaned forward. "Marek, can you remember *anything* that girl or woman might have said?"

Marek shook his head.

"Will you help us?" asked Clayton. "I'm making a personal, heartfelt appeal here."

"I don't see what I can do."

"Well . . . I'm planning on holding a seance, of a kind. Do you know what that is? When people hold hands and try to conjure up the dead. I'm planning on doing that, for the little girl you heard. To see if we can't maybe raise up her spirit, see what I mean, to help us discover what's been happening here."

Marek turned to Rej to make sure that this wasn't a leg-pull. But Rej shrugged and said, "It's a tough case. We're trying everything."

"A seance?" Marek asked him. "You mean, knock once if so-and-so killed you; knock twice if it was what's-his-face?"

"Not exactly," said Clayton. "But pretty close. And you could give us some real valuable input. You heard that child or that woman crying . . . you could have heard more than you realize. What do you say? Do you want to take part?"

A dark-haired, white-faced girl came back up the steps and wound her bangled arm around his neck and glared at Clayton defiantly. The young East challenging the middle-aged West. But Marek said, "Sure . . . okay,

I'll do it. If you really think it's going to help track down this Executioner character."

"I have to find a medium first," said Clayton. "But as soon as I do . . . well, tell me where I can get in touch with you, and we'll be ready to roll."

Rej stood up to leave. Marek looked up at him and said, "What happened, komisarz? You couldn't solve this case on your own?"

Rej looked across at Clayton, and then back to Marek. "Office politics," he said.

"Oh, really? So what happens if your boss finds out that you're still working on it?"

"I'll probably get the sack."

"Hey—so why are you doing it? I thought all you *gliny* wanted was a comfortable life and a pension."

Rej jabbed a finger at him. "You listen to me. My father fought the Nazis; and then he fought the Russians; and then he spent the rest of his life helping to put this city back together again. He couldn't stand time-servers and he couldn't stand bureaucrats, and neither can I."

Marek laughed. "Will you listen to this man? The next thing he's going to tell me is that he digs Nirvana."

"Better than digging graves," said Rej.

Ben said, "At last! New York's furious."

Sarah folded her umbrella and dropped it into the umbrella stand. "Of course they're furious. But there's nothing else that we can do."

"Can't we find *anybody* to get this contract moving?"

"Ben—even if we could, the police wouldn't let us. Not for two more days, at least. The whole site's been cordoned off."

"I thought you were pals with the chief of police, what's-his-name, Grabhandle."

"Grabowski. Yes, I am. But he's not going to interfere with proper police procedure; and neither can we. The only answer to this problem is to find the Executioner and have him arrested; and you know what we're doing about that."

"Jesus, yes. Bringing in some desiccated old flatfoot who happens to drink with your old man, and paying him $2,000 a week to bumble around a city he doesn't know looking for somebody he can't identify."

"Clayton Marsh is a brilliant detective. What's more, he's teamed up with Komisarz Rej, so he won't have any trouble finding his way around."

"Rej? That clown?"

"Rej isn't as stupid as you think."

"If you knew how stupid I think he is, you wouldn't even think that was a compliment."

Sarah slammed her briefcase down on her desk. "You listen to me, Ben. We have a problem here but it won't get solved by abuse. Nobody is going to work on that site until they're sure that they won't be attacked—and whatever you think about superstition, those men believe that if they upset that thing, they won't only lose their own lives, but their families will be killed, too, right down to the very last one of them. They *believe* it, Ben, and neither you nor I can change their minds."

Ben shook his head and propped one buttock-cheek on the edge of her desk. "I don't know, Sarah. What happened to that legendary ball-breaker I used to know?"

"You can't always get what you want by fear and intimidation, Ben. This is one of those times."

He picked a memo off her desk, read it, and then began to fold it into a paper airplane. "That's all well and good, sweetheart, but New York's furious. This thing is clocking up $395,000 a day, plus interest. If you don't start pouring concrete by the end of next week, then believe me, they're going to start looking for scapegoats."

"Ben, you simply can't force Brzezicki and his men to work; and you can't force anybody else, either."

"Turks," said Ben. "They'll do it. They don't give a shit for your so-called devil."

"If you try to bring in Turkish labor, you're going to antagonize everybody from the President downward. It was risky enough bringing in Germans. Besides, you won't get any of your major sub-contractors to cooperate. Can you imagine Wola Electrics allowing their ducting to be put in by Turks?"

"Well, you may be right," said Ben. "But New York's looking for somebody to blame, and the first somebody on their list is you."

"There have been four murders on that site, for God's sake. What do they expect?"

"They're four thousand miles away, Sarah. They expect their hotel to go up on time."

Sarah looked at him narrowly. The way he was sitting, the way he was folding his paper dart, the way he was setting up one obstacle after another, she began to suspect that Ben was up to something. It almost had a smell of its own, like scorched newspaper, or burned hair, or brimstone.

"What are you trying to tell me?" she said. "Are you trying to maneuver me out of this job?"

"Of course not. The total opposite."

"Then what is this all about?"

Ben put on a half-exasperated expression as if to suggest that he had been trying everything possible to protect Sarah's interests, but well, you know what they're like in New York . . .

"The fact of the matter is, sweetheart, I could manage to buy us a few more days. Jacek Studnicki says that Vistula Kredytowy could possibly waive interest payments so long as the Warsaw police are preventing us from continuing work. They're insured against certain types of delay, although whether they're insured against the site being cordoned off by the police . . .

well, that's arguable. I might have to offer him some kind of sweetener in return, and I'd have to spread a little sunshine around the insurance company."

"Then why don't you?"

Ben eased himself off the desk and came around so that he was standing only inches away from her. "The trouble is, Sarah, that I would be putting my ass on the line, and for what? You're in direct charge of getting this hotel built on time, why should I risk my whole career with Senate just for you?"

Now Sarah understood where this conversation was going. She was so shocked by what Ben was saying that the hair on the back of her neck started to prickle, and she began to wish she hadn't drunk her morning glass of tropical fruit juices so quickly.

"You don't have to risk your career for me. I didn't ask you to, and I don't expect it."

"Oh, no? You asked me to risk my career the moment you let Brzezicki and the rest of those superstitious morons walk off the job. Because once you'd allowed him to do that, somebody had to save you, and the only person around who could do it was yours truly."

His eyes softened and he tried to take hold of both of her hands, but she twisted them away. "You see?" he said. "This is the problem. I take risks for you and one day you may have to take risks for me. We're supposed to be team players. But how can we be team players if we're not a real team?"

Sarah said, "I've told you. We're colleagues; we're friends. That's as far as it goes."

"Oh, come on, baby—right now it doesn't even go as far as that. You treat me like I'm carrying some kind of disease."

"Maybe you are. It's called galloping presumption."

"Didn't that brooch mean anything to you?"

"It showed me that you've got more money than taste, and more taste than sense."

Ben said, "Sarah, I'm not asking you this. I'm telling you. I want you and me to try again. The spark's still there. You know it's still there. All we need is more time together."

Sarah stared at him for a long time without saying anything. He stared back at her, trying to read her expression. She saw hope in his eyes, and cunning, and self-pity, but most of all she still recognized the monstrous arrogance that had eventually broken their first relationship. It needed feeding, but she was determined that it wasn't going to feed on her.

She said, "Get lost, Ben. This is beneath both of us."

He lifted both hands. "I tried, sweetheart. You can't say I didn't try. I always thought you had spirit. I always thought you were the kind of woman who could seize the dream."

"What's that supposed to mean?"

"It means that I can't continue to work with you on this project because of your consistently hostile attitude and your refusal to cooperate with critical matters of policy. It means that you've mishandled labor relations and relations with local planners; and that you've cost Senate almost a million dollars in unnecessary delay. Its means, my tough little cookie, that I'm going to recommend to New York that Senate let you go. That's unless . . ."

Sarah was quaking with anger. "That's unless what? Unless I let you *fuck* me, is that it?"

Ben looked mock-shocked. "You said it, sweetheart. Not me."

Rej arrived at the office with a large plastic carrier bag from the children's department store Smyk. He sat down at his desk, laid the bag on top of his blotter, and almost immediately Matejko walked in and peered inside it. He took out a rolled-up sweater, turned it this way and that, and then put it back again.

"What the hell are you looking for?" Rej demanded.

"Sandwiches. I'm hungry."

"There's a bar of chocolate in my desk."

"I know. I ate it this morning. Well, don't look at me like that. You're supposed to be off duty. By the time you came back it could have gone stale."

Rej lit a cigarette. "How's the investigation?"

"Oh, dragging along. You know what Witold's like. No stone unturned, except that he keeps forgetting which stones have been turned and which haven't."

"Have you had any word from Dr. Wojniakowski yet?"

"On Antoni Dlubak? Nothing much. Decapitated with a sharp cleaver, like all of the others. But he says there's one noticeable difference. Dlubak was sexually assaulted. Somebody stuck a sharp-pointed instrument right through his penis."

"Ouch, painful," said Rej, his cigarette waggling between his lips. "But interesting, too. What does Witold make of it?"

"Witold thinks that he was tortured. Probably to find out what he knew about the money-laundering at Vistula Kredytowy."

"That makes sense. If he was, though, that means that he was probably killed by organized criminals, rather than a lone psycho. Mafia, maybe . . . or somebody working a scam through Senate Hotels."

Matejko nodded. "That's right. But if that's true, why were organized criminals interested in killing a tour guide, a mailman, a pharmacist and all those other people?"

"Well . . . they probably killed Kaminski for the same reason they killed Dlubak. The others . . . God knows. Listen, get onto Dr. Wojniakowski and ask him to put a rush on checking whether Dlubak was killed with the same weapon as all the rest of them."

Matejko shook his head. "You're off the case, Rej, or had you forgotten?"

"You can still do it. Witold would want you to do it."

"If Witold wanted me to do it, Witold would have asked me to do it."

Rej took his cigarette out of his mouth. "Why don't you just fucking stop arguing and do it?"

Matejko laughed and picked up the phone. While he was dialing, Rej said, "Listen . . . I left my towel in my locker. That's what I came in for."

He picked up his carrier bag, left the office and walked along the corridor. When he reached the end of it, however, he didn't turn right to the washrooms, but left to the stores where they kept all the evidence from recent cases. It was a long, narrow room, lined with olive-drab filing cabinets. A single police officer was sitting at a desk under the window, painstakingly writing in a ledger. On the desk in front of him stood a pair of cheap brown shoes, covered in blood.

The officer stood up when Rej came in, and clicked his heels. "Can I help you, komisarz?"

"Yes, the Executioner case. I need to see that doll again."

"Excuse me, komisarz. I was told that Komisarz Jar-czyk was conducting the Executioner case now."

"Of course he is. But that doesn't stop me taking a look at the evidence, does it?"

The officer looked uncomfortable. "Komisarz Jar-czyk specifically said that you were not to have access to the evidence, sir."

"For God's sake," said Rej, "I only want to look at it. And that was evidence that was found when I was still handling the case."

"Well . . ." said the officer, dubiously.

Rej offered him a cigarette. "Stop taking your job so seriously. I just want a couple of seconds to check if it's got any kind of label on it, then I'll put it back."

The officer accepted the cigarette and Rej lit it for him. "Well . . ." he said. "I suppose it can't hurt." Rej was still popular among the lower ranks. He always remembered their names and their birthdays, and he had a healthy disregard for pompous senior officers. The officer took out his keys, and beckoned Rej to follow him along the left-hand wall until they reached a filing drawer marked Hydra No. 1, which was their code name for the hunt for the Executioner. Hydra, because the case involved so many heads. Dembek's idea of a joke.

The doll was stored inside a large padded postal envelope. "There," said the officer. "Help yourself. I've got to get on with this Kepliz case."

"Oh yes, I heard about that," said Rej. "Some woman attacked her husband with a steam iron."

"That's right. You should have seen him."

"Looking a little depressed, I expect."

"Yes! That's a good one."

Rej eased the doll out of the envelope. She was completely dry now, but she was still grayish-brown. He guessed that she was supposed to be a little farm-girl. She was wearing a knitted bonnet and a knitted smock, and her feet were covered in little knitted boots.

He wondered what her name was.

The phone rang, and the officer picked it up. It sounded to Rej as if it were his wife or his girlfriend calling, because he started to get involved in a lengthy discussion about where they were going over the weekend. Whatever happened, he didn't want to go to her mother's.

As the officer talked, Rej gradually turned his back. He opened his carrier bag and dropped the doll into it. Then he lifted out his sweater and pushed it into the postal envelope.

He turned around again, held up the envelope in acknowledgment, and made a show of sliding it back into the Hydra drawer, and closing it. The officer, still on the phone, gave him a wave of thanks. Rej left the evidence store and made his way back toward his office. He was surprised how quickly his heart was beating.

Halfway there, he heard Matejko calling him, from behind.

"Stefan! I thought you were going to find your towel."

"Oh . . . I got talking to Dembek, and I forgot."

"What? Dembek's in Poznan today."

"Well, actually, it was one of the girls in filing," Rej blustered. "I didn't particularly want you to know."

Matejko gave him a suspicious frown. "I thought you didn't believe in officers getting involved with the secretarial staff."

"She's gorgeous, this one. I couldn't resist her. Come on. Jerzy, I'm a man. I've got needs."

"You'll have to point her out. All the girls in filing look like cows to me. Anyway, I managed to get through to the Department of Forensic Medicine. Dr. Wojniakowski wasn't there, but I talked to one of his assistants. They've just had the metallurgical results from Dlubak's neck."

He didn't even have to say what the results were. His face told it all. Rej pressed the heel of his hand against his forehead in frustration.

"God, Jerzy. This is like one of those damned nightmares—you know, when the faster you run, the further away everything gets."

10

They met at eleven o'clock that night outside a tall, narrow apartment block overlooking the market place on the corner of Banacha, only a few streets further south from the building where Ewa Zborowska and Kaczimicz Wroblewski had been killed. It was almost uncomfortably warm, but a strong breeze was blowing, filled with grit. It was one of those nights when you were conscious that you were right in the heart of Europe; breathing air that had blown over Austria, Germany and the Czech Republic, and which would blow over Russia and up to the Arctic Circle.

Clayton and Sarah had arrived first. Sarah wore a primrose summer coat and a sunflower-colored beret. Clayton looked somber in a black coat and gray slacks. "I always dress in mourning for seances. You're talking to the dead, after all."

Marek arrived soon afterwards, abruptly and very loudly, on the pillion of a motorcycle ridden by another black-leather-jacketed young man. He was wearing reflecting sunglasses and chewing a toothpick, and he walked with a conspicuous swagger. All the signs of nervousness, Sarah thought to herself, and she really felt for him.

She had always been shy when she was younger;

and even now she had to hype herself up before she spoke to an audience, or to reprimand anybody who had let her down; or to perform her notorious Ayatollah act, a fire-breathing performance of rage and hurt, followed by a display of inspirational encouragement that would have done credit to a television evangelist. She had a talent for making people feel that they had let her down; and an even greater talent for making them feel that they wanted to make amends. But it didn't come easily, and as Marek approached them she gave him a smile to make him feel relaxed.

"You found yourself a psychic, then?" Marek asked.

"A pretty good one, by all accounts," Clayton told him. "She writes a weekly horoscope for *Wszystko o Milosci*—that rag that's all full of sex and recipes and stuff. That's how I found her."

"Rej's late," said Sarah, checking her watch. "He promised he'd be right on time."

"Give the guy a break," Clayton calmed her. "He's probably knocking back a couple of vodkas to pluck up the courage to come at all. This isn't easy for him. He's lost half his god-damned finger. He probably knows more about this Executioner character than anybody else in Poland; yet they've bumped him off the case and told him to sit at home and watch *Knots Landing* dubbed into Polish. I know what it feels like. It happened to me once, back in 1985—. In fact it was worse for me because I had to watch *Knots Landing* in English."

Marek said, "All my friends said this psychic stuff was bullshit."

"Why did you come, then?" asked Sarah, sharply.

"Because I want to see if it works, that's why. You really believe it's going to work?"

Clayton shrugged. "I really have no idea. The odds are that I'm making a complete asshole of myself. But like I said before, why restrict yourself? If there's an infinitesimal chance that you can solve a case by using a psychic medium, then use a psychic. What's the harm? The worst that could happen is that we get a message from somebody else's long-dead Aunt Janina, telling us where she left the lottery tickets."

They talked a little more. Clayton's Polish wasn't very good, but he and Marek seemed to understand each other almost immediately. All through his professional life, Clayton had been dealing with disaffected kids from Polish families in Chicago, and he knew the frustrations that young men like Marek were up against: all the temptations of a material world, and not enough money to buy them. All the problems of living at home with their parents in an apartment that was two sizes too small, and where there was never enough hot water and the toilet always seemed to be occupied. All the disappointment of leaving school with a good degree and finding there was no work for them—or work that was so poorly paid they might just as well have been taxi drivers or gas station attendants or counter clerks.

"What I really want," said Marek, "you know, more than anything else, is to step out onto a stage in front of thousands of people, and they're cheering like crazy, and then I start playing this amazing guitar solo that blows everybody away."

"You play with a band?" asked Clayton.

"Sort of; but there's only two of us; and it's almost impossible to find anywhere to practice. All I ever get is, 'stop making that bloody awful noise, your sister's doing her homework!' "

"Sounds like the story of every great musician's life," said Clayton, and clapped him reassuringly on the back.

Just then, Rej's Passat came around the corner and jounced onto the sidewalk. Rej climbed out, carrying his plastic bag. "Sorry I'm late. I had a call from my mother's nursing home."

"Everything okay?" asked Sarah.

"Well, she hasn't been too well lately. Angina. I guess she's not bad, though, for seventy-six." He rummaged in the bag and produced the doll. "This is it, the original doll. If my boss finds out I've borrowed it, I'll probably end up in a nursing home myself."

"You did good," said Clayton. "Now, let's go see this Madame Krystyna."

They went up three shallow steps to the front doors of the apartment building. Through the wired-glass doors they could see a dingy vestibule with a mushroom-colored dado and a striplight that flickered like a migraine. There were two rows of bellpushes beside the doors, and Clayton picked out the one with Madame Krystyna's card tucked under it. Love, Health, Wealth: Your Fate In The Stars.

A crackly, expressionless voice said, "Madame Krystyna, psychic professional."

"It's Clayton Marsh, we have an appointment."

Madame Krystyna, psychic professional pushed the buzzer and the doors opened. They stepped into the vestibule and found a narrow elevator on their left, so small that they could scarcely squash into it. Rej was standing next to Sarah, and made a conscious effort to keep his arm behind him so that it wouldn't press against her breast. The lift slowly clanked its way up to the third story, and they extricated themselves with sighs of relief.

At the very end of the corridor they came to a purple door with silver stars pasted on it. The whole corridor smelled strongly of *bigos*, hunter's stew, and Sarah was reminded that she hadn't eaten all day. Still, it was good for the figure. Rej knocked on the door and they waited in the gloom for an answer.

Madame Krystyna opened up. She looked more professional than psychic. She was a handsome young woman in her mid-twenties, with curly black hair and wide blue eyes that were magnified by a pair of businesslike black-framed spectacles. She wore a white silky blouse and a smart charcoal skirt. The only clue to her calling was a silver pentagram hanging around her neck on a fine chain.

"Four of you, good," she smiled. "It always takes five to make the magic circle. Come on in."

Her apartment was furnished with dark oak antiques, and the windows were heavily draped with rich floral curtains. There were dried flowers and knick-knacks everywhere: glass paperweights and thimbles and stuffed birds in glass cases. In the far corner of the sitting room stood a tall, narrow bookcase indiscriminately crammed with paperbacks, leather-bound classics, magazines and newspapers. Next to it hung a strange oil painting of a woman in a long skirt and a veiled hat, flying through an orange sunset sky. Far beneath the painted woman stood a tabby cat and an alarm clock and a blank diary open at October, and a tiny figure of a man in gray, walking a white dog. For some reason, Sarah found the painting very melancholy and unsettling, and she kept turning back to look at it.

The middle of the room was dominated by a large, circular table, covered with a brown velvety cloth. In the center of the table an alabaster pyramid was placed, almost a third of a meter high, with a curious milky sheen to it, almost as if it were transparent and filled with congealed smoke.

"I adore this kind of work," Madame Krystyna told them. "I've helped the police before, you know. Not here in Warsaw but in Wroclaw. I helped to find a missing woman. She was dead, of course. But she told me where she was, in a turnip field. She wanted a coffin and a decent grave, not just a ditch. But here, sit down. Can I make you some tea?"

"Not for me, thanks," said Sarah. "I think I'd rather get on with it."

"I think we all would," said Clayton. "I told you the background to the story, Madame Krystyna. Is there anything else you want to know?"

"You've brought the doll?"

Rej laid his carrier bag on the table. Madame Krystyna didn't open it immediately, but gently laid her hand on top of it, almost as if she were trying to feel if it contained something living.

"This has very powerful emanations," she said. "It's very rare to feel latent emotions as strong as this."

"What can you actually feel?" Sarah asked her.

"Love . . . this poor little doll was very dearly loved. I can feel fright, too, and great distress."

"If I touched it, could I feel it?"

Madame Krystyna gave her a funny little sideways look. "You could, I think, under normal circumstances. At the moment, though, you might find it difficult to pick up—*blurred*, if you know what I mean, because you have so much distress of your own."

"I'm not distressed," said Sarah, rather crossly. "What do you mean?"

Madame Krystyna smiled. "I saw you looking at the painting. That painting has great significance for women . . . it means many things. It means escape, and freedom, but it also means instability and loss, the fear of falling and the fear of growing older. It was painted by a woman, of course, Maria Anto. No man could ever paint anything like that."

Rej sensed Sarah's embarrassment, because he quickly said, "Where do you want us to sit? Do we have to hold hands?"

Madame Krystyna continued to smile at Sarah for a few moments more. It was an extraordinary smile, penetrating but relaxing. It had the effect of making her feel that she had just unburdened herself of a painful secret. But then Madame Krystyna said, "Sit, yes. Anywhere will do . . . and, yes, you should hold hands. It isn't essential for any psychic reason but it will help us to concentrate."

They pulled out the chairs and sat around the table. Madame Krystyna took Marek's hand and immediately laughed. "Goodness! This young man is such a skeptic! He's wondering already why he came here!"

Marek pouted and slouched back in his seat, but Madame Krystyna said, "It doesn't matter. Airplanes fly whether people believe they can do it or not."

"Marek believes that airplanes can fly," said Clayton, with a grin. "He's just not sure about pigs."

Madame Krystyna held Sarah's hand. She didn't say anything, but somehow Sarah knew that her touch had confirmed what she had already seen in the way she looked at the painting. She tried not to think about the trouble she was having with the hotel, and with Ben, and the horror she had felt when Muller's three workers were cut up and killed; but the more she tried to empty her mind, the more luridly bright the images became.

Madame Krystyna gave her fingers the lightest of squeezes, and Sarah glanced at her and gave her a quick smile.

"Can you take out the doll, please?" asked Madame Krystyna. "Lay it on the table in front of me. I don't want to touch it just yet."

Rej lifted the doll out of the carrier bag and set it down. "Now everybody hold hands," said Madame Krystyna. "Complete the circle of five, and let's see what we can find out."

She close her eyes and stayed silent and unmoving for over a minute. Sarah could see that Marek was biting the inside of his lips to stop himself from laughing. Rej looked tired but patient. Clayton, on the other hand, was watching Madame Krystyna with an interest that was obviously sharpened by experience.

"A little girl has lost her doll," said Madame Krystyna, with her eyes still closed. "Somewhere in Warsaw, a little girl has lost her favorite doll. The doll is full of her love; but it is full of her fear, too. Can anybody help me to find out where this little girl came from, and where she has gone?"

More minutes went by. Marek let out an involuntary

snort, but Madame Krystyna ignored him.

"A little girl has lost her doll," she repeated. Her voice was becoming very slurred and dreamlike. "A little girl has lost her favorite doll. Can anybody help me to find her? Does anybody know where she is?"

Sarah was beginning to think that Marek was right to be skeptical. Another three or four minutes passed, and all Madame Krystyna could do was to murmur the same words, over and over. "A little girl has lost her doll. Can anybody help me to find her? A little girl has lost her favorite doll."

She was just about to pull her hand away from Madame Krystyna's and call it a night when the lights in the sitting room dramatically dimmed and flickered blue.

"Power cut?" said Rej, lifting his head.

"Ssh," said Clayton. "I've seen this before."

Sarah suddenly felt frightened. There was a strong sense that other people had entered the room. She could feel them, feel their clothes rustling, feel their breath, even though she couldn't see them. Rej gripped her hand more tightly and she knew that he, too, was aware that the five of them were no longer alone.

"... *favorite doll* ..." Madame Krystyna intoned. "... *anybody know where she* ..."

The sitting room was so dark now that Sarah could scarcely see the painting of the flying woman. But she was even more acutely conscious that people were moving around her, sighing, touching, whispering to each other, yet invisible. She had never believed in spiritualism. She had never believed that it was possible for anybody to "contact the dead." Yet here she was in a sitting room in Warsaw, surrounded by shifting and murmuring spirits. A chilly feeling crawled all the way down her spine, like a centipede that had been nestling in a freezer, and she sat up straighter, her eyes wider, and she dreaded to think what was going to happen next.

"You're here, aren't you?" asked Madame Krystyna, with her eyes closed. "Which of you recognizes this doll? Which of you knows the little girl she belongs to?"

There was a pause; and then a soft hurrying noise. Rej looked at Sarah and his eyes were wide. Marek turned his head this way and that, not laughing now.

"You're here, aren't you," Madame Krystyna repeated.

In the center of the table, the alabaster pyramid began to shine, so that it illuminated all of their faces like paper masks. The markings on its sides appeared to slide and shift, like a speeded-up movie of a cloudy day. Sarah felt that the sitting room was even more crowded, as if dozens of people had pushed their way in through the door; as if people had stepped out of the curtains; as if people were shuffling and pushing and filling up every available inch of space.

She began to feel claustrophobic and panicky, the way she did in the New York subway, even though there was nobody visible, and nobody was actually jostling her. She looked across at Clayton and she could tell from the expression on his face that he could sense these invisible strangers, too. Marek actually twisted around, looking for them.

"Can you *feel* that?" he asked. His cheeks were totally bloodless.

"Ssh," said Madame Krystyna. "They're here, you mustn't disturb them. Some of them are helpful; some of them are very aggressive."

"Who is?" asked Rej. "I don't see anybody."

"Can't you feel them?" said Sarah.

"I don't know. I don't know what I can feel."

"They're *souls,*" said Madame Krystyna. "And Warsaw has so many."

Rej opened his mouth as if he were going to say something, then closed it again. His hair bristled; his eyes were bright with alarm.

They heard voices. At first they sounded like nothing more than dead leaves, blowing across grass. Then they became more distinct, and Sarah was sure that she could make out words and phrases, and the sound of somebody praying. *". . . oh, God, protect me . . . so much suffering . . . bought him a waistcoat . . . never remembered . . . boated all summer on Zegrzynskie Lake . . . hurt me so much . . ."*

"They're souls," Madame Krystyna repeated. "And Warsaw has so many."

From the top of the alabaster pyramid, an inverted triangle of light began to shine, like a mirror image of the pyramid, reflected in thin air. Sarah could see through it—she could still see Clayton's face—but she could also see images inside it, clouds moving, and trees swaying; and then she could see people running along a city street. It was like watching an old black-and-white movie, silent except for the rustling voices of the spirits who were all around them.

The face of an old, bearded man appeared, angular and distorted. He didn't seem to understand where he was, or what he was doing. He stroked at his beard a few times, and then started to speak.

"That was Zofia," he said, in a distant, tinny voice, although his words didn't quite synchronize with the movement of his lips.

"Who was Zofia?" asked Madame Krystyna. "Listen to me . . . who was Zofia? Where did she live?"

"My wife gave her that doll, for her sixth birthday, when we took her to Urle. She loved Urle . . . she paddled in the river all day."

Sarah was frightened but fascinated at the same time. The old man's face flickered and shifted, as if she were seeing it from dozens of different angles, with long gaps of time in between. She was aching to ask Madame Krystyna if this was an actual spirit—the living image of a long-dead person—but she thought that it would be wiser not to interrupt.

"Where is Zofia now?" asked Madame Krystyna.

There was no direct answer, but a tiny, barely-audible voice saying, "... *paddle in the river* ..."

"Have we lost him?" asked Clayton.

"Jesus, I hope so," said Marek. "This is too fucking weird to be true."

"*Ssh,*" Madame Krystyna repeated. "He's showing us the way."

"The way to what?" asked Marek. "The way to where?"

"Just watch," said Madame Krystyna.

In the inverted triangle of light above the point of the pyramid, they could see a plain Warsaw street, with lime trees and automobiles parked on the sidewalk. They passed a food stall and a furniture stall, where sofas were arranged in the open air. They could even hear voices, and passing traffic. Somebody was arguing about the price of a fireguard.

They reached an intersection. Everything looked as if it were pitched at an odd slope. Sarah could see people walking past; housewives with shopping bags; men with briefcases. She could see cloud shadows crossing the road.

"Where are we?" she asked. "Does anybody know?"

"It looks like Swietokrzyska to me," said Rej. "Just past Jana Pawla II."

"Yes, you're right," said Madame Krystyna. "There's that cafe on the corner."

"I can't believe this," said Marek.

They crossed Jana Pawla II and continued along Swietokrzyska until they reached the door of an apartment building, with nine glass panels. Then they seemed to be climbing stairs. They could hear music and somebody arguing. They walked straight into a solid door and passed right through it.

"*My daw,*" said a high-pitched voice, like a very young child's.

"Is that you, Zofia?" called Madame Krystyna.

"My daw," the voice repeated; a little distressed, but very emphatic.

"It's her," said Madame Krystyna, gripping Sarah's hand even tighter. "It's the girl who owns the doll."

"Does this mean that she's dead?" said Rej.

"Of course she's dead. You can't find living people in the spirit world, can you?"

Rej said nothing but Sarah could see that he was upset. She pressed her thumb into the palm of his hand and said, "She probably didn't suffer."

"All the same," said Rej. "It's my job, isn't it, taking care of people like her?"

"Come on," Sarah urged him. "You're not going all soft and sentimental on me, are you?"

Rej looked at her intently; and for the first time she saw how good looking he was. Careworn, yes: and probably lacking the day-to-day attention of a bustling, supportive woman. But there was nothing that a sensible diet and two weeks in the gym couldn't cure. He reminded her so much of all those louche, battered European movie stars, Eddie Constantine and Alain Resnais. In fact, he could have been Zbigniew Cybulski, from *Ashes and Diamonds*, if Zybigniew Cybulski hadn't killed himself.

Madame Krystyna said, *"Look."*

Above the pyramid, indistinct and strangely-proportioned, they could see a living room, with a sofa and chairs and a coffee-table. On the wall hung a print of wild white horses leaping through a foamy sea. Two pairs of pantyhose were drying on the radiator. There was a small second-hand television with an aerial made out of a wire coat-hanger; and an ugly china troll.

"My daw," the child's voice insisted; and there it was, sprawled on the floor, the same knitted doll that was lying on the table in front of Madame Krystyna.

"This is it," said Clayton, breathlessly. "This is the place."

"My-my-my-my daw."

Sarah looked up. The room felt as if it were so crowded that there was scarcely any air in it. "My doll," she said. "That's what she's trying to tell us. She's only little. She's saying, 'My doll.'"

At that moment, they heard a muffled knocking. The room seemed to spin as the little girl looked around. The knocking was repeated, louder this time. They heard a blurry woman's voice say, "Zofia—stay there! Mummy will go!"

"What the hell is *that*?" said Rej.

There was more knocking: louder now, and much more furious. In the over-furnished confines of Madame Krystyna's apartment, it sounded muffled, but that muffled quality made it all the more frightening, like a wild drum-tattoo for the dead. Although the image was angled and distorted, Sarah was sure that she could see the door-frame shaking, and plaster cracking all around the architrave.

"Don't answer it!" cried the woman's voice. "Zofia— don't answer it!"

The knocking became thunderous. Sarah was digging her fingernails so deeply into the palm of Rej's hand that she was worried he was going to bleed. In the jumpy, erratic image above the pyramid, they could see the door coming closer, they could see a child's hand raised to open it. It was like a hologram, except that there was nothing to project it, only their own psychic energy; only their physical bonding, hands held tight; only their common need to know what was banging so violently on the other side of that hallucinatory door.

"Zofia, don't answer the door!" the woman shouted. But the door burst open and something dark rushed in. Something huge. Something terrible. Rej jumped back in his seat and lost his grip on Sarah's hand; and broke the circle.

There was a momentary sensation that the entire room was filled from floor to ceiling with pure evil, like chilled writing-ink. Then there was a thunderclap, and the five of them were dazzled right down to the core of their eyes.

Slowly, the room quieted, and the image over the pyramid melted away. Sarah leaned forward and shaded her eyes and tried to catch every last glimmer of it. But the lights brightened. Sarah heard footsteps rushing furtively away, and saw the curtains sway; and then they were alone.

Madame Krystyna looked around the table, at the four of them. For a moment, it was impossible for Sarah to tell whether she was angry or pleased. Then, without any drama, the psychic picked up the doll, and held it high above her head. The doll had been decapitated: its head remained on the table. More than that, the velvet cloth was stained with something dark. Madame Krystyna pressed the palm of her hand into it and then showed her palm to everybody sitting at the table.

"Blood. You see that? Blood. You can test it if you like; there's no trickery." She tugged a handkerchief out of her pocket and wiped her hand clean. "Whatever happened to this little girl Zofia, it was worse than we could imagine. It hardly ever happens that the spirit world can have an actual physical effect on the material world. Only when truly dreadful deeds have been done."

"So what does it all mean?" asked Clayton. He might have used mediums before, but he was plainly just as shaken as the rest of them.

"Oh, come on," said Marek. He was growing cockier now that the seance was over. "It was all done with mirrors."

"I don't think so," put in Rej. "That was a real street and a real apartment building. I can locate it, no trouble at all. And if I can do that, we can find out the name of the little girl whose doll this was; and whether she's really dead, and why."

"You honestly believe those images were real?" asked Sarah.

"There's only one way to find out."

"But even if they were real, and you find out who she was—what is that going to tell us? I mean, how is it going to bring us any nearer to catching the Executioner?" asked Sarah.

Rej grimaced. "I don't know. But as I said before, all I need is one connection. Just one."

Clayton said. "Whatever it was that broke through that door—did any one of you see that clearly?"

"It was big," Marek volunteered. "It was bigger than any man I've ever seen. And it was dark. Like it was dressed all in black. Except its face was dark, too. That's if it had a face. I mean I could see it but I couldn't see it. That's what made me think it was mirrors."

"I had that impression, too," said Sarah. "I felt as if I were looking at it but I couldn't decide what I was looking at. It was like one of those optical illusions— you know, when you have the silhouettes of two old witches, but it's not two old witches, it's a candlestick."

"That doesn't surprise me," said Rej. "Eye witnesses very rarely manage to make any sense out of accidents or violent crime. Their brain is too shocked and surprised by what's happening; and when they think about it afterwards, their imagination fills in a whole lot of detail they never actually saw. That's what makes eye witnesses so unreliable."

Clayton picked up the headless doll and turned it this way and that. "What *did* this?" he asked Madame Krystyna. "It looks like it's been cut with a very sharp knife."

"Maybe she's hiding a razor blade up her sleeve," Marek suggested. "And maybe that isn't blood. Maybe that's good old tomato ketchup."

"You want to taste it?" Madame Krystyna challenged him.

"Well, no thanks. But what we saw there . . . there's got to be a way of doing it with projectors or something like that."

Madame Krystyna slowly shook her head. "The young . . . you'd think they'd be receptive. Instead, they're more cynical than we are."

But Clayton said, "*Is* there a projector? Is your sleeve really empty? And is that genuinely blood?"

Madame Krystyna stared him directly in the eye. "You believe it was real, don't you? And you know what a disservice you'd be doing to that little girl if you didn't?"

Clayton stared back at her for a long time. Then he nodded, and gathered up his pen and his notepad, and stood up.

It was after midnight and Komisarz Jarczyk was still hunched over his desk reading witness reports. He had slept only three hours since taking over the Executioner case from Stefan Rej, and he felt gritty-eyed and exhausted. His case-solving methods usually owed more to inspiration than they did to legwork, and he had imagined that he would be able to read through Rej's plodding paperwork and almost immediately be able to divine who the Executioner might be. But he was beginning to admit to himself that Rej's work, even if it wasn't inspirational, was relentlessly thorough, and yet there was still no clue whatsoever to who the Executioner could be, and why he had embarked on such a strange and grisly series of killings.

Jarczyk's stomach growled like a mangy dog. He opened his sandwich-box but it was empty except for a bruised apple and two stale *paczki* that his mother-in-law had made for him. He picked out one of the doughnuts and began to chew it, but his stomach like that even less and let out another growl and a complicated gurgle. He could do with a hot shower and a good solid meal.

More than anything, he could do with a revelation, a blinding insight into the Executioner case. He had secretly hoped that he would solve it within a week and win instant promotion, or an award, or both. But the files remained as cryptic and as unrelated to each other as fourteen half finished jigsaws in an empty room, with no pictures on the boxes to tell him what they were supposed to look like.

He dropped the half eaten doughnut into his metal wastebasket. As he did so, there was a knock at his office door. It was Ligocki, a uniformed officer from the night shift. He had a neat black mustache and a reputation as a chaser of anything in skirts, even the ugly ones, of which police headquarters had more than the national average.

"Still working, komisarz?"

Jarczyk leaned back in his chair, clasping his hands behind his head so that he revealed his sweat-circled armpits. "If we're going to catch this bastard, Ligocki, we have to do our homework."

"We've just had a call from the Komenda Rejonowa Warszawa Mokotow. They've picked up a car thief."

"Well, good for them. What do they want, a presidential citation?"

"According to Mokotow, this thief says he knows who killed Antoni Dlubak."

Jarczyk slowly lowered his arm and sat up straight. "How does he know?"

"You can ask him that for yourself, komisarz. They're bringing him over."

Jarczyk beat on his blotter with his fist. "Shit! This is it! This is the break I've been looking for! I knew that somebody would have to crack in the end. Jesus! You can't cut the heads off fourteen unrelated people and expect to get away with it! Not in Warsaw! Not in *my* Warsaw!"

"No, komisarz," said Ligocki, looking absurdly suave. "You're absolutely right."

Jarczyk stood up. "When he gets here, take him straight to the interview room. Give him a cup of coffee and a cigarette if he wants one. Don't bully him, do you understand? I'm just going to freshen up."

He took out the plastic toiletries bag that they had given him on Lot airlines when he flew to Prague for a police conference. He went to the washroom, filled one of the basins, and stared at himself in the mirror. He thought he looked tired but determined: the kind of officer who stays at his desk, hunting down the truth, when everybody else has gone home. Nadkomisarz material; then inspektor; then—who knew? Nadinspektor?

If this car thief knew who killed Antoni Dlubak, then he knew who killed Jan Kaminski and all of those other poor bastards. The fourteen half finished jigsaw puzzles would assemble themselves into one large completed picture, and he, Jarczyk, would get the credit for it.

He shaved with his Russian Superbrytvo electric razor. It didn't cut much stubble off, but it gave him a fresh, pink look. He combed his hair, and used up his last two or three drops of aftershave by punching the tiny plastic bottle against his cheeks. Then he returned to his desk.

It was over twenty minutes before Ligocki called him to say that the suspect had arrived, and by then he was almost asleep. He had been dreaming of what he would say at tomorrow's media conference, when he announced that he had identified and arrested the Executioner, and that the streets of Warsaw were safe once again. Part of the dream had involved sitting in a dimly lit bar drinking cherry vodka and trying to attract the attention of a woman in a tight red dress. The woman had turned around, and her face was a smooth wax mask. He was quite frightened. He knew it was a death mask.

He arrived at the interview room looking smart but slightly stunned. A man was sitting at the wooden table in the center of the room, with an untouched cup of coffee in front of him and an unsmoked cigarette perched in an ashtray beside his right hand. Jarczyk put down his folder and pen, drew up his chair, and sat down. The man watched him with an expression like a venomous toad.

"So," said Jarezyk. "Lukasz Ruba, thirty-four years old, three previous convictions for larceny, two convictions for fraud, and one conviction for violent assault. Beat up your girlfriend, blinded her in one eye, broke both her arms. That's quite a record. Better than Miecyzslaw Fogg." Miecyzslaw Fogg was a corny and sentimental singer from the pre-war years. "Enough to bring tears to a mother's eyes."

Ruba said, "I saw them in Saxon Park, that's all. They were sitting on a bench by the fountain, talking. I didn't know Dlubak but I knew the guy who was with him. I was going to go up and say hello when all of a sudden they both stood up and hurried off; and I mean they hurried off. The guy had as gun, I'm sure of it."

"When was this?" asked Jarczyk.

"Lunchtime yesterday."

"Why didn't you say anything before?"

"I didn't know who Dlubak was, did I? But then I saw his face in the paper this morning."

"That was this morning. Why wait till now?"

"I wasn't arrested till now. You don't think I'd help the *gliny* out of the goodness of my heart, do you?"

"Did you have any reason to suspect that this 'other guy' might do Mr. Dlubak some serious harm?"

"Let's put it this way: he's the kind of guy who plucks out other people's nose-hairs, just for a laugh."

"You want to tell me who he is?"

Ruba crossed his legs and gave a loud, sarcastic laugh. "What do you think I am? A *kretyn*? First of all you have to give me a guarantee. No criminal charges; and protection afterwards. Yes, and two—no, two thousand five hundred—dollars."

Jarczyk shook his head. "What are you doing? Giving up car-stealing and taking up comedy? I'm not authorized to give you protection. And anyway, why should I? If you get killed, the police have one less problem. I'm certainly not authorized to give you any money. However, I *am* authorized to charge you with obstructing justice and wasting police time, for which you will be fined so much that you will have to steal three Mercedes every day for the next twenty years just to make enough money to pay it. Provided, of course, you don't get caught doing it. In which case, you'll be fined so much that you'll never live to pay it back."

"You can't do this to me. I know who killed Dlubak."

"You saw him do it?"

"Of course I didn't see him do it."

"You said he had a gun."

"Yes, but the guy with the gun didn't do it, did he?"

"Well how the fuck should I know? Especially if you won't tell me who he is."

Ruba picked up his coffee and sipped it noisily, as if he were determined to burn the inside of his mouth. "The name of the guy who picked up Dlubak doesn't matter."

"Oh, you don't think so?"

"No, I don't think so, because he only ran errands for the guy who *did* kill him."

"And who was the guy who *did* do it?" asked Jarczyk, with deeply sarcastic patience.

Ruba shook his head. His dark hair was cropped so short that his shingles scars showed through. "I'm not telling you that. Not unless you give me a guarantee. No criminal charges; and protection afterwards."

"I told you, I don't have the authority to do that."

"How about letting me go and buying me an air ticket to Stockholm."

Jarczyk rubbed the back of his neck, as if the price of an air ticket to Stockholm would jeopardize his entire career. "I don't know . . ." he said. "You're supposed to tell us who killed Dlubak because it's your public duty."

Ruba leaned forward, his eyes like nail heads. "If you don't promise to get me out of Poland I'm not saying one more word."

Jarczyk thought for a moment, then he nodded. "All right, then. An air ticket to Stockholm."

"You swear it?"

"Cross my heart and hope to die."

Ruba said, "You'd better not go back on that, because I'll kill you before they kill me. Give me some paper, and a pencil."

Jarczyk pushed his pad across the table. Ruba picked up his pen and wrote a name in Cyrillic letters. *Zboinski*.

"Roman Zboinski?" Jarowski asked him. He could feel the paper trembling in his hand.

"Now you know why I want a ticket to Stockholm."

"You're sure about this?"

Ruba nodded, again and again, and kept on nodding while he was talking. "The guy with the gun has worked for Zboinski for years, ever since they were stealing meat from the cold stores in Gdansk. I knew him because I dealt in Audis and Mercedes, and he always paid me top dollar. He does anything that Zboinski tells him. Zboinski says bring me a woman, he brings him a woman. Zboinski says bring me Dlubak, he brings him Dlubak. That day, he went to bring Dlubak, and Zboinski killed him."

"Do you have any proof of that?" asked Jarczyk.

"It said in the paper that Dlubak was sexually mutilated. That was Zboinski's specialty. He used a baling-hook, the same hook he used in Leningrad. He'd get hold of somebody's balls, and *uh*—" he made a strong twisting motion with his right wrist. "Sometimes he'd get them in the eye; or in the ear. But that was his specialty. To make you beg. To make you less of a man."

"That's right," said Jarczyk. "I've heard all about Mr. Zboinski. The Hook."

At that moment, Matejko came into the interview room. "What's up?" he asked. "I heard we made an arrest."

"I'm about to," smiled Jarczyk. "This gentleman here has given us the identity of the Executioner."

Matejko looked at him in disbelief. "Just like that?"

"Just like that. He's had a little difficulty with the police in Mokotow, and he's anxious not to face charges."

"Well, who is it?" asked Matejko.

"Roman Zboinski, our friendly neighborhood motor trader. This gentleman saw one of Zboinski's men abducting Dlubak at gunpoint."

"Is that all?"

"Oh come on, Jerzy, it's obvious, when you come to think of it. All we had to do was to find out who killed one of them, and then we would know who killed them all. All that paperwork that Stefan kept piling up. All those interviews, all that legwork. All that scribble, scribble, scribble."

"What's obvious? All of those fourteen people were completely innocent, as far as we know, and only two or three of them have any connection whatsoever. Why should Zboinski kill people like that?"

"To put us off the scent, of course. To confuse us. If he killed innocent people as well as the people he really wanted to get rid of, he thought that we'd never believe it was him."

"Witold," said Matejko, "you really have no—"

"I want twelve officers and two sharpshooters," Jarczyk interrupted him. "I want to do it as soon as possible, before it gets light. Let's catch Mr. Zboinski with his trousers down."

"But you don't have any serious evidence. You

haven't even had the full autopsy on Dlubak's body."

"His fucking head was cut off!" snapped Jarczyk. "What more of an autopsy do I need than that?"

"He was also tortured, which none of the other victims were."

"That, Jerzy, is a detail. Right at this moment, I'm not concerned with details. I'm not concerned with mountains of written witness-reports or searching the sewers inch by inch. I'm only interested in arresting the Executioner, and the sooner I do it, the sooner Warsaw is going to be safe for everybody."

Matejko hesitated. "Don't you think I'd better call Nadkomisarz Dembek? You know, before we . . ." His voice trailed away. Beads of perspiration were standing out on Jarczyk's upper lip and Matejko could tell that there was no arguing with him. "All right," he said. "I'll call the duty officer."

Jarczyk slapped him on the shoulder. "Good man. Let's have some positive policework around here, for a change."

Ruba said, "What about me? When do I get my ticket?"

"All in good time," Jarczyk told him. "You're a witness, remember. In fact, you're our *only* witness. We can't let you go flying off to God knows where, now can we? You might forget to come back."

"You promised me a ticket, you shit!" Ruba screamed at him.

"Yes," Jarczyk, leaning across the table so that they were practically nose to nose. "And when I get my sworn evidence that puts Roman Zboinski in jail, you'll get it."

"They'll kill me," said Ruba. "They'll do worse than kill me."

"I don't suppose your girlfriend will shed any tears."

11

hey drove to the intersection of Swietokrzyska and Jana Pawla II. Rej pulled up onto the sidewalk, his front bumper nudging a rusty Skoda, which immediately started a huge bull terrier on the back seat barking and hurling itself from one slobber-coated window to another.

Rej climbed out of his car, walked up to the Skoda and roared so fiercely at the dog that it sat down, whimpering, and tried to hide its head under a blanket.

"I see you have a way with animals," said Sarah.

Rej lit a cigarette. He hadn't attempted to smoke when Sarah was in the car. "Animals and people, they're all the same. They just need to know where they stand."

Clayton said, "This sure *looks* like the place. All we have to do now is find the right apartment block."

"I think it's that one," Rej told him, pointing with his cigarette-hand to a narrow six-story block with square concrete balconies. "I've been in there before. A man murdered his mother because she served him potato salad every evening for eleven years."

"You're kidding me," said Clayton.

Rej shrugged, as if Clayton could believe what he liked. Then he led the way across the sidewalk to the building's entrance, where a woman in a flowered housecoat was energetically scrubbing the front step.

"Police," said Rej, showing his identity card. "I'm looking for a little girl called Zofia. Do you know if she lives in any of these apartments?"

The woman knelt up straight, as if she were about to take communion. She had a circular face and a large mole on her chin. "There's two Zofias. One in 5 and the other in 11."

"This Zofia has a doll," put in Clayton. "A knitted doll, like a little farmgirl."

The woman shook her head. "I don't remember seeing a doll like that."

"Well, we'll just have to go in and ask, won't we?" said Rej.

"There's no point in trying number 5," the woman told him. "They've been away for over a week."

"Away? Do you know where they are?"

She shook her head again. "She never tells me anything. She's always very quiet, coming and going like a mouse. She's a single mother, see. Her husband left her and went off with some tart."

"Did she say when she was coming back?"

"I didn't even know that she was going. She didn't say a word. She just went."

"Do you have a key to that apartment?" Rej asked her.

"Yes, but she won't like it if I let you in. She keeps herself to herself."

Rej took out his wallet and handed her ten zlotys. "That's for your expenses."

"What do you think I am?" the woman asked him, one eye slitted against the sunlight. "A tart, too?"

Rej looked at Clayton completely deadpan; and then they both laughed; and Sarah laughed, too.

"Just give me the key," said Rej; and the woman stood up and fished a huge bunch of keys out of the pocket of her housecoat.

"Here," she said, fussy and embarrassed, and laughing, too, and pried a long brass key off the ring. "But don't tell her I gave it to you."

"All right," Rej agreed. "So long as you don't tell her that I gave it to *you*."

The woman couldn't resist grinning and slapping his arm. "It's men like you. . . !"

They entered the apartment block. Inside the lobby, there was a red vinyl-covered chair with knobby gold feet and, on the wall, a faded photograph of John Paul II celebrating mass in Pilsudskiego Square. They pressed the button for the elevator, and rose together to the fifth floor. Sarah looked at herself in the mottled mirror and wished she hadn't worn her pink linen suit: it creased so easily, especially in Rej's sticky-seated car.

Number 5 was right across the corridor from the elevator. There was a name-card pinned to the brown door: *Wierzbicka*. Rej knocked, waited a few seconds for an answer, and then opened the door with the key. "Anybody home?" he called; but it was obvious that nobody was.

Inside, there was a cramped little entrance hall with overcoats and woolly hats hanging on pegs. To the right, an open door led to a kitchenette, with a small electric cooker and a collection of cheap plastic jars for sugar and tea. There was a door at the end of the kitchenette, with a small wired-glass window in it. Sarah peered out through the window and saw darkened service stairs. They reminded her of the service stairs in the apartment building that she had lived in when she was little: she had always imagined Morlocks and other monsters shuffling up and down them.

On the right side of the entrance hall, there was a drab, brown-wallpapered living room, furnished with a sagging green couch, a small television set and two mismatched armchairs, one plum and one lime green. Sarah went to the window to look out over the street, but what caught Clayton's attention was a coffee mug lying on its side next to the couch, and a dry brown stain of coffee on the carpet. He beckoned to Rej and nodded at it without saying anything.

Rej carefully searched the room from one end to the other, going down on his knees to look behind the couch, lifting the cushions, peering under the chairs.

"What's he looking for?" Sarah asked Clayton.

"Anything," Clayton told her. "People don't usually leave their apartments without cleaning up."

Rej stood up and brushed the knees of his trousers. "Nothing else," he said. "Let's try the bedroom."

They went through to the single bedroom. It smelled of lavender talcum powder and damp. There was a double bed on one side, covered with a knitted bedspread, and a single bed on the other. Above the double bed hung a crucifix. Above the single bed a poster of Michael Jackson had been taped, and on the pillow there were three more knitted dolls, all of them bearing a striking family resemblance to the one they had found in the sewer.

Clayton said, "This is it all right, Zofia's house. But where the hell is Zofia?"

Rej opened the rickety chipboard closet. It was crammed full of clothes, and a purple plastic traveling-bag was wedged into the bottom of it, next to the shoes.

"These people didn't go on holiday." he said. "These people just upped and left. Or else they were kid-napped. Or worse. That was why nobody reported a girl missing on the night that Kaminski was killed."

Rej cautiously opened the bathroom door and peered around it. A tap was softly dripping into a brown-stained bath. On a plastic shelf under the cabinet, he found a glass with two toothbrushes in it, one adult size, one smaller. Sarah came and stood beside him while he opened the cabinet and sorted through it. De-odorant, shower gel, L'Oreal shampoo, tweezers, three false eyelashes, tampons.

"They're dead, aren't they?" said Sarah. She found their cheap, abandoned belongings infinitely poignant.

"We won't know that for sure until we find their bodies. But, yes. Even if you're running out on your unpaid rent, you take your toothbrush with you."

They went back into the living room, where Clayton was searching through the drawers of a small varnished bureau. There was nothing much: a few untidy bundles of letters, five or six envelopes stuffed with photographs. A carefully-folded communion gown, beautifully embroidered, silky and stale, in tissue paper. A red tin chocolate box with sewing materials in it. Half a dozen different-colored balls of wool.

Rej looked through the photographs. He came across one of a blond-haired young girl in a yellow flower-printed dress, standing by the concrete bear pit at Praga Zoo. One hand was lifted to shield her eyes from the sun, which cast a dark shadow on her face. Rej shuffled through the pictures and found several more of the same young girl.

"Zofia?" he asked, passing one of them to Sarah.

Sarah nodded. "She must be."

Without a word, Rej passed her another one. It showed the girl sitting on the steps outside the apartment block, hugging the same knitted doll that they had found in the sewer. The same knitted doll that had bled on Madame Krystyna's table.

"The question is," said Clayton, "how did one man manage to abduct both Zofia and her mother without anyone seeing him?"

"Who says it was one man?" Rej countered. "Maybe that's the key to this case . . . it wasn't just a lone psycho. It was two people, or possibly more."

"I don't know . . . we only saw one figure in those psychic images."

"Clayton, those were nothing more than pictures in the air. Intuition. Magic, if you like."

"They led us here, though, didn't they?"

"Yes," Rej admitted. "They led us here. But we still have to have substantive evidence. Even if we find the Executioner, we can't make an arrest on the basis of psychic images, can we?"

"Let's find him first," said Clayton. "We can worry about the evidence later."

Rej opened another packet of photographs. These were older, black-and-white and sepia, with folded, dog-eared edges. There was a picture of a pretty teenage girl in a black coat and white ankle socks, standing self-consciously in a park. Whoever had taken the photograph had cast their shadow across the path. Then there was another picture of the same girl, wearing a one-piece bathing-costume. He turned it over. Pencilled on the back were the words "Iwona, 1976."

"This must be Zofia's mother," said Rej. "You can see the resemblance."

Clayton nodded. "She must have been about fourteen here, by the look of her, which would make her early to mid-thirties now. So Zofia must have been—what, six or seven?"

Rej found photographs of Iwona as a very small girl—then pictures of her parents, and her grandparents. Then he came across three pictures which had obviously been taken in wartime. One showed three girl couriers who had somehow managed to find themselves Polish Army uniforms, complete with peaked caps, standing next to a broad-shouldered man in a jacket and a beret. Another showed the same man shaking hands with another man who was wearing a dark military uniform. In the third, he was standing next to a barricade of asphalt blocks, smoking a cigarette. He was trying to look nonchalant but he succeeded only in looking hungry.

Only the second photograph bore a caption. In slanting writing, it said "K. Kucma & J. Z. Zawodny, August 7, 1944."

"Home Army," said Rej. "J. Z. Zawodny was one of their main leaders."

"What does that mean?" asked Clayton.

"I don't know yet. But this fellow Kucma must have been related to Iwona and Zofia. He could have been Iwona's grandfather . . . maybe her father, even. He looks pretty young in this picture. No more than twenty or twenty-one."

"And? So?"

"When I looked over Ewa Żborowska's apartment— you know, that girl who was murdered on Grojecka— she had a picture of her father from 1944, with General Bór."

"So two victims out of fourteen had parents or grandparents in the Home Army. That can't be too statistically unusual, surely?"

"I don't know. Many of the Home Army were shot. Many were taken prisoner. But a lot of them survived. And it's a connection, isn't it?"

Clayton said, "Why don't you follow it up? You know, check on the family backgrounds of every single victim?"

"That's going to take days. You think it's worth it?"

"Of course. It rings a little bell in the back of your head, doesn't it? A little tinkle-tinkle-tinkle. It may come to nothing, but you're a cop, just like me, and when those little bells start tinkling, it's time to find out why."

"You're right," agreed Rej. He took out a Marlboro but Sarah gave him the ray and he didn't light it.

"Question is," said Clayton, "what did the Executioner do with Zofia and Iwona's mortal remains? It's difficult enough to abduct somebody who doesn't want to be abducted. It's even harder to get rid of two dead bodies."

Sarah said, "There was a service door in the kitchen, wasn't there? Maybe he took them out that way."

They went back to the kitchenette. The service door

was locked. Clayton and Sarah searched through the cupboard and peered in all of the plastic spice-jars, but they couldn't find a key. While they did so, Rej placidly produced a worn black leather wallet full of lock picks, and took less than a minute to open it.

"That's very effective," said Clayton. "In Chicago, if we couldn't find the key, we always use to kick them down."

"In Warsaw, doors are expensive," said Rej. "We 'reat them with respect."

The service stairs were gloomy and smelled of dust. On the far side of the landing, there was a battered metal flap, with a handle. "Garbage chute," said Rej. He opened it up and they were overwhelmed by a warm, foul draft. "Straight down into the basement."

They all looked at each other. "What do you think?" said Clayton.

"I don't even want to think," Sarah told him.

"We have to face it. He could have killed the mother, thrown her down the garbage chute and abducted the little girl. That wouldn't have attracted so much attention."

"Jesus," said Rej.

"Come on, Rej," Clayton told him. "We have to sift through the trash; there's no other way of knowing; not for sure."

"I'm on suspension. I can't call out for a search squad, not without consulting Nadkomisarz Dembek. I can't even call out for a pizza."

"Then we'll have to be the search squad, you and me."

The garbage from the apartment building was stored in four large galvanized metal bins in a small high-walled yard, right at the rear. There was a strong smell of rotting cabbage and burning. The woman with the mole came down to show them where they were. "They're supposed to come to collect them once a week, but they never do. And kids are always setting fire to it, look." One of the bins had been burned out, its sides scorched and all of the rubbish inside it turned to ash.

Rej said, "Iwona didn't go on vacation, you know. You see these ashes?"

The woman stared at him for a long time. Then she turned toward the trash bins. Rej said nothing, didn't even blink. After a while the woman turned and went back up the steps to the apartment block's rear entrance. The door closed behind her with a vibrant bang. In Warsaw, for people of a certain age, there were things that didn't bear remembering, and among those things that didn't bear remembering were killings, and ashes.

Clayton opened the top of the burned-out trash container. It was heaped to the brim with grayish-white ashes, as well as an odd assortment of objects that wouldn't burn, like blackened cans and bottle tops and spoons and wire coat hangers. He dug his hand into the ash and let it run through his fingers. "God, this must be five feet deep. We're never going to find anything in this."

"We're the search squad," said Rej.

Sarah said, "Tip the bins over, that's all you have to do. If there's any charge for clearing up, Senate will pay for it."

Rej looked at her with respect. "Okay. That's the best idea I've heard all day."

Between them, he and Clayton took hold of the bins, one by one, and threw them onto their sides. They made a thunderous banging, and their lids flew open, and heaps of garbage spread all across the yard, until they were ankle deep in it. The woman with the mole came to the back door and stared at them for a while, but then she went away again, still without saying a word. Rej and Clayton used a sweeping-brush and a garden fork, and started to comb through the ash.

"God, I never thought that I'd ever have to do this

again," said Clayton, in disgust, as he flung away a filthy discarded diaper. But Rej was too busy raking through twisted bottles and cans and springs.

Sarah found a spade with a broken handle and started sorting through the ashes, too. Working with Clayton and Rej was so unlike anything that she had ever done before that she felt quite amateurish and inexperienced. She had misjudged Rej, in a way. He was cautious, yes, and deeply suspicious of anything novel, especially if it came from the West; but he had a persistence that she had never found in anybody else before, a single-mindedness that was both sad and admirable at the same time.

Rej said, "For God's sake, how many jars of sauerkraut do these people eat?"

Clayton said, "Look—I think I've found a ring. Is this somebody's ring?"

He held it up and Sarah and Rej came to look at it. It was a thin circlet, deeply discolored by fire, but it was undeniably a woman's ring. Not a wedding band, necessarily, but something similar. The kind of ring that a single woman might wear to ward off unwelcome approaches.

All three of them concentrated their efforts on the heaps of ash close to where Clayton had discovered it. They found more bottle tops, more cans, more half incinerated newspapers and magazines and potato peelings. Then Rej tried to dislodge the next heap with his sweeping-brush. There was a terrible soft lurching sound, the ash dropped, and a ribcage was revealed, a scorched ribcage, with part of a shoulder blade.

"Oh, God," said Clayton. "I was right."

"I don't think we should touch this anymore," Rej told him. "We could mess up the evidence. Let me call Matejko and have him come down here with the guys from forensic."

"I agree," said Clayton. He reached out and took hold of Sarah's hand. "Besides . . . I think you've probably had enough of this kind of stuff for one lifetime, haven't you?"

Sarah dropped her shovel. Her mouth felt dry and she felt as if she had a temperature. All the same, she couldn't stop looking at the ribcage lying in the ashes, and thinking of the photographs of Iwona in her bathing-costume, smiling into the sunlight.

"Do you think that's her?" she asked Rej.

He put his arm around her shoulder and led her through the spilled ashes, back to the steps. "I don't see how it could be anybody else. But the forensic people will tell us for sure."

"Iwona," said Sarah, under her breath, almost as if she had known her.

Jarczyk's pre-dawn raid on Roman Zboinski's apartment had gone badly wrong, but only because Roman Zboinski's hadn't been there. Six police cars had arrived simultaneously at the corner of Targowa Street and Solidarnosci Avenue, their lights flashing, and a group of seven armed officers had burst into the apartment block with a battering-ram and two police dogs. They had knocked open the door of Zboinski's apartment, to find it dark and completely deserted, although there were signs that Zboinski intended to return, such as a video-recorder timed for *Gliniarz i Prokurator*, the American cop show on Channel 1.

Now, at 11:07 in the morning, Jarczyk and Matejko and twelve other officers were waiting impatiently in four unmarked cars for Roman Zboinski to come home. The sky was hazy, but the sun was almost unbearably hot, and they sat with the windows wide open, sweating and smoking and passing around cans of Coke. Matejko kept checking his watch. He had promised Helena that he would drive her to the clinic this afternoon, but unless Zboinski showed up soon, it looked as if he were going to have to let her down.

Jarczyk was nervous, jumpy, and kept drumming his

fingers on the dash. "It's typical," he kept saying. "He lives in that apartment 364 days of the year; but the one day I want to arrest him, he isn't there."

"Actually, he only lives here in August and September," Matejko told him. "The rest of the time he's in Holland; or else he's in Spain."

"What are you, a friend of his?" asked Jarczyk.

"No . . . but I pulled his file as soon as I knew you wanted to arrest him."

Jarczyk said, "Good. Fine. Good work," although he was obviously irritated.

They waited another hour. There was scarcely any breeze through the trees around St. Mary Magdalene Church. Two of the men were sent to a delicatessen on Targowa for sandwiches, and returned with broad smiles and armfuls of ham, salami and salad rolls.

"Very subtle," said Jarczyk, as they went from car to car, handing out the food. "You don't suppose this looks anything like a stake-out, do you?"

"I doubt if he's coming," Matejko told him. "Somebody must have tipped him off by now."

"Do you know somewhere else to find him?" Jarczyk retorted.

"Sometimes he hangs around the Zebra, on Sobieskiego. That's his unofficial office."

"Why didn't you say so before?"

"Because you're in charge of this operation, komisarz, not me."

"Meaning what?"

"Meaning that Ruba's confession doesn't amount to solid evidence."

Jarczyk twisted around in his seat, his mouth full of sandwich, and jabbed his index finger at Matejko. "When it comes to evidence, Jerzy, your opinion doesn't count. All you have to do is do your duty and do what you're damn well told."

He told the driver, "Get onto Nadkomisarz Dembek. Ask him to send two officers around to the Zebra, to check if Roman Zboinski's there. If he is, tell them to leave him well alone, but to get back to me immediately."

He looked back at Matejko and shook his head. "You could have compromised this entire fucking operation, do you know that?"

Matejko turned his head away and said nothing. He didn't want to end up on a disciplinary charge; or being suspended; especially now he and Helena had the new baby to look after. He knew that Jarczyk mistrusted him because he had worked so closely with Rej, and because he knew so much more about the Executioner case than he did, and because he had expected to take over the case when Rej was relieved.

He was trying to be co-operative, but he wanted the Executioner caught, the real Executioner, and he knew that Jarczyk's hunches were far too flimsy. Jarczyk had a reputation among his superiors for breaking cases within two or three days, sometimes in hours, but there was more than one officer at Wilcza Street who suspected that Jarczyk often arrested people not because they had committed any crime, but because they couldn't prove that they hadn't.

"Rej would have taken a century to solve this case," said Jarczyk, as if he had been following Matejko's train of thought.

Still Matejko said nothing, but thought to himself: Rej wouldn't have been wasting time sitting in this stifling car eating sandwiches. Rej would have been searching through the city, bar by bar, casino by casino, until he found the man he was looking for, who wouldn't have been Zboinski.

Another hour went by. Jarczyk leaned his head against the door pillar and started to snore. The driver whistled an irritating tune between his teeth. Over on the other side of the street, in a beige Polonez, another four officers were deeply asleep. Even from a distance, they looked like four police officers, deeply asleep.

Matejko thought that this must be the most obvious
stake-out ever. He didn't know why Jarczyk didn't set
up a large sign announcing "Quiet! Police Stake-out in
Progress!" He checked his watch again, and wished
that he could call Helena.

It was almost 12:30 and the day was warm and
glazed like an earthenware jug. There was only one
cloud in the sky, in the shape of a duck. It was so warm
that even Matejko was finding it hard to keep his eyes
open. But it was then, while they were all dozing, that
a black BMW with black-tinted windows rolled almost
silently past St. Mary Magdalene Church, with its onion domes, and parked outside the apartment block opposite.

The doors of the BMW opened, and it was only because one of them reflected a flash of sunlight in Matejko's eyes that he came abruptly to his senses.

"Zboinski!" he hissed, slapping Jarczyk on the
shoulder. "Zboinski's here!"

"What?" said Jarczyk, staring at him with unfocused
eyes.

"For Christ's sake, *look*!" Matejko urged him, and
on the other side of Targowa they could see Roman
Zboinski heaving himself out of the back seat of the
BMW, huge and bulky, in a flapping black linen suit
and a purple shirt. Three other men climbed out of the
car, too—one in a faded green polo shirt, another in a
Hard Rock T-shirt, and the third in a shapeless brown
suit.

Jarczyk snatched his transmitter from the top of the
dash, knocking the remains of his salami roll into his
lap, and screamed, *"Go! Go! Go!"*

He pushed open the car door, wrenched his gun out
of his shoulder holster, and started running across Solidarnosci shouting, *"Police! Freeze! Put up your
hands!"*

Matejko couldn't believe what he was seeing. Christ,
you never challenged an armed suspect on your own,

especially on open ground, with no cover at all. The four officers in the beige Polonez had only just woken up, and the other two cars were out of sight. He could see Zboinski and his men turn around in surprise. He could see their driver ducking back into the BMW. He could see Jarczyk running wildly toward them with his gun in his hand, screaming at Zboinski like a madman. But he still couldn't believe it.

He kicked open his door, dragged his automatic out of its holster, and ran after Jarczyk as fast as he could. A white car blared its horn at him wildly, and he had to swerve sideways to avoid a clanking, thundering truck. But then there was nothing between him and the BMW but Jarczyk, waving his gun and shouting at the top of his voice.

He saw the man in the shapeless brown suit lifting what looked like a cudgel from under his coat. He was running so fast that he didn't realize exactly what it was until he had almost caught up with Jarczyk.

"Witold!" he shouted, and shoved Jarczyk's shoulder with the palm of his hand, like a quarterback. Jarczyk staggered, almost lost his balance, and turned around with his face clenched with anger.

A dull boom echoed around the intersection, echoing from the buildings and sending the pigeons flying from the onion domes of St. Mary Magdalene. A puff of smoke hung above the BMW, in the windless air, reflected in its highly-waxed finish like a cloud in a lake.

Matejko fell backward, his arms outspread, Christ crucified in front of Mary Magdalene, blood spraying in thousands of tiny droplets all over the roadway. His jaw was blown open in a wide, exaggerated scream, his brains sprayed out of the back of the head in a knightly plume. He collapsed with a loud, complicated thud, and then suddenly the afternoon was silent.

Matejko lay staring at the sky. His last thought was: I'm late, Helena will kill me.

The silence lasted only for a few seconds. Zboinski

and his men tried to hustle themselves back into their
BMW; but a police car came skittering around the corner and blocked it off. The four officers finally managed to climb out of their Polonez and approach the
BMW with their guns drawn. Jarczyk pushed himself
forward, too, holding his gun in both hands, American-style, his knees bent.

"Out!" he shrieked. *"Get out of the fucking car!"*

There was a lengthy pause. Matejko lay bleeding in
the road, but nobody looked at him. This was too exciting; this was too much like *Gliniarz i Prokurator*.

Eventually, Zboinski climbed back out of the car
with his hands raised half heartedly. He was followed
by the man in the brown suit, who tossed his sawed-off shotgun into the road. The others followed, grinning
with amusement.

Jarczyk approached Zboinski, walking stiff-legged
around the BMW, his eyes bulging with excitement.
Zboinski, in his outsized linen suit, stood and watched
him with terrible equanimity.

"You bastard, you're under arrest," said Jarczyk.

"On a charge of what?" asked Zboinski.

"What the fuck do you think? Multiple homicide!
You're the Executioner!"

Zboinski's face slowly cracked open into a smile.

"I'm the Executioner?" He turned to his companion.
"What a joke. *I'm* the Executioner."

"Just put up your hands! Right up! And keep them
up!"

"You're making a bad mistake here, my friend,"
Zboinski told him. "First you attack me without any
warning. Now you accuse me of serious crimes. You
know who I am? I'm not one of your cheap toughs.
I'm a businessman; an important businessman."

"You've just killed one of our officers," said Jarczyk.

"Self-defense. What we were supposed to do, when
men with guns came running toward us?"

"We called out 'armed police.' "

Zboinski, still smiling, shook his head. "I don't think so. And even if you did, the traffic's too loud."

Jarczyk came closer, and unhooked his handcuffs. "I want you to turn around and put your left arm behind your back. Wasilkowski! Did you call for an ambulance?"

Zboinski said, "I won't need the handcuffs. I'm a professional businessmen. If you want me to come with you to sort this matter out, then I will."

There was a long moment of high tension between them. Somehow Jarczyk began to feel that Zboinski was right, and that he *had* made a mistake. But it was too late now. He had made his arrest and Matejko was lying dead in the middle of the street. He was committed.

Zboinski's men were handcuffed and taken to the Polonez. Jarczyk escorted Zboinski to the Fiat and opened the door for him. Zboinski heaved himself into the back seat and gave Jarczyk a grin that he would have nightmares about.

An ambulance arrived, its siren honking like a jackass. Jarczyk walked over to Matejko's body and stood over it. The other officers looked at him and it was difficult for Jarczyk to read in their eyes what they were thinking; but he sensed that he wasn't too welcome here, and he turned and went back to his car.

"I'm sorry about your man," said Zboinski, with relish.

"You will be," Jarczyk told him, and nodded to the driver to take them back to Wileza Street.

Sarah had showered and washed her hair and she was just making herself a cup of coffee when her front doorbell rang. She went through to the hallway and called, "Who is it?"

"Ben."

"I'm sorry, Ben. I don't want to talk to you right now."

"This is business. You have to."

"I have a day off and I don't have to."

"But Gawlak's agreed to all the specs. In fact, he's agreed to even less demanding specs, especially with the poured concrete. So soon as we can get Brzezicki back on the job, we can start catching up on our schedule."

Sarah said nothing, but waited. She knew that Gawlak's first list of construction criteria had been far too high; and she had been prepared to argue with him over the stress that he expected the hotel's main frame to be able to withstand. But she also knew that Senate's quantity surveyors had cut building costs down to the bone. It was what they were good at, and many of Gawlak's criticisms had been justified.

On the other hand, if she could deliver the completed hotel on time, it would certainly enhance her career, and she might even be offered a vice-presidency back in New York. She had always wanted to build a landmark hotel in the United States, but if the Warsaw Senate ran over-time, she would most probably end up in charge of the Baltic States, or Albania, or somewhere worse.

She opened the door. Ben was standing outside in a smart tan coat with matching necktie and handkerchief, holding a huge bunch of orange roses and a bottle of champagne.

"I also came to apologize. I acted like a total barbarian."

"Yes, you did," said Sarah, bluntly. "You'd better come on in."

Ben laid the roses on the kitchen table and held up the bottle of champagne. "How about a toast to celebrate?" Without waiting for a reply, he went searching through her cupboards until he found two tulip glasses. "Everything's going to be fine. All we have to do now is persuade Brzezicki that there isn't any devil."

"Oh, yes? And how do you propose to do that? No champagne for me, thanks."

Ben opened the bottle and poured out two glasses all the same. "It's all superstition, this devil business. It's all hocus-pocus. So how do you fight it? Not by being logical. You can't fight insanity with logic. So what do you do? You give the poor suckers what they want. An exorcism. Bell, book and candle."

"You need a priest for an exorcism."

"All arranged. I found a priest in Mokotow who's prepared to do it."

"For a fee, of course?"

"What does that matter? The point is, Brzezicki gets his exorcism and we get back on schedule."

"It matters because Senate has a policy of not corrupting people who are financially vulnerable. Besides, what happens if the Executioner strikes again—even *after* your exorcism?"

Ben handed her a glass of champagne, and lifted his own glass. "Come on, sweetheart, what are the odds of him killing in the same place three times over? Besides, I've arranged a little insurance. An armed security guard to keep an eye on the site until the sewers are fully repaired and the foundations have been poured. He'll be dressed as a company site inspector."

"Well, well, you think of everything, don't you?" said Sarah. "But what happens if I don't agree?"

Ben looked perplexed. "Why shouldn't you agree?"

"Can you imagine the adverse publicity this is going to attract? 'Senate Hotels arranges exorcism for possessed hotel site.' It's bad enough that we're building the hotel where four people were murdered. That's going to put off quite enough potential guests. But if we admit that there's something spooky going on . . ."

"Do you know something?" said Ben, swallowing champagne. "You're like all women. All you ever see is obstacles. No wonder women talk about a glass ceiling. But it isn't men who stop them from rising to the top. It's them, themselves. There is no glass ceiling, but women always want to believe that there's something in the way—something preventing them from fulfilling their potential. Let's put it this way: it wasn't women who landed on the moon."

"That's right. They were too busy doing something useful."

Ben came closer. "You're creating obstacles now, between you and me. It seems like you want me but you don't want to let yourself have me. It doesn't have to be that way."

"What's this? Your revised seduction technique? You hold a phony exorcism with a bribed priest so that you won't have to report me back to New York, and then you want me to be so grateful that I throw myself back on the bed with my legs open?"

"Damn it, Sarah, why do you have to make it sound so goddamned crude?"

"Because it is. Because I used to love you, but I don't love you anymore, and the way that you keep harassing me and trying to bully me, I don't think I even *like* you anymore, either."

"I'm still holding the exorcism."

"Do what you like, Ben. Just leave me alone."

Ben shook his head as if Sarah were mentally deranged. "I'm not asking you for anything, Sarah. Just to recognize your own feelings."

He put down his glass, and then took her glass, too. He held her arms, and said, "I want you, baby. That's the long and the short of it."

"Ben—" Sarah began, but without any warning he pressed himself forward and clamped his mouth over hers. She twisted her face away, and tried to wrench herself free, but Ben gripped her arms even more tightly, and swung her from side to side. He tried to kiss her again, but she kept her mouth tightly closed and stamped on his feet.

"Ben, get off me!"

His eyes were starey and mad. "Get off you? Get *off* you? Is that what you really want? Jesus, Sarah, I know what you really want. You've been dreaming about you and me ever since we broke up. We were always perfect, you and me. The perfect couple. And what the fuck were you doing, walking right out on me like that. I mean I was practically your husband."

He pushed Sarah with the flat of both hands, pushed her across the living room, and pushed her backwards onto the huge, brocade-upholstered sofa. "You know what you need? You need to remember who took care of you, who taught you everything you know. They call you the Ayatollah because *I* taught you how to do business the hard way, didn't I? *I* taught you when to bully and when to connive; when to refuse to compromise and when to give in. And now you're turning around and saying that you don't want me? I mean— what is this? Have you turned dyke or something?"

Sarah tried to sit up, but Ben pushed her flat on her back again.

"What's the matter with you?" he demanded. "I came over here specially to see you again. I could be back in New York now, taking care of business, watching my back. But oh no, I came here to stick my neck out and protect little baby green-eyes. But what do I get? I get fucking permafrost, that's what I get."

"Ben," said Sarah, "I simply don't want you anymore. Can't you understand that?"

He looked down at her for a long time with an expression like a broken mirror. Then, abruptly, he loosened his necktie, and threw it across the room. He took his coat off, too, and threw it onto the chair. He started to unbutton his shirt.

"Shit, Sarah, don't you remember those nights on Lafayette Street?"

"Yes," she said. She could feel her heart beating faster and faster. "But they're gone now, Ben. They're history."

"You're calling me history? Is that it? You're calling me history? Let me tell you something, sweetheart, I'm richer now than I ever was before. I'm richer, and I have more clout. I'm twice the man I used to be."

"You think so?" asked Sarah. "So why don't you attract me anymore?"

Ben stared down at her and she could almost hear the rumble of his anger rising, like a volcano about to erupt. He didn't say anything, but he stripped off his shirt, and then he unbuckled his belt.

"Ben," Sarah warned him, "don't get any ideas. I'll call the police if you do, and I mean it."

"Ideas? What fucking ideas? You think you're so incredibly smart. You think you're so incredibly together. You would have been nothing, if it hadn't been for me."

He pulled off his Gucci loafers and dragged off his pants. He wasn't drunk. He wasn't high. But he was intoxicated with frustration and rage. He stood in front of her with his penis sticking up at an angle. It looked thinner than she remembered, with lots of wiry ginger hair around it, and a glans like a plum tomato. She thought it was extraordinary how erotic a man's genitals were if you were in love with him, and how ridiculous they looked, if you weren't.

"Go on," Ben challenged her. "Tell me that everything's different. Tell me that everything's changed. Tell me I'm history."

Sarah looked him up and down, as coolly as she could manage. "I'll tell you one thing, Ben. You've put on a hell of a lot of weight."

Ben's eyes widened. Then he went for her. He slapped her across the face, twice. She lifted her arms to protect herself, so he punched her on the shoulders and hit her on the ribs.

"You shit!" he bellowed at her. "You stuck-up, hy-pocritical, pretentious shit!"

"Ben!" she screamed at him. *"Ben, for God's sake, stop it!"*

He was about to hit her again when a harsh voice shouted out, *"Stop! Don't you touch her!"*

Ben turned around, his eyes unfocused. He hardly saw the stubby, white-haired man who took four quick steps across the room and punched him directly in the jaw. Something cracked inside his face, and he fell back against the sofa. Then another punch hit him on the bridge of his nose, and he felt blood spurting onto his chest like a warm, wet poultice. He found himself lying on his back on the floor, deafened, half blinded, looking up with his one good eye at Sarah's bare foot, protruding over the arm of the sofa.

He heard a voice say, "Are you all right?" and the voice wasn't talking to him.

Sarah, bruised and shaking, climbed off the couch. "He went crazy," she said, rubbing her arm. "He came here to talk about business, and then he went crazy."

"You want me to arrest him?" asked Rej. He was trying to sound matter-of-fact but he was panting, and rubbing his knuckles over and over.

Sarah looked down at Ben, lying on the floor, his white-haired chest sprayed with nostril-blood, his penis all curled up. "I don't think so," she said. Her voice was wobbling like a cup on an ill-fitting saucer. "I don't think he'll try it again."

"It's lucky for you I came around to see you," said Rej. "And it's even luckier that you didn't close your front door properly."

"I thought I—" Sarah began; but then she remembered how quickly Rej had picked the lock at Zofia's apartment, and said nothing.

"It's all right. I heard shouting," Rej reassured her. "That's all. We have the legal right to break in if we suspect domestic violence of any kind."

For some reason, Sarah reached up and took hold of his hand. It reminded her of holding her father's hand when she was little. It had always made her feel so secure. So long as they were hand-in-hand, she was safe, and well protected. She had loved cuddles with her father when she was small, but there was never anything quite like walking along the street together, holding hands, as if they were prepared to show everybody that they loved each other, and that they wanted to protect each other, and that they were safe.

Ben awkwardly climbed to his feet, and struggled into his clothes. They both watched him, giving him no privacy. He glared at them from time to time, but said nothing.

"Use the bathroom," Sarah told him. "And don't leave blood on the towels."

Ben limped off without a word, and closed the bathroom door. Sarah sat down and gently patted the side of her face. She was beginning to feel her lip swelling out, and the bruises on her cheeks began to puff up. She had a meeting with International Travel Bureau tomorrow morning, and she knew that she was going to look great. A bulging mouth, a half-closed eye, and cheeks like Marlon Brando.

Rej sat next to her. "Let's take a look," he said. "You're not too bad. Once your boyfriend's gone, you can put a cold facecloth on that."

"Believe me, he's not my boyfriend."

"He used to be, once?"

"That was a long time ago, in a galaxy far, far away. Now he's my boss, and an all-around pain in the ass."

"He still likes you, then?"

"I don't think 'like' is the word for it. He wants to have me, that's all. He lost me, because I walked out on him, and that's rankled ever since. 'No woman walks out on me.' You know the deal."

"Of course. My woman walked out on me."

Sarah reached across and picked up one of the

glasses of champagne. She took a long drink, and then put it down again. "Ugh, that was far too fizzy. I should have had a brandy."

"You want to know the best brandy in the world? Lancut, from the Tatra Mountains. That's beautiful. You must try it some day. In fact, I don't know why you don't try some today, with me."

Sarah sensed that there was something wrong. She grasped Rej's hand and said, "What's wrong? Has something happened?"

Tears began to roll down Rej's rough-cast cheeks. He wiped his nose with the back of his hand. "I came back to tell you that Komisarz Jarczyk has arrested one of our local gangsters on a charge of murdering all fourteen of the Executioner's victims."

"He's caught him? He's really caught him?"

"I don't know . . . the evidence doesn't seem to be very strong. Jarczyk has an informant who saw one of this gangster's stooges abducting Dlubak from the Saxon Gardens . . . armed with a gun, as far as we know. The next thing we knew, Dlubak's dead body was found in a sewer underneath Powstancow Warszawy Square." He sniffed, and waited until he had managed to recover himself. Then he said, "Minus his head, just like all the others."

He stood up, and shrugged, as if he were too choked up to speak at all. "Dr. Wojniakowski assures me that Dlubak was killed in almost exactly the same way as the other victims, but there are two important differences. One—he was sexually tortured. His penis was pierced all the way through by a very sharp hook. None of the Executioner's victims was ever tortured before, and none of them was interfered with, sexually."

"Go on," said Sarah. She glanced toward the bathroom door but there was still no sign of Ben.

"Well, second, Dlubak's head was cut off with a different knife from all of the rest. That doesn't mean conclusively that he wasn't killed by the same person.

The Executioner could have dropped his knife when he was killing those Germans of yours, and found himself another one."

"What else?"

"That's all . . . except the man they've arrested didn't have any known motive for murdering any of those fourteen people except for Dlubak."

"So he may have killed Dlubak, but there's less chance that he killed any of the others?"

"That's the way it looks to me."

Rej was silent for a time, his hand pressed over his mouth. Sarah watched his eyes filling with tears, and then said, "What's wrong? What's happened?"

Rej swallowed. "They arrested this man . . . he's a well-known racketeer, Roman Zboinski. A very hard case, we've been watching him for years. During the arrest, one of his men shot at my partner, Jerzy Matejko. Jerzy has a young wife, a new baby."

He paused, and then he said, in a light, despairing voice, "Killed him. The bastards killed him."

Sarah put her arm around him. Through his jacket she could feel him shuddering.

"It's crazy," said Rej. "I don't even know if Zboinski is the right man. Supposing Matejko died for nothing at all . . . just for some stupid mistake?"

"You don't know that," Sarah soothed him. "Surely Jarczyk wouldn't have tried to arrest this Zboinski for no good reason?"

"I don't know . . . I haven't had the chance to talk to him yet. I'm not sure that I will. Now that Matejko's dead, they're shutting me out of this case completely."

Ben reappeared from the bathroom. His face was puffy and bruised, and he looked as if he were still concussed. He ignored Rej, but walked right up to Sarah and stood over her, still sniffing blood up his nose. "I'm not going to forget this in a long time," he told her. "In fact, I'm not going to forget this as long as I live."

"So what does that mean? You're going to call New York and tell them I can't hack it? You do that, and I'll call New York and tell them that you've sexually assaulted me and that you've gone way over the edge."

Ben said, "I won't have to call New York. Once they've worked out the figures, you'll be catmeat."

Rej stood up. "I think it's time you left now, sir. That's unless you want to face charges."

"I'm going, all right? I have an exorcism to arrange."

"You won't need to do that now. Apparently the Warsaw police have caught the Executioner, and he's safely locked up behind bars."

"You've *caught* him?" asked Ben, incredulously.

Rej shrugged. "Lots of hard work, plus a lucky tip-off. You know how these things go."

Ben hesitated for a moment, his lower lip curled down in contempt, as if he really wanted to say something sarcastic, but couldn't think of it.

"You people," he said at last. "You goddamned self-righteous people, you make me sick."

With that, he turned around and left the apartment, but not before making a short detour to the kitchen, picking up the champagne bottle, and taking it with him.

After he had gone, Rej took out a pack of cigarettes, but then he put it away again. Sarah said, "It's okay. You can smoke if you like."

"No . . . you're right. I should give it up." He paused, and then he said, "I hope I haven't interfered . . . I saw him hitting you and I had to do something."

Sarah shook her head. "I'm glad you did. I used to love him. I used to think that the sun rose in his eyes. But I was younger then. I didn't know the difference between love and dependence. I didn't know what bastards men could be."

"Well, we're not all bastards," said Rej. "But when it comes to women . . . we're none of us very clever."

Sarah went to the bathroom and switched on the light

over the mirror. Ben had bled copiously into one of her hand-towels and just dropped it on the floor. She ran the cold water, soaked a facecloth, and pressed it against her cheek.

"Does it hurt?" asked Rej, reflected in the mirror.

"I expect I'll live. They don't call me the Ayatollah for nothing."

"I should have arrested him."

"No . . . I don't want to make waves, not until we've finished building this hotel. Believe me, komisarz, I'll get him back for this one day, when he's least expecting it."

Rej said, "Why don't you call me Stefan?"

She looked up at him, first with her left eye closed, and then her right. The vision in her left eye was still a little blurry. "All right, Stefan, if that's what you want." She squeezed out the facecloth. "I guess you're off this case for good now, what with this Zboinski guy being arrested."

"Officially, yes."

"Do you really think this is the end of it? After all, I'm paying Clayton over two grand a week, and if you guys really have found the Executioner . . . I could save myself a whole lot of money."

"It's hard to be sure," said Rej. "Nobody saw Dlubak being taken to Zboinski's apartment, nobody witnessed him being killed, and nobody saw his body being dumped. Of course, we still have a mountain of forensic evidence to look at. We've been searching Zboinski's apartment since seven o'clock this morning. Maybe they'll come up with something which might connect him with one of the other murders, or maybe all of them, if we're lucky. But somehow I don't think so. Zboinski likes to think of himself as a businessman. He wouldn't kill anybody at random, just for the sake of killing them."

"That's your theory, anyhow," said Sarah.

"It's more than a theory, Ms. Leonard. I know more about this case than anybody."

"So in your opinion they haven't arrested the right man? And why don't you call me Sarah?"

Rej nodded. "All right, Sarah. It's *not* Zboinski. I'm ninety percent sure of it."

"So even if I could persuade them to go back to work, Brzezicki and his men could still be at risk?"

"We're all at risk."

"Ben thinks we ought to have an exorcism."

"An exorcism? With a priest?"

"I don't know how serious he is. He *sounds* serious; but then there were times when he sounded like he loved me. Most likely it's all for show . . . a way to convince Brzezicki that he's driven out the devil for good."

"Well, who knows," said Rej. "Maybe an exorcism might work. There's much more to this case than we know. Look at that seance we did with Madame Krystyna. Did you ever see anything like that before?"

Sarah shook her head.

"No, me neither," said Rej. He was silent and reflective for a moment, as if he were trying to make up his mind about something. Then he said, "Listen . . . I'm going back to police headquarters to find out what's going on. Matejko was supposed to be organizing a search of the sewers, I want to know what's happened to that. I also want to know if the lab has come up with any more information on how Dlubak died. If there's any chance that Zboinski killed all of those people, I'll be the first in line, buying Jarczyk a drink. But if there isn't . . . well, we're just as much in jeopardy as we were before."

"I have some free time," said Sarah. "Is there anything I can do?"

"Well . . . you could push Vistula Kredytowy to give you more information on Zboinski's money-laundering affairs. You're the client, you could be quite tough about this. Threaten to go to the Ministry of Finance if they don't cooperate. Do it today, if you can. Jarczyk's bound to start poking around at Vistula Kredytowy within the next twelve hours, and I'd like to get my hands on that information before he does."

"Do you really think this whole Executioner business is about money-laundering? Nothing else?"

"No, Sarah, I don't. But there's something else you could do for me. As far as I know, we haven't yet interviewed Hanna Peszka. She was Jan Kaminski's girlfriend. She was too shocked to talk to us before, and it looks as if Jarczyk has forgotten all about her. Maybe you could go out to Mokotow and talk to her. She lives on the Ursynow development: I've got the address here."

He took out a cheap ballpen and scribbled Hanna Peszka's address in his diary, ripping out the page and handing it over. "Ms. Leonard—Sarah—you and I both have vested interests in finding the real Executioner. I don't think he's a devil, and I don't think he's a gangster. But he's something in between, and I want to find him. If I don't—well, I might as well put in my resignation, and spend the rest of my life growing tomatoes. I don't have anything else in my life."

"What about your daughter?"

"Katarzyna? When do I ever get to see her? I'm always too busy."

"Make yourself some time. You're off the case now, aren't you? Listen . . . arrange to see her. Do it as soon as you can. It'll make you feel better."

Rej looked doubtful. "I don't know . . . I never know what to do with her. She's fourteen now, all she's interested in is ponies."

"Take her horseback riding, then, I'll come with you."

Rej stared at her as if he had never seen her before in his life. "You? Why would you want to do that?"

"Because . . . I don't know. Because you saved me from Ben. Because I love horseback riding and I haven't ridden in a coon's age. Because your friend got killed. Because we're two human beings and we're not dead yet."

Rej couldn't stop himself from smiling. "That sounds like more than enough reasons to me. Listen . . . there's a cottage we go to, in a little village near the Kampinos Forest. You could come with us one weekend."

As soon as Rej had left she called Piotr Gogiel and asked to visit Vistula Kredytowy. Piotr seemed flustered and upset.

"What's the matter?" Sarah asked him. "I just want to go through this month's accounts with you, that's all."

"I won't be here. I have to leave the office in ten minutes."

"Then send the accounts to me here. You have my e-mail address, don't you? Then we can talk about them on Monday. Or tomorrow, if you have the time."

"Well, ah . . . the mainframe's offline, just for the moment."

"Mr. Gogiel, I'm coming over to the bank *now* and I want those accounts up on screen and ready to scroll."

Piotr Gogiel audibly swallowed. "You'll have to talk to Mr. Studnicki."

"In that case, I'll talk to Mr. Studnicki, and if there's anything funny going on, I'll do more than *talk* to Mr. Studnicki, I'll have him for a late lunch and eat you, Mr. Gogiel, for dessert."

Sarah put down the phone, and sat for a long time, thinking. Something was seriously wrong here. She had the feeling that, behind the curtains of Vistula Kredytowy's secrecy, scenery was being rapidly shifted, and that when lights came up again, everything would have been transformed, so that it looked bright and innocent.

But she could sense deception, and trickery, and ill-intent; and for the first time in her business career she felt out of her depth, and frightened.

12

arek and Olga and three of their friends came bursting out of the Green Cat Billiard Club on Piekna Street, laughing and slapping at each other. They had been playing billiards for most of the afternoon, and Marek had won eleven zlotys. He was supposed to have gone for a job interview at a hi-fi store on Grzybowska, but in the end he hadn't bothered. The pay was crap, and the pasty-faced assistant manager had treated him as if he was something he had stepped in. Not only that, the store had playing old Wojciech Mlynarski records, which had been enough to make Marek feel like tying a plastic bag over his head and ending it all.

"You coming to Zbylut's tonight?" asked one of Marek's friends. "His parents have gone to Cracow."

"Pa-a-arty!" screamed Olga, and danced a little wiggling dance right there on the sidewalk.

"I don't know," said Marek. "I'm supposed to be meeting up with Clayton Marsh."

"Oh, excuse me," his friend retorted. "Kurt's on a case with the great American detective. You can see it now, can't you? *Marsh and Maslowski*, crime-busters!"

"They've caught the Executioner, anyway," put in Olga.

"Clayton says they've made a mistake."

"Oh come on, Kurt. How does he know?"

"He just does, that's all. He says the *gliniarze* are rushing this through because they're embarrassed."

"So what's it got to do with you?"

Marek took out a cigarette. "I said I'd help, man, that's all. Think how many people the Executioner's murdered. I mean, he's the mass-murderer of the century, practically. If we can catch him—the *real* Executioner—think of the fame, man. TV interviews, pictures in the paper. There's a reward, too."

"You're dreaming," laughed another of his friends.

"So? What's wrong with dreaming?"

"Nothing—when you're asleep."

They scuffled and pushed each other as they walked along Piekna. It was just after four o'clock in the afternoon now and the sky was heavy and gray. There was no wind, and the city was warm and humid and hazy with pollution. They started singing, badly off key.

"You'll still come to Zbylut's?" asked Olga, grasping Marek's arm.

"Maybe later. It depends what Clayton wants to do."

"Clayton, Clayton, Clayton! Why don't you do what *you* want to do?"

They crossed the street, dodging in between the cars and the buses. And it was then that Marek glanced back, just to make sure that all of his friends were following him, and saw something on the opposite side of Koszykowa that brought him to a halt, even before he had reached the sidewalk. He stood in the road frowning, trying to see between the passing buses and trucks, and the crowds of pedestrians on the other side of the road. A man in gray overalls was lowering the last triangular section of a four-pointed sewer lid. Passers-by were walking around him without taking any notice; and in a moment he had joined the crowds himself, and disappeared. But Marek stood and stared and felt a cold crawling sensation down his spine. The man might have been wearing overalls, but he was white-haired, and very old—in his late seventies, at least. What sewer worker was as old as that?

Not only that, he must have simply climbed out of the sewer onto the sidewalk. If he had been inspecting the sewer, or working on it, he would have put up a guard rail and a warning sign. What genuine sewer worker appears like a stage genie in the middle of a busy street? And where was his van, and his equipment?

A car blew its horn at Marek. He turned around and gave the driver the finger. The car blew its horn again, but Marek had already started to run back across the road.

"Kurt! Where the hell are you going?" called out one of his friends.

"Marek! Come back!" shouted Olga.

But Marek ran flat out across Koszykowa and along the opposite sidewalk. He collided with a woman carrying her shopping and then he almost knocked over an elderly man with a suitcase. They shouted out after him, but he kept on running—jumping up now and again to see if he could catch sight of the white-haired man in the overalls. He was sweating and panting, and his leather jacket made a squeaking noise with every step.

He had almost reached the end of the street when he glimpsed the man turning into the front doorway of a large apartment building. Now he knew for certain that he wasn't a real sewage worker. He hurried up to the apartment doors, trying to reach them before they closed, but when he was only two meters away, a woman stepped in front of him, and the two of them performed a futile little waltz before Marek was able to get past. Just as he got to the apartment door, it clicked shut, and Marek could see very little more through the reflections in the wired-glass windows than a brown-painted elevator door closing.

However, he could also make out the illuminated floor numbers. It must have been a very slow elevator, because it seemed to take an age to rise from 1 to 3. At 3, it stopped, and stayed; so at least Marek knew what floor the man lived on.

He looked at the bell-pushes beside the front door. Only a third of them had names, and only one of those was on the third floor: *Gajda*. He stepped back. He wondered what he ought to do. This may be nothing more than a ridiculous wild goose chase; his imagination working overtime. But Clayton and Rej had both been sure that the Executioner used the city's sewers in order to get about without being detected, and who else would climb in and out of manholes like that, except somebody who knew his way around?

He could call Clayton, but if he were wrong he would be wasting Clayton's time; and more important than that, he would look like an idiot. He hesitated for a while. At one point he almost gave it up and walked away. But then he pressed the bell-push marked *Gajda* and waited to see what would happen.

For almost a minute there was no reply. Then he heard a clicking noise, and a woman's voice said, *"Tak?"*

"Hello?" said Marek. "I'm here to replace the light-bulbs."

"What?"

"The landlord sent me, but he forgot to give me the key. I have to replace all the light-bulbs."

"What's the matter with the light-bulbs?"

"Wrong wattage. They could cause a fire."

There was another clicking noise. Then abruptly the buzzer sounded, and the door was unlocked. Marek stepped inside.

The entrance hall was airless and totally silent. Marek walked across to the elevator and pressed the call button. Immediately there was a complicated clattering and a penetrating hum, and the elevator began to sink slowly down the shaft. Marek glanced back toward the street. A plump woman in a brown flowery dress was standing outside the apartment door, her brown head-scarf fluttering. For some reason she was staring at him as if she thought she recognized him.

Marek was still looking back at her when he heard the elevator door open. He turned around and jumped in shock. The white-haired man in the gray overalls was standing in the elevator, right in front of him.

He was much taller than he had appeared on the street; and much more emaciated. His head was like a skull with thin mottled parchment stretched tightly over it, so that Marek could see every wriggling vein in his forehead. Beneath brambly white eyebrows, his eye sockets were as hollow as caves, and his eyes were pale and expressionless, as if too many years of living had worn all the color out of them, and all of the sensitivity. His nose was bony and narrow: his mouth was a lipless slit. All the same, Marek could see that he must have been handsome once, in a cold, chiselled kind of way. His overalls must have been black originally, but years of washing had reduced them to a patchy gray.

"Can I help you?" he asked. His voice was high and tensile, like a steel saw cutting an iron pipe.

Marek blurted, "Gajda. I was looking for Mrs. Gajda."

The pale eyes blinked, as slowly as a lizard's. "You must mean Mr. Gajda. He's a widower." The man stepped out of the elevator with a strange, gliding movement. "I can't think what you would want with him."

"Well . . . I have a message for him."

"A message? I see. I can't think who would want to send a message to Mr. Gajda, can you?"

"It's private."

"I see. Private. We all have to have our privacy, don't we?"

Marek nodded. The man was still watching him, so he had no alternative but to step into the elevator, and press the button for 3. The man didn't move as the elevator door clunked shut and the elevator began to judder its way upward. *Shit*, he thought. This was ridiculous. Here he was, stuck in an elevator in a strange building, delivering a non-existent message to somebody he didn't even know.

What was even more absurd, the white-haired man in the gray overalls was probably completely innocent. Maybe he wasn't a sewage worker, but who was to say that he wasn't authorized to go down in the sewers and test for gases, for instance, or rat infestation, or toxic chemicals; or that he wasn't a harmless nutcase who enjoyed walking around Warsaw knee deep in other people's excrement? The elevator came to a halt, the door opened, and Marek found himself in a high, gloomy corridor, with brown gloss-painted walls, and a single grimy window at the very end, through which he could just make out the buildings on the opposite side of Koszykowa, like buildings in a faded photograph.

He walked cautiously along the corridor with his leather jacket creaking. He found a scaly brown door with the name K. Gajda on an old business card fastened to the door with a rusty thumbtack. Maybe this was all he needed to do: wait here for a while, and then go back down to the ground floor and get the hell out of here. But supposing the white-haired man asked Mr. Gajda if he'd been given a message? He'd be suspicious, wouldn't he? And if he *was* the Executioner—well, he'd be well forewarned.

There was no doorbell so Marek knocked with his knuckles. After a while he heard an internal door open and the brief blare of a television turned up loud—*Stop* magazine on TVP 1. Then he heard a chain sliding back and a bolt being drawn. The apartment door opened and he was confronted by a handsome middle-aged woman with graying black hair, and a slight cast in her eyes.

"I'm looking for Mr. Gajda," he said.

"Are you the light-bulb man?"

"Well, not exactly. But I have a message."

"I don't understand. Who from? Mr. Gajda isn't well."

"We're going to be cutting off the electricity for two hours next Wednesday. For maintenance purposes."

"Is this a joke? You don't look like somebody from the electricity company. Where's your identification?"

Marek said, "They're short staffed. And they have to tell everybody, by law. So I'm telling you."

"All right," said the woman, suspiciously, and began to close the door.

"Wait!" said Marek. "There are two other people on this floor, aren't there?"

She looked at him through the inch-wide gap. "That's right."

"The problem is I've, uh, lost the list with their names on, and I have to report back that I've told everybody, or else they'll sack me."

The woman said nothing, but continued to stare at him through the gap.

"Please," Marek begged her. "I really do need to know."

The woman opened the door a little wider. "Down there, in number 1, that's Mrs. Krajewska. Over there, in number 3, that's Mr. Okun. But Mr. Okun went out. I heard him go."

"He went out? What does he do?"

"He's retired. He doesn't do anything. Can't a man go out?"

"Of course he can. I just wondered what he did."

"I told you. He doesn't do anything. He sits in his apartment and listens to music."

"Does he have any friends?"

The woman frowned at him. "You're asking a lot of questions. I thought you worked for the electricity company."

Marek shrugged, and grinned. "We're supposed to prepare this customer profile. You know . . . how often they cook, how often they entertain. It all helps us to give you a better service."

"You're lying," the woman told him.

"What?"

"You're lying. If you don't go, I'll call the police."

"All right," said Marek. "If you can't cooperate . . ."

He started to back away; but as he did so, a thin voice called out, "Stop!"

The woman hesitated, and opened the door a little wider. As she did so, an old man in a wheelchair came into view, pushing himself laboriously across the red-and-green patterned carpet. He looked like a scarecrow: wrapped in a thick mustard-colored dressing-gown with dried soup caked onto the lapels. His hair stuck up in all directions, and his eyes were rimmed with soapy red.

"Why are you asking questions about Mr. Okun?" he demanded, in a high, phlegmy voice.

Marek started to say, "We're having a power cut next week—I just have to—" but he could tell at once that Mr. Gajda didn't believe him, either. "I'm helping some people look for a criminal," he said.

"And Mr. Okun is a criminal?"

"No, no. I didn't say that. It's just that we have to check out a whole lot of people."

"And Mr. Okun is one of them? About time, too."

"What do you mean?"

Mr. Gajda coughed, and wiped a long dangling string of saliva from his lower lip. He looked as if he shouldn't be alive at all. "Mr. Okun . . . he's one of *them.*"

"Andrzej, don't be ridiculous," the woman interrupted. "I'm sorry . . . he's old, he's not very well. He gets these ideas."

"What does he mean by 'one of them?' " asked Marek.

"I mean one of *them*," spat Mr. Gajda. "One of von dem Bach's bastards. Oh, he calls himself Okun, but he doesn't fool me. He never has. Sometimes, in the night, I've heard him talking on the telephone, and what does he speak? Not Polish, you mark my words. He's one of *them*."

"Don't take any notice," said the woman, trying to close the door. "He's old . . . he lost all of his family in the war."

Marek said, "All right. Thanks for your help, anyhow."

"He's one of *them*!" screamed Mr. Gajda. "If you're looking for a criminal, start with him!"

The door closed and Marek was left alone in the half darkness. He heard Mr. Gajda and his caregiver arguing for a few moments, then he heard the television again, then silence.

He didn't know what to make of this. He hadn't paid much attention in history lessons, but even he knew that Erich von dem Bach-Zelewski was the SS general whom Himmler had appointed to crush the Warsaw Uprising in the summer of 1944. It was von dem Bach who had killed tens of thousands of Home Army insurgents, as well as women and children, and it was von dem Bach who had supervised the ruthless reduction of the entire city to rubble. Churches, hospitals, houses, hotels—all pounded into dust.

Maybe the woman was right, and Mr. Gajda was rambling. Marek knew a lot of old people whose sanity had been affected by what had happened during the Uprising. You didn't easily forget the bodies of your friends and neighbors lying in the street, covered in nothing but newspaper for lack of coffins. You didn't easily forget young children, shot by snipers, bleeding to death in the dust. You didn't easily forget the screeching dive bombers and the massive howitzers, a hundred times too powerful for the job they were supposed to be doing, steadily battering your city into mountain ranges of bricks and slates and moonscapes of broken stones.

Marek turned to leave; and as he did so, he found Mr. Okun standing in the gloom, watching him. He shivered with surprise. He couldn't help it. He hadn't even heard the elevator.

"Delivered your message?" asked Mr. Okun. His eyes were concealed in shadow.

"Yes, thank you."

"He's a sick man, Mr. Gajda. He shouldn't be disturbed."

Marek said nothing, but edged past Mr. Okun on his way to the elevator. When they were shoulder to shoulder, Mr. Okun said, "Who are you, really?"

"What's it to you?"

"You could be a burglar, or a con man. You could be anybody."

"I'm just delivering a message, that's all."

Mr. Okun stared at Marek with those rinsed-out eyes and he was almost sizzling with menace and distrust. Marek returned his stare for a few seconds, and then pressed the elevator button. The elevator opened immediately, and he stepped inside.

"I don't want to see you back here," said Mr. Okun.

Marek didn't reply, but waited for the elevator door to slide shut; and the elevator to make its way down to the entrance hall. His heart was beating so hard that he pressed his hand over it, and closed his eyes, and tried to breathe slowly and deeply, to calm himself down.

The hall was utterly silent, but when he opened the door the noise of Koszykowa burst onto him like a welcome shower of rain. He stood on the sidewalk for a moment, still breathing deeply. Then he started to walk north, toward Jerozolimskie Avenue, and the Marriott Hotel. He was less than half way there before he was sweating, and so he took off his leather jacket and slung it over his shoulder.

ℜej sat in the back room of the Medusa food store on Nowogrodzka Street and watched the bulky gray-haired manageress slicing and wrapping sausage. He was dying for a cigarette but there were No Smoking signs everywhere. The room was bright and clean and overlit, which made him feel more like a character in a 1960s art movie than ever. In the far corner there were stacks of cans of Krakus sauerkraut and Pek meat and Hormex cherries. There was also a calendar with a color photograph of the Annunciation from the church of St. Elisabeth in Cracow: a riot of gilded angels and trumpets and exultant shepherds.

The manageress kept on slicing and wrapping. She was fat now but once she must have been pretty in that strong, challenging, clearly-defined way in which only Polish girls can be really pretty.

Rej said, "I didn't really come to talk about Barbara."

The manageress weighed another 250 grammes of sausage, wrapped it, and stuck a price label on it. "Nobody does. Not the police, not the press. Not anybody. Nobody cares what happened to her."

"I do. That's why I'm here."

"You've caught your Executioner. Why should you worry?"

"Because I don't think we *have* caught him. I mean the man we're holding . . . he's a car thief, and a murderer, too, more than likely. But he's not the Executioner. He didn't kill your Barbara."

The manageress stopped slicing and frowned at him. "Why are you saying that you've caught him, if you haven't?"

Rej gave her what he hoped was a disarming smile.

"They took me off the case. I was the expert . . . but they didn't want expertise. They wanted quick results. They arrested this local gangster because he chopped some poor innocent accountant's head off. Who knows why he did it? Maybe he thought that everybody would believe that the Executioner did it. Maybe it was just a joke. That's the kind of joke that gangsters enjoy."

The manageress came up close to Rej and there was a coronet of clear perspiration on her upper lip. "My sister was beautiful, komisarz. She wasn't bright, but she was beautiful; and she would have had a happy life."

"I know," Rej told her. "I saw her pictures. I would have married her myself."

"Not if *I* had anything to do with it."

Rej was silent for a moment. Then he said, "Was your family here in Warsaw during the war?"

She nodded.

"Do you have any idea if your father or your mother was involved in the Home Army?"

"Both. My father wouldn't talk about it, but my mother used to tell me stories about it when I was small. She was a courier during the Uprising . . . you know, carrying messages from the Old Town to Srodmiescie, the city center. Lots of her friends died in the sewers, but somehow she always managed to find her way through. They used to call her Little Rat because she knew her way around the sewers so well."

"You don't know what your father did?"

The manageress shook her head. There were tears in her eyes. Not sentimental tears, but tears of frustration, and regret. "He wouldn't talk about it. He fought with Colonel Karol Ziemski, in Zoliborz, that's all he said."

Rej took hold of her hands, which were surprisingly elegant and long-fingered. She could have been a pianist, rather than a slicer of sausages.

"He never told you anything else?"

"No. He said it was all too terrible. He wanted to forget."

Rej put his arms around her and hugged her. He didn't know what Nadkomisarz Dembek would have thought, if he had seen him like this, but he didn't care. The manageress had lost her sister and Rej had lost Matejko; and both of them had been victims of the same madness. Sometimes Rej despaired, and thought that Poland would never escape from violence and lunacy, both her own and that of her neighbors. The only answer was affection; and consideration; and sharing the pain.

He missed the comradeship of communism, no matter how restrictive it might have been. He missed the bureaucracy, and the predictability, and the feeling of brotherhood and sisterhood.

The manageress wept on his shoulder, and made a damp patch on his brown checkered shirt. "Why did it have to happen to her?" she repeated, over and over again.

Rej didn't answer, because he wasn't so sure that it wouldn't happen to her, too.

An hour later he was sitting in a cramped apartment in Wola, only two blocks away from the corner of Gorczewska and Zagloby Streets. It was here, in 1944, that the Germans had taken three hundred patients and staff from Wolski Hospital and shot them, all of them.

He was drinking tea and trying, politely, to eat poppyseed cake, although he hated poppyseed cake and he wasn't at all hungry. Poppyseeds always lodged in his teeth, and he had nightmares about interviewing homicide suspects with little black specks between his incisors. The room was airless and over-furnished. A polished sideboard was crammed with ruby-colored brandy glasses and silver-plated coasters and plastic figures of the Virgin Mary. Mrs. Slesinska was fussing and weeping, taking off her glasses again and again to wipe her eyes. She was a small, fraught woman with tightly-permed hair and freckles everywhere, as if somebody had sprinkled her with cinnamon. She never stopped talking and tutting and brushing her skirt. She had even brushed the dandruff from Rej's collar, the moment he had stepped into the room. He supposed, gloomily, that she was missing her husband very badly, but that nobody had counselled her. Nobody had tried to help.

On the wall above the sideboard were five large black-and-white photographs, arranged in a star shape. All of them showed a smiling, balding man in his mid-fifties, with a large nose and a heavy chin, and eyes that were bright with simplicity.

"I need to ask you something about Bronislaw," said Rej.

"Bronislaw never did one thing wrong, in the whole of his life. Sometimes I wish that he had. But he was such a saint. He was a choirboy at St. Lawrence's, and that's where we met; and we were married at St. Lawrence's when I was seventeen, and we had eight children. Eight! But it would have been nine, if little Darek hadn't died."

"I'm sure he was a very good man," Rej reassured her.

"Once his supervisor accused him of throwing letters away, so that he wouldn't have to deliver them. You haven't come about that, have you? It wasn't true. He treated the mail like his sacred duty."

"I'm sure he did. I expect somebody was trying to cover up for their own inefficiency. They lose letters all the time; or steal them if they look as if they've got money in them. You know that."

"Bronislaw never stole anything. He was a saint."

Rej said, "Tell me about his parents."

"His parents? I don't know anything about his parents. His father was a welder, I think. I don't know what his mother did. She came from Lublin, I think.

They both died about two years after we were married. They were quite old, you see. Bronislaw was an accident."

"You don't happen to know what his parents did, during the war?"

Mrs. Slesinska noisily blew her nose. "Bronislaw never talked about them. He didn't talk much about anything. He liked his peace and quiet. Please—eat your poppy-cake."

Rej took the smallest bite he possibly could, and sat chewing for a while, his tongue hunting into every crevice of his teeth. "Would *anybody* know what his parents did, during the war?"

"Well, of course Staszek."

"Who's Staszek?"

"His older brother. He had two older brothers and one older sister. The sister and the other brother, they're both dead now, but Staszek's still alive. He lives in the Iron Gate housing estate. I can tell you what *he* did in the war. Bronislaw was very proud of him. Staszek fought against the Germans, during the Uprising. He helped to capture the railway headquarters, something like that. Bronislaw always used to say that Staszek was a real Pole."

Rej leaned forward. "So Staszek fought with the insurgents?"

"That's right. Do you want to see a picture of him? I have one somewhere. We took it when we went on holiday to Italy. That was two years ago. I didn't like the Italians. In the hotel they shouted at us because we brought all our own food. What's wrong with that? Not everybody's a millionaire."

"Don't worry about the picture," said Rej, standing up. "You've been very helpful."

Mrs. Slesinska looked up at him, her face pinched. "It's more than I can bear, you know, losing Bronislaw like that."

"I promise you . . . we're doing our best to find out who did it."

"I had to bury his body, without his head, that was what made it so terrible. It's just as if I haven't been able to bury him at all."

Rej laid a hand on her shoulder, almost as if he were giving her benediction. "Maybe when we find out who did it, we'll be able to put him to rest."

But as he stepped out into the street, and lit up a cigarette, he was already beginning to doubt that he could find out who or what the Executioner was—and, even if he could, that he would be able to catch him. The Executioner was beginning to sound more and more like Brzezicki's devil, who pursued every last member of a man's family in its hunger for revenge.

That afternoon, he managed to make two more calls—to the travel guide's offices at the airport, and to the clinic on the outskirts of Ochota where the ear-nose-and-throat doctor had practiced. None of the travel guide's colleagues knew anything about his family or his past, although they believed he had a sister living in Poznan. But the garrulous old receptionist at the clinic knew everything about her late employer, even down to his shoe size ("he used to ask me to buy him socks . . . he was always too busy to buy his own socks").

She also knew that, as a boy, he had been a courier for "Radoslaw"—the *nom-de-guerre* of colonel Jan Mazurkiewicz—when the Germans began to force the Warsaw insurgents back into the Old Town in a fierce fighting retreat.

"He didn't talk about it very often . . . just now and then, at the end of the week's work, when we were clearing up. He had a bottle of cherry vodka in his desk and we'd have a glass each."

"Can you remember anything he told you?"

"Some of it. I think he said he was fourteen, in 1944.

He said that what he did was so dangerous that after the war he went freezing cold just thinking about it, he'd sit and shiver for hours, worse than catching the flu. At the time, though, he was so young and so cocky that he wasn't frightened. The only thing was, he fell in love with a girl. She was a courier, too. I don't remember what her name was, although he did tell me. When the insurgents finally surrendered, he took off his Home Army armband and pretended that he was just another civilian. But this girl kept her armband on, like a lot of them did, and the Germans sent her off to a concentration camp. He never saw her again. But he said he had never loved anybody, before or since, as much as he had loved her."

"You're very kind," Rej told her.

"It's nothing," said the receptionist. "In any case, haven't you caught him? It's in the paper this morning."

"We've caught *somebody*," said Rej.

"Somebody's better than nobody, isn't it?"

Rej looked away. "I'm not so sure about that."

Outside, just as he was unlocking his car, the receptionist came bustling out after him. "Komisarz, I've remembered!"

"What have you remembered?"

"The girl's name. The girl that he fell in love with. Her name was Ewelina!"

Back at police headquarters, the atmosphere was feverish and festive, and Rej had to push his way through a crowd of press and television reporters. He had almost reached the doors when he was dazzled by a camera-light, and Anna Pronaszka elbowed her way through the crowd toward him.

"Well, komisarz? How do you feel now that the Executioner has been arrested?"

"We don't yet know if he *is* the Executioner. If he is—well, of course, I'll be delighted."

"Sour grapes, komisarz?"

"Realism, Ms. Pronaszka."

Inside, the building bustled. Rej made his way to his office through hurrying police officers and excited secretaries; and everywhere phones were ringing and people were shouting.

Nadkomisarz Dembek had just announced that the President himself had sent them a message of congratulations (although some of the officers had responded to this news by blowing loud and extended raspberries). Roman Zboinski and his associates had already been formally charged with murder, conspiracy, kidnap, fraud and the possession of illegal firearms and stolen goods. They had all denied it: in fact the man whom Ruba had identified as the man who had abducted Antoni Dlubak in the Saxony Gardens had claimed that he was in Budapest at the time, visiting his cousins.

But all that Nadkomisarz Dembek wanted was Roman Zboinski's head on a plate, and he said so, again and again, on national television.

Rej reached his office and stood for a long time staring at Matejko's empty desk. Matejko's scribbled notes were still there. His coffee mug was still there. In a small glass bottle, a pink rose had shed the last of its petals. Matejko's wife had given it to him to take to work.

Jarczyk came in, with a bottle of beer in his hand. "Stefan! We're celebrating! Do you want some?"

He saw what Rej was looking at, and put the bottle down. "I'm sorry. Jerzy was one of the best. We're having a collection for his wife and kid."

There were all kinds of corrosive remarks that Rej could have made to him then. But until he knew more about the Executioner, he didn't want to fall out with anybody at police headquarters, not even Dembek, and so he bit his lip and said nothing at all.

"Even the President sent us a message," said Jarczyk. "Come on, Stefan . . . it was just one of those things. It could have been you. It happened to be me."

"I suppose so," Rej replied, in a voice that wasn't much more than a whisper. "By the way, did he finish searching the sewers?"

"They searched up to a point, but they didn't find anything significant."

"What do you mean, up to a point?"

"It isn't easy, you know. Those sewers are like a maze. And who knows what you might come up against."

Rej held up his little finger, still protected by a bandage and a plastic finger-stall. "Been there, Jarczyk. Done it. Got the stump to prove it."

"I'm sorry, Stefan. I'm sorry that Dembek took you off the case and I'm sorry about Jerzy. But you mustn't put too much of a dumper on things. We've scored a big success here, and most of the groundwork was yours. You've got to take some of the credit, too."

"That's all right, Jarczyk. The credit's all yours. Now . . . do you know how far Jerzy managed to search?"

"What does it matter? It's over. We've got three witnesses and all the forensic evidence we need."

"For Dlubak's murder, maybe."

"So long as they give Zboinski one life sentence, that's enough for me."

Rej said, "Do we yet have any evidence at all that could connect Dlubak's murder to any of the rest of the Executioner's murders?"

Jarczyk counted on his fingers. "Number one, method. Their heads were all chopped off. Number two, motive, which I'm working on. Kaminski and Dlubak were both investigating Zboinski's money-laundering operation, so it's obvious why he went for them. And I've found out that the mailman Slesinski worked in the sorting department which dealt with Zboinski's postal district. Apparently he was accused of stealing mail . . . which means that he could have taken something valuable which Zboinski wanted back."

"That's a bit tendentious, isn't it?" Rej interrupted. "What about the girl from the grocery store? Did she give Zboinski some out-of-date sausage? And how about the travel guide? Maybe he gave Zboinski the wrong directions. And Ewa Zborowska? And all those German workers?"

"As I say," said Jarczyk, testily, "I'm working on it."

"All right, then," said Rej, tiredly rubbing his eyes. "You work on it. Meanwhile, did Jerzy leave any kind of map of the sewers, to show how far he'd got?"

"It's in my office," said Jarczyk. "But as far as I remember, he didn't get much further than Zurawia in the south and Zelazna in the west. Only a dozen square blocks."

"How about forensics? Anything more from Dr. Wojniakowski?"

"Yes ... the sharp instrument that was used to torture Antoni Dlubak was definitely the baling hook that we found in Roman Zboinski's kitchen."

Dembek came in, and said, "Stefan! You haven't got a beer!"

Rej said, "That's all right, Artur, I'm not staying. I think I need something stronger."

So help her find her way to see Jan Kaminski's girlfriend in Mokotow, Sarah's secretary Irena had drawn her a dramatic map covered in instructions such as *Turn Right Here*!!! and *Don't Go This Way*!!! but Sarah still managed to get lost three times. In the end she had to ask directions from a weather-beaten old man with white bristles and scarcely any teeth, who told her she was the most beautiful woman he had ever seen in his life, and would she like to come to bed with him for an hour or two?

Hanna Peszka lived in a large family apartment with

a balcony overlooking a quiet, well-tended garden. Although it was past seven o'clock, the evening was still oppressively warm, and all the windows were open, so that they could hear the traffic. Hanna's father wasn't yet back from work but her mother was in the kitchen making a cucumber salad. One of her brothers was in his bedroom laboriously practicing "Satisfaction" on the guitar. Hanna took Sarah into the living room and they sat side by side on a huge couch upholstered in red brocade, next to a grotesque porcelain planter filled with pink-dyed feather-grass.

Hanna was a mousy blond, shy and thin-wristed but deceptively attractive. The dark circles under her eyes showed how much she was still suffering from the shock of her boyfriend's murder. She spoke in quiet, quick whispers, and only occasionally looked up.

"You're not a policewoman, are you?" she asked.

"Well, no . . . but Komisarz Rej asked me to talk to you. He thought you might find it easier."

"I still can't believe Jan's gone. It's funny, isn't it? I keep looking at the phone and wondering whether I ought to call him."

"It's going to take you a long time to get over that."

"Do you want tea, or coffee?" asked Hanna. "I don't really know what to say to you now. They've caught him, haven't they, the man who killed Jan, and all those other people?"

Sarah gave her a reassuring smile. "They think so, yes."

Hanna was clutching a folder of papers in her hands. "Jan left these here . . . he didn't like leaving his papers at the radio station because people used to pry through his desk. I had a look at them, after he died. I don't know whether they might help you. You see here—" she licked her thumb and leafed through four or five sheets "—he mentions this man Zboinski again and again. I can't understand all of it, but it looks as though

Zboinski was using Vistula Kredytowy to help him sell his stolen cars."

"Could I see that?" asked Sarah; and Hanna passed it over.

The first few pages were nothing but rough, scribbled notes that Jan Kaminski had made while he was preparing his investigation into the way that Senate's contingency account had been used to launder money from Zboinski's car business in Gdansk. But the meaning was very clear. Zboinski stole luxury cars in France and Germany and Britain, Senate Hotels "bought" them as anything from "courtesy cars" to "kitchen ranges" to "air-conditioning equipment," and then "sold" them as surplus or damaged goods to a bewildering variety of salvage companies, some in Bulgaria, some in the Czech Republic, some in Romania. The huge losses they sustained were written off, but in fact they weren't losses at all. They were Zboinski's profits, which seemed to have run into well over $3.5 million.

But it was the second-to-last page that caught Sarah's attention more than anything else. A bald, pencil-written memo that read: "A senior Senate executive *must* be involved, because Antoni Dlubak says that all of these transactions need top-level authorization. Sarah Leonard? Possibly, because she speaks flawless Polish and has v. good contacts in Warsaw. But Dlubak seems to think it was somebody higher up, in New York. Also that odd fax re the Senate contingency account that was sent to Jacek Studnicki but given to Antoni Dlubak in error."

The last page of the file was a photocopy of "that odd fax." It was typed in English, and it read: *Everything in place for next month's transfer from Gdansk. Find out what's happened to the shipment from Rotterdam. I'm very pleased with the way things are going. There's nothing I like better than getting rich by taking my revenge on that Lewandowicz bitch.*

Sarah said, "You see this? About 'that Lewandowicz bitch?' "

Hanna shook her head. "I didn't really understand it. I don't know anybody of that name; and I never heard Jan mention it."

"I know somebody of that name, all right," said Sarah, in a grim voice. Through the open french windows, far to the east, the sky was coppery green, and lightning was flickering. "That 'Lewandowicz bitch' is me. My family name is Lewandowicz, but my father changed it when he emigrated to America after the war. Nobody could pronounce it, so we called ourselves Leonard, instead."

"So you know who wrote this fax?"

"I can guess. Only two people in the New York office knew that my name used to be Lewandowicz ... my secretary and my boss, Ben Saunders. I'm ashamed to say that he was more than my boss, too."

"Then you think that Zboinski *did* kill Jan?"

"He had a motive, didn't he? But I'll have to talk to Ben about that. Not to mention the police."

13

$\mathfrak{M}$arek met Clayton on Koszykowa, a few meters away from the apartment block where he had bearded Mr. Okun in his elevator. Clayton was wearing a short-sleeved, blue check shirt with a broad stain of sweat across his back, and he wasn't looking very happy. "Don't ask," he said, before Marek could even say hello. "I've had a crappy day all round. Everybody I try to talk to, they give me sweet smiles and no information whatsoever. My Polish isn't up to it, that's the trouble."

"Your Polish is excellent, man," Marek told him.

"Don't flatter me, kid," said Clayton, in English. "I'm not in the mood. Now, where did you see this guy coming out of the sewer?"

Marek tapped the four-pointed manhole cover with his running-shoe. "He just appeared, just like that, as if he did it every day."

"Maybe he does do it every day. He could have been a sewer inspector, couldn't he?"

"I don't think so. It just didn't look right. I never would have noticed it if you and Komisarz Rej hadn't been talking about this Executioner using the sewers, but—I don't know, there was something strange about him. Kind of an *aura*, you know?"

"An aura? I'm not surprised. You try walking around in those sewers, and see if you don't come out with an aura."

"No, I'm not kidding. He had a look about him. It was the way he climbed out of there as if it was the most natural thing in the world."

Clayton said, "Keep a look out." Then he knelt down on the sidewalk and opened up the pointed flaps of the manhole cover with his pocket-knife. A few passers-by turned briefly to see what he was doing, but most of them took no notice at all. Clayton peered down into the pungent, echoing sewer, and Marek did, too. In the darkness they could just make out the reflection of slowly-running water, and their own shadowy faces, like drowned souls.

"This manhole has been regularly used," he said, swinging one of the flaps backward and forward. "There's no grit in the grooves around the edges, and the hinges are shiny . . . look, where they've been constantly opened and closed. The rungs of the ladder are shiny, too, from somebody clinbing up and down them."

"So what do you think?"

Clayton started to drop the flaps. "Either this is the most inspected manhole in the whole of Warsaw, or else your new friend Mr. Okun is using it as a highway to heaven-knows-where. That doesn't mean he's the Executioner, of course. But it's worth checking out."

"You think we ought to go down there?"

"Not just yet. Let's keep a watch over the weekend; see if Mr. Okun repeats the performance. Do you have any friends who'd help you mount a stake-out?"

"A stake-out?" said Marek. "That'd be so cool!"

"Sure," said Clayton. Expressionlessly, he dug into his back pocket and produced a thick roll of zlotys. He stripped off more than a hundred dollars' worth, and stuffed them into the pocket of Marek's leather jacket. "That's to keep you going. Give some to your friends, too, if you can persuade them to help you. If you want my advice, you'll use that coffee shop opposite. You'll be able to see most of the street from there. If you see him come out of the manhole, or go down into the manhole, just call me, and I'll get here pronto with a couple of flashlights." He looked down at Marek's studded, high-heeled boots. "And if I were you, I'd change into the crummiest shoes you can find. You don't want to be wading in second-hand meals in a fancy pair of Cuban dancing-pumps like those."

"Cool," said Marek. "I'll talk to you later."

He crossed the street to the Welcome Bar, and pushed open the door. It was hot and tawdry inside, with red plastic seats and a deafening coffee-machine, but it would be perfect for keeping an eye on Mr. Okun. Marek found a seat by the window and ordered a cup of coffee and a raisin pastry. He could see Clayton still standing thoughtfully by the manhole, turning around from time to time and frowning.

After three or four minutes, Clayton walked off without waving or even looking at him, and disappeared. Marek settled down for a long evening on his own.

21 t eleven o'clock, five cups of coffee later, the waitress came up to him carrying her pocketbook and said, "You have to go now. We're closed."

"What time do you open tomorrow?"

"Seven o'clock. Why? Don't you have anywhere else to go?"

Marek gave her a daft, desperate grin. "I like it here, that's all. That's not a crime."

The waitress looked slowly around the Welcome Bar in disbelief. "Well, no . . . I suppose it isn't a crime. But don't you think you should see a doctor?"

S arah was working on her word-processor when the doorbell rang. She let out a little hiss of annoyance and went to answer it. She had been trying to complete her weekly progress report on the Senate Hotel development for the past two days, and apart from the time she had spent in helping Stefan Rej, everything had conspired to interrupt her—from a long, tedious lunch with a committee of urban planners from Katowice to a promotional presentation to the association of British travel agents, most of whom had been disheveled and unshaven and suffering from catastrophic hangovers.

She opened the door and a tall, slim girl of about fourteen was standing outside, in jeans and a Björk T-shirt. She had fair silky hair that came down to her waist. She was thin faced, with big, sensitive brown eyes and a slight overbite, which gave Sarah the impression of a nervous woodland creature from a Disney cartoon. But she wasn't nervous when she held out her hand and said, "Daddy says are you ready yet?"

"Ready? Ready for what?"

"Daddy said we were all going riding. He said you won't need much: just clothes for one night, and a toothbrush."

"You're Katarzyna Rej," said Sarah, taking her hand. "Come on in. Where's your father now?"

"He's downstairs, waiting. He said you'd understand why he didn't come up."

"You bet I understand. He didn't tell me he was taking you riding *today*."

"Oh. I didn't know. But it is all right, isn't it? You *will* come?"

Sarah looked across the living room at her word-processor, with her half-finished report glimmering on it. She also thought about Ben, and Brzezicki, and all the other problems she had to deal with. But it was Saturday, damn it, and she hadn't been riding since she was in Prague. She could always finish her report on Sunday evening when she came back, and e-mail it.

The phone rang, and that convinced her. She left the answer-phone to take care of it, went through to the bedroom and tugged down her overnight bag from the top of the closet.

"Do you know where we're going?" she asked Katarzyna.

"Somewhere in the country, that's what he said. One of his friends has a cottage."

Sarah packed her Versace jeans and the Charles Tyrwhitt polo shirts she had bought in London; a white skinny-rib sweater, clean underwear, and toiletries. Katarzyna sat on the side of the bed watching her, and kept picking up her Chanel lipsticks and—most important—her Guerlain face recontouring serum—*"wyniki mowia same za siebie."*

"Your daddy tells me you don't get to see each other very often," said Sarah.

"He's always busy, that's what he says."

"He's not so busy right now."

"Well, yes, but I don't think he likes being a father very much."

Sarah tossed in her hairbrush and closed her case. "That's not the impression that he gave me. I think he loves being a father, especially your father; but the trouble is that he hasn't had the chance to see you grow up. He doesn't know what it's like, when you're fourteen, and everybody seems to think that you're still a child, but you know for sure that you're a woman already."

Katarzyna gave Sarah the strangest look: partly defensive, but mostly wondering. Sarah guessed that even her mother had never spoken to her like this. She remembered that when she was growing up, five or six of her friends had come from broken homes, and she knew how insanely possessive their parents had been: each of them trying to pretend that their daughter was still their little precious girl, their property, their very own baby, long after their very own baby had grown into a questioning, developing young woman.

"Come on," said Sarah. She checked that everything

in the kitchen was switched off, closed the windows, and left.

Rej was waiting for them outside, quietly sweating in his parked Passat. He was wearing a new white sports shirt which was still creased across the front where it had been folded in its wrapper. He jumped out as soon as Sarah and Katarzyna appeared, and opened the trunk. Sarah came up to him, carrying her overnight bag, and said, in a deadly whisper, "You didn't tell me you were one of those men who takes people for granted."

Rej took off his sunglasses. He looked hurt. "I'm sorry. It was you who suggested that I take her riding. I just didn't know how to ask you."

"It's all right, komisarz," said Sarah; and for the first time she felt really gentle toward him. "I'm looking forward to it."

"You're sure?"

"I'm here, aren't I? And packed? Besides," she smiled, "Katarzyna and I are friends already."

Rej didn't say anything, but stowed her overnight bag next to the spare wheel and hurried around to open the passenger door for her. She climbed in, and gave him the quickest of smiles. Katarzyna climbed into the back.

"You'd better tell me where we're going," said Sarah, as they drove through the city. "Just in case the office needs to get in touch."

Rej shook his head. "You won't want anybody to get in touch. We're going to Czerwinsk, a village that my parents used to take me to, when I was a boy. It's beautiful."

Sarah said, "I went to see Jan Kaminski's girlfriend last night. I tried to call you, but you were out."

"That's right. I was fetching Katarzyna. What did she say?"

"Can we talk off the record?"

"It depends. If you're going to tell me that you know

the real identity of the Executioner, then no, we can't."

"Well, I don't know. It may lead to that. The fact is, Jan Kaminski's girlfriend showed me some of his research."

As they drove north on Marymoncka Street, Sarah explained how the Senate contingency account was being used to launder the profits from Roman Zboinski's stolen cars; and how Kaminski had suspected that somebody in Senate's New York office was guilty either of complicity in what was going on, or was actually organizing it.

Last of all, she told him about the fax that had mentioned "that Lewandowicz bitch," and for the first time he turned and looked at her.

"Lewandowicz? That's you? Your name's really Lewandowicz?"

"Yes. What's so funny about that? Plenty of Poles changed their names when they went to America."

"Somehow it makes you more human, having a Polish name."

"I'm not sure how to take that."

Rej shrugged, glanced at her, and gave her a sloping smile. "When I first met you, you were a representative of American capitalism. You were like a corporate robot, yes? You shouted at people because you knew you had the power to shout. If people didn't obey you, you had all of those resources behind you, Senate International Hotels; so they'd *have* to obey you. But I don't think that's the real you. Sarah Leonard may be tough and outspoken, but I've been watching you, you know. And listening to you, too; and so it doesn't surprise me that your real name's something different, something Polish. I've heard you talking human; and I've suspected that you might be human; and now you've told me what your name is, Lewandowicz, I know that you *are* human, after all."

Sarah stared at him as he drove out through Zoliborz, once a genteel suburb of 1920s "officer's quarters" and "civil servants' residences"—now self-consciously over-developed with cul-de-sacs of new detached houses with neat greenery and well-cropped lawns. Parts of it reminded Sarah so strongly of the outskirts of Chicago that it was hard for her to believe that she was *here*, and not there. But then why shouldn't it? All the Polish immigrants who had settled in and around Chicago had a little part of Poland with them. The elaborate net curtains at the windows. The Polonez, part-rusted, part-polished, parked proudly in front of the driveway, nineteen years old if it was a day. The hanging baskets of pink and white flowers. The mother in her head-scarf walking hand-in-hand with her child, in the same way that Sarah had walked with her mother when she was a child and the world was nothing like this. No Senate, no Ben, no Mr. Brzezicki; no devils and murders and deadlines she couldn't meet. For the first time in years, she began to feel quite sorry for herself; and ashamed that she had called herself Leonard.

Rej tried to swerve out to overtake a huge tractor-trailer loaded with breezeblocks, but an equally huge truck was coming in the other direction, and so he had to swerve back in again, with only centimeters to spare. The Passat dipped and bucked on its worn-out suspension and Katarzyna complained, "*Tato* . . . !"

"All right, all right," Rej appeased her. He dropped his speed and allowed the truck to pull further ahead. "So who do you think this was, this man who wanted to get his revenge on this Lewandowicz bitch?"

"I can't be one hundred percent certain, but I believe it's Ben Saunders. I trod on lots of people's fingers, when I was working with Senate in New York, and there are quite a few people who would call me a bitch. But only a few people would have called me Lewandowicz because only a few people knew what my real name was. Ben, of course, was one of them."

Rej stuck a cigarette between his lips but made no

attempt to light it. "So there's a real possibility that Ben could have been responsible for laundering Zboinski's money?"

Sarah nodded. "I'm not sure why he would take the risk. I always thought his family were pretty rich."

"The rich are as greedy as anybody else. But if he was involved with Zboinski and Zboinski killed Antoni Dlubak to conceal that involvement . . . well, it could be that your Ben is more than just greedy. He could be an accessory to murder, or conspiracy to murder, as well as a racketeer."

He paused, and then he added, "As well as a shit."

Sarah laughed and plucked the cigarette out of his mouth, and tucked it back into the pack. She had been wondering why she felt so much better, and of course it was being with Rej that was doing it. He made her feel protected in a way that no man had made her feel protected since her father, Victor. In fact, there was quite a lot about him which reminded her of her father, something bruised, yet deeply determined, although her father was frailer and thinner and much more elegant than Rej, and her father had never been a communist.

They drove through Zoliborz, past the Bielany Woods. The trees looked as dark and rich as broccoli; and they could see runners and hurdlers exercising in the fields. Then they drove out into the countryside, and opened the car windows so that the warm air buffeted in. Sarah took off her shoes and rested her bare feet on the dash. Rej switched on the radio and all three of them sang along with Tina Turner: *"You're simply the best . . . better than all the rest . . ."*

Sarah stepped out onto the cottage verandah and said, "I didn't have any idea."

Rej came out behind her, carrying two beers. "Everybody has to have someplace where they're still a child, and they can behave like a child; and this is mine."

The cottage was built in the traditional old-Polish style, with thick white-plastered walls and an orange tiled roof. It had its own small fenced garden, over-grown with weeds and poppies, with four dilapidated beehives and a dovecot. It was at the end of a narrow lane, on the outskirts of Czerwinsk, on the escarpment overlooking the Vistula. Through a thin screen of silver-birches, Sarah could see the wide silver curve of the river; and across to the opposite bank, to the Kampinos Forest, over four hundred square miles of pines and oaks, alders and bird cherries.

The early afternoon breeze lifted Sarah's hair. It was as soft as being touched by somebody who loves you. And there was a *sound* in the air, like the greatest clock-shop you had ever walked into, the chattering of thousands of distant birds, singing in the forest, and millions of branches whispering and rustling, aspens and alders, birches and oaks.

"You like it here?" Rej asked her. "We can go for a walk in a moment. There's a little place where we can have something to eat. Then maybe we can ride."

"Do you have your own horse?" asked Katarzyna, coming out of the cottage with a can of Coke.

"I used to, when I was your age. My father used to spoil me."

They sat on fraying old basketwork chairs and raised their glasses to each other. Butterflies blew in and out of the open cottage door. "Tell me about your family," Rej asked her. "Is your father rich?"

"Well . . . he did quite well for himself. He came over to Chicago in 1947, when my grandfather died. He was only sixteen. My great-uncle and my great-aunt took him in. They had a carpet business on Milwaukee Avenue . . . there are lots of Polish families there. When my great-uncle retired, my father took over the business, and turned it into one of the biggest carpet wholesalers in the midwest."

"Your mother?"

"She's Polish, too. Her parents brought her over to Chicago in 1949."

"They're both from Warsaw?"

"No, no. My mother came from Czestechowa, but my father came from Warsaw. He used to tell me these stories of how he used to run messages for the Home Army, during the Uprising, and load their guns for them. He was lucky he wasn't killed. You wouldn't think of a thirteen-year-old boy doing anything like that today, would you?"

Rej wiped his mouth with the edge of his hand. "It's funny you should mention the Home Army. So far I've talked to the relatives or the friends of three of the Executioner's victims—the mailman, the girl who worked in the grocery store, and the the ear-nose-and-throat doctor. And all of them had either fought or carried messages during the Uprising, or else they were related to somebody who had."

"Zofia's mother . . ." said Sarah, sitting up straight. "She had photographs of the Home Army, too, didn't she?"

"That's right. Her father, with J. Z. Zawodny. And Ewa Zborowska, she had pictures of *her* father with General Bór."

"But not *all* of the victims had a connection with the insurgents, did they? Those German workers couldn't have, could they?"

"Well, it's doubtful. And I can't find any evidence to link Mr. Wroblewski to the Home Army . . . he was the old man who tried to save Ewa Zborowska's life. But that doesn't mean the connection isn't worth following up. When your Al Capone tried to kill his enemies, there were plenty of occasions when innocent people were standing in the way, weren't there?"

"*My* Al Capone?" Sarah retorted.

"You know what I mean. Innocent people are always getting hurt."

"But who would want to murder people, just because

they happen to be related to somebody who fought in the Uprising? That was over half a century ago . . . I mean, little Zofia, and Ewa Zborowska, and Jan Kaminski . . . most of those people weren't even *born* then!"

Katarzyna went back inside. Rej waited until she had gone, and then he said, "I came away this weekend for four reasons. One was to have a rest, which I badly need. The second was to see Katarzyna, and see if I couldn't try to be a better father. The third was to think some more about this Executioner case."

"I've been thinking about it, too," said Sarah. "In fact I had a nightmare about it last night."

"Go on, tell me about it."

Sarah crossed her arms over her breasts. "I had a nightmare about those German workers. I was standing by the sewer pipe and bits and pieces of them kept flying out . . . but each of the bits and pieces was still alive, and lay on the ground struggling. There was a heart, still beating, and a hand, trying to crawl across the concrete like a spider, and part of a knee that kept bending and unbending."

"What you saw was worse than anything I've ever seen," said Rej. "It's hardly surprising that you're having nightmares."

"No—there was something else. Something that made it seem like *more* than a nightmare. I kept staring and staring into that sewer pipe and it was so damned *dark* in there, darker than any place I'd ever seen before. I walked toward it, even though I didn't want to. I thought, *I have to go in . . . I have to go see for myself.* Because I knew there was something inside that pipe that wasn't wholly human, and I needed to see what it was."

"So," said Rej. "Maybe it *is* a devil, after all."

"And if it is? How do we get rid of it?"

"Who knows? Perhaps your boyfriend's exorcism will do the trick."

Katarzyna came out, with a flowery red scarf tied around her head. "Are we going to have something to eat soon?" she complained. "I'm starved!"

"Sure," said Rej. "Why don't we go now?"

They left the cottage and walked together down the path. Sarah swatted at occasional midges. The smell of evaporating pine-sap was so heady that it was almost like a drug. Katarzyna walked a little way ahead of them, thrashing the bushes with a stick.

"You think she's pretty?" asked Rej.

"I think she's terrific. Does she look like your ex-wife?"

Rej nodded, and said nothing.

As they approached the village they could see the silhouette of the 12th-century abbey of the Canons Regular—a soaring church in the Ramanesque style, with a fifteenth-century belfry in front of it, and a Gothic monastery attached. The sun shone so brightly from the abbey's spires and rooftops that it had the look of a building seen in a mirage. As they passed nearer, pigeons clattered from the roof-ridges and swung out over the Vistula.

"Some people say that wherever people believe strongly in God, they also believe strongly in devils, and give them both much more substance," said Rej.

"Does that mean that *you* believe it's a devil?"

"I'm keeping an open mind. But I think your friend Clayton understands this better than we do. These are real murders, happening in the real world. But neither of us believes that this is some psychopath, running madly through the sewers, and jumping out at people at random. We don't believe that it's gang killings, either—although poor old Jarczyk is trying to prove that it is."

"What is it, then? Ritual murder? Sacrifice?"

"I was beginning to think that it was, until I found so many connections with the Home Army. No—my opinion now is that this is something else altogether. I think this is a *hunt*."

"You mean somebody's trying to execute the families of anybody who fought with the Home Army? But who would do that?"

"I don't have the slightest idea. It's a theory, that's all; and I'm not usually given to theories. But that day we went to the seance at Madame Krystyna's—well, that opened my eyes to all kinds of different possibilities."

"But it would be pretty *extreme*, wouldn't it, to murder somebody's children and grandchildren in punishment for something that happened all that time ago?"

Rej shrugged. "In Old Testament times, that was the way that people took their revenge. If you killed my brother, I would wipe out your entire family to the very last child. When it says in Deuteronomy that you should take an eye for an eye, and a tooth for a tooth, that wasn't being extreme—that was a plea for people to be reasonable."

"I'm surprised you know your Bible so well."

"My ex-wife, she's very religious. Besides, one should always know one's enemy, don't you think?"

Sarah stopped, her hand lifted to her forehead to shade her eyes from the sun. "This is hard for you, isn't it, all this talk of devils?"

Rej said, "If you show me the evidence, I'll believe in anything. Even God. And I'm off duty now: you don't have to salute."

They walked along the side of the road until they reached the first houses. A horse and cart clattered past them, loaded up with fresh-cut grass and wild cornflowers.

"What do you feel like eating?" asked Rej. "There's a place here where you can get wonderful pancakes."

"I feel like *kotlety*," said Katarzyna. "And french fries. And ice-cream."

It was then that Sarah saw an old woman walking

toward them. She was dressed entirely in black, and
very small, although her arms seemed to be too long
for her body, giving her an ape-like silhouette. Katarzyna stepped out of her way, and as she did so, it became apparent to Sarah that the woman was blind, or
purblind, at least, because her eyeballs were as milky
as a boiled cod's, and although she was walking quite
quickly. She was walking at an odd diagonal across the
road.

She passed Rej, but when she came to Sarah she
abruptly stopped, lifted both hands, and swivelled her
head from side to side. Under her black headscarf, she
had fraying gray hair, and a flat, almost Mongolian
profile, with a small sharp nose and cheeks as withered
as one of last autumn's apples. There was a silver ring
on every one of her fingers, and her thumbs, too—rings
with strange designs on them, like knots and crescents
and interlocking triangles.

"What are you doing here?" she asked, in a harsh,
country accent. "Why do you bring that face with
you?"

"I'm having a weekend vacation," Sarah smiled.
"It's beautiful here, isn't it? So quiet."

"Why do you bring that face?" the woman de-
manded. Her sightless eyes stared somewhere over
Sarah's left shoulder. "What are you trying to do?
Show us what a martyr you are?"

"I'm sorry," said Sarah. "I really don't understand.
What face are you talking about?"

"The face that follows all of you! The face that never
lets you go!"

"Come on, Sarah," said Rej, reaching out and taking
hold of her hand. "She's cracked, that's all. Every
country village has to have one, and she's Czerwinsk's."

They started to walk away, but the woman followed
them, and suddenly snatched at the sleeve of Sarah's

blouse, clutching it between her fingers and twisting it tight.

"Hey, come on, old girl," said Rej, and took hold of her shoulder. But Sarah said, "Wait, Stefan . . . I want to know what she's trying to tell me."

The old woman licked her lips and noisily swallowed. "I may be blind, Miss Lewandowicz, but I can see much more clearly than you."

Sarah gave Rej a quick glance of complete perplexity. "How do you know my name?" she asked.

"You *are* a Lewandowicz?"

"Yes . . . but I've never met you before, have I? I've never been to Czerwinsk before."

The old woman twisted her sleeve even more tightly. "They all have names. Many, many names, and I know them all. Inside my head, instead of songs, I have a cold black memorial, engraved with names. Not one forgotten: not one. Rataj and Niedzialkowski; Kusocinski and Lewartowski; on and on! But not all dead. Not dead yet. But *marked* for death, because the face follows all of them."

"I'm sorry, I still don't understand what you mean."

"You will, Miss Lewandowicz. I can see your face as clear as day. But I can see the face behind you, too. I can see the face that's been close behind you all your life; and now it's even closer still. You shouldn't be here, Miss Lewandowicz, and you shouldn't have brought that face with you. Not here."

Rej reached over and pried the old woman's fingers away from Sarah's sleeve. He took out his old plastic purse and gave her five zlotys. "Go on, now. Leave us alone."

The woman swallowed more saliva, and then let out a contemptuous laugh. "What will you do, *pan*, if I don't? Call a policeman?"

Again, they started to walk away, and this time the old woman didn't attempt to follow them. But they hadn't gone more than a few meters when she called out, "Miss Lewandowicz! You listen to me!"

Rej said, "Ignore her, Sarah," but Sarah stopped.

"If you want to *see* the face that's following you, put five aspen berries under your pillow before you go to sleep; and one piece of silver; and one piece of amber; and a cutting from your own hair."

"I knew it," said Rej, shaking his head. "She's a witch. A genuine certified witch."

"A witch?" the old woman screeched at him. "Who are you calling a witch? Who else could remember every name? Who else could remember every single name, except a mother, and a grandmother, and a griever?"

"Goodbye, old woman!" said Rej. "Have a wonderful afternoon!" He took Katarzyna's hand and together they crossed the village street.

But Sarah couldn't help hesitating, and turning back. The old woman was still standing by the side of the road, staring at her blindly. *Five aspen berries*, she whispered to herself, *one piece of silver, and one piece of amber. And a cutting from my own hair.*

As though she had heard her, and was satisfied, the old woman turned around and went on her way.

Sarah caught up with Rej and Katarzyna, who were talking about riding this afternoon, but she couldn't get the old woman off her mind.

"Really—how do you think she knew my name?"

"I don't know, Sarah. Maybe you reminded her of somebody called Lewandowicz. Maybe there's a Lewandowicz family resemblance. Who knows?"

"And what did she mean by a face following me?"

"Sarah, she was old and mad. The war didn't only cause physical injuries."

"Maybe I should do what she said, and put all that stuff under my pillow tonight."

Rej gave her an odd look which she couldn't quite interpret. His smile was obviously meant to be amused; but his eyes were saying something else altogether.

* * *

𝔐arek was onto his fourth cup of coffee and his seventh comic when he saw Mr. Okun appear on the front steps of his apartment building, dressed in his faded overalls, with a large untidy bundle under his arm. Mr. Okun paused for a few moments, looking left and right, and then he began to walk quite slowly toward the manhole from which he had appeared the previous day. Marek dropped his copy of *X-Men* and sat up straighter. Mr. Okun kept glancing over his shoulder, as if he were making sure that he wasn't being watched. As he approached the manhole he walked more and more slowly, until he reached it, and stood still.

He bent down, and carefully laid his bundle on the sidewalk. Then he took a key out of his overall pocket, and lifted up the manhole's four triangular flaps. It was Saturday afternoon, and Koszykowa was even busier than usual, but nobody stopped to ask Mr. Okun what he was doing—not even a policeman on a motorcycle who drove straight past him. But who would believe that anybody would voluntarily go down a sewer unless it was their job?

Marek watched Mr. Okun climb down into the manhole and close the flaps over his head. It was all over in less than twenty seconds. Then Marek went to the payphone next to the toilets, dug an A token out of his jeans, and dialed Clayton's number. He urged, "Come on, come on . . ." as the phone rang and rang and nobody picked it up. But at last he heard Clayton's deep voice saying, "Yes . . . what is it?"

"This is it . . . I just saw Okun go down the manhole. He was carrying a big bundle with him. No, I don't know what it was."

Clayton said, "Give me ten minutes. Stay there. Keep your eyes open. Don't try to follow him; and whatever you do, don't try to tackle him."

"Are you kidding me?"

While he waited for Clayton, Marek combed his
hair, finished his coffee, rolled up his comics and
pushed them into the back pocket of his jeans, and paid
the check.

"Don't tell me you've had enough of us at last?"
said the waitress.

Marek looked around. "To tell you the truth, I think
I'm actually beginning to like it here."

The waitress said, "You were watching for somebody, weren't you?"

Marek didn't say anything, but his expression gave
him away.

"Don't get involved in anything dangerous, that's
all," she told him. "I had a son who was all mixed up
with Solidarity. The police beat him up so badly, he's
like a vegetable now. That's why I have to work here."

Marek cleared his throat. "Don't worry," he told her.
"This thing that I'm involved in . . . it's nothing."

All the same, she took the cheap silver crucifix from
around her neck, and handed it to him. "Wear it," she
said. "I took it to Pilsudskiego Square, the day the Pope
celebrated mass, and he blessed it for me."

"I can't take that," Marek protested, in embarrassment.

"Take it for now, and bring it back when you're sure
that you don't need it anymore. I'll still be here."

She kept on holding it out; and in the end, Marek
took it, and hung it around his neck. "Thanks," he said,
and kissed her cheeks.

"If I'm not here," she said, "just ask for Ewelina."

It was then that Clayton arrived. He was wearing a
check lumberjack shirt and jeans, and he was carrying
an olive-green knapsack over his shoulder. He was
sweating because of the heat, and out of breath, but he
looked all fired up and ready to go.

"You ready, Marek?"

Marek pointed to his feet. He was wearing the old
gray rubbers that his father used to take whenever he

went fishing. Clayton gave the waitress a mystified grin, and then the two of them crossed the street to the manhole.

"Your ma mind you staying out so long?" asked Clayton. Then, "*Spierdalai*—piss off!" as an oil-burning Volkswagen nearly ran him over and hooted at him.

Marek shook his head. "So long as she knows I'm not stealing automobiles, or smoking crack. Besides, my friend Michal took over at eleven o'clock, and I went home for lunch."

Clayton gave him a friendly clap on the back. "That's good. A boy should always take care of his ma, no matter what."

They reached the opposite sidewalk, and approached the manhole. Clayton crouched down beside it, and ran the tips of his fingers over the cast-iron patterns. "I'll tell you, Marek, I have a feeling about this case. I have a real strong feeling that we're getting close."

"You think this Mr. Okun really could be the Executioner?"

"Who knows? He could be just a fruitcake who likes going down into the sewers. But I've been doing a whole lot of research over the past couple of days, and things are beginning to fall into place. Not the whole picture yet. Not even half a picture. But a kind of sketchy outline, you know."

He handed Marek a flashlight with a looped cord to tie around his wrist, and then switched his own flashlight on and off to make sure that it was working. "I've spent most of the time in the National Library, looking up criminal case histories and then cross-referencing them with real historical events, and then cross-referencing both of them with legends and myths. I've come up with some stuff that you wouldn't believe. Apart from the Executioner, I found five murderers in the area defined by present-day Poland who cut off their victims' heads. One was in Lublin, in the 1920s;

one was in Wroclaw, just before the First World War;
another was in a little village up in the Tatra called
Zebryzdowice, that was in 1952. Both of the other two
were in Warsaw. Out of those two, one beheaded his
landlady, that was in 1895—but the other was supposed to have killed at least nine people, maybe more,
and *he* was never caught. He beheaded his first victim
in the late summer of 1881 and his last in the spring
of 1882. The newspapers called him Mr. Guillotine."

He took out his clasp-knife, and opened the manhole
cover. He made no attempt to hurry, or to conceal what
they were doing, but nobody took any notice.

"Before that, the earliest historical reference I could
find to any kind of mass beheading was way back in
the 15th century, after the Battle of Grunwald."

Marek gave him a shifty, uncertain look.

"You never heard of the Battle of Grunwald?" said
Clayton, in surprise. "That's the same as me never
hearing of Bull Run."

"What's Bull Run?" Marek asked him.

"Come on," said Clayton. "Let's just get down this
hole before anybody starts wanting to know what the
hell we're doing here, having a history seminar next to
an open sewer. You go first . . . I'll close the cover after
us."

Marek peered dubiously into the darkness. "How do
we know that Mr. Okun isn't on his way back?"

"We don't, kid. But there are two of us and only one
of him."

Marek cautiously climbed down into the manhole.
The iron rungs were worn, and he slipped on the third
and almost fell, but Clayton caught his sleeve. "So long
as you don't wind up in the shit."

When Marek was sufficiently far down, Clayton
climbed in after him, and closed the cover. Section by
triangular section, with emphatic metallic clangs, Marek saw the sky disappear like a cut-up cake, until they
were swallowed in darkness. He could hear echoing

and gurgling and huge bellowing whispers, and noises that sounded like distant cries. He kept on climbing down, trying to direct his flashlight beam so that he could see his feet. He was terrified of missing the last step and dropping blindly into raw sewage, over his boots. He was already beginning to regret that he had agreed to get involved with Clayton and Rej. It had seemed cool and different at the time, but now he felt seriously apprehensive. Supposing Mr. Okun *was* the Executioner? He had already cut off Rej's finger and scarred his face: what would he do to *him*, if he caught him, especially since his only escape route was blocked by Clayton's panting bulk and a closed manhole cover.

"You okay, kid?" Clayton asked him, in a tubular-sounding voice, and Marek had to answer, "Fine. I'm really fine."

They reached the main sewer pipe. Marek's flashlight illuminated a wide arched ceiling, in the style constructed immediately after the Second World War, although the thick encrustations of yellowish salts that streaked its sides made it look much older—more of a hermit's thousand-year-old cave than a municipal sewer. The salts sparkled and glittered, and although it was noisy with clattering water and the air was almost unbreathable, it looked almost enchanted. Marek stepped down in the slowly-moving sewage, and was relieved to find that it was less than three centimeters deep.

"It's okay, it's shallow," he called. Then he took two steps forward and plunged up to his crotch.

"Ja pierdole!" he shouted. He was so angry that he couldn't even move. "My Levis! My fucking Levis!"

Clayton reached the bottom rung, and splashed over to help him out. "Don't make waves!" Marek screeched at him. "Don't make waves!"

Clayton gripped his hand and hauled him back onto the shallower shelf at the side of the pipe. "Most of these type sewers have a deep central channel," he remarked, flicking his flashlight beam right and left.

"Yes, well, thanks for telling me. Shit!"

Their flashlights criss-crossed, and they could see that the sewer went off in three different directions—a wide main drain running north-west toward Piekna; and south-east toward Ujadowskie Avenue; and then a lower, narrower drain running off southwest, although they couldn't tell how far because it curved to the right after only twenty meters. This drain must have been very much older than the main sewer, because it was built of brick, and its curved walls were covered with dripping stalactites of curdled grease. Marek saw a humped gray shape wriggling in the sewage that ran down it, and took two steps back in fright. Only Clayton gripping his sleeve saved him from dropping back into the deep central channel.

"Did you see that? What the hell was that?"

"Rat," said Clayton laconically. "Small one, too."

"Shit, I forgot about rats."

Clayton was examining the bricks where the older sewer joined with the post-war sewer. "Somebody's been walking up and down this pipe fairly regular," he remarked. "Look at the long horizontal scratch marks in the grease. Some of them are old but are some of them are fresh. There—look—on the ceiling. Somebody's been trailing a hand along the ceiling to make sure that they don't bump their head. Gloved hand, probably, the marks are too wide for bare fingers . . . and besides, who'd want to drag their bare fingers through this stuff?"

"So what do you think?" asked Marek, edgily. The cold sewage was beginning to trickle inside the legs of his jeans, and he could hardly wait to pull them off and wash himself. "You think that Mr. Okun came this way?"

"Looks like it. Not just today, but on a regular basis."

Marek said, "Maybe it's time we called the *gliny*."

Clayton shook his head, still shining his flashlight from left to right, scrutinizing the brickwork and the channelling peering at the stalactites to see if any had been broken. "People don't realize what trails they leave behind. You know something, I was six months in Arizona once, training up Native Americans as police officers. They were shit when it came to paperwork, believe me. But when it came to seeing where people had passed by, it was like they had X-ray eyes, you know, like Superman. They could point to a stone that somebody must have displaced, by stepping on it; or a broken weed that couldn't have been broken by the wind. It wasn't magic. It was observation, and sheer out-and-out logic, but it taught me a whole lot about hunting people down. You see here? You see these semicircular scuff marks, on the sides of the brickwork. Those are shoe-marks, the edges of somebody's shoes, you can see the same marks on automobile carpets, or the lower part of well-used doors."

He peered down into the darkness of the sewer. "That part wasn't magic, the analytical part; but they did have magic. I saw a Pima Indian officer find a wanted man in two hundred square miles of desert, just by following the smoke from this little burner he had. Whichever direction the smoke blew, he followed it; and I can swear to you, kid, there were times when that smoke was blowing upwind. It was ever since then that I decided that crimes could be solved all kinds of different ways, occult included."

"What do you think we ought to do now?" Marek asked him. "If Mr. Okun's gone down there—"

"I'm pretty sure he *has* gone down there. And if that's the case, what do *you* think we ought to do?"

"Um, go back up top and wait for him to come out?"

"And say what? 'You went in that sewer and now you've come back out again—I'm calling the cops?' Do me a favor. If this guy's the Executioner, we're got to find some proof, and the only way we're going to find any proof is by following him."

Marek looked into the narrow, curving sewer. He couldn't see the rat any longer, but that was no guarantee that it wasn't still there, slick and gray and crowded with diseases, and waiting to bite at his ankles.

"What if we meet him, face-to-face?"

"I told you. There's only one of him, and there's two of us."

"Clayton, for Christ's sake. He chopped three big Germans into little bits."

Clayton beckoned him forward, into the sewer. "That's because they didn't know what to expect. They didn't have any inkling what they were dealing with."

"And I suppose you do?"

Clayton walked a little way ahead of him, silhouetted by his flashlight like a character from a *cinema noir* movie. "You know the trouble with you kids today?" he told him. "You always think you know everything; and because of that, you never learn anything. When I was your age, I was a filing clerk; and being a filing clerk meant wearing a shirt and necktie and keeping my hair cut. I was right at the bottom of the ladder and they gave me all the crap jobs, emptying wastebaskets, making coffee, running errands, and all the time I had to be polite to everybody in the office, yessir, nossir, certainly sir, even the total assholes. And do you know something? I took a pride in myself, and I took a pride in my work, and I never gave backtalk to nobody. In three years I knew the whole damn business better than anybody there, and they made me a manager."

"So what's the moral?"

"The moral is, keep your mouth shut when you're young. Never stop listening, and never stop learning. Read the clues, kid, the same way I always had to. Read the fucking clues."

"What clues?"

"The clues to life, kid. Like staying angry on the inside but always being quiet on the outside. And these clues here, you didn't even see them, did you, you were so damn worried that your pants were wet. The finger marks, the shoe marks—the simple fact that Mr. Okun came down here. I mean, people just don't disappear down manholes, do they?"

"Maybe they do. Maybe I never noticed it before."

"They don't, believe me. But you were smart enough to spot him. Which means that you're smart enough to work out what you're dealing with."

By now, they were over twenty meters into the sewer, crouching down slightly so their hair wouldn't touch the black glutinous stalactites that hung down all around them. The stalactites had the consistency of axle grease and they smelled so foul that Marek's mouth filled with saliva and he had to keep on spitting.

Clayton said, "You're dealing with something that's got used to living down here in the dark. In fact, maybe it *always* lived in the dark, that's what you have to say to yourself. You have to free your mind, you understand, and not make assumptions. This could be man or beast or monster."

Marek said, "Ssh! Did I hear something?"

Clayton stopped, and listened too. After a few moments, however, he shook his head. "You get real weird noises, down in the sewers. Most of the time they're echoes . . . you know, trucks driving over manholes, nosy kids getting their heads chopped off."

"You told me to read the fucking clues," Marek objected.

Clayton turned around and grinned at him. "Don't take it to heart, kid. It's called stupid American humor."

They kept on splashing ahead. By now the sewer had curved so far that, when he glanced back, Marek was unable to see the main drain. He didn't know where Clayton was taking him, or what he expected to find, but he was feeling breathless and sweaty and desperately claustrophobic. He kept thinking about the manhole cover, which was shut tight, and wishing he were climbing up those iron rungs at double-quick speed and forcing it open, and climbing back out onto Koszykowa. But Clayton pressed on, his back hunched, his flashlight reflecting in curves and spangles from the walls and the sewage-water.

"Are you okay?" Clayton called back, and Marek said, "Fine. Why shouldn't I be?"

Ahead of them, they heard the rushing sound of cascading water. After thirty more meters, they found themselves in a large, arched chamber, almost the size of a small church. On one side, brownish sewage was foaming down a series of steps, into a large pool in the center, which lazily circled before tipping its contents down a shallow slide, into total darkness.

"So where do we go from here?" asked Marek, raising his voice so that Clayton could hear him over the confusion of pouring and gurgling and gushing.

"I don't know . . . I've been trying to work out why the Executioner comes down here, whoever he is. That's why I've been reading up all of this history, and all of this mythology. Most of it may be bunkum, but in every legend there's usually some grain of reality, you know. Some essential truth."

"Maybe Mr. Okun is just a thief, you know, and hides his stolen property in the sewers."

Clayton shook his head. "Would you come down here, if it wasn't totally necessary? No, kid, the sewers are the key to this. The sewers is what this is all about."

Their flashlights reflected on the dun-brown surface of the water. Then they probed the various pipes and entrances all around the sides of the chamber. There was no indication that anybody had been here, or where they might have gone. Marek was more than ready to leave right away; but Clayton stayed where he was, his eyes narrowed, his flashlight systematically searching the walls.

"There has to be something. You can't pass through anyplace without leaving something."

"But he could be anywhere," said Marek. "He could have left by another manhole, and be back at home by now."

Clayton ignored him. "I was telling you about the Battle of Grunwald, wasn't I? That was back in 1410, when King Ladislaus Jagiello gathered his soldiers in the Kampinos Forest, and beat the living crap out of the Teutonic Knights." He continued to scrutinize the chamber, his flashlight beam descending every step of the foaming cascade, step by step. "It was a victory, but it wasn't an easy victory. Two of those Teutonic Knights fought so madly that the Poles thought they were possessed. They rode right through the middle of King Ladislaus' men. Cutting their heads off like they were asparagus. Heads, arms and legs flying everywhere.

"And the story goes that when it was all over, and the king's men searched the battlefield, trying to find the bodies of these guys, they found their armor scattered around, but that was it. No bodies, nothing. At first they put it down to magic—you know, the way that anybody would have done in the fifteenth century. But then they found some burrows in the ground nearby; and they dug up one of these burrows, and two or three meters down they found a 'thing like a child, yet the size of a man, with broad hunched shoulders and legs like those of a cricket.' It had a face 'so terrible that none could look on it.' When they first found it, they thought it was dead; but after a while they realized it was deeply asleep, like it was hibernating. So they did what any self-respecting fifteenth-century soldier would do, and they hung it, and disembowelled it, and chopped it up, and burned it, and had a priest sprinkle holy water all over the ashes."

Marek was straining his ears. He thought he could hear footsteps, faintly splashing along one of the pipes.

Clayton cleared his throat. "A few days later, though, they found another one of these 'things,' another one of these so-called 'children,' and they sealed it in an oak box and brought it back to Warsaw. They put it on display for two or three weeks, but people started complaining about sickness and nightmares, and the church bells started ringing in the night when there was nobody there to ring them. They brought John XXIII, the Anti-Pope, from Rome, and he recommended that they bury this 'thing' as deep as they could, and never speak of it, which they didn't."

Marek said, "Are you trying to scare me, or what?"

"I'm just telling you what I've been reading about. You can read it for yourself. It's all in the National Library. Why do people never use their own libraries? You should see the stuff they've got in there, brilliant."

"I can hear something," said Marek.

"You can hear your brains working, for the first time in your life."

"No, seriously. I can hear something."

They listened, and waited. Over the rushing of the water, Marek was sure that he could hear a high, plaintive wail.

"Can't you hear that?" he asked Clayton; but Clayton shook his head.

"It's like a kid crying. I'm sure of it."

"Which direction is it coming from? Any idea?"

Marek listened again, but the wailing had stopped. He pointed tentatively toward a narrow tunnel on the far side of the chamber. "I couldn't be sure, but I think it was coming from over there."

"Let's check it out, then," said Clayton.

There was only one way to reach the other side of the chamber, twenty-five meters away, and that was to walk across the third highest step of the thirty-step cascade.

"We can't go across there!" Marek protested.

"How else?" asked Clayton. "Come on, kid, it'll be a breeze. Just follow me."

Clayton went first, cautiously placing his left foot onto the narrow concrete ledge. Sewage splashed over his boot in a bubbling flurry, and he almost slipped. He placed his right foot ahead of his left foot, like a tightrope walker, and then began to inch his way across, his arms extended to give himself balance.

"Be careful, kid!" he called back. "This concrete's real slimy."

Marek took a deep breath and then wished that he hadn't, because the air was so fetid. He stepped out onto the cascade, and went teetering across it, the water rushing against his ankles and chilling his feet. Ahead of him, Clayton made it across and was leaning against the curved wall, emptying sewage out of one of his boots.

"Just take it as it comes!" he called. "Don't try to rush it!"

Marek was more than half way across when his left foot slipped off the ledge and he had to seesaw from side to side to stop himself from falling. He managed to lift his foot back up again, but then he found that he had frozen. He had lost all momentum, and his legs refused to move.

"Come on, kid, just put one foot in front of the other!" Clayton exhorted him. But all Marek could do was stand in the middle of the cascade, his arms outstretched, biting his lip in panic. He couldn't move, he couldn't breathe: all he could do was to think that he was going to fall.

"Come on, Marek, get your ass over here!"

Marek heard another tremulous noise, but this wasn't the sound of a child crying: this was him, whimpering. He thought with an odd sense of dispassion that he sounded just like a dog whose paw had been run over.

Clayton came back to the edge of the cascade and

tried to reach out for him, but he was still too far away.

"All right!" said Clayton. "I'm coming out to get you! All you have to do is stay still!"

Clayton stepped back onto the foaming ledge and began to shuffle his way toward Marek with his right arm extended. It took him seven or eight shuffles to reach him, but when Marek tried to snatch at his hand, Clayton stepped back.

"Don't just grab like that, you're going to have to take my hand real easy. Get a firm grip, and then just shuffle your way along like I'm doing. Don't try to walk the way you were before, and don't look down. If this ledge was painted on a floor, you could walk along it easy. It's plenty wide enough."

Marek stiffly reached out and took Clayton's hand. Then he began to shuffle his way forward, a few centimeters at a time, trying not to think where he was, trying to believe that he wasn't going to fall.

They had almost reached the far edge when a huge dead rat suddenly appeared over the top of the cascade, and tumbled down the steps to lodge against Marek's ankle. Marek jerked his foot up in disgust. The rat fatly slithered away down the cascade, but Marek began to sway backwards, and he knew that he had irrevocably lost his balance.

"Hold on!" Clayton bellowed. But it was too late, for both of them. Marek toppled down the cascade, splashing and bumping against the steps, and Clayton came splashing after him.

Marek was jarred and jolted and bruised by every slithery concrete step. Then Clayton rolled past him, his arms and legs flying, and kicked him in the cheek. The two of them plunged into the deep cold pool of sewage at the bottom of the cascade, and Marek found himself deep underwater.

It seemed to take him a long, slow century to swim up to the surface. He let out an explosive burst of air, and then spat and spat. Clayton surfaced a moment later, his hair plastered flat over his skull.

Together, they swam to the edge and clung onto the rusted rungs of a service ladder.

"Why the hell didn't you let go of my hand?" Clayton gasped.

"You told me to hold on!"

Clayton climbed up the ladder with sewage streaming from his clothes. "I bet I've contracted every damned disease known to Western civilization! I bet I've caught cholera and typhus and hepatitis and plague!"

He reached the concrete platform at the top of the ladder, and furiously kicked away a condom which was draped over his boot. "I stink!" he shouted. "I absolutely stink!"

Marek climbed after him and knelt down on his hands and knees, coughing. "Listen," he said, "I'm sorry. I just lost my balance."

They trudged back toward the tunnel entrance. "Do you still want to go on?" asked Clayton. "I don't mind quitting while we're ahead."

"Let's quit," said Marek. "I feel sick."

Just as they reached the tunnel, however, they heard a quick, scuffling noise. Clayton immediately shone his flashlight down it, and caught the back of a shadowy, fleeing figure, more like a ghost than a man.

"Is that him?" he asked Marek.

Marek nodded, his heart beating in long, suspended thumps.

"Right then. It looks like we don't have much choice. Let's get after the bastard."

14

Once the sun had gone down, the country air became chilly and Rej lit the log fire in the living room. They sat in front of it drinking honey vodka and eating plum cake. They were all tired, because they had been riding all afternoon, hiring horses from a stable on the other side of the village. They had ridden through the woods where it was almost completely silent except for the birds and the jostling and jingling of the horses' harnesses. Sarah and Rej had ridden slowly because Rej was so inexperienced, and held his reins as grimly as if he were careening down a mountain on a runaway bobsleigh; but Katarzyna had cantered way ahead of them, right up through the birches and the shivering aspens, until all they could see was an occasional glimpse of her horse's bright chestnut flank.

Now Katarzyna was in her pajamas and ready for bed, and Sarah and Rej were trying to soothe some of the unexpected muscles that they had discovered. The living room was small and whitewashed, with heavy oak furniture and heaps and heaps of huge cushions, some velvet, some crochet, some embroidered with buttons and beads. On one wall there was a painting of the Vistula in autumn, with knobbly rows of pollarded trees in the foreground and tall wistful poplars in the background. Above the fireplace hung a silver icon of the Blessed Virgin Mary.

"I wish I could go to America," said Katarzyna, her eyes reflecting the flames from the birch logs.

"There's no reason why you shouldn't," Sarah told her. "You could come and stay with me."

"Do you live near Disney World? I'd love to see Disney World!"

"No, I don't. But we could always fly there."

"How about daddy? Could he come too?"

Sarah turned to Rej and smiled at him. "I don't know. It depends whether he's interested in going on rides and talking to giant mice. He would probably find it far too silly."

"Well . . ." said Rej, "it might be worth visiting, purely for research."

Katarzyna kissed them both goodnight and Rej went to tuck her in. When he came back, "You like it here?" he asked.

Sarah nodded. "It's beautiful. I wish we were staying longer."

"We could always come again. My friend hardly ever uses the place these days. His wife died of cancer two years ago. A place like this, well, it's not the same when you're on your own."

Sarah sipped more vodka and then lay back against the cushions. "I can't stop thinking about that old woman today. She wouldn't have frightened me so much if she hadn't have known my name."

"Coincidence. Inspiration. Magic. It doesn't matter which, does it? She can't do anything to harm you."

"Do you believe in magic?"

Rej looked at the fire. The flickering light cast a strong shadow under the scar on his cheek, where the thing in the sewer had cut him with its knife. "I'm not sure. My mother was very superstitious. She was forever tossing salt over her shoulder and making sure that she didn't walk under ladders. If ever she had a wart, she used to rub it with a stone, then wrap up the stone in paper, and drop it at the crossroads at the end of our street. Whoever picked it up was supposed to get infected by the wart instead of her." He laughed. "I can't remember if it ever worked."

"But this *face* that's supposed to be following me."

"Oh, that's just rubbish. Country people love making fools out of us townies."

"You think so? After that seance, I think I could believe in just about anything."

Rej was silent for a while. Then he reached over and took hold of her hand. Oddly, it didn't come as any surprise.

"If you could believe in just about anything . . . could you believe that I think you're very attractive?"

She found herself smiling. "I think you're attractive, too. So there."

"Me? I'm ugly. I've got a face like a block of rock."

"I happen to like blocks of rock. You know what they say. Inside every block of rock, there's a beautiful sculpture, just waiting to be discovered."

"That's very poetic."

"Maybe you make me feel poetic. Maybe you make me feel all kinds of things that men haven't made me feel before. Like, safe. No man ever made me feel so well-protected."

"Just because I lost my temper with that boyfriend of yours."

"No, it's more than that. Every other man treats me as if I'm some kind of ball-crushing Amazon. All right—I'm doing a very hard job in a very competitive world, but that doesn't mean that I don't need looking after in the same way that any woman does. And you do it."

Rej looked into her eyes for a very long time. "They're green," he said. "They're like the sea, where it's very shallow; almost transparent."

He leaned forward and kissed her. It was a gentle, caring kiss at first, almost the kind of kiss that you give to someone you love while they're asleep. But then Sarah put her arm around his shoulders, and drew him closer, and opened her mouth.

She had never been kissed like this before. He was strong, and he was firm, and his tongue dived between her teeth like a muscular seal. But there was none of the crushing and slobbering that she was used to. He kissed to please her; he kissed to excite her; and she suddenly realized what it was that made him so different: he wasn't afraid of her.

He cupped her breast through her soft pink checkered shirt, and she could tell how much it aroused him. He kissed her cheeks and her chin and her eyes and her nose. His hands were broad and his fingers were stubby, but he stroked her hair and her neck so gently that she had to close her eyes, as if she were dreaming. He kissed her shoulder, and started to unbutton her blouse.

"I knew you wanted to do this," she whispered, kissing his craggy cheek, and grinning at him.

"How did you know?"

"You gave up smoking . . . and you knew I wouldn't like kissing you so much if you smoked."

He eased the blouse from her shoulders. "Everybody has to make sacrifices to get what they want."

She knelt up to face him, and they kissed some more, but much more hungrily now. They wanted each other and there was no need for them to pretend. Rej reached around Sarah's broad, pale-skinned back, and released the catch of her bra. Her breasts swung free from the cups, heavy and wide-nippled, with the palest branches of blue veins. Rej took them in his hands and gently squeezed them, rolling her nipples in between finger and thumb until they crinkled.

They dragged piles of cushions in front of the fire. Then Sarah unbuckled her belt and stepped out of her jeans. Rej stripped, too, wrenching off his shirt and kicking off his corduroy trousers. His body was slabby and muscular, not a young man's body, but the body of a man who keeps himself tolerably fit and lives off nervous energy. His chest was marked with a small crucifix of gray hair.

He tugged down Sarah's white silk panties, revealing a soft turf of blond hair. He touched her with his finger between her legs, and she was already slippery. He kissed her with his eyes closed. Then he opened them again and said, "I told a lie. You're not attractive. You're beautiful."

His blue boxer shorts were rearing in front. Sarah gripped his erection through the cotton and gave it a hard, playful squeeze. "What's under here, komisarz? Don't tell me this is where you keep your nightstick?"

He laughed, but at the same time he couldn't hold back a little gasp. She tugged down the shorts and his penis bobbed up, big and swollen and emphatically veined. She delicately scratched his balls with her fingernails, and they wrinkled up in reaction like big crimson walnuts.

"Has it been long?" she asked him, kissing him, and slowly rubbing his penis up and down.

"It's never been like this, ever," he told her, close to her ear.

She lay back on cushions, her big breasts spreading sideways. He climbed over her and kissed her more and more frantically—her mouth and her neck and her shoulders. He cupped her right breast as if it were a full glass of champagne, and kissed her nipple.

She kissed him just as frantically in return—his chest, his Adam's apple. She bit at his nipples, too.

"Condom," he said, reaching to his trouser pockets.

Sarah lay back while he located the packet. She held his penis in her hand while he tore the foil open, and stretched the rubber over his glans. She helped him roll it right down, and then she slowly massaged him, while all the time she looked him directly in the eye, challenging him, arousing him, with eyes as green as shallow seas.

With the fingers of her left hand she parted her lips, and he entered her. His whole body was tense, and the muscles around his buttocks felt like rope. He was thick and hard and she felt herself opening up to take him in. She wanted him in, as far as he could, as deeply as humanly possible, and more. They made love in silence, in front of the fire. She dragged her fingernails down his back, and clutched his buttocks, and pulled them apart as if she were breaking bread. She probed inside him and he winced, but he didn't push her away. He thrust harder and harder, and deeper and deeper; and although his rhythm was unfamiliar at first, it began to carry her away, until she matched it with her own movements, and the two of them were pushing at each other, hip to hip, as if they were trying to force themselves to occupy the same space at the same time, in defiance of physics, in defiance of reality, in defiance of everything else except that they needed each other.

Sarah felt the room beginning to contract. The fire was far too hot and far too bright, and the cushions were far too prickly. But Rej kept pushing and pushing, and the feeling was so good that she didn't want it to stop, ever. His face, looking down at her; his block of rock. His muscular chest, with its hairy cross and its gloss of perspiration. The relentless squeaking of his condom. He pushed and he pushed and she felt as if the soles of her feet had suddenly opened up, like floodgates, and allowed a gush of pleasurable darkness to fill her lower legs, and then her knees, and then her thighs.

"*Stefan,*" she whispered, and she loved the sound of the name. The darkness filled her completely, and she began to shake, and shake, and grip his shoulders. He kept on pushing and the feeling was so intense that she lifted her head from the pillows as if she were having a fit. *"Stefan."* Her nipples were rigid and her whole body was tight.

Then Stefan quaked, too, and arched his back; and deep inside her she felt his condom bulge.

He took himself out, very carefully, and lay on the cushions beside her. They looked into each other's eyes for reassurance and explanations; but they were deeply pleased with each other, too.

"You won't believe me if I say that I love you," said Rej.

"Why shouldn't I?" she said. She propped herself up on one elbow and traced a cloverleaf pattern on his bare shoulder with her fingertip, over and over.

"Well . . . you don't seem like the kind of woman who believes in love at first sight."

"What kind of woman is that?" she challenged him. "As a matter of fact, I believe in romantic accidents. Two people, who should never have met, discovering each other completely by chance. Three years ago I was working in New York. If somebody had come up and told me that in three years' time I'd be making love to a Polish detective in a cottage overlooking the Vistula, I'd have told them they were crazy."

He kissed her, and touched her forehead and her hair. "Sarah Lewandowicz," he said, with satisfaction.

"I'm only Lewandowicz in bed," she retorted. "Up, and dressed, I'm Leonard."

Rej got up and poured them two more glasses of honey vodka. She lay back looking at his naked body. He was so sinewy and strong, and yet he looked vulnerable, too. When he came back and lay beside her, she licked her fingertip and touched each of his nipples; and then she reached down and massaged his penis and his balls, feeling his stickiness.

"Do you know what I would like now, more than anything else in the world?" he asked. His eyes were very serious.

"Tell me," she said, and kissed his lips.
"A cigarette. I would die for a cigarette."

The logs gradually collapsed and died, until there was nothing left of the fire but sparks and ashes. Rej fell asleep on the cushions, one hand holding his penis, like a small boy. Sarah covered him with one of the home-woven blankets that were draped over the back of the sofa, and kissed him. He didn't even stir. A whole afternoon of horseback riding had obviously exhausted him.

When she was sure that he was asleep, she tippytoed across the room and opened her Gucci satchel. She took out a twist of newspaper, and opened it up. Five aspen berries rolled into the palm of her hand. Then she opened her purse and took out a silver-and-amber bracelet that Piotr Gogiel had given her after her first meeting with Vistula Kredytowy. She hoped that it wouldn't matter that the amber and the silver were joined together. Finally, she took out her nail scissors and carefully cut off a centimeter from her fringe.

She glanced back at Rej: still deeply asleep. He had been so warm and protective toward her that she felt incredibly cheap for trying out the old woman's charm. But Madame Krystyna's seance had opened up a door for her; and made her realize that there was another world; just as real and just as tumultuous as the so-called "real world"; and if the old woman's charm could show her what this *face* was that was supposed to be following her, then she wanted at least to try it.

Naked, she crept back across the room, lifted a large brocade cushion, and arranged the berries underneath it in the pattern of a five-pointed star. She laid her amber bracelet right in the center of the star, and her hair clipping right in the center of the amber bracelet. She lowered the cushion, and then rested her head on it, settling down to sleep.

It was over an hour before she finally closed her

eyes. She kept thinking about the old woman snatching her sleeve and screeching at her. *"Why do you bring that face? What are you trying to do? Show us what a martyr you are?"*

What had frightened Sarah the most was that the old woman had known her name, when she *couldn't* have known, no matter what excuses Rej had come up with. But the word *martyr* had frightened her too. *Martyr* conjured up images of painful, self-sacrificial death, like Joan of Arc, or Catherine broken on the wheel. The old woman's words had sounded more like a prophecy than a taunt, as if Sarah had already committed herself to a course of action which would lead her inevitably to martyrdom. She couldn't imagine what cause she would possibly die for, but then few martyrs do.

She watched Rej sleeping, and wondered about him, and what kind of man he really was. She knew that he wasn't much of an intellectual, and that he wasn't particularly sharp, but she had to admit to herself that his lack of flash was part of his attraction. If he didn't know anything, he didn't try to pretend that he did. He never carried crisply-laundered handkerchiefs, only small packets of tissues. And he didn't seem to know the meaning of the words "pressing your pants."

She touched his cheek with her fingertips. Without waking, he brushed them away, as if he were walking through his father's garden and a midge had settled on his face. She herself was Polish; but she knew that she could never be Polish in the way that Rej was. Although she was working here now, Poland was still a faraway homeland, remote and romanticized, a reality that never was.

It was a land of dreams: a land of dawns and dusks, a land of blossoming orchards, colorful musk thistles, large and dark branchy trees, glittering streams and dark woodlands, silver spruces, bridges in the middle of nowhere, and dark windmills over swelling waters.

There was a Poland of emotion. A Poland with old monuments, and churches, and fragments of town walls, palaces and huge parks, shrouded in mists rising from park ponds, roads leading somewhere into the distance, tracks running through villages. All gone; all imaginary; and yet never forgotten. A Poland that existed only in the minds of Poles; and yet a Poland that they would die for. Perhaps that was what the old woman had meant by martyrdom.

Sarah slept. She lay on her back, one hand raised, her hair spread across the cushion. The glowing fire limned her naked body, her flat stomach and her long slim legs. The last logs on the fire gave a soft lurch, and sparks were whisked up the chimney.

She dreamed that she was walking across a wide, sunlit barley field, with the ripe barley whipping against her calves. She was wearing a thin flowing dress with large poppies printed on it, which had once belonged to her mother. In the far distance she could see a line of trees, and smoke drifting between them. Although the day was so warm and the wind was so soft, she felt strangely unsettled, as if she had forgotten something important. She wondered what time it was, but she had no way of telling.

High above, a V-shaped flight of cranes flapped their way south. She had the feeling that the summer was coming to an end, and that winter would soon be here, sooner than anybody could imagine. She started to walk more quickly. She didn't want to be caught out in the open when the weather turned and it started to snow, not in this flimsy dress. The barley field seemed to stretch ahead of her forever. She knew that she had already been walking for several hours, and that she was late. She could see people on the horizon, cutting the barley with scythes, but they were so far away that even if she had called out to them, they wouldn't have been able to hear her.

The sun began to sink, and in some way, to *darken*.

The wind began to rise and blow chaff across the field, although it was still quite warm. Sarah turned around, and saw, far behind her, a large hunched figure in a cloak or a cape. The figure was following her across the field, its cloak billowing in the wind, and dust rising from its footsteps. It was almost black, this figure, and although there was nothing around it with which she could compare it for size, it looked huge, as if all the perspective in the field had been reversed, like a medieval painting, and objects grew bigger the further away they were.

She stopped for a moment and shaded her eyes, and watched the figure approaching. Not only was it very large, it was walking very fast, too, unnaturally fast. She had caught sight of it only a moment ago, and yet already it seemed to have reduced the distance between them by a third. She began to feel that she didn't want to let it catch up with her—that it intended to do her some harm.

She carried on walking, as fast as she could. She was wearing no shoes and her feet were scratched and bruised by thistles and barley stalks and stones. She ran for a little while, and then walked some more, and then ran for another few minutes, until she was out of breath. All the same, the edge of the field seemed just as far away as it had before, and when she turned around, she was astonished to see that the figure in the cape was less than a hundred meters away from her, and closing on her fast.

I can see your face as clear as day, Miss Lewandowicz. But I can see the face behind you, too.

Although she was tired, Sarah started running again. She knew that she was fit, but it was almost impossible to run barefoot across this dry, broken soil, and the heat was almost unbearable. Apart from that, she was naked under her dress so that her breasts bounced uncomfortably as she ran, and the dress itself seemed to cling to her like a winding-sheet.

The sun sank lower and lower, until it looked as if it were burning the trees. Sarah glanced over her shoulder and saw that the figure was only a few paces behind her, looming over her like a huge shadow. All the same she tried to keep on running, her breath coming in parched, rasping gasps, her legs scratched into criss-cross patterns by the thistles, blood sticking her toes together.

I can see the face that's been close behind you all your life; and now it's even closer still.

Now the figure was so close that she could hear its cape rapidly dragging over the barley, and the insistent chop-chop-chopping of its footsteps. She was bursting for air, bursting with panic. She tried to leap over three deep furrows and she fell, bruising her elbow and scratching her cheek. She rolled over onto her back and looked up. The figure was standing over her and it was immense. It must have been three meters tall, maybe taller.

She was too exhausted to move. All she could do was lie on the soil, panting for breath. She couldn't understand what this figure was, or what it was going to do to her, but she had never felt such dread in her entire life. The figure seemed to *emanate* dread, as if everything that Sarah had ever been afraid of was concealed beneath its cape. Fear of the dark; fear of spiders; fear of being alone. She felt that it would only have to sweep open its cape, and she would be overwhelmed in terror.

"Don't," she whispered. "Please don't."

The figure stepped even closer. Then it reached up, and cast back its hood, so that the last light from the disappearing sun illuminated its face.

Sarah's whole body was locked with fright. The face was very pale, and unnaturally small, like the face of a child or a china doll. It had black, unblinking, expressionless eyes—eyes as dead as a hammerhead shark's—but its little nose was exactly modelled, and so was its tiny mouth.

Although its face was so small, the rest of the figure's head was in proportion to its huge body—a pale domed skull with hanks and patches of diseased-looking hair on it. The contrast between the coarseness of the head and the miniature perfection of the face was so extreme that Sarah couldn't stop staring at it, too horrified to turn away.

The figure stared back at her, quite motionless. Then, slowly, it began to lean toward her. It leaned as if its feet were on silent hinges, not bending its body. The little face came closer and closer, until Sarah could have reached out and touched it. There was a long moment of supreme tension. Then suddenly the face distorted. The jaw dropped and the mouth stretched open. Sarah could hear the crackling of bones and muscles, and the glutinous cacophony of wet flesh. The tiny black eyes stayed staring and steady, but the mouth opened so wide that it was inside-out, revealing purplish, swollen gums, and thousands of tiny needle-sharp teeth. A long purple tongue rolled out of his lips, and strings of thick saliva swung from its jowls.

The sun disappeared, and darkness swallowed everything: the sky, the barley field, the figure in the cape. But in the very last instant of fading light, Sarah heard the metallic sliding sound of a blade being drawn out of a scabbard, and glimpsed a huge steel blade being lifted into the air.

She couldn't scream. She couldn't breathe. The night exploded inside her mind, like a black glass window breaking. She felt herself dropping through the ground, through layers and layers of time and history, through countless harvests, through woods and bushes and battles and blood, buried by centuries of grief, buried by soil that was crumbled in summer, frozen in winter, sodden in spring.

She thrashed from side to side, suffocated, crushed;

and it was only when Rej seized hold of her arms and shouted at her that she opened her eyes.

It was still very dark. The fire had died out, but she could see the outline of his shoulder.

"What the hell's wrong?" he asked her. "I thought you were having a fit."

She lay back for a moment. She was dripping with perspiration. Even her hair was wet. She couldn't believe that she wasn't covered in thousands of tons of soil; and that what she had just been dreaming was just a dream.

Rej said, "You all right now?" and she nodded. He climbed off her. He fumbled for his trousers and found his cigarette lighter, and lit the oil-lamp next to the couch. His hair was sticking up and he looked almost boyish.

"I was all ready to call an ambulance."

She drew the blanket over herself. "Honestly . . . I'm fine now. I'm okay, I promise."

He sat watching her, one hand on her thigh. "What was it, a nightmare? You kept saying 'don't.' "

"It was nothing. Sleeping in a strange place, that's all. Why don't you turn out that lamp and come back to sleep?"

"Do you feel like a drink? How about a cup of tea?"

She dabbed her forehead with the blanket, and smiled at him. "Listen, I'm fine. I really am. I just need to get some sleep."

He looked like a man who would have done almost anything for a cigarette. But he nodded, and patted her leg, and said, "Okay . . . if that's what you want."

He reached over, lifted her head, and plumped up the cushion that she had been lying on. As he did so, the aspen berries rolled out. He lifted the cushion completely, and saw the amber bracelet, and the snipping of hair. He let the cushion drop back, and looked down at her with a disappointed expression on his face.

"What?" she demanded.

"You tried it, didn't you? That stupid spell."

"Of course I tried it! What did you expect? I wanted to find out what she was talking about. She knew my name, Stefan! I mean, what are the odds against that?"

"There are no such things as spells, for God's sake. Magic, superstition—it's all in the mind."

"Oh, stop talking like an *apparatchik*. She knew my goddamned name!"

Rej turned his face away and didn't say anything; but Sarah could see a muscle working in his cheek. "I'm sorry," she said. "I didn't mean to call you that. But I had to know."

After a while he turned back again. "So what did you see?" he asked her. "Or was it nothing but a nightmare?"

"I was walking in a field, and something was chasing me. In the end, it caught up with me. It was horrible. It was all covered in a kind of a cloak, and it had a huge head and a tiny face. A tiny face, just like a little child. It leaned over me—it tilted right over me—and then its mouth opened so wide. It had a knife, too. Well, more of a sword than a knife. It pulled it out, and God knows what it was going to do to me—but then I woke up."

"A cloak?" asked Rej. "What color?"

"I'm not sure. It could have been black; it could have been very dark blue."

"Any buttons on it?"

"Buttons? I don't know. I can't remember. I was too terrified."

"*Think*. Did it have buttons on it?"

"Maybe it did, maybe it didn't. Why is it so important?"

Rej said, "Listen—if what you dreamed was only a dream, then it isn't important at all. But if the spell really worked—if you really saw this face that's been following you—then every single detail that you can remember is just as important as if you saw this person in the flesh."

"I'm not sure that it was a person. Well, not in the usual sense of person."

"So what was it? Some kind of . . . thing?"

"I don't know," said Sarah. "Its face was actually beautiful, but in a very cold, dead kind of way. Its eyes were totally blank, they didn't have any expression at all. But its head, its scalp—it was horrible, all tufty and balding and scaly. It looked as if it was suffering from ringworm, or something like that."

"Could you draw it for me?" asked Rej.

"I'm not sure that I'd want to. It frightened me to death."

Rej leaned over her and kissed her, first on the forehead and then on the lips. She touched his cheek, and said, "I'm really sorry. I shouldn't have called you an *apparatchik*."

"Hunh!" he shrugged. "Maybe I was, once. Maybe old ideological habits die hard." He stroked her shoulder as if he couldn't quite believe that it was real. "You're used to freedom," he said. "I can smell it on you. It's exciting."

Sarah had a feeling then, quite unexpected, that she and Rej would never be able to have anything more than a fleeting relationship, a night here in Czerwinsk, maybe one or two nights more back in Warsaw, but nothing permanent. He was strong, and he was kind, and she was almost in love with him. But he had so many years of catching up to do.

"This *thing*," she said, "whatever it was, came following me over the field. It was so frightening that I couldn't find the strength to get away from it. It seemed to drain all of the strength out of me. It even drained the light out of the sky."

Rej said, "When I was down in the sewers, and I was attacked, my flashlight went dead. It was just as if somebody had sucked all the power out of it."

"It was so fast," said Sarah. "I was running, but it still managed to catch up with me."

"This thing in the sewers was fast, too. I only managed to escape because they were dragging me out with a rope."

Sarah closed her eyes, and tried to picture the figure that had been pursuing her. Its exquisite, diminutive face. Its raggedy, diseased-looking skull. Its heavy, windblown cape. She could see it as clearly as if it were tilted in front of her, the way it had in her dream. And there were two buttons, holding its cape together; two buttons, connected with a chain. And on each button, the face of a snarling beast.

"Yes," she told Rej. "It *did* have buttons. I can draw them for you."

Rej sat beside her while she sketched one of the buttons in the margin of yesterday's *Super Express*. He drummed his fingers and she was dying to tell him that he could smoke; but she didn't. When she was finished, she passed over the newspaper and watched while Rej examined it.

"No doubt about it," he said, after two or three minutes. "That's exactly it."

"That's exactly what?"

"The same button that we found after Jan Kaminski was killed. It was attached to a piece of very old velvet." He looked intently at her. "Your dream or your nightmare or whatever it was . . . it was real. There was no way you could have drawn this button without seeing it first."

Sarah said, "Oh, God," and covered her mouth with her hand.

"What are you worried about?" said Rej. "This is one step nearer to finding out who the Executioner is."

"But how could I *do* that? How could I know what this button looked like, just from a dream?"

"I take back what I said before. I don't think it *was*

a dream. Not in the conventional sense. I think you actually saw the Executioner."

"That creature? With his great big cloak, and his eyes, and his mouth and everything? How could that be real? And supposing it *is* real?"

"Then we find it," said Rej, "and we arrest it. And if we can't arrest it, we'll kill it. Then you and your workers can get on with building your fancy hotel, and I can go back to work."

"But why is it looking for *me*?"

"For the same reason that it went looking for all of those other people . . . little Zofia and Ewa Zborowska and Bronislaw Slesinski. They were all connected with the Home Army. It wants to hunt down every last one, and kill them, though God alone knows why."

Sarah was silent for a moment. She felt deeply tired, but she knew that she wouldn't be able to sleep. "Let me draw it for you," he said. "Then at least you'll know what you're looking for."

Rej leaned over and kissed her cheek. She had a feeling that it would be one of the last kisses that he would ever give her.

Clayton and Marek hurried Indian-file along the narrow oval sewer, their shoes splashing rhythmically in the water. Their flashlight beams jiggled and jumped as they ran, until the sewer became a kaleidoscope of dancing reflections.

"Can you see him?" Marek panted. "He can't have got too far ahead."

Clayton tried to steady his flashlight as he ran. At the far end of the sewer, it looked as if a shadow was disappearing around a corner. "There! That's him! Did you see that? Just caught a glimpse of him!"

"How come he doesn't need a flashlight?"

"I don't know," said Clayton. "Probably knows his way by now. Less'n he can see in the dark."

"Oh, come on. This is total darkness, down here. Nobody can see in total darkness."

"Don't believe it, kid. They have lizards back in New Mexico, live all of their lives under the ground, in prehistoric caves. They can *see*, these critters, they've proved it, whether by infrared or ultra-violet or what have you. Don't tell me that a human being couldn't do the same."

They went on jogging for another two or three minutes, and then they came to a branch in the sewer— one leading south, one leading southwest. "Ssh, stop, listen," said Clayton, so they stood completely still, suppressing their breathing. From the southwestward tunnel they heard the unmistakable slapping of feet in several centimeters of water, and a single, barking cough. "Got the bastard," said Clayton, and they set off jogging again.

They had no idea how far they had traveled. Marek guessed that they had probably run right under Marszalkowska and crossed Trasa Lazienkowska; but they had been running for so long that they may have gone very much further. The air in the sewer was growing increasingly fetid, and Marek couldn't stop himself from spitting and coughing. His wet clothes clung to his skin, and he felt sick and exhausted. If Clayton hadn't kept on jogging ahead with such determination, he would have found the nearest manhole and climbed out as soon as he could.

"I see him!" said Clayton. "Come on, kid, we're closing in on him!"

Only sixty or seventy meters away, pinned in the dazzling beams of their flashlights, Mr. Okun turned and stared at them, and his eyes reflected red, like a partygoer caught by a Polaroid. Then he was gone, and they were running again.

"Guy's guilty as hell," Clayton gasped. "He wouldn't be running, else."

Marek said nothing but continued vehemently to wish that he wasn't here.

They reached the place where Mr. Okun had disappeared. Here, there was a narrow pipe half way up the side of the wall, only a meter in diameter, and utterly dark. Water poured out of it in a constant, irritating dribble. Clayton pointed his flashlight down it, and said, "This is it . . . this is the way he went."

"In *there*?" said Marek. "That's only a drainpipe."

"That's where he went. Look, you can see the marks he made with his shoes."

"So what do we do now?"

"What do you think we do? We go after him."

"I don't think so," said Marek. "I think this is just as far as I go."

"What are you? Chicken?" Clayton challenged him. "He's just a little weedy old mass-murderer. What are you afraid of?"

"No way, man! Absolutely not!"

"Listen," said Clayton, "I've done much more frightening things than this. Remind me to tell you about the time I had to climb right inside a gas-fired coke furnace to look for some lunatic who was holding a young girl hostage."

"I don't care. I'm not going down that drainpipe."

"You are, kid, and I'm coming with you. We didn't come all the way down here for nothing, did we? We didn't get plastered in shit for nothing, did we? And you just remember those little kids in the war, they used to crawl down these pipes for miles, and do you think *they* were scared?"

"Yes I do, as a matter of fact."

Clayton rubbed the back of his neck to ease the tension that was locking up his back muscles. "So you really want to throw in the towel? When you might have found the Executioner? You're throwing away a lot of glory, kid."

Marek peered down the drain again. He wouldn't

have dreamed of crawling down a narrow pipe like this, even in daylight. But this was pitch dark, and coated in slime, and a thin rivulet of dark brown sewage trick-led down the middle of it. And God alone knew what was hiding in there, waiting for the first foolish intruder to come blundering within its reach.

He looked back at Clayton, and Clayton shrugged. "It's up to you, kid. I'm going, even if you're not."

"All right," said Marek, even though the sensible side of his brain was furiously thinking *Shit! shit! Why did you say that?* And then he made things even worse by saying. "Why don't I go first? I'm a little faster than you." At the same time, thinking *You're crazy, you're totally crazy, you must be out of your mind.*

There were two rungs on either side of the pipe and he used them to heave himself up. There was barely room enough for him to be able to turn his head around.

"What happens if I meet up with him?" he asked, in a muffled voice.

"Just hold onto his feet. He won't be able to do much, in this confined space."

"Just hold onto his feet," Marek muttered, as he started to elbow his way along the sewer. "Easy!"

As soon as Marek had climbed completely into the pipe, Clayton hauled himself up and came after him. "My guess is, this is just an interconnecting pipe he uses to make his way from one main drain to another," said Clayton. His voice boomed like a man with his head in an empty water tank.

"So long as it goes *somewhere*," Marek called back. He hadn't crawled more than fifty meters, and he was already beginning to feel desperately closed-in and panicky, especially since the only way back was ob-structed by Clayton, bulky and coughing and very much slower than he was.

His flashlight illuminated a pipe that ran dead straight for as far as he could see; and beyond the range of the beam there was nothing but darkness. To begin with, he was disgusted by the slime on the sides of the pipe, but after a while, when he had worked out a regular rhythm with his knees and his elbows, he began to be grateful for it, because it enabled him to crawl and slide at the same time, and made his progress much faster. *Who needs to go rollerblading*, he thought, *when you can skate on your belly on human grease?*

"See anything?" asked Clayton.

"Darkness and more darkness, that's all."

"Stop for a while. Let's listen."

They stopped crawling for a moment and strained their ears. They could hear the faint whistling of air through a ventilator shaft, and a distant, deep grinding noise, but that was all. "Traffic," said Clayton. "Let's go on a bit further."

Marek was sweating now. The effort of crawling along the pipe was beginning to exhaust him. His knees and his elbows were sore, and his sewage-wet jeans were chafing his thighs. But if the only way out was to go forward, he didn't have any choice but to continue. He cursed himself for having agreed to do this; and he cursed himself even more for having volunteered to go first. "You know what you are, you're a *menda*, a pain in the ass."

"Say what?" called Clayton.

"Never mind," said Marek. "Talking to myself."

At that instant, he heard a frantic clicking, clattering sound, coming straight toward him. His flashlight beam caught a huge black shape, almost as big as a dog, with slicked-back fur. He screamed, "*Gaaaaaah!*" and whipped up both hands to cover his face. The largest rat that he had ever seen in his life jumped onto the back of his head, its claws scrabbling in his hair. It was so heavy that it knocked his forehead down into the sewage. Then it ran along his back, and all the way down his legs. He lay flat on his stomach, quaking with shock. He didn't even hear Clayton saying, "Shit!" and hitting the rat with his flashlight. He just stayed where he was, his eyes squeezed shut, his teeth gritted, his whole body convulsing as if he had stuck his fingers in an electric socket.

"You okay, kid?" asked Clayton.

Marek nodded, forgetting that Clayton couldn't see him. And even then he thought, *Why did I do that? I'm not okay. I'm up to my armpits in shit and I'm shitting myself. I want to go home.* He thought of his mother taking apple mazurka cake out of the oven. He thought of Olga and his little brother, and he could have cried.

"Didn't hurt you, did it?" Clayton wanted to know.

"No, no. I'm terrific. I've never seen a rat as big as that before, that's all."

"They feed good down here. It's a non-stop banquet as far as rats are concerned."

They continued to crawl along the pipe, but this time Marek kept his flashlight pointing steadily at the darkness in front of him. He didn't intend to be surprised by any more rats. If he was growing tired, Clayton was almost at the end of his strength. Marek could hear him gasping and wheezing as he dragged himself forward, and every now and then he had to stop for a rest.

"Are you *sure* this goes somewhere?" asked Marek. "I don't fancy crawling all the way to the river."

"If your Mr. Okun managed to come this way, then so can we."

"What if he didn't come this way? What if he tricked us? What if this is a dead end?"

"If this is a dead end, then we'll just have to crawl out backwards, won't we?"

Almost twenty minutes went past as they grunted and scuffled their way through the interminable darkness. Marek's flashlight beam began to weaken, and he had to shake it to keep it bright. They were both aching and numb, and the air was so foul that they couldn't stop themselves from coughing up sour-tasting saliva. They stopped repeatedly, and listened for any sound that might indicate that Mr. Okun was up ahead of them, but there was nothing. Marek was feeling so claustrophobic that he had to keep closing his eyes and pretending that he wasn't here at all. What was worse, he was sure that the pipe was becoming even narrower, so that he had to keep his head down all the time, and his shoulders rubbed against the sides.

He thought, *If this gets any tighter, I'm going to have to tell Clayton that I can't go on. Because I can't go on.*

He struggled on for five minutes more, and then another five, but then he stopped.

"What's the matter?" asked Clayton. "You hear something?"

"I've had enough. I want to go back."

"Come on, kid, you'll get a second wind in a minute. You're tired, that's all."

"And you're not?"

"Just give it a little further. We're bound to hit a main drain soon."

"That's what you said an hour ago. I can't stand it. I just can't stand it. I'm having one long panic attack."

"Wait," said Clayton. "Switch off your flashlight."

Marek hesitated, but then he switched it off. Clayton switched his off, too, so that they were plunged into darkness. All Marek could see were greenish after-images floating in front of his eyes like bacteria under a microscope.

"What is it?" he asked. His heart was beating so hard against his ribs that he felt as if he were being punched.

"There . . . I thought I saw light," said Clayton, and pointed up ahead. Marek looked, too, and saw the faintest glimmer.

"Looks like daylight."

"I don't care what it is, so long as it's a way out of this goddamned pipe. Come on, let's haul ass."

They switched on their flashlights again, and kept on crawling, their knees and elbows sliding on the thick

greasy residue that coated the pipe in thicker and
thicker layers. In some places, it was like slimy lard,
more than five centimeters in depth. Up ahead of them,
however, the light grew gradually more distinct, until
they could actually see the curve of the pipe that it was
illuminating, like a crescent moon reflected in a pond.

"It's a ventilation shaft," said Marek. "I can feel it
. . . I can feel it already."

He arched his neck back as much as he could, and
he could feel a soft sour current of air playing against
his face—tainted not just with sewage, but with diesel
fumes, and the smell of the world above, of the streets.
For the first time in over an hour he took a deep breath,
and then another. As he kept on crawling, he heard
buses, and car horns, and the distant nagging of an
ambulance siren.

"It's okay, we're going to make it," he said, twisting
his head around so that Clayton could see him.

"Maybe we are. But what happened to your friend
Mr. Okun?"

"Who gives a shit? Let's just get out of here."

But Clayton was adamant. "Listen, kid, I didn't
crawl all the way down this toilet pipe for nothing. I
wanted that bastard before, but I really want him now.
I'm going to make him eat this grease for breakfast."

Marek reached the ventilation shaft, and eased himself, bruised and aching, to his feet. It was nothing
more than a circular, brick-lined shaft which led up ten
meters to an iron grating. Marek saw tyres passing over
it, and heard the rumble of heavy trucks. He couldn't
guess exactly where they were, although it must be
underneath a main route, probably Pulawska or Nie-
podleglosci.

What amazed him was that night had fallen, and that
the light which filtered through the grating wasn't daylight, but the light from streetlamps. He checked his
watch, shook it, and realized that it must have stopped.
He and Clayton must have been crawling for hours.

Clayton's filth-caked hands appeared in the sewer pipe, and then his face. Marek was shocked by how haggard he looked. His eyes were rimmed with red, and his features seemed to have collapsed, like an old brown paper bag, smudged and worn and criss-crossed with creases.

"I guess you're going to have to help me out of here," he said, holding out his hand. "I'm not as sprightly as I thought I was."

Marek took hold of his hand, and began to heave him out of the pipe. As he did so, however, he became aware of a thick shuffling sound, somewhere in the distance, almost a *chuffing*, like an approaching locomotive. He stayed still for a moment, and said, "*Listen*—what do you think that is?"

Clayton listened. "How should I know? Maybe a train."

"A train? It sounds like it's coming down the pipe."

Clayton listened again. "At that speed? Nothing can come down this godawful pipe at *that* speed."

But the shuffling was coming closer and closer; and faster and faster; and Marek was suddenly aware that the airflow had changed direction. It wasn't blowing *in* from the grating, but *out* of the sewer pipe—and it began to rush so forcefully that it ruffled what was left of Clayton's hair.

Clayton listened a few moments longer, and then he said, "Holy Jesus, kid, something's coming up behind me."

"What?"

"He's tricked us, the bastard! He's got us trapped! He never came this way! But he's sent the Executioner after us!"

Marek was so shocked and panicky that he stumbled back against the brick ventilator shaft, bruising his shoulder. But Clayton yelled at him, "Get me out of here! For Christ's sake get me out of here!" and Marek seized both of his black, greasy hands, and tried to pull.

"It's okay, I'm okay," said Clayton. "It's just that I—"

The shuffling, chuffing sound was so close now that it seemed to fill the whole sewer. The walls shook, and iron grids started to rattle. Marek could feel the Executioner through the ground, through the soles of his feet, and it was like standing in the middle of a highway waiting for a truck to hit him (which he had once, in a moment of teenage despair, and every vehicle had driven around him, frustrating him at first, but then making him laugh, as if he were a seriously failed matador, at whom the bulls refused to charge).

But there was nothing laughable about the way that the sewer was literally *quaking* as something came close. "Get me out of here, for Christ's sake!" Clayton begged. "He's almost here . . . I can feel him! Jesus, can't you hear that knife?"

And sure enough, Marek could hear the off-key ringing of a long, sharp blade. If the Executioner was approaching them like an unstoppable locomotive, then this was its bell, its clanging, repetitive bell, warning everybody who stood in its way that the Executioner was coming through the night, and that they had better hide, or run, or stay well out of its tracks, because it was coming through, and nothing in the world could stop it.

Marek tugged at Clayton's hands again, but their fingers were so greasy that they slipped. Clayton seemed to be wedged, maybe around the waist, and it was going to take a whole lot of pulling and wriggling to work him free.

"Listen, Clayton, just try to relax," he said in a high, off-pitch voice. "All you have to do is to let the air out of your lungs. You got me? Let it all out, exhale; and then I'll pull you!"

Clayton made a face like a drowning swimmer. But even as he tried to breathe out, the ringing stopped, and

Marek heard a sharp chopping sound. Then another. Then another.

Clayton screamed, "No!" and twisted around and around in the pipe. He was staring at Marek in agony and utter horror, but there was nothing that Marek could do, except to grab hold of his hands and try to pull him out.

"No!" screeched Clayton. "No!" He was thrashing around so violently that Marek couldn't get a grip, although he tried to seize the collar of his jacket.

"No! God! No!" Clayton repeated, his eyes wild with shock. "It's cutting my feet off! It's cutting my fucking feet off!"

Marek bunched the fingers of his left hand into Clayton's collar, and grasped his wrist with his right, and heaved. There was a moment when he thought he might have succeeded in dragging Clayton free. They were face to face: eye to eye. Clayton was staring in pain and desperation; Marek was straining as hard as he could. *God forgive me for coming down this pipe. God give me strength.*

He pulled at Clayton until he heard the muscles in his back cracking. But Clayton wasn't just wedged in the pipe. Something was holding him fast, and something wasn't going to let him go. There was more chopping, and Clayton shouted, and jerked from side to side, and said, "Please, Marek, please Marek, please don't let it do this Marek! It hurts, Marek! *For Christ's sake, Marek it's cutting my legs off! Don't let it— aaah—don't let it—AAAAAH—Marek—don't let it—*"

The chopping noise quickened, and Clayton looked at Marek in absolute horror. He was almost beyond pain now. All he could do was stare, open-mouthed, as his legs were chopped up, and then his buttocks; and then he screamed in a way that Marek had never had a man scream before.

"Marek—it's—*aaaaahhhh!*"

Clayton's face dropped forward, and at that moment

a huge surge of blood and sewage poured into the bottom of the ventilation shaft, and lazily swirled around Marek's feet. Marek let go of Clayton's collar, and stepped back, mewling in fright. Clayton seemed to shudder for a moment. One hand looked as though it might be appealing for help. But then he was dragged away into the darkness of the sewer pipe, and Marek heard the noises of such an appalling act of butchery that he couldn't do anything at all, but stand with his back to the brickwork and his eyes wide open, listening to the brisk, decisive bite of steel against bone.

Suddenly, there was silence. Marek waited, trying not to breathe too loudly, trying not to cry. More blood swelled from out of the pipe, streaked with sewage. It carried fragments of bone with it, and ribbons of pale beige intestine, and a huge dark clot of bloody-looking offal that could have been part of Clayton's liver.

Marek listened and listened, but he couldn't hear anything at all. No shuffling, no ringing, no breathing. He reached out with his left hand and clasped the nearest of the iron rungs that led up the ventilation shaft. He made no noise at all. He waited, and then he reached out with his right hand. With any luck, the thing would be satisfied with Clayton, and wouldn't even realize that he was here.

He lifted his foot out of the pool of blood and lifted it onto the very first rung. He didn't want to shake, he didn't want to tremble, but he couldn't help it. *Please God let me not make a noise, Please blessed Virgin Mary may the ventilator grille not be locked.* He suddenly thought of the ending of *The Third Man*, with Harry Lime's fingers protruding through a sewer grille that he couldn't open. He didn't want to die like that. He didn't want to die down here.

He climbed silently up to the second rung, and then the third. He was sweating so much that he could hardly keep a grip on the ironwork. Every now and then, a car or a bus would drive over the grille, momentarily blocking out of the light and filling the ventilation shaft with fumes. Marek was desperate to cough. His throat felt as if it were crammed with burrs, and his eyes were watering, but he didn't dare to make a sound. He thought he heard the sound of a knife-blade scraping across concrete; and a shifting, dragging noise. But then another bus blared over the ventilation shaft, and he couldn't hear anything at all.

He climbed up two more rungs. He was more than halfway up the shaft now, but his arms were juddering with fatigue, and his legs seemed to have lost all of their strength. *Please God help me get out of here*, he prayed. *Please God don't let me die.*

He managed to drag himself up the last four rungs, and at last he reached the ventilator grille. He pushed upward with his right hand, but he couldn't move it. He could actually see a streetlight and part of a building, and traffic flashing past. A truck drove right over the grille, with a deafening rumble and a sizzling of tyres, and Marek almost lost his grip.

He pushed again. He was sure that he could feel the grille shift a little, but he wasn't able to get enough leverage to lift it right up. He cautiously took his left hand off the top rung, too, and balanced on the ladder with his feet and his knees, so that he could try pushing upward with both hands. Again, he could feel the grille shifting slightly in the roadbed, but it was far too firmly lodged.

He glanced down the ventilation shaft. There was nothing down there but darkness, and blood; but he didn't dare risk going back the way he had come. The thought of crawling along that pipe again was like a dark, jangling nightmare—especially after what had happened to Clayton.

One lesson he had learned from breaking into derelict buildings was that if you wanted a door open, you didn't try to beat it with your fist or rush at it with your shoulder, the way they did in police movies. That way, all you got was badly bruised. You kicked it, as hard as you could, and even the strongest doors could only withstand two or three determined kicks.

He leaned back on the ladder until his shoulders were resting on the opposite side of the ventilation shaft. Then he took his feet off the rungs, and began to "walk" up the brickwork, his arms splayed behind him to give him support, and to prevent himself from falling. He was grunting with effort, and he couldn't stop himself from coughing, but he kept on "walking" until he was doubled-up, and his left foot was nearly touching the grille. He took a deep breath, and then he swung his left leg and tried to kick upward. But his position was too awkward, and he slid down the shaft for two or three horrifying meters, his jacket slithering against the bricks. He snatched for one of the rungs and managed to stop himself from sliding any further, but after that he clung to the ladder, shivering and panting.

Maybe he should wait here until he was sure that the Executioner had gone, and then try to attract attention by shouting and poking his fingers through the grille. But how did he know that the Executioner wasn't going to stay here all night, and all the next day, listening and waiting for him?

Painfully, he started to climb up the rungs again, until he reached the top. He took out his flashlight, switched it on and waved it backward and forward underneath the grille. The batteries were dying, but maybe somebody would see it, and call for help.

Another truck ran over the grille, blasting Marek with thick black diesel smoke. He lifted his hand to cover his face. And dropped his torch.

He heard it rattle all the way down the ventilation shaft, and echo as it hit the bottom. He waited, clinging tightly to the rungs. At first, there was nothing but silence, no response at all. Marek hoped and prayed that the Executioner had been satisfied with slaughtering

Clayton, and had gone back the way it had come. But then he heard a thick, shuffling sound, and the springy tap-tap-tapping of a knife-point.

He gave the ventilator grille another effortful push. It shifted almost half a centimeter, and he heard the crunching of grit against metal as it settled back again. He pushed it again, using the heel of his hand, clenching his teeth and straining his back. The grille lifted—it actually lifted—and then it violently slammed back down again as a car ran over it, almost breaking Marek's wrist.

Gasping, he pushed yet again. And it was then that he heard the knife-point scratching against the sides of the bricks, and a soft draft of air *rising* all around him, faster and faster, as if something huge were climbing up the ventilation shaft after him. He looked down, and what he saw frightened him so much that his mouth stretched open but he couldn't find the breath to articulate a scream.

It was a bulky shape, in a voluminous black cloak. But for all its bulk it had a tiny, delicate face, as white as porcelain, with dead black eyes—a face that would have been beautiful if it hadn't been so horrifying.

It was scaling the rungs of the ventilation shaft hand over hand, and its hands were white and spindly, almost transparent, like long spider's legs scuttling up toward him.

Marek stared at this creature for one frozen instant, and then he bent his head down and rammed the metal grille with his shoulders. The grille burst out of its setting and clanged into the roadway. Marek scrambled after it, just as one spidery hand caught at the heel of his boot.

He was right out in the middle of the street, with traffic roaring on either side of him. A taxi swerved to avoid him and almost collided with a bus. A truck bellowed its horn at him. He knew how dangerous it was to leave the ventilation shaft uncovered, but he didn't look back. He ran right down the middle of the street, his arms and his legs going like scissors. His throat hurt, from dragging in warm, polluted air. He had a pain in his stomach and a pain in his chest. But he kept on running and running, regardless of the traffic. He ran right across a major road intersection, followed by hooting and shouting and drivers waving their fists at him.

He didn't know where he was, or where he was going. All he knew was that he had to put as much distance between himself and that creature as he possibly could. He kept turning around, fearful that it was following, but all he could see was traffic signals and automobile lights and fluorescent signs.

At last, exhausted, he crossed to the sidewalk, and sat down with his feet in the gutter, his head between his knees. He was gasping for breath and caked in rapidly-drying sewage. An old man came up and asked him if he was all right, but all he could do was shake his head. In spite of the traffic, he couldn't get the noise of Clayton's butchery out of his ears.

Eventually, however, he looked up, and realized where he was—on Ujazdowskie Avenue, by the Ujazdowski Park, right across the street from Koszykowa, where he and Clayton had first entered the sewers. They had crawled around in a circle, and arrived back only two or three blocks from where they had started; and it had taken them hours.

Marek climbed to his feet and walked unsteadily into the park. It was quieter here, and he could breathe. He made his way along the path, with shrubs and herbaceous borders on either side, their flowers closed and secretive now that it was dark. He felt as if his whole life had been turned inside out, in nothing but a few hours. He had climbed down into the sewer in innocence and optimism, in a spirit of adventure; and come out of it shocked and distressed, and ten years older. He had known that Jan Kaminski had been horribly killed, but that had been easy to accept compared with Clayton's death. He had liked Clayton: he was almost an uncle. But he had heard the Executioner chopping him up like butcher's meat, and that was more than he could take.

He passed a colorless lawn where ducks were sleeping, their head furled under their wings. His feet dragged, and he felt like falling onto the grass himself, and closing his eyes. But at last he arrived at the park's main gate, facing onto Roz Avenue. Right inside it stood the statue of Ignacy Jan Paderewski, the pianist and politician, who had fought so hard for the reconstruction of Poland. Marek leaned against its plinth and bowed his head. He felt like crying, but he couldn't cry. He didn't even know if he would ever be able to speak.

15

Warsaw was humid and hazy the next day, when they returned. It looked like a city seen in a foggy mirror: the Viceroy's Palace, St. Anne's Church, and the Palace of Culture and Science. Even though they had driven with the car windows wide open, Sarah's green crepe dress was sticking to the seat. Rej looked unusually jaunty in a white short-sleeved shirt and sunglasses, and he had been singing for most of the way back, and drumming his fingers on the steering wheel.

Sarah knew why he was so happy. He felt that he made a catch, a wonderful catch. She knew that he was going to ask to see her again; as soon as tonight; but she also knew that she couldn't. He had given her everything: warmth, protection, humor and such old-fashioned courtesy—opening doors, pulling out chairs, and walking on the outside of the sidewalk. He had made her feel as if he had wanted her because she was a woman, and nobody had done that to her, not for a very long time. But they came from different planets, and their lovemaking had been like the lovemaking of two species that were only similar to look at, not to know.

She knew why he was so happy, and she knew that

she was going to hurt him; but she had no choice. She couldn't afford another traumatic affair, not now. She would be better off with another rock singer.

They reached her apartment, and Rej lifted her bag out of the trunk and opened the car door for her. It creaked like a door in Castle Dracula.

"I hope it's been good," he told her. He took off his sunglasses and his eyes were filled with the need for reassurance.

She kissed him, once on each cheek, and then on the lips. "The best weekend I ever had, I promise. Thank you, Stefan. And I love Katarzyna."

"Do you want me to carry your bag for you?"

"No, no. You don't have to do that. You have to get Katarzyna back to her mother, don't you?"

Rej looked at his watch. "I was wondering... maybe I could see you later."

"For sure. I'd love to. But not today. I'm going to have so much work to catch up on. I haven't even written my weekly report for *last* week!"

"You don't want dinner tonight?"

She shook her head. "Let me get my nose back to the grindstone first. I have so much to do."

Rej said, "That dream you had . . . that didn't upset you too much?"

"It was a dream, that's all. Too much honey vodka, too much country air."

"Ah, yes. The honey vodka."

She reached out and touched his face. She thought that it was terrible that human beings found it so difficult to love each other: she could have cried. She turned around and saw Katarzyna in the back seat of the car, smiling because she liked her, and because she made her father happy, and she felt so sad that she almost relented, and said that she *could* have dinner. But she knew where that would lead; and she didn't want to go that way, not yet, and probably not ever.

"I always want you to tell me the truth," said Rej, in English, pronouncing it "troot."

"I will," said Sarah, in Polish, and picked up her bag. Rej was still standing beside his car when she entered the building. She went upstairs to her apartment, opened the door, and flung her bag on the sofa. First she needed a shower: the washing facilities in Czerwinsk had been primitive, to say the least—a china jug in a big china basin. She crossed the living room and opened up the French windows to get rid of some of the weekend's staleness, and when she went out onto the balcony she was surprised to see that Rej was still there, standing in the same position, as if he expected her to come back out again, and say that she *would* have dinner with him after all, and that she loved him.

She went into the kitchen, opened up her breadbox, and found half a stale loaf and a hard bialy roll. She took out the bialy, went back to the balcony, took aim, and dropped it neatly right in front of his feet. It bounced right into the street, and was flattened by a passing taxi. She saw Rej jump back, startled; and then look up at the sky, turning around and around, as if he thought that a passing bird had dropped it on him.

Sarah fell back on her sofa, convulsed, her hand clamped over her mouth to stop herself from laughing too loudly. She was still laughing when the phone rang. She climbed off the sofa and picked it up, carrying it over to the balcony so that she could see whether Rej was still there. She was just in time to see his Volkswagen pull out into the traffic and head south. She saw Katarzyna turn her head and look toward her balcony; but she doubted if Katarzyna could see her.

The voice on the phone said, "It's Marek. I've been trying to call Rej, but he wasn't there."

"Marek? You sound dreadful! What's happened?"

"It's Clayton, he's dead. We went down into the sewers and the Executioner got him."

Sarah felt as if her whole body had been immersed

in freezing water. "Clayton? I can't believe it! Are you sure?"

"He's dead! The Executioner chopped him up, just like those Germans! I don't know what to do!"

"Come on, Marek, try to stay calm. Have you told anyone else?"

"I tried to call Rej at the police station but they told me he hadn't arrived."

"You didn't tell any other police officers?"

"I didn't know how to explain it. I mean, there was *this thing*—and it killed Clayton, and it came right after me."

"Marek—try not to get too excited. Try to tell me what happened."

"I saw this man go into the sewers; that was yesterday. I just wondered what he was doing so I followed him home. I called Clayton and Clayton told me to watch him, so I did. Then yesterday evening I saw him again and we followed him. We went right into the sewers—down this really narrow pipe. But the Executioner came after us, and he chopped Clayton into little bits, I mean he chopped him up! And I don't know how I got out of there, I really don't."

"It's okay," Sarah soothed him, although she was already beginning to make terrible sense out of what he was babbling at her. "Marek—it's okay. Rej should be back at his apartment by eleven o'clock, I'll call him up then, and we can meet."

"But Clayton . . . I liked him so much. I still can't believe it. We were crawling along this pipe and it just came after him."

"How about you?" asked Sarah. "Are you all right?"

"I j—j—." Marek began, and had to stop.

"Where are you now? Do you want to come around here?"

"I think I'm all right. I'm at home. My mother made me some tea."

"Marek, listen to me, where did you go down the sewer?"

"Koszykowa, half way down. But we crawled around for hours. It was daylight when we went down there, and when I managed to get out, it was dark."

"Where do you think Clayton was killed?"

"It's down this really narrow pipe . . . somewhere under Ujadowskie Avenue."

"All right," said Sarah. "I'll talk to Rej as soon as I can." She was just as upset as Marek, but she tried to sound calm. "Don't call the police just yet. The police think they're holding the Executioner already, and they won't want anybody telling them different. If I know anything about police politics, they'll probably lock you up, too, and accuse you of killing Clayton."

"But the Executioner killed him! He chopped him up, I could *hear* him, chopping him up!"

"Did you see him?" asked Sarah.

"What?" said Marek. His voice was as pale and crazed as pottery glaze.

"Did you see the Executioner? That's what I want to know."

Marek was silent for almost half a minute. Then he said, "Not very clearly."

"Did he have a cape, Marek, a large black cape?"

"A cape, yes, Kind of a cloak."

"What about his face? Did you see his face?"

"I don't think so. I was just trying to get out of there."

"Did he have a *small* face, Marek? A really tiny face, like a child's face, totally white? Did he have jet-black eyes?"

The moon could have changed quarter in the time that it took Marek to reply. But at last he said, "Yes. A really small face . . . really pale."

"Then she was right," said Sarah; in sorrow, but also in relief. "The old woman was right, and Rej was right.

It's the same face that I saw in my nightmare, except
that it's not a nightmare."

"What?" said Marek. "I don't understand."

"I'll tell you all about it when we meet. But this
thing is real, Marek; and it's looking for us. Looking
for *us*—anybody who fought against the Germans in
the Uprising, and their children, and their grandchildren, and their cousins, and maybe their friends, too.
It doesn't want anybody left, Marek. It wants to kill *all*
of us."

ej left Katarzyna with her mother, after an awkward tango in the hallway involving Rej and Katarzyna and Katarzyna's suitcase. Her mother proffered
her cheek, with its soft blond hairs like a peach. Rej
had managed to miss kissing it, in case he was being
unfaithful. "Next weekend," he promised Katarzyna,
raising his hand. "We'll go to Pomiechowek. We can
ride there, too."

Katarzyna clung to his sleeve for a moment. Perhaps
she, too, had seen that Sarah didn't love him as much
as he thought she did; but *she* loved him, because he
was her father.

The door closed in his face and Rej went back downstairs to his empty Volkswagen. He searched in the
glove box for a cigarette but there weren't any.

He pulled out into the traffic. He felt hot and sweaty
and he needed a shave, but there were a couple of calls
he wanted to make before he went back home. The
first was to Oczki Street, to talk to Dr. Wojniakowski.
He wanted to know what had happened to Zofia's
mother. She may have ended up as nothing more than
a scorched ribcage in the bottom of an ashcan, but Rej
had seen her pictures when she was young and pretty;
and that young and pretty girl deserved as much justice
as anybody else.

Dr. Wojniakowski was just starting an autopsy on a
young girl who had hanged herself in a room at the

Dom Chlopa hotel. She was plump and fair with freckles all over her. She looked as she were sleeping, rather
than dead, and Rej felt embarrassed for her, lying on
that metal table with nothing on, while Dr. Wojniakowski stood over her and smoked. Today he had a
young assistant with him, a greasy-haired boy with a
startling cast in his eyes and an earring.

"Tomasz," said Dr. Wojniakowski, pointing toward
Rej with his scalpel, "meet the best detective in Warsaw."

"I don't need flattery, Teofil," said Rej. "I need a
cigarette." Dr. Wojniakowski passed him his crumpled
pack of Extra Mocne and Rej shook one out and lit it.
The smoke was so strong that he coughed and coughed,
and couldn't stop coughing.

"A man's cigarette," said Dr. Wojniakowski. "I've
taken the lungs out of Extra Mocne smokers. They look
like lumps of brown coal. So much tar in them you
could put them on the fire, and they'd burn for a week."

"What about my friend Iwona?" asked Rej. "Have
you finished your report on her?"

Dr. Wojniakowski nodded. "Obviously there were
no internal organs remaining, so it's impossible to de-
termine if she was stabbed or shot, but three of her ribs
were cracked, either by several hard punches or a beating with a stick. By the way, we found her pelvis and
her leg bones, they were deeper down in the ashes.
They don't tell us much, either, although I've sent the
whole lot off for bone-marrow analysis, in case she was
poisoned."

"What about her skull? Did you find that?"

"Not a sign of it. Someone cut her head off, with a
very sharp instrument."

"The Executioner?"

"Judging from the evidence of previous autopsies,
I'd say yes, almost certainly. I've examined her upper
vertebrae and her head was cut off with a single right-
handed blow, the same as all the others."

"Would you say that she was killed by the same knife as Jan Kaminski, and all the rest of the victims, or the same knife as Antoni Dlubak?"

Dr. Wojniakowski blew two long tusks of smoke out of his nostrils. "I don't understand the question," he said, uneasily.

"What do you mean, you don't understand the question? You said before that Dlubak was killed with a different knife than all of the other victims. You said the metal traces didn't match at all."

"Oh, that! That was a mistake! Two samples were switched."

Rej stared at him. "A *mistake*? What are you trying to tell me, Teofil?"

"It's nothing complicated. We had metal traces from Antoni Dlubak's neck, and on the same day we had metal traces from a stabbing in the student hostel on Narutowicza Square. They were side by side, waiting for spectroscopic analysis. They were accidentally mixed up, that's all."

"Teofil, when did your department ever accidentally mix up anything?"

"There's always a first time," said Dr. Wojniakowski, turning his face away.

Rej walked around the autopsy table so that he could confront him. "So what are you saying—that Antoni Dlubak was killed by the same knife as all of the others?"

"It looks that way, yes."

"So if Witold Jarczyk can prove that Roman Zboinski killed Dlubak, we can assume that he killed all the rest of the victims, too?"

"Well, there's a problem with that, too."

"Oh, yes? What problem?"

"Jarczyk was on the phone to me early this morning. It seems that Zboinski has independent alibis for at least five of the murders, and his accomplices are prepared to testify that he couldn't have committed any of the others."

Rej stood and stared at Dr. Wojniakowski in silence. His assistant Tomasz shuffled his feet and gave an uncomfortable cough.

At last, Rej said, "Tell me the truth, Teofil."

"I'm telling you the truth! Why shouldn't I? Antoni Dlubak was probably killed with the same knife as the rest of the Executioner's victims, and if Zboinski can establish that he didn't kill any of the others, then the likelihood is that he didn't kill Dlubak, either."

"So what's happening now?"

"You'll have to talk to Witold."

"What's happening now, Teofil?" Rej snapped at him.

Dr. Wojniakowski shrugged, and crushed out his cigarette in a stainless steel kidney bowl. "They're taking a statement from Zboinski, then they're probably going to let him go."

"They're going to let him go? For Christ's sake, Teofil—even if we can't prove that he's the Executioner, even if we can't prove that he killed Dlubak, he shot Jerzy Matejko, blew his brains out in the middle of the street!"

"As I said, you'll have to talk to Jarczyk. But from what he was saying this morning, Matejko had his gun out and Zboinski's bodyguard was frightened for his life."

"I don't believe what I'm hearing," said Rej. "First you mix up the slides, then Zboinski has a whole sheaf of alibis, then you're trying to tell me that those bastards shot Matejko in self-defense."

Dr. Wojniakowski stared down at the green-swirled linoleum floor and said nothing. Rej came up close to him and said, very softly, "How much are they paying you, Teofil?"

Dr. Wojniakowsi quickly looked up. There was an

expression on his face that Rej had never seen before—defeat, and shame, but desperation, too.

"It isn't only the money," he said.

"How much?" Rej repeated. He was standing so close to Dr. Wojniakowski that he could smell his breath, cigarettes and peppermints.

"You know about my sister, she's in the nursing home. It's been very hard to make ends meet. They said they'd help to make her better—or, if I didn't agree to that—"

Rej looked as if he had put a bad mussel in his mouth. "I know. They'd help to make her very much worse."

"Come on, Stefan. You know what these people are like."

"Yes, I know what they're like. And I know that they only get away with it because people like you won't stand up to them."

"Would *you?*" hissed Dr. Wojniakowski. "Would *you*, if they threatened Katarzyna?"

Rej looked down at the dead girl lying on the autopsy table. Her lips were blue, her fingernails were black. There were freckles on her thighs, and three bruises that looked like thumbprints. Her eyes were closed, but they looked as if they might open at any moment. But common sense told him they wouldn't; and that whoever she once had been, she was gone now, and lost forever.

He stroked her hair with the back of his hand, and while he was stroking it, he said, still very softly, "I don't suppose you might be kind enough to give me some indication as to who they were? These people?"

Dr. Wojniakowski gave a small, quick shake of his head.

"I could sort them out for you," said Rej. "No questions asked."

"No," said Dr. Wojniakowski. "They're out of your league. You'd just be asking for trouble, that's all."

"I'm a police officer," Rej reminded him. "Nobody is out of my league."

"Your superiors are out of your league. Nadkomisarz Dembek, for example."

"What does that mean?"

"It means, Stefan, that you're on your own. It means that you're swimming against the tide. You always were stubborn. You never knew when to call it a day. Forget Zboinski. Forget the Executioner. Enjoy your suspension. Go fishing. Go to the Teatr Wielki and listen to some opera."

Rej was filled with such rage that he could barely speak. He jabbed his finger on the side of the autopsy table as if he were going to make a point, he jabbed it again and again, but he couldn't find the breath, and he couldn't find the words. In the end, he turned around, and pushed his way out through the swing doors, past the portrait of Marie Sklodowska-Curie, and along the corridor toward the stairs.

Dr. Wojniakowski came out after him, and called, "Stefan! Stefan, stop!"

Rej stopped at the head of the stairs. The thin light that filtered down from the clerestory windows made him look old, and haggard, and very gray.

"I'll deny it, Stefan, every single word!"

Rej looked at him, and felt a sadness that Dr. Wojniakowski would never understand. The terrible sadness of losing a friend, because of principles. The terrible sadness of being right; and of never giving in; but of being powerless, too. His ex-wife had always accused him of being weak, but she didn't know the difference between weakness and justice.

He stood there in his crumpled summer slacks and his jazzy red-and-yellow short-sleeved shirt, and for a moment he felt beaten. But then he thought of Sarah, and how Sarah never gave in, in spite of being a woman in a man's world, having to get up every morning and face up to prejudice and bullying and suggestive remarks. He thought of the cushions in front of the fire, in the cottage in Czerwinsk, and the roundness of her breasts.

He went down the stairs, and the sharp-faced woman was sitting in reception, pecking away at her word-processor. He stopped by the counter and stared at her.

"I'm leaving now," he announced. "You're supposed to know that I've gone. Security."

She stared back at him, her mouth pinched. "Very well, then. Goodbye."

He waited, and waited. Eventually, she managed to say, "Sir," and he left, without a word.

He walked into his office and found Jarczyk with his feet on his desk, drinking coffee and laughing with two of his junior officers. As soon as Rej came in, the laughter stopped, and one of the younger officers suddenly remembered that he ought to be checking up on a Romanian car registration plate. The other retreated into a corner by the filing cabinet.

"Stefan!" said Jarczyk. "Can't stay out of the office, can you?"

"I'm trying to," said Rej. His voice was dry with tightly-contained anger, and Extra Mocne tobacco. "But I hear that you're letting Roman Zboinski go free."

Jarczyk let out a nasal whinny, and tried to challenge Rej with his eyes. "We didn't have any choice, did we? You said yourself that the evidence was far too slim."

"I did, yes, you're absolutely right. Because I never thought for one single moment that Roman Zboinski was the Executioner, and neither did you. You thought you could sweep all of those killings under the carpet, just because Zboinski chopped one man's head off."

"It turns out that he didn't chop *anybody's* head off," Jarczyk retorted.

Rej banged his fist on the desk, and glared at Jarczyk as if he could incinerate him with a single, concentrated stare. "You know damned well that he did; and you know why he did it; and you know that Teofil was bribed and bullied into changing his forensic evidence; and for all I know you've been bribed and bullied too."

"Now look here!" Jarczyk shouted, swinging his feet off the desk and standing up. "You can't come in here making accusations like that! I had a good lead. I had every possible justification to make an arrest. At least I collared *somebody*, for Christ's sake! You didn't even have a suspect!"

"No, you're right," said Rej. "I didn't have a suspect. And the reason that I didn't have a suspect was because I didn't have sufficient evidence; and neither did you. But you organized a stake-out, didn't you, like some half-baked Hollywood movie, and you bungled it, you damn well bungled it, and you killed Jerzy Matejko. *You*! You killed him, you asshole, as much as if you blew his head off yourself!"

Jarczyk came storming around the desk, his fists raised, his eyes bulging with anger. "Come on, then!" he demanded. "Come on, then! Come on! Let's see who's the asshole, shall we?"

Rej faced him with his arms by his sides and didn't flinch. "How much?" he said, in the same quiet voice that he had used when he spoke to Dr. Wojniakowski.

"What the hell are you talking about, how much?" Jarczyk shouted at him.

"Just what I said. How much did they pay you to say that Roman Zboinski had a watertight alibi for five of those murders?"

Jarczyk flourished his fists; but then he realized that Rej wasn't going to put up any kind of a fight, and slowly lowered them. He was sweating, and his cheeks were burning crimson. "I don't know what you're trying to imply, but nobody has paid me anything."

"Payments have been made," said Rej. "Payments, and threats. Carrots and sticks, they call it."

"I don't know anything about that."

"Who gave Zboinski his alibis?"

"Independent witnesses . . . people who saw him out and about. The Zebra Club, he's always there. Sometimes the Valdi, on Piekna Street."

"That was good work, Witold. And quick, too. How many witnesses did you manage to find?"

"Several. What's it to you? You're off this case."

"No, I'm not. The day you killed Jerzy Matejko, you gave me an open invitation to come back on this case, and I'm never going to be off it, ever, until it's solved, and I find out what the truth is, or else I die."

"Christ, you're over-dramatic," said Jarczyk, pacing backward and forward.

"You've taken money," Rej told him. "If you hadn't taken money, you wouldn't be so agitated."

Jarczyk stopped pacing and took a deep breath. "Listen to me, Rej. I made a mistake. Roman Zboinski didn't kill any of those people. He may have killed Dlubak, but you try proving it. There's no forensic, and nobody's saying anything, except some small-time car thief who may or may not have seen one of Zboinski's runners take Dlubak away. It's all hypothetical!"

"How much?" Rej repeated. In the corner, the junior officer had pressed himself against the wall, desperate not to get involved.

Jarczyk took three deep breaths. Then he said, "Are you going to repeat that accusation in front of Nad-komisarz Dembek?"

"I'll repeat it in front of the Pope, if you like."

Jarczyk said nothing for a while. Then he snapped his fingers at the junior officer, and flapped his hand at him to leave the room. When he had gone, Jarczyk said, "Listen, this is one of those situations where we have to turn a blind eye."

"Go on," said Rej. He reached into his pocket for his cigarettes and then he realized that he didn't have any.

"This is all tied up with the government . . . with foreign investment. There's millions of dollars involved. Antoni Dlubak was just a little boring clerk who got the idea that he was some kind of—I don't know, some kind of medieval knight, charging into battle against the evil dragons of international business. He found a technical irregularity at Vistula Kredytowy. They were writing off losses when they shouldn't have been writing off losses. No big deal: no investors suffered. Nobody lost any money. But of course Antoni Dlubak had to make it into a crusade."

"So he deserved to be tortured, and to have his head cut off? He asked for it?"

"It was unfortunate," said Jarczyk. "But it wasn't Roman Zboinski who did it, and nobody can prove that it was."

"I seem to remember you telling me that the sharp instrument that was used to torture Dlubak was the same baling hook that you found in Roman Zboinski's apartment."

"Mistake."

"He stuck it right through his goddamned cock, for God's sake!" Rej roared at him. *"How could that be a mistake?"*

"It was another baling hook. Just ask Teofil Wojniakowski."

"Another baling hook? I don't think I'll bother. Teofil has been fed with the same carrots that you have; and threatened with the same stick."

"Don't insult me, Stefan."

"I don't have to," said Rej. "You insult yourself. You insult your job. You insult your colleagues, and you insult your friends. You insult me."

Jarczyk said nothing, but kept pulling at his face as if he expected the skin to tear off, like it did in horror movies.

"How much did they pay you?" Rej demanded.

"Why? Are you jealous, because they didn't make an offer to you?"

"How much, Witold?"

Jarczyk couldn't help smirking. "More than you'll make in the next ten years. That's how much."

"So who was it?" asked Rej.

Jarczyk let out a loud, false laugh. "They always said you were obstinate, and they were right! Dogged, determined, they always allowed you that much. You plodded and you plodded and you got your man. It didn't matter that it took you six months to make a case that most of us could wrap up in six days."

Rej was about to bellow back at him; but then he clenched his fists, and took a deep, snorting breath, and decided not to Jarczyk was right, in a way. He *was* stupid, not to have realized who was paying off Dr. Wojniakowski, and who was paying off Jarczyk, and who knew how many other city and government officials. He had guessed, of course—he had *known*, really—but he had a natural aversion to jumping to conclusions, and a deep suspicion of "hunches." A long time ago, he had shot a young skinny student in front of the statue of St. John of Nepomuk, close to Bankowy Square, based on a "hunch," and he had stood alone waiting for an ambulance while the young men bled across the sidewalk, and a crowd gathered all around, and he had known that he was wrong.

Who would have arranged for an exorcism on the site of the Senate Hotel, if they hadn't known that Roman Zboinski was going to walk free? After all, if the Executioner had been caught, and imprisoned, why bother? Who had the power to use Senate's contingency account as a way of laundering Roman Zboinski's profits? And who was determined to bring down "that Lewandowicz bitch," and make himself rich, both at the same time?

Of course Rej couldn't have known that he was echoing the words of the old lady who had approached Jan Kaminski, trying to catch a bus to Czerniakowska. But he said, bitterly, "It's worse than the old days."

* * *

He was half way across the lobby when Roman Zboinski appeared, surrounded by police officers and bodyguards. The lobby echoed with footsteps; but nobody spoke. Zboinski wore a gray Hugo Boss jacket slung over his shoulder, a black shirt, and flappy black trousers. He looked tired and angry; as if his boulder-like face had been beaten overnight with a quarry hammer.

Nadkomisarz Dembek flanked him on one side; his lawyer on the other. They marched toward the revolving doors at a steady, relentless pace, but Rej stepped out and stood right in front of Zboinski, so that he was forced to stop.

"What's this?" Zboinski demanded. "You told me I was free to go. What's this shit doing?"

Rej said, "This shit is reminding you that you may escape the police, but that you'll never escape what's coming to you."

"Some kind of threat, is it?" Zboinski growled. "Get him out of my way."

"Take it from me, Roman," said Rej, "I'll never get out of your way. I'm going to haunt you, right up until the day you die."

"I want to complain!" Zboinski shouted. "I'm free, yes? I'm innocent, yes? Tell this asshole to get out of my way!"

Two officers moved toward him, but Rej stopped them both with a stare that equaled Sarah's notorious ray. He stepped right up to Zboinski and stabbed him in the chest with his finger.

"You listen to me, you fucker. I know who you are, and I know what you've done. I'm going to get you one day, when you're least expecting it. So if I were you, I'd spend the rest of my life being frightened."

"Of you?" Zboinski retorted. "Let me tell you some-thing about you, little old white-haired man; the day that I'm frightened of you, I'll kill myself, for being such a chicken-shit."

"I'm looking forward to it," said Rej.

Nadkomisarz Dembek came forward and said, "Come on, Stefan, this is all over now. We made a mistake, that's all. Mr. Zboinski is free to leave."

"He shot Matejko," said Rej. He made no attempt to move out of the way.

"How could I shoot?" Zboinski protested. "I didn't even have a gun!"

"You told your bodyguard to shoot him. That's the same fucking thing."

"I said nothing! This is insane! I said nothing!"

Rej seized hold of Zboinski's lapels and pulled him until their noses were only inches apart. It didn't matter to Rej that Zboinski was so much taller than he was: he was fire, he was justice, he was *gliny* and prokurator, both.

"I'm going to make you one solemn promise," said Rej; right in Zboinski's ear, so that nobody else could hear him. "One day soon, I'm going to kill you, or have you killed; and you won't know when to expect it. But I will. What Antoni Dlubak suffered, that's going to be nothing, compared to what happens to you. Baling hooks? I'm going to tear you to fucking pieces."

"You're insane," said Zboinski. He turned, in feigned amazement, to Nedkomisarz Dembek. "This man's insane! Does he still work here? I can't believe it!"

"He's, um, on suspension," said Dembek; and gave Rej a convulsive jerk of his neck, trying to indicate that he should stand aside.

Rej massaged his knuckles, as if he were considering whether to punch Zboinski or not. Zboinski glared at him, and kept on glaring at him, until he was jostled away.

At that moment, the revolving doors revolved, and the press came pushing in, manhandling their cameras and their microphones. Rej stepped away. He had delivered his promise to Roman Zboinski and he meant to keep it. He smiled at Zboinski; but the expression that Zboinski gave him in return was like a death mask. Rej couldn't help smiling even more broadly. He had always thought that there was no greater compliment than to make your worst enemy scowl.

Anna Pronaszka was one of the first television reporters into the lobby. She caught sight of Rej as he turned to leave and she lifted her microphone.

"Komisarz Rej—?" she began. But in some mysterious way she knew that he had been proved right, and that she had been proved wrong, and she lowered her microphone and watched him leave without saying a word. All she could think of asking him now was who cut his hair so ineptly; and where he had bought such a loud and terrible shirt.

ℜej went back home, opened the refrigerator, and looked for something to eat. All he could find were a few slices of salami, a withered apple and a yellowing segment of farmer's cheese. He decided against eating, and poured himself a beer. He went out onto the balcony, and sat down. The day was hot and dazzling, and the shadows had been filled in with India ink. The sound of children playing on the scrubby grass below reminded him of seagulls mewing on the Baltic coast, one summer, long ago, when his mother had taken him for a week's vacation. He didn't know where his father was: his father with his big iron-gray mustache, shaped like the cow catcher on an old-fashioned locomotive.

He hadn't sat there for more than a few minutes when the phone rang, and he had to go inside to answer it.

"Stefan? It's Sarah. Something's happened."

"What? You sound terrible."

"Marek saw a man going down into the sewers—on

Koszykowa I think it was. He called Clayton and the two of them followed him." She suddenly stopped, and sobbed, and said, "Clayton's been killed."

"You're not serious."

"Clayton's been killed, Stefan; and it was the Executioner. Marek's sure of it."

"I can't believe it. When did this happen?"

In bits and pieces, Sarah managed to tell him what Marek had told her. Then she said, "Marek *saw* the Executioner, he saw it with his own eyes. It came so close to him that it almost caught him. It was the same creature I saw in my dream, in Czerwinsk. It was exactly the same. The tiny white face, like a little doll; the big black cape."

For the first time in his life, Rej heard somebody say something completely preposterous, and thought to himself, *You're right, I believe you.* He believed now that the Executioner was something far more de- monic than Roman Zboinski could ever aspire to; something far more terrible and far more vengeful; and that it was still hurrying through the sewers, street by street, avenue by avenue, smelling out victims like some mindless bloodhound.

"I presume that Marek hasn't told the police yet," said Rej. "I was around at the station only about a half hour ago, and nobody said anything about it then."

"Poor kid—he's scared they're going to think that *he* did it."

Rej said, "Well—up until today, I would have told him to go ahead and report it, and not to worry. But something very odd is going on."

"What do you mean?"

"I mean that Roman Zboinski is going to be released this afternoon; no charge. Apparently there was a mix-up at forensics, and he couldn't have killed anybody, not even Antoni Dlubak. Not only that, the bastard who shot Jerzy is probably going to walk free, too. It suddenly turns out that he killed him in self-defense."

"Stefan, what's going on?"

"Somebody's been spending a great deal of money to persuade certain people to change their minds about Roman Zboinski; and those that weren't interested in money were offered something even more persuasive—like having their ears cut off."

Sarah was silent for a long time, and then she said, "You sound like you know who it is."

"I'm sure I know who it is. It's just a question of proving it."

"You're talking about Ben, aren't you?"

"Yes," said Rej. "I'm talking about Ben. Why do you think he arranged this exorcism? He knew right from the beginning that Jarczyk wouldn't be able to charge Zboinski with being the Executioner, or even of killing Antoni Dlubak. And he knew because he was going to make goddamned sure that nobody came up with any evidence, or any witness statements, or any proof whatsoever. My guess is that your Ben has been making a steady fortune out of laundering Zboinski's money, and he's not going to let anybody mess up a steady earner like that. Especially not you."

"He really wants to destroy me, doesn't he?" said Sarah. " 'That Lewandowicz bitch.' "

"Well, yes. That's the way I read it. He's going to hold his exorcism, and get Brzezicki and his men back to work, and you'll end up looking like the dithering female who couldn't get the job done. Senate will sack you, or demote you; and your Ben will carry on running his money-laundering racket, and probably dozens more rackets, too—all in the glorious name of Western enterprise."

"You're sounding like a communist," said Sarah.

"I *am* a communist. But I'm a police officer first of all."

"Just like Clayton," said Sarah. "He was eccentric. He believed in spirits, and things beyond. But he was a cop, too, wasn't he?"

"Are you all right?" Rej asked her.

"No," she said, "but I can manage. I *have* to manage."

He paused for a moment, and then he said, "Listen, you should be very careful with Ben Saunders."

"I'm always careful with Ben Saunders."

"I know. But be *particularly* careful. Has Vistula Kredytowy sent you your statements yet?"

"They promised to, but they didn't. I'm going around there later."

"Can we meet? I need to talk to Marek. I thought you might like to come along, too."

"Yes, I would. Let me call him, and arrange a rendezvous."

"You're sure you're all right?" Rej repeated.

"Come on, Stefan. I'm a big girl now. I can take care of myself."

There was a pause, and then Rej said, with a hint of regret in his voice, "Yes. Of course you can. I shouldn't have doubted it."

She walked briskly into the office and opened her briefcase. Irena came hurrying in after her, looking flustered. "Ben says he wants to see you."

"That's good. I want to see him. Tell him to come on up, would you?"

Irena said, "I don't think he's in the mood for that."

Sarah hung up her tailored linen coat and sat down at her desk. "I don't care what kind of a mood he's in. If he wants to see me, he knows where I am."

Irena said, "I'll try." Then, "Are those bruises on your face?"

"Yes," Sarah told her. "They're bruises."

"Ben has bruises, too. And a plaster on his nose."

"Precisely. And that's why *he* has to come and see *me*."

"All right," Irena nodded. She retreated to the door,

and was just about to go out when she turned and said, "How *was* your weekend?"

Sarah looked up and said, "Frightening. How was yours?"

She sorted through all her mail and all her papers. There was no sign of the promised bank statements from Vistula Kredytowy; although there was a long fax from Senate New York demanding to know why construction hadn't yet started, and a letter from Mr. Gawlak with a long list of questions about piles and stress and staircase dimensions. She was still reading it when her office door opened and Ben walked in, wearing shirtsleeves and Donald Duck braces, carrying a thick *mille-feuille* of computer printouts.

"Well, well," he said, dropping the printouts onto Sarah's desk, and dropping himself in a chair. Irena was right: he had two black eyes, a swollen red bruise on his cheek, and a plaster across the bridge of his nose. "I'm surprised you had the balls to come back in."

"Ditto," said Sarah, without looking up.

Ben said, "You know what your trouble is? You think you're a businesswoman; but the fact is that you're not very good at business, and you're not very good at being a woman, either."

"You're probably right," said Sarah, leaning back in her chair. "I'm too honest when it comes to money; and I'm too discriminating when it comes to men."

"There are the bank statements you wanted," Ben told her. "I want you to know that you caused us considerable embarrassment with Vistula Kredytowy. They're supposed to be our partners in this project; and we should treat them with courtesy and respect. Instead of that, you practically tell them to their faces that they're criminals."

Sarah looked at the sheaf of printouts as if Ben had dropped a box of week-old haddock on her desk. "I don't suppose there's the slightest discrepancy in any of those statements. I bet they all balance out exactly, credit for credit, loss for loss. I bet that none of them mentions shiploads of stolen BMWs, offloaded at Gdansk. I bet none of them accounts of convoys of Mercedes, driven through the Czech border; or top-of-the-range Toyotas, driven in from Berlin. I bet I could search through these statements for the rest of my life, but I'd never find any evidence of what you're up to."

Ben said, "You're demented. You know that? You're completely demented. Not only that, you're totally incompetent. As soon as I've got Brzezicki back to work, I'm going to have you kicked out of Eastern Europe so fast your eyes are going to water."

"So when are you holding this exorcism of yours?"

Ben jabbed a finger at her. "Don't you mock me, Sarah. All I'm doing is what you should have done right from the very start. If your work force believe that they're plagued by a devil, you give them a religious ritual. It's the only way to make them see sense."

"And what happens if your police force believe that they've caught a murderer? Do you give them money, in the hope that *they're* going to see sense?"

Ben stood up, and looked around Sarah's office. "You'd better enjoy yourself here today, Sarah, because this is the last day you're going to be sitting here acting like you're the Queen of Warsaw. By the way, where did you go over the weekend? New York were screaming for their weekly report and I couldn't contact you anywhere."

"I went to the country, not that it's any of your business."

"Not with that scruffy detective?"

"Yes, with that scruffy detective. And that scruffy detective is protective and graceful and twice the man that you'll ever be."

Ben curled his lip in what he must have imagined was a look of pity. "Gone native, huh? I don't think New York will take very kindly to that, either. 'Senate executives are expected to maintain cordial but detached personal relationships with the inhabitants of the countries in which they are employed. Senate executives represent Senate International and as such should be models of decorum.' That's what the rules say. Not very decorous, is it, humping Warsaw's answer to Columbo? Anyway—" he added, checking his wristwatch—"that's all pretty academic now, isn't it? Are you going to come to the exorcism tonight? Eleven o'clock. I'm sure you don't want to miss all the fun."

"I'll come," said Sarah tightly.

"Good. And bring your Polack policeman, too. There's nothing like going out with a bang."

He went, leaving the door open. Her eyes filled with tears. Not because Ben had enraged her, he hadn't, she was too contemptuous of him for that. They were tears for Clayton which she hadn't wanted to let out until Ben had gone, in case he thought that he had really hurt her.

She spent two hours going through the bank printouts, and as she suspected they were in immaculate order. In fact they were so perfectly balanced that they couldn't have been real. There was no sign of any large sums of money coming from unexplained sources; no sign of suspiciously heavy losses; no writeoffs; no mysterious expenses. Whoever had doctored the accounts had expertly removed all trace of Roman Zboinski's money as if it had never existed.

Sarah left the office and took a taxi to Vistula Kredytowy, carrying the printouts with her. She went up the steps, and across the marble-floored reception area, with its bronze statue of a mermaid holding a sword in one hand and a balance in the other. The receptionist called out, "Madam! Madam, can I help you?" but she ignored him and walked right through to the corridor at the back, and into Piotr Gogiel's office.

He was talking to a customer on the phone, but she

threw the printouts onto his blotter, and said, "Are you responsible for this?"

Piotr Gogiel said a hurried goodbye and put down the receiver. "I don't understand what you mean. This is your bank statement, that's all."

"Is this what Antoni Dlubak died for? This treachery?"

"Please—it's nothing to do with treachery, Ms. Leonard. It's—the way that the statement came out."

"Did Ben pay you off, too? Is that it? Or did he threaten to cripple you for life?"

Piotr Gogiel said nothing, but sat behind his desk looking miserably at the printouts, swallowing and swallowing as if he had a biscuit-crumb stuck in his throat. Sarah leaned forward on his desk and stared him directly in the face. He kept trying to look back at her, but he couldn't.

"I'm going to find out who did this," said Sarah. "I'm not going to rest until I do. And when I do, the worst torture that Roman Zboinski is capable of handing out will seem like a friendly scratch on the back compared with the pain that I'm going to inflict. And that's a promise."

Piotr Gogiel said, "I'm sorry, that's all I can say."

"Oh, you're sorry. Well, I suppose that's a start. Now where's that greaseball Studnicki?"

"He had to go to Brussels . . . some kind of financial meeting."

"All right. But when he gets back, you can tell him what I just said to you."

Piotr Gogiel stood up and walked with her to the door. He was perspiring with heat and embarrassment. "I want you to know . . . I didn't want things to happen this way. But sometimes you don't have a choice."

"Mr. Gogiel, you always have a choice. One is marked 'wrong' and the other is marked 'right.' "

"It isn't as easy as that, Ms. Leonard. I have a wife, and a family. I have people who depend on me."

"I thought *I* could depend on you. But never mind. It's your decision, isn't it?"

She left the bank, her shoes rapping on the floor. Piotr Gogiel watched her leave, glumly mopping his face with his handkerchief.

16

Sarah and Rej met Marek shortly after five o'clock, at a corner table in the Welcome Bar. There were dark circles under his eyes but he was jumping with nervous energy. The waitress brought them two cups of strong coffee and a Russian tea for Sarah.

Marek described how he and Clayton had followed Mr. Okun down into the sewers, and how the Executioner had caught up with them, right underneath Ujazdowskie Avenue.

Rej said, "I didn't see it, when it cut off my finger, but it sure sounds the same."

"It's *exactly* the same as my nightmare," said Sarah. "I was absolutely terrified, but I couldn't wake up."

"Do you think it was human?" asked Rej.

"I don't know," said Marek. "It had a human face, but so small. I thought it was a mask, at first, but it couldn't have been. It came after me so damn *fast*, man—I don't know how I got out of that grating."

"Do you think that it could have been this Mr. Okun of yours—changed, somehow?"

"I don't understand what you mean by 'changed.' "

"Well, *changed*, you know, like a werewolf. A what-do-you-call-it: a shape-shifter."

Marek shook his head. "Clayton definitely saw his

shoe marks leading into that narrow tunnel, and that must have meant that he was ahead of us. The Executioner came up from behind. Anyway, they were so completely different. Mr. Okun's skinny. Just a skinny white-haired old man. The Executioner—it's huge."

"What do we do now?" asked Sarah, sipping her tea.

"I think we ought to pay Mr. Okun a visit."

"He's *very* creepy," warned Marek. "Even his next-door neighbor is scared of him."

"How do you know?"

"I talked to him. He said that Mr. Okun was 'one of von dem Bach's bastards.' He said his name wasn't Okun at all, and that he didn't speak Polish when he was alone in his apartment. He was 'one of *them*,' that's what he said."

" 'One of von dem Bach's bastards?' Are you absolutely sure?"

Marek nodded. "He kept on shouting that Mr. Okun was a criminal, and 'one of *them*.' "

"Von dem Bach?" said Rej. "He really mentioned von dem Bach? This could be the best connection yet!"

"What do you mean?" asked Sarah.

"Von dem Bach was the German general who was given the job of putting down the Uprising. He hated Poles so much he was almost like a maniac. He hunted down every man, woman and child who had anything to do with the Polish Home Army, and he shot them, thousands of them. There's one other thing—he was particularly furious when the Home Army managed to escape through the sewers. He was the one who filled drainpipes with barbed wire, and dropped tear gas and burning gasoline down manholes, even though he knew there were children down there. He had another invention, too: the *Taifun-Gerat*. It was an apparatus for pumping gas into the sewers and then setting it off in a massive explosion. The 'typhoon machine.' "

Sarah said, "You don't think that Mr. Okun could

still be hunting down the Home Army . . . all these years after the war?"

"Why not? The Jews are still looking for Nazis."

"Clayton wasn't a member of the Home Army, though, was he?" said Marek. "Why do you think the Executioner killed him?"

"He was a threat," said Rej, "just like you were." He finished his coffee. "Let's go see what Mr. Okun has to say for himself."

"Are you sure it's going to be okay?" asked Marek, doubtfully.

"Don't worry." said Rej. "There's two of us. There's only one of him."

They crossed the street and Marek guided them to the entrance of Mr. Okun's apartment building. Marek pressed the bell-push marked "Gajda" and they edgily waited for an answer. After almost a minute, Marek rang again; but there was still no answer.

"Maybe he went out," Sarah suggested.

"I don't think so. He's in a wheelchair, and he's really old and sick. Maybe he switched off his hearing-aid."

Marek pressed the bell-push again and again, but without success. After a while, Rej said, "Which bell do you think could be Okun's?"

"He lives right next door. I guess it's either the bell directly above it or the one directly below it."

Rej pushed both of them.

"What are you going to say if he answers?" said Sarah, wide-eyed.

"I'll say, 'Are you Mr. Okun? You've just won a two-week vacation to sunny Auschwitz.' "

"No, seriously."

"I don't think I'm going to have to say anything," Rej told her. "There's nobody in."

"What do we do now? Wait?" asked Marek. "That waitress is beginning to think that I've moved in."

But Rej was already working on the lock. Within six

or seven seconds, he had sprung the levers, and the doors opened. "What we do now is, we go take a look at Mr. Okun's apartment while he's out."

"What if he comes back?"

"Then we'll make up some stupid excuse; or hit him. How should I know?"

They crowded into the elevator and Marek pushed the button for 3. The elevator wearily dragged them up to the third floor, and they climbed out. The corridor seemed even gloomier than Marek remembered it, and there was a strong, unpleasant smell.

"Which one's Okun's?" asked Rej, and Marek pointed to the door at the very far end of the corridor. They walked toward it, but as they passed Mr. Gajda's door, the smell became so strong that Rej stopped where he was, and looked the door up and down.

"Is that a gas leak?" asked Sarah, with her hand cupped over her face. "It smells totally disgusting."

Rej said, "You'd better go back downstairs. I think we've got ourselves a problem."

"What kind of problem?"

"That smell . . . I think that something could be dead in there. Maybe it's just a dog or a cat, but I'll have to take a look."

"If you're going to take a look then I want to take a look too."

"Believe me, Sarah, you'll regret it. Why don't you and Marek go back outside until I've seen what this is. Otherwise, I promise you, you're going to lose your lunch at about twenty times the speed that you ate it."

"I can take it."

"All right," Rej shrugged. "But if you do feel sick, make sure you're pointing the other way. I just washed and pressed these trousers."

He took out his lockpicks again, and opened Mr. Gajda's door. A steady, warm draft blew out of it, sickly with the smell of corrupted flesh. Marek gave a cackling retch, and said, "Sorry," and had to turn away.

Rej took out his crumpled pack of Kleenex and covered his face. Sarah had only a small lacy handkerchief in her bag, but she took it out and sprayed Giorgio perfume on it, and held it to her nose.

"You don't have to do this," said Rej, in a muffled voice.

"I want to, Stefan. I've come this far."

"All right, then. It's your funeral."

They entered the hallway. It was cramped and dingy, and crowded with coats and walking-sticks and old, bunion-distorted shoes. Rej nudged open the kitchen door. The kitchen was better lit, because it had a frosted-glass window facing to the south, but the sunlight revealed how filthy it was in the way that old people's kitchens become filthy, through semi-blindness, and lack of strength, and forgetfulness. Rej glanced around it, without saying a word. Then he stepped across the corridor and opened the living room door.

The living room was shabby, too, although there were some homely touches like a hand-woven blanket over one of the chairs, and a gilded statuette of the Virgin Mary on the mantelpiece over the electric fire, and a reproduction of a painting by Jacek Malczewski, called *Christ Washing His Disciples' Feet*, although it was a woman in a white blouse who was doing the washing, and the disciple had the abstracted, sombre look of a careworn father, or a soldier returned from the war.

Rej paused for a moment, looking, listening. Then he went further along the corridor to the bedroom; and by his stiff-legged movement, and the jerky way in which he opened the door, Sarah could tell that he knew what he had to expect. Except that she didn't expect it: a torrential swarm of fat green blowflies, thousands of them, pouring out of the open doorway and pattering against the walls. Rej stepped back, and

swatted at them, but all Sarah could do was shut her
eyes and cover her hair with her hands.

"Oh, God!" she cried out. "Oh, God, no!"

Blowflies tapped against her hands and dropped from
her sleeves and crawled on her shoulders. One flew
right into her lips, and she spat and furiously wiped
her mouth with her handkerchief. But at last the storm
began to subside, with flies on the ceiling and flies on
the walls, and more flies circling around the kitchen.
Rej didn't even look back at Sarah, but stepped into
the bedroom alone. Sarah swallowed, and felt as if she
were swallowing flies, but she knew that she had to
go, too. She was never going to let Ben bring her down;
she was never going to let Piotr Gogiel cheat her; and
she was never going to let Stefan do something which
she couldn't do.

She walked down to the bedroom, and forced herself
to go through the door. Her eyes were open, but at first
she was blind with panic; and even when the room did
come into focus, she couldn't understand what she was
looking at.

A double bed stood against the right-hand wall, with
a pale green coverlet slewed across it. Above the
wooden bedhead, the wall was literally hosed in blood,
all the way up to the picture-rail, and beyond the
picture-rail, and across the ceiling. The coverlet, too,
was covered in massive, dark-brown stains, all dried
now, like maps of terrible continents, and islands, and
places where no sane man would ever dare to travel.

In the middle of the bed lay two glistening black
mounds, side by side. They seemed to move and glitter;
and it was only gradually that Sarah could see what
they were. Two headless human bodies, smothered in
blowflies, thousands and thousands of feeding, egg-
laying, green-glistening blowflies.

Vomit rose up in her throat, sharpened with bile; but
with an effort she managed to swallow it back down.
Rej was standing at the end of the bed, looking at her.

He seemed to be transformed; a different kind of Stefan altogether.

"Somebody's cut off their heads," he said.

Sarah couldn't do anything but nod, and nod, and try to stop herself from being sick. She was perspiring so much that she could feel it trickling down the small of her back.

Rej flapped away another fly. "Don't tell Marek this, but this could have happened because of him. If Mr. Okun knew that Gajda had identified him as one of von dem Bach's SS men . . . and then Marek and Clayton chased him down the sewers . . . well, he could have decided to shut Gajda up."

"Are you going to call the police station?" asked Sarah, her voice muffled behind her handkerchief.

"In a minute. I want to take a look in Okun's apartment first, although I'll bet you ten million zlotys that he's gone. Old zlotys, that is, in case he hasn't."

He walked around the bed, and as he did so, his toe accidentally chipped against the left-hand leg. Instantly, the blowflies billowed up from both of the bodies in a thick, noisy cloud, and for a split-second Sarah could see what they really looked like. Headless, horribly anonymous, their stomachs distended with gas. Every inch of them was bobbly-white with flies' eggs, and their crotches and armpits were alive with maggots.

Then, like a glittering veil, the blowflies covered them up again, and preserved the modesty of their awful death.

Sarah managed not to be sick. She didn't know how. But when she reached the corridor she went directly to the window and pushed it open, and took a deep, thankful breath. Marek came up behind her and laid his hand on her shoulder. "They're dead, huh?"

"Yes," she nodded. "They're dead. A man and a woman, both with their heads cut off."

In a surprisingly mature and gentle movement, Marek drew her hair away from her face. "Are you sure you're all right?"

"It was my choice," said Sarah. "I knew that it was going to be bad. I just wanted to face up to it."

Rej came up the corridor jingling his lock-picks. He was trying to appear nonchalant, but he too was looking ashen. "Let's take a look into Okun's apartment. Maybe it'll give us some clues."

Deftly, he opened the door, and they all stepped inside. They could see at once that the apartment was empty. There was no furniture, no pictures on the walls, no curtains, no lampshades, nothing. All that was left of Mr. Okun's tenancy were some rusty circular marks on the pea-green carpet where his chairs had stood, and a tiny triangle of paper stuck to the opposite wall. Rej walked across the room, pulled out the thumbtack that was holding it, and turned the little piece of paper this way and that. On one side it had a fragment of dark-blue border, and a beige-and-white pattern that could have been streets, on a street map. On the other side, the words *"Powstanie Warszawskie postawilo ponownie w koncowej fazie wojny przed swiatem problem Polski . . ."*

"This is a part of a map of the Warsaw Uprising," said Rej. "You can buy them in all of the tourist shops."

Marek was in the kitchen. "He's left most of his food behind. Sugar, coffee, black cherries in syrup. Phff, this milk's off."

"So where has he gone, I wonder?" asked Sarah.

"More to the point," said Rej, "who the hell is he?"

Sarah paced around the room, looking for anything that might give them a clue. She found a single white shirt-button; a used postage-stamp with a picture of the Pope on it; a small spring; and a desiccated toenail clipping.

She went into the bathroom—and there, in a cloudy glass, was a yellow plastic toothbrush with widely-splayed bristles. "I've suddenly thought of something," she said. "Madame Krystyna managed to use Zofia's doll to show us where Zofia used to live. Maybe if we gave her this toothbrush?"

Marek came across and wrinkled up his nose at it. "You're not serious, are you? That's disgusting."

"It worked before; why shouldn't it work again?"

"But Zofia's doll, that was something she loved . . . something personal."

"What's more personal than somebody's toothbrush?"

"I don't know," said Rej. "Zofia was dead, and the spirits wanted to help us. So far as we know, Okun's alive; and I can't see *him* being very popular, especially with the spirits in Warsaw."

"All the more reason for them to help us to track him down."

"Well . . ." said Rej, taking the toothbrush between finger and thumb. "I guess we can only try."

Marek said, "What are we going to do about them? Mr. Gajda, and that woman? We can't just leave them there."

"No, we're not going to," said Rej. "We're going to the nearest call-box and make an anonymous phone call. I don't want Nadkomisarz Dembek to know that I'm involved. I'm supposed to be on temporary leave, remember? I don't want Dembek making it permanent."

"You're still coming to the exorcism tonight, though, aren't you?" asked Sarah.

Rej gave her the grimmest of nods. "I wouldn't miss it for the life of me."

She called her father. In Chicago, it was only 9:30 in the morning, and he was still reading the morning paper. She could see him with her mind's eye, sitting on the porch at the back of the house, wearing his striped blue-and-white bathrobe, handsome in a slabby,

Jack Palance kind of way, his gray hair combed straight back from his forehead.

"Dad? It's Sarah."

"Sarah? Are you back in the States?"

"No, I'm still in Warsaw. Yes, I know it sounds clear. I'm sorry I haven't called for so long. How are you?"

"I'm fine, your mother's fine. We're taking a short vacation at the end of next week: we're going to Tampa to see your Aunt Clara."

"Dad—I called for a reason."

"You don't want to borrow money, do you? I thought you were loaded these days."

"No, it's nothing to do with money. It's something I'm trying to find out. You were in the AK, weren't you, the Polish Home Army?"

There was a short silence. "What suddenly brought this up?" her father asked her.

"I know you don't like to talk about the war. But something's been happening here in Warsaw, people have been murdered, and the police think it may be connected with the Uprising."

"What does Clayton think about it?"

"He—ah—Clayton thinks the same."

"How's he getting on, by the way? He's a great character, isn't he? Clayton and me, we go way back."

"He's fine. He's out of town right now, doing some research."

"Well, you have him call me, soon as he gets back."

"Okay, I'll do that," Sarah said sadly. She didn't want to tell him yet that Clayton had been killed. It would upset him far too much—and, besides, the police hadn't even recovered his body yet, if they ever could.

"So, what is it you want to ask me?" said her father. She heard him cup his hand over the receiver, and say to her mother, "It's Sarah . . . she just wants to ask me something. I'll put her on in a minute."

Sarah said, "You ran messages, didn't you, down through the sewers?"

"That's right. Mainly I used to take them from Stare Miasto, that's the Old Town, right along the main sewer that runs under Krakowskie Przedmiescie, and out at Warecka, in the town center. Sometimes I went as far as Marszalkowska . . . right underneath that hotel of yours, I shouldn't wonder."

"The Germans tried all different ways of stopping you, didn't they, like gasoline down the sewers, and blocking them with barbed wire?"

"Smoke they used, too. Thick black smoke. Once I nearly died from breathing in smoke."

"Dad—was there anything else they used? Like somebody specially trained to hunt you down?"

This time the silence was even longer. "I don't know, Sarah. Those were terrible days, and they're best forgotten."

"This is important, Dad. This is really important. If I don't find out about this, I may lose my job."

"How can this have anything to do with your job? This all happened fifty years ago."

"I can't tell you now, but please."

"Well . . ." said her father, with obvious reluctance. "I never saw it . . . I only heard about it. The Uprising started on August 1, but by the middle of the month the Germans had pushed us right back into the Old Town. We tried to join up with the other insurgents in the town center. Our 'Zoska' battalion actually managed to do it. But the rest had to escape through the sewers—nearly four and a half thousand of them, and that's when we started to hear stories."

"Go on," Sarah urged him. "What kind of stories?"

"Maybe the older men made them up to frighten us messenger-boys. As if we weren't frightened enough! Maybe they invented this thing to make sure that we ran our errands as quickly as we could. As if anybody would dawdle down those sewers! The way they told it, this thing had first appeared after the Germans took the last building in which the Home Army were holding out, in Ochota—60 Wawelska Street, that was a famous address! Most of the insurgents managed to get through the sewers safely, back to the town center. But a few of the stragglers didn't make it.

"The last man to come out of the sewers said that he and his friends had been chased through the sewers by something dark. He didn't know what it was, but he said that his friends had all been killed. The next day a party of volunteers went back to look for them, and found them with their heads cut off. After that, it was supposed to have happened again, and again. Usually, there were no witnesses—or none that survived. But occasionally we'd hear these reports that men had been found beheaded, and that something dark had hunted them down. Once or twice, people said that they had seen its face, this thing, but I expect they were pulling our legs. They said that it looked like a child, almost like an angel, or a saint, so we took to calling it the Tunnel Child. Of course, we surrendered on October 2, and that was the end of that. I never heard about the Tunnel Child, ever again."

"Do you think it could have been real?"

"I don't know. But it scared me, all the same. I had nightmares about it for years and years. I kept seeing this tiny white face and this huge black body, and it was chasing me through the sewers, night after night."

"Thanks, Dad," said Sarah. "I didn't mean to upset you."

"I only get upset because I think of all the good people who died. Eighteen thousand insurgents, all dead; and six thousand badly wounded. What was far worse, 180,000 civilians were killed. Can you imagine that many people, if they stood in the street outside your apartment?"

"I'm sorry, Dad."

"Oh, come on . . . I don't want to start getting morbid. But you're a Pole, too. Once in a while, you should remember the people who fought for you."

He passed Sarah over to her mother, who clucked at him for talking about such depressing things. Sarah chatted for a while about her new apartment, and told her that everything was well; but it was difficult for her to concentrate. She kept thinking of the pale, child-like face that had pursued her father through so many nightmares, and which was now pursuing her.

When she was finished, she called Irena and asked her to go to the Marriott Hotel, pack Clayton's belongings, and settle his account. She hung up, and gave Clayton a silent apology for treating him as if he had simply ceased to exist; but she promised him a proper funeral later.

At eleven o'clock that night, the Senate Hotel site on Marszalkowska was brightly lit. Three police cars were parked outside, but the police had only been called to keep sightseers away, and they were standing around laughing and smoking. Rej parked half way up the sidewalk, and a policeman sidled over to move him on. Rej showed his badge, and snapped, "Take that dog-end out of your mouth. You're supposed to be a law officer."

"Yes, komisarz. Sorry, komisarz."

"Slobs," Rej growled, helping Sarah out of the car.

They entered the site through the door in the hoarding. Nothing had been done since the three German workers had been killed, and the rough, brick-strewn soil was already overgrown with nettles and dock-leaves. Ben was already there, in a dramatic black Armani suit with flappy trousers. So was Jacek Studnicki, his hair shinning in the lights; and two other executives from Vistula Kredytowy. Over to one side, to Sarah's consternation, stood Roman Zboinski, surrounded by four of his shell-suited bodyguards. He grinned at Sarah when he saw her, his mouth opening up like a fissure in a limestone cliff, and said something to one of his bodyguards. She couldn't lip-read, but from his expression she could have sworn that she saw him mouth something filthy.

Over to one side stood Jozef Brzezicki and his work-men, most of them dressed in their church-going clothes, although a few wore jeans. Brzezicki gave Sarah a solemn nod, and one or two of his workmen took off their hats. It was good to know that she was still respected somewhere.

Ben came over to Sarah and Rej with his hands in his pockets. He still had a sticking-plaster across the bridge of his nose. "Glad you could make it, sweet-heart," he said.

"What's *he* doing here?" asked Sarah, nodding to-ward Zboinski.

"He's a businessman. What sort of people do you think are going to be staying in this place, once we get it built?"

"Murderers? Racketeers?"

"What is it about women?" said Ben, ignoring Sarah and turning to Rej. "They have no sense of humor whatsoever. I mean, when was the last time a woman made you laugh, apart from taking her clothes off?"

"It sounded like a pretty good joke to me," said Rej. "Anyhow, thanks for inviting me. I never went to an exorcism before: it should be very enlightening."

Ben slapped him on the shoulder. "I don't know about enlightening, komisarz, but it might get these su-perstitious suckers back to work. Ah—here's my priest now."

Senate's public relations director appeared, ushering in front of him with some embarrassment an elderly, painfully thin priest. The priest had a cockatoo's-crest of fine white hair, and a sharp beak of a nose. "Father Xawery, over here!" called Ben, and the old man came limping slowly up to them. He wore a long traditional cassock, buttoned all the way down, and shiny with wear.

"Father Xawery has kindly agreed to conduct the exorcism for us," said Ben, as if an exorcism were nothing more exceptional than opening a new shop. He took a folded memo out of his pocket, and said, "He studied in Rome, didn't you, Father Xawery; and then under Father Souquat, S.J., Superior of the Jesuit house at Strasbourg. So he might be old—you're getting on a bit, aren't you, Father Xawery?—but he exorcised a young woman in Cracow who left bloody footprints wherever she walked, and a farmgirl in Biala Rawska who kept having fits and talking in voices, in languages that nobody could understand. Are you listening to this, Mr. Brzezicki? Our man here has a pretty damned impressive c.v. There won't be anymore devils on *this* site, not after tonight."

Father Xawery approached Sarah and clasped her hand with fingers that felt like dry bones loosely wrapped in tissue paper. His right eye was glass, and stared all the time at a fixed point just over Sarah's shoulder, so she kept thinking that somebody must be standing close behind her.

"Something is troubling you," he said. "I don't trouble you, do I?"

Sarah shook her head. "I'm worried about what's going to happen here tonight."

"Perhaps you don't believe in devils, is that it? Or are you doubtful about my experience and my reverence?"

"I don't question your reverence, Father. I just don't think that you know what you're up against. This isn't a question of young girls with epileptic fits; or children with Tourette's syndrome, swearing and scratching and jumping around."

"I realize that," said Father Xawery, still staring over Sarah's shoulder. "I realize that men were killed here,

by something unknown. I intend to confront that unknown being, and dismiss it."

"There you are, you see," said Ben, taking hold of
Father Xawery's arm. "A couple of prayers, a sprinkle
of holy water, and we can start construction again. This
way, Father. We've rigged up an altar for you, and
everything you wanted. One Bible, one silver bowl, one
medal of Saint Benedict, one picture of Our Lady of
Perpetual Succour."

"Thank you, excellent," said Father Xawery. "And
I've brought with me a special relic of my own. It was
given to me by Monsieur Ignace Spies, the mayor of
Selestat, and a man of great piety." He took a small
brown bag out from under his habit and held it up.
"The ring finger of Saint Gerard Majella, the great Re-
demptionist thaumaturge."

"Well, whatever," said Ben, and led Father Xawery
up to the makeshift altar—one of the tables from the
workmen's huts, draped in a white tablecloth with a
purple-and-gold border. Ben had found a large silver
cross which he had set in the center of it, along with
all the other sacramental objects that Father Xawery
had asked for. Father Xawery took out his stole, kissed
it, and draped it around his neck. Then he kissed the
Bible, and closed his eyes in prayer, to show that he
hated sin in his heart. Brzezicki and some of his men
closed their eyes, too.

Sarah glanced across at Roman Zboinski. He caught
her eye and gave her a slow, suggestive wink. Rej saw
it, too, but said nothing, and Sarah was amazed at his
self-control, in the presence of the men who had shot
his partner. She didn't know that he was grinding his
teeth.

At last, Father Xawery approached the edge of the
excavations, right above the broken sewer pipe, and
began to criss-cross the ground with holy water. "Remember not, Lord, our offenses, or the offenses of our

forefathers neither take Thou vengeance of our sins. Lord, hear our prayer."

"And let our cry come unto Thee," muttered the workmen, in response.

Now Father Xawery stood with his arms wide apart and his head thrown back. "I exorcise thee, most foul spirit, every coming in of the enemy, every apparition, every legion; in the Name of our Lord Jesus Christ be rooted out, and be put to flight from this place. He commands thee, Who has bid thee to be cast down from the highest heaven into the lower parts of the earth. He commands thee, Who has commanded the sea, the wind and the storms. Hear therefore, and fear, thou injurer of the faith, thou procurer of death, thou destroyer of life, kindler of vices, seducer of men, inciter of envy, origin of avarice, cause of discord, stirrer-up of troubles.

"Depart; be humbled and be overthrown; the wilderness is thy abode. There is no time now for delay. For behold the Lord thy Ruler approaches closely upon thee, and His fire shall glow before Him and shall go before Him; and shall burn up His enemies on either side."

Again, he sprinkled holy water on the ground. Then he began the "Our Father," starting it aloud, but continuing it secretly.

He had reached the words ". . . and deliver from us evil," which were spoken aloud, when one of the arc lamps burst, sending out showers of orange sparks. Then another burst, and another, until the entire excavation site was plunged into darkness.

"Brzezicki!" roared Ben. "Get those emergency lights working!"

Brzczicki said, "We don't have fuel for the generator."

"Well, replace those damned lamps then!"

"I don't know how many we've got. I'll have to go to the stores and look for them."

"I want some light in this place, God damn it! Somebody's going to get hurt!"

Everybody was jostling and pushing, so Sarah stayed close to Rej. Gradually, her eyes became accustomed to the dim glow from the streetlamps outside the site, and she could make out the white tablecloth and the shapes of the workmen's huts. For a moment, however, she thought she saw a large shadowy shape moving across the ground, just beside the mounds of rubble where Brzezicki's men were standing.

"Rej," she said. "Do you see that?"

"What? What am I supposed to be looking at?"

The shadow ran fluently across the makeshift altar, and then disappeared, swallowed into all the other shadows.

"I'm sure I saw something. It was like a shadow, only it wasn't."

"I think your imagination must be working overtime. Come on—why don't we get out of here? This is a farce."

"Lights, for God's sake!" Ben was bellowing. "We're trying to hold an exorcism here—a religious sacrament—not a goddamned slumber party!"

A single arc lamp was replaced, and snapped on. A ribald cheer went up from Brzezicki's workmen. Another lamp snapped on, and then another. The excavation site was lit up again, and Jozef Brzezicki walked back to his position, dusting his hands in satisfaction.

It was then that everybody realized that Father Xawery had disappeared. "Did you see him?" Ben demanded. "He was standing right here when the lights went out. He couldn't have been more than two meters away from me!"

Zboinski and his men approached the altar but Rej got there first and warned them off with a look. "You didn't see him moving, in the darkness?"

"How could I, komisarz? A priest in a power cut? That's like a crow in a coal mine."

Rej gestured everybody to stand away, and he slowly walked around the altar, looking for footprints. Just by the hem of the tablecloth he found the small brown bag containing Saint Gerard Majella's ring finger. He picked it up, and laid it on the altar next to the Bible. "I'll tell you one thing," he said, "he didn't leave on purpose. This relic is priceless."

He raised the side of the tablecloth, and Father Xawery's magical disappearance was solved. He was crouched in the dirt, his bony hands covering his head. At first Sarah thought that he was dead, but then Rej laid a hand on his shoulder. "It's all right, Father. You can come out now. Here—let me give you a hand."

Father Xawery crept out from under the altar on his knees and elbows. He hadn't looked very well when he first arrived, but now his face had the color and texture of a wasps' nest, papery and pale. He was trembling so violently that he could hardly stand, and Brzezicki had to come over and support him.

"So what happened to you?" Ben wanted to know. "The lights went out, it was dark, that's all. Don't tell me you spend your life exorcising demons, and you're afraid of the *dark*!"

Father Xawery stared at him in horror. "I *saw it!*" he wheezed. "*It was coming straight for me! It was going to kill me, cut off my head!*"

"Oh, here we go," said Ben, throwing up his hands. "Of all the exorcists in the whole damn world, I have to pick one who actually sees demons! Great!"

"Then you didn't believe in any of this?" Brzezicki challenged him. "You just set this up to make us feel that the devil had gone?"

"What's eating you?" Ben retorted. He squared up to Brzezicki and tapped the foreman's forehead with his finger. "Devils exist in here, Brzezicki. No place else. But I reckoned that if took an exorcism to persuade you bozos to get back to work, then I was more than happy to arrange it. Father Xawery's a genuine exorcist . . . what the hell more did you want?"

"I saw it!" gasped Father Xawery, swivelling his head from side to side, his single eye staring. "It came rushing right up to me! All I could do was hold up my hands and pray to God to spare me."

"Hiding under the tablecloth wasn't a bad move, either," said Ben.

Sarah took hold of Father Xawery's arm. "I saw it," he repeated. "In all my years . . . I saw it!"

"Are you all right?" Sarah asked him. "Maybe you'd like some tea."

Brzezicki said, "Why don't you let me take him home? He's had a serious shock. Listen, Ms. Leonard, why don't you come, too? I asked you before if you wanted to talk to my mother. She knows all about this thing . . . she can tell you, so long as you're prepared to listen."

"I've booked Father Xawery into the Solec-Orbis," Ben interrupted. "One of our people can drive him back."

"It's all right," said Sarah. "I think he'd be better off at Mr. Brzezicki's house. Besides, the Solec-Orbis isn't exactly grande-luxe, is it?"

"For God's sake, he's a priest. He's used to deprivation."

Brzezicki helped Father Xawery to gather up his things, and then he and Rej took his arms and half carried him off the excavation site.

"What happened?" asked a young girl newspaper reporter, as they stepped out onto the street.

"A short circuit, that's all," Rej told her. "Nothing to worry about."

"And the exorcism?"

"Father Xawery decided there was nothing to exorcise."

"So the site isn't possessed?"

"Only by Senate Hotels," said Sarah. "And we'll be restarting construction as soon as possible."

Ben and Roman Zboinski came out onto the street, too, and watched Rej and Brzezicki helping Father Xawery into Rej's car. Ben looked distinctly angry; but as they drove away from the kerb, Sarah turned around and saw Zboinski lay a reassuring hand on his shoulder.

$\mathfrak{I}$t was well after midnight by the time they reached Jozef Brzezicki's apartment, on the fifth floor of one of six identical blocks overlooking the Ursus tractor factory in Ochota. It was a bleak, windswept development, with floodlights glaring everywhere. Even though it was so late, Brzezicki's mother was still up, and she was more than happy to make Father Xawery a cup of tea, while Brzezicki poured vodka for everybody else.

Brzezicki's mother was a fat, cheerful woman with frizzy hair that looked as if it had been permed within an inch of its life; and a laugh like an organ bellows. "This poor priest," she said. "Look how thin he is!"

Her flat was crowded with massive Socialist-realist furniture, an immense sofa and bulbous chairs. Pieces of offcut carpet had been laid on top of the carpets to protect them from wear; and every table had a mat or a tablecloth or a plastic coaster to prevent it from being marked. Inside a large glass cabinet, her best tea service was arranged, as well as all the dried-up crosses she had been given on Palm Sundays for the past twenty years.

Most poignant of all, though, was an oval picture of a good-looking man with a big mustache and his hair extra-neatly parted, and a curiously defensive look on his face, as if he wasn't used to being photographed.

"Jozef's father," said Mrs. Brzezicki, picking it up. "He died in 1982. A good Solidarity man."

"I can see the resemblance," said Rej.

"So, how was the exorcism?" asked Mrs. Brzezicki,

sitting down on the sofa so close to Rej that he could feel her corsets.

"The exorcism, pfff!" said Brzezicki.

"I saw it," said Father Xawery, his single eye darting from one side of the room to the other. "I was saying the Our Father; and everything went dark; but then it came right at me, with its face shining and its knife held high . . . and I was never so frightened in my whole life. I held—I held up the relic—that was all I could do—and then it was gone. I hid myself under the table and I prayed like I've never prayed before."

"It was the Tunnel Child," said Brzezicki. "My mother said it was, as soon as she heard about Jan Kaminski. I know that it's hard to believe in such things; but it's true."

Sarah said, "I didn't believe you before, Mr. Brzezicki. But I believe you now. I talked to my father this afternoon, in Chicago, and he knew about it, too. My father used to carry messages for the Home Army during the war. He said that there was something in the sewers . . . something that used to chase them, and cut off their heads if it caught them."

Mrs. Brzezicki sat back and nodded. "My great-grandfather told me all about it. He helped to build the sewers and the drains. One day they were digging close to the city center and they found it buried in the ground. A child, but not a child. Dead, but not dead. They left it in their hut, but in the morning it was gone. Afterward, nine or ten people were killed in the middle of Warsaw, and their heads cut off. Some of the sewer workers said that they could hear children crying in the sewers, and the sound of somebody rushing along the pipes. They were always frightened to go down into the sewers alone, and who can blame them? But the next year, the killings suddenly stopped. My great-grandfather didn't know this for certain, but some of the old men said that they found the creature sleeping, whatever it was, child or monster or a bit of both, and they buried it, and stamped down the earth, and called in a priest to say the sacrament over it."

She patted Brzezicki on the thigh, and laughed. "This poor boy, I used to tell him such frightening stories, when he was little! It isn't surprising he thought of a devil, when Mr. Kaminski was killed. But I think he was right. It *is* a devil, and it's the same devil. They've been digging up Warsaw right, left and center—digging all these deep foundations. I think they've set him free, that's what they've done. Dug him out of the ground, without even realizing it. And that's who your Executioner is; or whatever you call him; your Tunnel Child."

Father Xawery rattled his teacup back into his saucer, and sat up straight. "I didn't realize what they were asking me to do. They offered me money, to restore my church, and said that they needed an exorcism. I imagined a bad smell, perhaps; or oozing walls; or something of that kind. I didn't realize it was *that*."

"You knew about it already?" asked Sarah.

"Of course. When the Germans invaded, I was a novice at Our Lady of Grace, Patroness of Poland. I'm afraid to say that I wasn't so holy in those days. I did everything I could to help the Home Army. I knew 'Karol' very well—Lieutenant-Colonel Rokicki. He was fighting to hold Upper Mokotow, but in the end he had to order an evacuation through the sewers—and it was then that we were attacked. That creature went through twenty or thirty at a time, cutting off their heads, and there was nothing that anybody could do to stop it."

He paused, and then he said, with infinite sadness, "I didn't go down the sewers. I surrendered to the Germans. Because I was a priest, they let me go. They beat me, and kicked me, and then they said, 'Go on . . . go away,' and I never felt so defeated in my life. They shot so many of my friends; and those they didn't shoot they sent to the camps."

Rej said, "That thing down the sewers, did you ever find out what it was?"

Father Xawery nodded. "After the war, I devoted many hours to trying to discover what the Tunnel Child might have been. It was like a dreadful fairy tale, you know; a terrible story to frighten your children; and nobody dared to speak of it; but I knew it was true. I went right back through all of the history books, and in the end I think I understood what it was. The trouble is, it seems impossible. Yet I think to myself, if Christ is capable of miracles, perhaps the Anti-Christ is capable of miracles, too."

Sarah laid her hand over his, and she felt as if she were laying her hand over history; as if his papery skin was a palimpsest of years gone by, rubbed out but never completely erased.

"In Checiny, in the 13th century, there was a small order of monks, the Recondites, who concerned themselves with discovering the mysteries of life. They were self-sufficient, and spoke to nobody, but there were many stories told about them; and the things that they did in search of earthly and supernatural knowledge. They were supposed to have joined two pigs together, to make one; and to teach a bull to walk on its hind legs. The legend says that the Recondites found a girl in a nearby village who was deaf-mute and malformed at birth. They bought the girl from her impoverished parents, and kept her at their monastery until she was old enough to conceive. Then they tried to impregnate her with a mixture of human semen and cockroaches, to see if a woman could give birth to a child that had the attributes of both species. Intelligent, like a human being. Reverent to God, and obedient to its masters. But possessed of enormous strength, and longevity, and a merciless turn of mind."

"You're not trying to say that it *worked*?" asked Rej.

"It's legend. We don't have any proof. And you know what it's like, trying to find historical evidence in Poland. The Swedes invaded, and took everything away. Then the Russians swept in, and took everything away. Then the Prussians, then the French, then the Russians again, then the Germans, then the Germans again, then the Russians. It's very difficult to trace such old documents."

"But you're saying it worked," Rej repeated.

Father Xawery nodded his head. "I believe that it did. I don't know how; but the Recondites had extraordinary scientific skills, far in advance of the age in which they lived. I believe it worked more than once; and that the Order of Recondites produced six or seven children who were human, but not quite human. Like humans, they could think. Like humans, they needed companionship, and someone to love. But just like cockroaches, they abhorred the light, and they needed to live in damp, dark places. They could bury themselves in the soil and they could hibernate for months. I don't know, perhaps they could hibernate for years, if you can believe that such a thing is possible."

"But how did they get into the Warsaw sewers?" asked Sarah.

"It all started in 1409. The Teutonic Knights heard stories that the Recondites were capable of working magic. They racked the monastery and killed all the monks. However, they spared the lives of these six or seven children, because they discovered that they would fight like demons for anyone who fed them and protected them while they hibernated. They clad them in armor, and sent them off to fight in eastern Pomerania. There are many stories about that. They fought so fiercely, with no regard for anything but killing, that many Polish soldiers ran away as soon as they saw them. It was only when King Ladislaus defeated the Teutonic Knights at the Battle of Grunwald that the children were left without anybody to protect them. Most of them escaped, but one was brought back to Warsaw, and buried."

"That's exactly what Clayton told me!" Marek put in. "He'd been in the library, looking up everything he could find about people who were killed by having their heads cut off. He mentioned the Battle of Grunwald—and, what else? Somebody the newspapers called Mr. Guillotine. I don't know when that was."

"Oh, I know when that was," said Father Xawery. "That was in the autumn and winter of 1881 and 1882. There were nine murders then, all by beheading, and in every case the head had been taken away. They bore all the hallmarks of the children's killings, but it took me a long time to work out why there had suddenly been such a spate of them. When I realized what the answer was, it seemed obvious. In 1881, the British engineer William Lindley was constructing Warsaw's first sewage system. That was the time that your great-grandfather was talking about, Mrs. Brzezicki.

"I didn't know that the sewage workers managed to find the Tunnel Child and bury him. I'd always assumed that he simply crawled back into the soil and continued his hibernation. But it seems clear that the Germans found him again, when they started to bombard Warsaw. Somehow they must have discovered who or what he was, and used him against the insurgents.

"For the sewers, you see, the Tunnel Child is a perfect predator. He can sense his prey in almost total darkness, and he is completely at home in damp, polluted places. He has enormous strength in his arms and legs, in the same way that a cockroach has enormous strength. Yet he has the intelligence of a human being, and he can wield a knife."

"Would he be hard to kill?" asked Rej.

"He seems to have proved almost invulnerable, up until now. Remember that cockroaches are one of the few creatures on earth who have shown themselves to be capable of surviving a nuclear explosion."

Sarah finished her vodka and stood up. "You're

looking tired, Father Xawery. Why don't we take you back to your hotel?"

"Oh, no, I won't hear of it!" said Mrs. Brzezicki. "The Father must stay with us! I have a good soft bed in the spare room, Father. You'll sleep like a baby!"

"Well, I'm not so sure of that," Father Xawery told her, trying to smile. "It's one thing to know the history of something terrible, like the Tunnel Child. It's quite another to meet it face to face."

Sarah and Rej and Marek shook Father Xawery by the hand, and said goodbye to Mrs. Brzezicki. In the hallway, Jozef Brzezicki said, "You believe me now, that it's a devil?"

"I should never have doubted you, should I?" said Sarah.

"You're going to try to hunt it down?"

Sarah nodded. "We have some leads. We're going to follow them up in the morning."

"If there's anything you need—"

Sarah kissed his stubbly cheek. "Thanks, Mr. Brzezicki. I appreciate it more than you know."

They dropped off Marek and then Rej drove Sarah back to her apartment.

"I'd ask you up for a drink, Stefan, but I desperately really need to get some sleep."

He shrugged. "It doesn't matter. I'll see you in the morning. How about ten o'clock? I'll call Madame Krystyna and see if she can help us to track down Mr. Okun."

She squeezed his hand, and kissed him lightly on the lips. They both knew that they would never sleep together again.

"Goodnight," said Sarah, and climbed out of the car.

Rej waited until he saw her putting her key in the door and then he drove away. Sarah had already opened the door and was just about to go inside when she heard somebody calling her in a hoarse stage whisper. "Miss Leonard! Over here, Miss Leonard!"

She turned. A man was standing in the narrow dark alley beside her apartment building. He was wearing a creased blue suit and holding a large brown envelope.

"Who's that?" she asked.

"Over here, quick! I don't know whether anybody followed me!"

Cautiously, Sarah stepped across to the alleyway, making sure that she stayed in the light. The man came forward, and the streetlamp illuminated his face. It was Piotr Gogiel, looking sweaty and tired.

"I've been waiting for you for two hours. I was just about to give it up and go home."

"You could have come to the office in the morning."

"Not to give you this," he said, handing over the envelope. "This is your proper bank statement . . . I found a copy in Antoni Dlubak's filing cabinet. It shows you how all of Roman Zboinski's money was run through the Senate contingency account, and who authorized it, everything."

"Ben Saunders?"

Piotr Gogiel said, "Yes, I'm sorry to say. He had another account, too, with a Russian gangster—a man called Shtemenkov. I asked one of my friends about Shtemenkov, and apparently he's a well-known drug dealer."

Sarah grasped Piotr Gogiel's hand and said, "Thanks, Mr. Gogiel. I know how risky this was. Believe me—you'll get your reward for it."

"Sometimes there are only two choices," said Piotr Gogiel. "The right one, and the wrong one."

17

She undressed, put on her silky blue Japanese robe, and made herself a cup of herbal tea. She opened the French windows and went out onto the balcony, leaning on the balustrade and looking at the lights of Warsaw. Although it was nearly two o'clock in the morning, a warm wind was blowing from the west, carrying with it the distant clanking sounds of trains being marshalled.

She kept thinking of Ben's abortive "exorcism," and everything that Father Xawery had told them about the Tunnel Child. She didn't think it was possible that any human being could really have hibernated through hundreds of years; but she believed in the Tunnel Child's existence, and she knew that she was going to have to find it and destroy it. The very thought of going looking for it made her feel queasy, but there was no other choice.

As she was sipping her tea her eye was caught by a black Mercedes parked in a line of cars on the opposite side of the road. She was sure that she had seen the brief orange flare of a match in the windscreen, as if somebody were sitting inside it, smoking a cigarette. All the other cars were parked facing the kerb; the Mercedes was parked so that it was facing outward, toward her.

She stared at it for more than a minute, and she was sure that she could distinguish a man's arm, resting against the driver's window. Then she saw the pinprick glow of a cigarette tip, and a waft of smoke blew out of the window.

She went inside and rang Rej. He had only just come through the front door, and sounded flustered.

"Stefan? It's Sarah. There's a car parked opposite my apartment and I think the driver may be watching me."

"Hold on. What kind of car?"

"Black Mercedes. I don't know what model."

"Can you see the registration plate?"

"Not from here."

"How do you know he's watching you?"

"I don't, not for sure. I just have a feeling. But Piotr Gogiel was here when you dropped me off. You know, from Vistula Kredytowy. Would you believe it, he gave me all the printouts from the Senate account. The *real* printouts, not the doctored ones that Ben gave me. The trouble is, I'm wondering if he was followed."

"Gogiel actually gave you the printouts? I thought you told me he was stonewalling you."

"Obviously he changed his mind. He's one of the few executives at Vistula Kredytowy who don't think they're Gordon Gekko."

"That's excellent," said Rej. "Maybe things are starting to look up at last. Listen—I doubt if anybody would make it so obvious that they were watching you, but I'll ask a patrol car to take a look. All I can say is, keep your doors locked. I'll call you if I find anything out. If not—well, sweet dreams."

Sarah put down the phone and went back to the window. The Mercedes was still there. After a few moments, the driver tossed his cigarette out of the window, and sparks drifted across the road. She was probably being paranoid; but she couldn't forget the way that Roman Zboinski had winked at her during the exorcism. He frightened her almost as much as the Executioner, or the Tunnel Child, or whatever it was called. In some ways, he frightened her more.

Shortly before 2:30, she closed the French windows, and locked them, even though her apartment was so high up. She went into the bathroom, dropped her robe, and stepped into the shower. She switched it on full and rested her back against the tiles, letting the water gush through her hair and over her shoulders. For the first time in a long time, she realized that she was lonely, and it was an unfamiliar and unwelcome feeling. She didn't love Stefan. She knew that she never could. But he had given her such strong companionship, and listened to her with such respect, that she found that she was missing him.

Just to be able to turn around to him and say, "What did you really think of Father Xawery?" or "Children and cockroaches . . . I mean, was this guy *serious*?"

Slowly, she soaped herself, her eyes half closed with tiredness. Tomorrow she would have to go through all of the printouts that Piotr Gogiel had given her; and then she would probably have to talk to Senate's lawyers. At least she had a way of defending herself against Ben's attempts to oust her from Eastern Europe. In fact—depending on what she found—she probably had enough incriminating information to have Ben arrested for major fraud. She wouldn't have chosen to see him prosecuted. She was hard, but she had never been vindictive. All the same, she thought that Ben had made himself a bed of barbed wire, and so there was no injustice in making sure that he lay on it.

She was rinsing her hair when she heard a ring at the doorbell. *God*, she thought, *it must be Stefan*. He was so damned protective that he had driven all the way from Ochota to see how she was. She turned off the shower and found herself a large green towel. Then she left the bathroom and padded across the living room to see who it was.

The bell rang again, long and loud. "All right, all right! Keep your shirt on!" she said. She peered through the spyhole but all she could see was the landing outside, and the curving art-nouveau banister rails.

"Stefan, is that you?" she called out.

"Open the door," said a muffled man's voice. She wasn't sure whether it was Stefan or not.

"Stefan?" she repeated. "Stefan . . . go to the spyhole, so that I can see your face."

"Open the door, quick," the man repeated.

Against all of her instincts, Sarah opened the door, although she kept it on the security-chain. "Stefan, I can't see you! I just wanted to make sure that it was you! I don't think you needed to—"

She didn't have a chance to say anything else, because the door was kicked with such violence that the security-chain was torn out of the architrave. It slammed backward against the wall, and Sarah was confronted with a fat man in a purple shell-suit, holding a sawn-off shotgun. He had a flat, masklike face with a white crewcut, and there was a huge brown wart on his cheek.

"Give me the papers!" he demanded, in English. He was as nervous as she was. "Come on, papers, or gun!" and he cocked the shotgun to show that he meant what he said.

Sarah retreated from the front door and the man followed her. "Papers," he kept repeating. "Papers."

"What papers?" said Sarah. She didn't know whether to be frightened or furious. "I don't know what you're talking about."

The man kicked the door shut behind him and advanced on Sarah until she had reached the living room wall, under a silver-and-enamel icon of the Blessed Virgin. "Papers! Papers!" he kept shouting at her. His voice was half strangled with asthma. "Bank papers! Gogiel!"

"Listen, I've called the police," Sarah told him. "They'll be here in two minutes . . . maybe one minute," and she tapped her wristwatch and lifted a single finger.

"Bank papers, now quick," the man repeated. He came up closer, holding the shotgun one-handed. Sarah feinted to the right, and the man shifted to the right. But when she tried to duck to the right, he grabbed her hair and slammed her back against the wall, so that the icon dropped onto the parquet floor. He pushed the shotgun barrels right up against her nose. She could smell nothing but gun oil, and far too much Obsession for Men. She didn't move. She had been in business long enough to know when people were bluffing and when they weren't, and this man wasn't bluffing. He had everything to gain, and nothing whatsoever to lose.

He made an extraordinary face, as if he were trying to dislodge a shred of meat from between his front teeth. Then, very slowly, he said, "You, must, give, bank. Papers, to, me. I, will. Shoot, your, head."

Sarah looked him in the eye and the bastard meant it. She nodded toward the coffee table in the center of the living room. "There," she said. "Take them, if you want to. I'm not arguing."

The man glanced at the brown envelope. For one long moment, Sarah thought that he was going to blow her head off, and then walk out with the printouts. *Dad*, she thought, *mom*. There wasn't even time to say a prayer. But the man lowered his shotgun, and eased back the hammer, and grinned at her.

"Dobrze," he said; and went across to pick up the envelope.

At that moment, there was a devastating knock at the door. It was so hard that the upper right-hand panel split in half, and pieces of plaster dropped from the architrave. The man jumped back in shock. He turned around to Sarah, and then looked at the door, and half lifted his shotgun as if he couldn't decide whether it would be wise to be caught with a weapon in his hand, or not.

"What?" he asked, in alarm.

Sarah was about to say, "*Gliniarze*, what else?" when there was another knock, and another. Massive, timber-cracking knocks that wrenched the hinges out of their sockets.

The man snatched the envelope and hurried toward the French windows. He furiously rattled the handles, but Sarah had locked them. The knocking went on: heavy, regular blows, as if somebody were determined to beat the door down, no matter how long it took.

"What?" the man screamed, coming back across the room. *"What?"*

Sarah shook her head, and retreated away from him, one hand held up to fend off his shotgun. She didn't know what it was, either. But oh God, she could guess.

The man hesitated; and then he obviously decided that it was worth trying to shoot his way out. He edged his way toward the front door, and stood beside it, his shotgun cocked, while the deafening banging went on and on. The top hinge had almost broken free, and the screws were hanging out. Plaster sifted from the ceiling, and cracks appeared in the wall.

God help me, thought Sarah. *It's come for me, too. It must have picked up my scent at the exorcism. It must have smelled what I was; the daughter of one of its enemies.*

The banging quickened, until it was a thunderous drumming. Suddenly, the door broke open and twisted sideways. At the same instant, all the lights in the apartment dimmed until they were nothing more than fitful points of light, no brighter than fireflies.

In the doorway stood the same dark shape that Sarah had seen during the seance at Madame Krystyna's. The same dark shape that had pursued her through her

dream. She was so frightened that she could hardly
move her legs. She stepped backwards toward the
kitchen, but she felt as if she were wading through
syrup.

There was a long silence. The shape remained where
it was, silhouetted in the doorway. Beside the door, the
man with the shotgun was poised, obviously assessing
his chances of getting out. Sarah took another step
back, and then another, but then she found herself
against the wall.

The shape came through the doorway, with a deep
dragging noise from its cape. The man with the shotgun
pushed past it, and tried to get out onto the starkly lit
landing.

Sarah wasn't sure what she saw. But it looked as if
a thin, spidery hand leaped out from underneath the
cape and snatched the man by the shoulder. The man
twisted around, and shouted out, *"Help me! Jesus
Christ, help me!"* The shotgun went off with an ear-
cracking explosion, and fragments of black cape flew
everywhere. But the shape kept its grip on the man's
shoulder, holding him so tightly that Sarah was sure
that she could hear his collarbone slowly cracking.

The two of them wrestled on the landing, thickly
wreathed in gunpowder smoke. The spidery hand released the man's shoulder and seized his hair, and the
man screamed out again, *"Help me! For God's sake,
help me!"*

The shape appeared to hunch up, as if it were lifting
its arm. Then Sarah caught the bright, excited flash of
metal. There was an extraordinary noise, like a whip
cracking.

The shape moved away from the man with the shotgun, and left him standing on his own on the landing,
under the bare bright light of the chandelier. The man
couldn't have stood there for more than a split second,
but to Sarah it seemed that it was almost an eternity.

He had the strangest look on his face, as if he were about to say something amusing.

But then his knees began to buckle, and his arms dropped by his sides, and his head tilted sideways and dropped off his neck. A huge gush of blood spouted up unto the air, and then another, and then the man fell to the floor and lay on his side, quivering and twitching. His head rolled across the landing and came to rest in the doorway of the apartment opposite.

Stiff with shock, Sarah shifted along the wall, feeling behind her for the kitchen door. If she went through the kitchen, she could make her way out onto the fire escape, and at least she would have a chance of getting away. For a while, the shape stayed motionless in the hall, but then it turned toward her, and came back through the shattered door.

"Oh God," she said, and tried to run. But the shape came so swiftly across the room that she was much too late. She heard its cape dragging, she heard its breath whining. It stood between her and the kitchen, exuding the deep, sweet stench of sewage and death, and she knew that she could never make it to the fire escape before it caught her. She backed away. She could hear herself whimpering, almost as if she had a child with her, a terrified child who wasn't her at all.

The shape came closer. She thought she could make out the paleness of its face, beneath its cape, its dead black eyes. She tried to say, "Don't hurt me," but her lips were numb.

She backed away even further. The shape shuffled after her. It was exactly like her dream, only far worse, because this time she could smell it, this time she could hear it whispering and whining, and this time it was real, and it meant to kill her.

She heard the dreadful metallic dragging of a huge knife being drawn out of its scabbard. The fact that she couldn't see the knife made it all the more frightening.

"Go away," she managed to whisper. *"Go away, please go away."*

The shape's breathing began to quicken. It came closer still: so close now that it blotted out almost all of the light from the landing. For one instant Sarah saw its face, its perfect childlike face, with its black impenetrable eyes. It could have been a wax effigy or a religious statue, like one of the eerily serene Virgins sculpted in the 15th century by the Master of Beautiful Madonnas. She was so terrified that she felt as if the whole room were slowly imploding, as if darkness were flooding in on her from all sides.

She saw the creature's jaw drop, and its mouth stretch open, and suddenly that eerie beauty was transformed into a nightmare.

"Get away from me!" she screamed at it. *"Get away from me!"*

She collided with the telephone table, snatched up the phone and threw at it the shape, but it seemed about as ineffective as throwing it into a heavy velvet curtain. She picked up the brass table-lamp and threw that, too. Then she tried to pick up the table, but she lost her balance and fell back against the wall.

Gasping, she reached for anything she could find. A fallen cushion, a glass paperweight. Then she picked up the silver icon that had dropped from the wall, and threw that, too.

Immediately, she heard a high, desperate cry, like a child in distress. It was the same cry that she had heard at the excavation site, when the German workers were killed. It was so sad and filled with such pain that she couldn't believe that it had been uttered by this huge, menacing shape.

It tried to come nearer, but it seemed as it couldn't. It stepped forward two or three times, its robes swinging and swaying. Every time, it cried in anguish; a heartbreaking cry that came straight from the soul.

Sarah said nothing, but sat on the floor staring at it

in horror. It tried one last time to approach her, but then it turned away, and swept back across the room as dark and as swift as a cloud-shadow crossing the moon. It didn't pause for a moment, but hurried out onto the landing, and was gone. At the same time, the lights came back on.

She heard the street door bang, and then she knew that she was safe.

ej came into the room and gave her a hug. Jarczyk, unshaven and disheveled, looked the other way. Out on the landing, photoflashes flickered like summer lightning, and police ran up and down stairs.

"Are you all right?" Rej asked her. "It didn't hurt you at all?"

Sarah shook her head. "It came right up to me. It took out its knife . . . but I kept on throwing things at it, and it started to cry this terrible crying, and then it went away."

"You saw his face?" asked Jarczyk.

"Only for a split second."

"But you'd know him again?"

"Oh, yes, komisarz. I'd know him again." The idea that she would have any trouble identifying the shape that had attacked her almost made her smile.

Rej said, "You know who that was—the man it killed?"

"No. I don't think I'd ever seen him before."

"His name was Lukasz Wlosowicz: another of Zboinski's heavies. I think he was under orders to get back those printouts: and then to kill you. It seems as if the Executioner saved your life, in a way—even thought *it* was trying to kill you, too."

Jarczyk said, "We're taking the printouts for blood and fingerprint tests, but you can have them back after that." He ruffled his hair, which was already sticking out in all directions, as if he hadn't had the chance to comb it. "Anything to get that bastard Zboinski."

Rej looked around the room. He picked up a cushion and righted the fallen telephone table. Then he saw the silver icon on the floor. "Did you throw this at it?"

"That was the last thing I threw."

Rej turned the icon over in his hand. "This is genuine, isn't it?"

"Yes. I bought it when I visited Poland last year. It came from the church of St. Elisabeth, in Wroclaw."

"You threw a religious symbol at it, and it started this crying, and went away?"

"I suppose so, yes."

Jarczyk went back out onto the landing, where the medical examiners were ready to take away Wlosowicz's body. Rej said, "You remember what happened at that so-called exorcism? Father Xawery was holding a religious relic, wasn't he? St. Gerard Somebody's ring finger."

"What do you mean—that religious symbols could actually ward the Executioner off?"

"It makes sense, in a way."

"But how you can believe that? You're a communist!"

"I believe it simply because it makes the best logical sense. I mean, if Father Xawery's story is true, and these children were bred and brought up by monks, they would be bound to have a fear of anything holy, wouldn't they? The Executioner may have hibernated for five centuries, but it must still have a medieval sense of heaven and hell."

"I don't know. I suppose you could be right."

Rej said, "We have to go after it. You know that, don't you? Otherwise you're never going to be safe in Warsaw, ever again."

"You want to go *now*? It's 3:30 in the morning!"

"No time like the present. Let me call Madame Krystyna, and see if she'll do us a seance."

"We're going to need five people."

"Then I'll call Marek, too, and get him to bring that

Olga of his." He held up the icon and said, "You don't mind if we take this with us, do you?"

"Of course not. It always gives me a good feeling to see somebody converted."

They were still talking ten minutes later when Jarczyk came back from the landing, shutting the aerial of his mobile phone with the palm of his hand. "Miss Leonard, I'm sorry, I've just had a call from headquarters. They found the body of Mr. Piotr Gogiel, on waste ground in Praga South."

"Oh, no," said Sarah. "Oh, no, not him."

"I'm sorry. Can I get one of my men to make you some tea, or coffee, perhaps?"

"It's all right. I have things to do."

Sarah went into the bedroom, closed the door, and changed into jeans and a checkered cotton shirt. As she brushed her hair in the mirror, she couldn't get over how bloodless she looked, but she made a deliberate effort not to think about the Executioner, or the way that Lukasz Wlosowicz's head had tumbled from his shoulders; nor to think about Piotr Gogiel. "It's a story," she told herself. "None of it's real."

She pulled on a pair of calf-length leather boots, and then she came out of the bedroom and took hold of Rej's arm. "Ready," she said.

Jarczyk said, "I may want to talk to you again later. You won't be going far, will you?"

They passed the building supervisor, the grumpy, bullet-headed Mr. Sprudin, who was hammering nails into the door frame as a temporary repair. "Do you know how much this is going to cost?" he demanded. "Doors like these, they cost thousands!"

Sarah and Rej went downstairs. The street was crowded with emergency vehicles, their lights flashing under a lightening sky. They climbed into Rej's Volkswagen and headed off in the direction of Marek's house, to pick him up.

"I'm really sorry about Piotr Gogiel," said Rej, resting one hand on top of Sarah's hand. "I know how much you trusted him."

"He had a family, that's what makes it worse. I feel so guilty, because I shouted at him for giving me the doctored printouts. God—why didn't I just let it go? I didn't think that they would actually kill him."

"Come on, Sarah. He made his own decision."

The streets were almost deserted, although a few early morning buses were beginning to bring in haggard-faced office cleaners and shift workers. "How did he die?" asked Sarah.

"They cut his head off. Zboinski's idea of a joke."

Sarah covered her mouth with her hand and said nothing more until they reached Marek's apartment. She was filled with so much grief that she was right on the very edge of tears, but she was determined not to cry, not yet, until she had found the Executioner, and not until she had made sure that Ben and Roman Zboinski were both punished for what they had done.

They found Marek and Olga both waiting on the kerb, sharing a cigarette. Olga was wearing a black mini-skirt and her face was painted as white as the Executioner's. They climbed into the car, and Marek said, immediately, "You've seen it? You've actually seen it?"

"Yes," said Sarah. "I've actually seen it."

"Is it really awful?" asked Olga, excitedly.

Sarah turned around in her seat. "Let's put it this way. I'm not going to have nightmares about it. It's far too frightening, even for nightmares."

Madame Krystyna was surprisingly charming and equable, considering that they had got her up at four o'clock in the morning. She bustled around in a smart silk robe of amber and blue, making them strong mocha coffee.

"This is a good time for contacting the spirit world," she said. "It's very quiet, a time when the spirits like to reminisce about the life they left behind. Do you have a talisman?"

Rej produced Mr. Okun's yellow toothbrush. "I'm afraid this is all we have. I hope it's going to be enough."

Madame Krystyna held it disdainfully between finger and thumb. "Hardly a sentimental object, is it? Still, I suppose I can try."

They sat around the table. Between the thick floral curtains, there was a narrow isoceles triangle of wan, early morning light. It softly illuminated the painting of the woman flying through the sky. It also fell on the sides of the polished alabaster pyramid in the center of the table, so that it gave off a milky, suffused shine. Rej laid the toothbrush in front of Madame Krystyna, and then held hands with Sarah and Olga.

"Are you ready to begin?" asked Madame Krystyna. "This isn't going to be easy. You must try to empty your minds of everything else except the matter at hand ... which is to find the owner of this toothbrush, wherever he may be."

She paused, and closed her eyes, and squeezed Sarah's hand very tight. Almost three minutes passed by in which she said nothing at all. Olga kept glancing at Marek as if she wanted to laugh; but Marek had experienced Madame Krystyna's seance before, and this time he was deadly serious. Sarah turned to Rej and thought how old he was looking. It didn't occur to her then that losing your beliefs is always a deeply aging experience; and so is losing your heart.

She looked at the painting of the flying woman, and suddenly realized that she understood what it meant. Freedom, at a price. That's why it had saddened her so much when she first saw it. That's why it saddened her even more, when she looked at it today.

"I am trying to find the owner of this toothbrush," said Madame Krystyna. "I am trying to find a man in black, who calls himself Mr. Okun. You must help me find him . . . he has hurt so many souls."

They waited and waited, Madame Krystyna repeated her incantation. "I am looking for the man who owned this toothbrush . . . I am looking for Mr. Okun."

Still nothing. Only the noise of traffic, from the street outside, and the chatting of Madame Krystyna's clocks. Madame Krystyna was gripping Sarah's hand so tightly that Sarah thought that her fingernails were going to penetrate her skin. But abruptly, Madame Krystyna released her hold. She looked around the table, her eyes alight. "Somebody here has *seen* Mr. Okun!"

"Yes," said Marek, uncomfortably. "I did. I saw him two or three times."

"Then you can really help us! What I want you to do is to place your hands on the sides of the pyramid, and I want you to *think* what Mr. Okun looked like. I want you to imagine him, as clear as day. Then the souls will know who we're looking for."

"Well, okay," said Marek, dubiously, but Olga nudged him and said, "Go on. I want to see what happens."

Marek stood up; and Madame Krystyna guided his hands so that he was holding the pyramid with his fingers splayed. "Now . . . you must think of Mr. Okun as if you were seeing him for the first time . . . you must remember the moment when you first caught sight of his face. Close your eyes; see him in your mind. How was it? How did it happen?"

Marek closed his eyes, although his eyelashes still fluttered. "We were coming out of the Green Cat Club . . . we were crossing Piekna. I turned, and there he was."

"Why did you notice him?" asked Madame Krystyna.

"He was climbing out of the manhole . . . just like it was a door to another room. He closed it behind him, and then he walked away."

"Think of him," urged Madame Krystyna. "Imagine that moment, the way he looked. Try to believe that you're back there now, crossing the street, turning around, and—"

Above the pyramid, another pyramid began to shine, a pyramid of light. Inside this pyramid, Sarah could see shapes moving, just like before, shadows and reflections and patches of sunshine. Gradually the picture began to clear, until she could see a wide street, with traffic passing backward and forward. It was all angular, strangely distorted, but she could still distinguish the figure of a man on the opposite sidewalk, climbing out of an open manhole. He looked elderly, and emaciated, yet he closed the manhole covers with efficiency and confidence, and walked like a man who has a mission in life.

The next second, the picture changed, and the man was walking out of an elevator door, and staring at them, right in the face. He was so close and so vivid that Sarah couldn't help shifting her seat back, and Olga whispered, "Oh my God . . . this is so *real*? Is he really *thinking* that?"

The image wavered and changed, so that one moment it looked as if Mr. Okun were smiling; and the next it looked as if half his face had melted, and he was looking at them with an appalling snarl.

"Who is this?" Madame Krystyna appealed. "Is there anybody there who knows who this is, and where we can find him? He has destroyed so many souls. He has caused so much pain. Please, show us where he is!"

The picture of Mr. Okun danced and flickered. Sarah could tell that Marek was straining hard to keep it focused. His finger joints were spots of white, and he was sweating.

"Please!" begged Madame Krystyna. "All you homegoing souls, returning to your cemeteries to sleep! All you saddened spirits, sinking into your memories! We need you, my darlings, we need you! Please help us to find this man!"

There was a moment of utter silence. Above the pyramid, the image of Mr. Okun was beginning to twist and collapse, like a dying tornado. Madame Krystyna pressed both hands against the sides of her head, and squeezed her eyes tight.

The room was shattered by a cracking explosion. The alabaster pyramid burst apart in Marek's hands, and shards of broken plaster rattled around the room like shrapnel. Marek stepped back, his hands bleeding from dozens of tiny cuts. The air was thick with dust and settling fragments.

Then a dry, attenuated voice said, *"Gerhard von Zussow."*

Rej looked at Sarah in alarm, and then at Madame Krystyna. "What did it say?"

The voice repeated itself, as dry as unoiled hinges, as dry as autumn leaves. *"Gerhard von Zussow . . . and you will find him here."*

Although the alabaster pyramid was shattered, a tilted picture appeared directly above it, like a slide displayed on a slanted ceiling—an apartment block, with a statue of a soldier in the forecourt. They all watched as they appeared to enter the apartment block and climb two flights of stairs. They turned left, and reached a door marked 277. Then, without warning, the picture faded.

They all sat back. Madame Krystyna opened the curtains, and the room was filled with morning sunlight. "I'm sorry," she said. "There was so little to go on."

"I'm sorry about your pyramid," said Marek, trying to collect up the lumps of broken alabaster. "Was it really expensive?"

"I'll find another," smiled Madame Krystyna. "It isn't often that I see a force so strong. It's a privilege, not a problem."

Sarah looked at Mr. Okun's toothbrush, lying amidst

the dust. Its handle was warped, as if it had been held over a fire, and its bristles were thick with blood. She laid a hand on Rej's arm and said, "Look . . ."

But all Rej did was to nod, and stand up. "Madame Krystyna, I want to thank you for everything. When you find a new pyramid, send the bill to Wilcza Street, addressed to me. I'll sort it out. Come on, Sarah, we have to go."

"Go? Go where?"

"Lazienkowska Estate. To look for Gerhard von Zussow."

"You know who he is?" asked Madame Krystyna, in surprise. "He sounds German to me."

"Oh, yes. He's German. He was an SS Major-General, during the war. He was one of those who helped to crush the Warsaw Uprising. A war criminal. After the war, everybody thought that he was dead."

"Mr. Okun?" asked Marek, wiping the sweat from his forehead with the back of his hand.

Rej nodded. "One and the same, I'd say."

"And how do you know where he is?"

"Didn't you see the picture? Some soul knew who he was, and where he is now. That soldier statue stands right outside the center block of the Lazienkowska Estate. Whoever that soul was, he even gave us von Zussow's apartment number."

Sarah tiredly stood up. "So what now? We go to pick him up?"

"You got it," said Rej. He looked down at the toothbrush with its blood-clotted bristles. "It's about time we cleaned Major-General von Zussow out of our system, what do you think?"

They drove through the early traffic toward Ochota. Hazy sunlight filled the interior of the car. Rej kept flicking his eyes up to his rear-view mirror, and after a while Sarah turned around and looked out of the back.

"You don't think we're being followed?"

"I don't know," said Rej. "You see that black BMW? It's been two or three cars behind us, most of the way."

"It's not Zboinski, is it?"

Rej made a face. "Who knows? You still have the printouts, don't you? Or you will, when Jarczyk's finished with them."

Marek said, "Listen, I don't want to get involved with that Zboinski guy. Absolutely no way. You can let us off here if you like."

"He won't do anything," Rej reassured him. "It's daylight. Too many people around. Besides, I've got hold of a gun."

"Oh, that makes me feel a whole lot better—not."

They reached the Lazienkowska Estate and Rej parked with his bumper nearly touching the statue that they had seen in Madame Krystyna's apartment. "There you are," said Rej. "A soldier of the 1939 barricade. I knew I recognized it."

As they left the car and walked toward the apartment block, the black BMW passed them by, and kept on driving southwest. Both Rej and Sarah saw it, and Sarah raised an eyebrow; but Rej simply shrugged. All the same, he knew whose BMW it was. There were dozens of black BMWs in Warsaw, but only one with totally black-tinted windows. Roman Zboinski was watching them.

They climbed up to the second floor. The Lazienkowska Estate had been ultra-modern in 1965, with its concrete stairs and its wired-glass windows and its decorative wall panels in turquoise and yellow. But now it was shabby and worn out. The elevators kept breaking down and the walls in the lower hallways were dense with graffiti. All around them, the building sounded like Babel: televisions jabbering, men and women arguing, children crying. And everywhere the smell of sauerkraut, as if that was all that the inhabitants of Lazienkowska ever lived on.

They reached the chipped, salmon-painted door numbered 277. Rej said, "Stand right back: let me do this. I don't want anybody getting injured." He clenched his fist and beat a furious tattoo on the door.

They waited—Marek and Olga almost ten meters down the corridor, hiding behind a pillar. Rej knocked again, and shouted, "Gerhard von Zussow! I know you're there! Open the door, this is the Wyzdial Zabostwj!"

They waited two or three minutes more. Then Rej braced his back against the corridor wall, and gave the door a deafening kick. Nothing happened, so he kicked it again. A disembodied voice from the next apartment called, "Shut up, will you, some of us are trying to sleep!"

Rej was about to kick the door a third time when they heard a chain being drawn back, a lock being turned, and a latch clicked out of its socket. The door opened and there stood Mr. Okun, in a brown wool robe, looking red-eyed and cadaverous. Rej immediately kicked the door wide open, stepped inside, and seized Mr. Okun's lapels.

"I want you to understand something!" he shouted at him. "You make one unpredictable move and I'm going to blow your head off!"

Mr. Okun looked at them all with his glittering, cavernous eyes. "And what is this?" he asked, in sharply-accented Polish. "The circus has come to town?"

Rej said, "I am Komisarz Stefan Rej. This is Miss Sarah Leonard, of Senate Hotels. And this is Marek Maslowski, who first saw you coming out of the manhole cover on Kosyzkowa."

"Well, I see," said Mr. Okun. "And what does this prove?"

"You know what it proves," said Rej. "We have enough evidence to connect you to the Executioner, and to every one of the Executioner's murders. You feed it, don't you? You take care of it. And in return, it hunts down all of the insurgents you hate so much, and their children, and their cousins, and their children's children."

Mr. Okun smiled, and passed his hand over his hair in a curiously effeminate gesture. "I suppose it's good to know that one's efforts are appreciated."

"You'll have to show us where it is," said Rej.

"Oh, it's not an 'it,' by any means. It is most definitely 'he.' He's a boy, a child . . . an innocent creature who lives his life according to his nature."

"You'll still have to show us where it is."

Mr. Okun frowned. "This is very difficult. You have to understand that this is very difficult."

"Just show us where he us, Major-General von Zussow, before he hurts anybody else."

"Then you'd better come in, while I change."

They all entered the small, dingy apartment. Mr. Okun had obviously arrived here in a hurry. There were two unpacked suitcases in the living room, and a stack of cardboard boxes crammed with books and newspapers and magazines. There was no carpet, only a dark brown vinyl floor, like cheap chocolate, and a bedsheet hung up at the windows in place of curtains. Mr. Okun went into the bedroom and tried to close the door, but Rej kicked it open and told him to get changed in full view.

"Well, there's no privacy any more," said Mr. Okun, resentfully.

"You didn't give anybody much privacy in Treblinka, did you?" Rej retorted.

"That was a very long time ago, komisarz."

"But the Polish people haven't forgotten it, and it seems that you haven't either."

Mr. Okun turned his back while he stepped into his droopy cotton underpants. "You seem to have forgotten that you killed ten thousand Germans, and that seven thousand went missing, and never reappeared, and that nine thousand were seriously injured. It was madness, that Uprising! Madness! I lost all of my boyhood friends. I lost everybody! I saw my brother lying in the street with his throat cut!"

"Perhaps you shouldn't have occupied Warsaw in the first place," said Marek.

"Who are you to speak of destiny?" Mr. Okun retorted. "Warsaw has been occupied again and again, by the Russians, by the French, it's history! You deserved what you got, and you still deserve more!"

"You mean you're not going to rest until you've beheaded us all," said Sarah.

Mr. Okun buttoned up his plain shirt. "That is what you should expect, yes. I was in charge of the Executioner, during the Uprising. An SS patrol found him half buried in a cellar, in the Old Town. He was alive, yes, but we didn't know what he was. The Poles said that he was a basilisk, do you know what that is? A monster that can hypnotize you, just by staring at you; and then kill you with its poisonous breath. But that was just stories. When I saw this poor creature, I knew that it wasn't a monster, but a child, a strange and interesting child; and I asked General von dem Bach-Zelewski if I could find out what it was, and why the Poles were so afraid of it."

Smartly dressed now, he came back into the meager living room. "I talked to our historians in Berlin; and our theologians in Dresden; and I soon discovered what we had unearthed. A child bred to survive forever. A child bred to carry the word of God from century to century, so that the word of God would never die . . . even after the holy order of monks who had created him had been dead for centuries.

"I discovered that he was obedient to anybody who said that they spoke the word of God, and that he would serve anybody who cared for him, and fed him. So when the insurgents began to escape through the sewers . . . well, I thought, who better to catch them for me? A devoted child who can slide through the sewers quicker than they can; and will bring me their heads."

Sarah said, "The war was over fifty years ago. Why are you doing it again now?"

Mr. Okun stared at her and his eyes glittered like black beetles in a pool of freshly spilled ink. "We lost so many young men . . . we lost everything. I tried to forget, but I couldn't."

"What happened?" asked Rej. "I mean, what happened to this child of yours, at the end of the war?"

"He didn't even survive that long. General von dem Bach-Zelewski brought in howitzers, and started to bombard Warsaw with shells that were almost a meter in diameter. On the same day, I sent my child down the sewers to search for insurgents trying to escape from Mokotow back to the city center. Those shells could penetrate two meters of concrete. One of them hit Koszykowa, exactly at the intersection with Piusa XI. It went right through the roadbed into the sewer, and my child was buried under tons of rubble and tons of earth. There was no hope of digging him out, not then. We had too many other problems to deal with. And then, of course, the Russians crossed the Vistula, and that was that."

"But you never forgot?" asked Sarah. "And you never *forgave*? The Polish Home Army were fighting for their own city!"

"No," said Mr. Okun.

"Is that it?" asked Rej. "Just 'no'—you never forgave, and you never forgot?"

"No," said Mr. Okun.

"So what happened to this so-called child of yours?"

"Why do you ask? You know the rest. I came back to Warsaw two years ago, when you started to redevelop and to dig up your sewers for your fine new hotels. And I found my child, with the help of some of my friends. He was buried in five meters of rubble and mud, still hibernating, still alive, on the site of the US Insurance building."

"And you revived it?" said Rej. "You revived it, and fed it, and gave it a knife, and sent it out looking for former insurgents, and their families, too?"

Mr. Okun tugged repetitively at his cuffs. "I saw my brother lying in the street with his throat cut."

Rej held up his hand, with half of his little finger missing. "You see this? Your baby did this! And you want me to understand why you did it? You want me to feel sympathetic? You *cwel!*"

"What does that mean?" Sarah asked Marek, but Marek shook his head, as if to say "You don't want to know."

"Everybody has their own view of history," said Mr. Okun, licking his lips. "We carried out our orders. We would have been shot if we didn't, and what was the point of that? And our young men suffered too. Seven thousand Germans disappeared in Warsaw, in just a few weeks. Where are they? Where are their graves? How can their families ever mourn them?"

Rej said. "We're going to get rid of this child of yours, once and for all. And you're going to take us down in the sewers to find him."

Mr. Okun sniffed, and coughed. "Don't you know how dangerous that is?"

"On past experience, yes."

"And if I refuse?"

"I won't have the slightest hesitation in blowing your brains all over the wallpaper."

There was a long silence, in which they all stood like figures in a tableau. Then Olga said, "You wouldn't really shoot him, would you?"

Rej lifted his automatic, cocked it, and pointed it directly at Mr. Okun's left eye. "The answer to that, Olga, is yes."

They were about to push their way out of the doors of the apartment building when Rej said, "Stop! Look! Wait!"

Across the street, barely visible in the shadows, a black BMW was parked, its windows gleaming in blue-and-white waves.

"Zboinski," said Rej. "He's waiting for us."

"Zboinski?" asked Mr. Okun. *"Wer ist Zboinski?"*

"There are some people who make your life a little sunnier every day," said Rej. "Roman Zboinski isn't one of them."

Mr. Okun said, "The best way into the sewers is on Krucza, right in the town center."

"In that case, show us the way."

Marek touched Sarah on the shoulder. "Listen," he said, "I don't want Olga involved in this. Let me take her home, and I'll join you later. Is that okay?"

"Of course it is," Sarah told him. "And—thanks, Olga. You've really been a help."

Olga gave her a shy smile, and Marek ushered her away. Mr. Okun called after him, "You can't miss the manhole, it's eighty meters south of Jerozolimskie Avenue, on the west side of the street. We look forward to seeing you!"

Rej dug his automatic into Mr. Okun's shoulder blade. "Stop being so goddamned happy," he ordered him.

"Happy? Why shouldn't I be happy? I'm bringing the people I hate the most to meet the worst fate that they could ever imagine."

"Well, we'll just have to see about that, won't we?" said Rej.

They squeezed into Rej's car, and Rej handed Sarah his automatic so that she could keep Mr. Okun covered.

"I've never fired a gun before," she told him.

"It's easy. Just point, and pull the trigger. Imagine it's Ben."

They drove back toward the city center. Rej glanced in his mirror from time to time, and sure enough the black BMW was following them, making no pretense of staying out of sight.

* * *

Rucza was busy with pedestrians and traffic by the time they arrived. The early mist had cleared and it looked as if it was going to be another warm day. Rej drove half way onto the sidewalk and parked, and they all noted with satisfaction that the black BMW had to pass them by in search of a parking space.

"You see that?" said Rej. "One of the biggest criminals in Eastern Europe, and he's afraid of getting a parking fine."

Mr. Okun led them over to a large inspection cover. It was one of the earliest type, with a double-headed Polish eagle embossed on it, and the name of the steelworks in Katowice. Mr. Okun took two special keys out of his pocket and heaved the cover out of its frame. Inside, Sarah could see a rusted iron ladder leading downward.

"He's here?" asked Rej.

"Not far," said Mr. Okun.

"Well, you lead on," Rej suggested.

The morning breeze caught Mr. Okun's white hair and he brushed it back with his hand. "I hope you understand what could happen. This is no ordinary being, and he respects and protects only me."

"Just shut up and get down the hole," Rej told him.

Mr. Okun shrugged, and began to climb down the ladder. Rej had his regulation flashlight, but Mr. Okun didn't seem to be concerned about the dark. He disappeared almost immediately, and although they could still hear his feet clanging on the rungs, Rej had to hurry to catch up with him.

"You stay here," he told Sarah. "Make sure that nobody falls down the manhole."

"Don't be ridiculous, I'm coming too. This is just as much my affair as it is yours."

"That thing nearly killed you last night."

"Yes, but you've got the icon, haven't you?"

"All right, then. But you'll have to close the cover after you. And make it quick."

He disappeared, and Sarah heard his feet go clang-clang-clang on the ladder as he went after Mr. Okun. She climbed into the manhole herself, much to the amazement of two old women who were passing by, and she dragged the cover back over it. God, it stank down here, and it was so dark that she couldn't even see her hands on the ladder.

Rej was at the bottom now, and he shone his flashlight up to help Sarah climb down. When she reached the foot of the ladder, she found that they were standing in a large arched chamber, with dry footing on either side, and a deep channel of sewage flowing sluggishly down the center. Mr. Okun said, "It isn't far now. But I warn you, he won't take kindly to your coming down here. There's nothing that I can do to save you, you know."

"You said you wanted us to get what was coming to us," said Rej, grimly. "So, come on, then—let's go get it."

Mr. Okun led the way along the main sewer. Their footsteps echoed and when they spoke, their voices were hugely distorted, like the voices of lost souls down the bottom of a well. Every now and then Mr. Okun would turn around to make sure that they were following him closely, and there was an expression on his face like nothing that Sarah had ever seen before. It was more than pleasure: it was glee.

As they walked, he marked arrows on the walls with a small stick of chalk. "You see? Your friend can follow us now."

They crossed the central channel by a small steel bridge, and then turned down a narrow, brick-clad side tunnel. A faint draft blew down it, and it carried a cloying, sickly smell, like bad pork. Although she wanted to see the end of this business, Sarah was beginning to wish that she had obeyed Rej's instruction, and stayed up on street-level.

"Not far now," said Mr. Okun. "Speak quietly . . . don't alarm him. He will attack anybody and anything that alarms him."

They reached the end of the tunnel, and came out onto a concrete landing, with a railing around it, and concrete steps going down into the darkness. Even before it was lit up by Rej's flashlight, Sarah realized that they were standing in a huge vaulted chamber. Every drip and splash of sewage echoed in chorus, and there was a feeling of empty vastness.

"It's immense," she said. "I never knew that—"

She stopped talking as if she had been struck dumb. Rej's flashlight beam was slowly moving across the walls of the chamber, and what it illuminated filled her with such horror and disgust that she was unable to speak. Hundreds and hundreds of human skulls were nailed in rows to the brickwork. Some of them were so old that they had turned to the color of mahogany, but many were much whiter. Right at the top, nearly reaching the highest part of the vaulting, there were heads which still had remnants of hair and flesh on them.

One by one, Rej lit up the puffy, decaying faces of all of the Executioner's recent victims—Jan Kaminski, Mr. Wroblewski, Zofia's mother Iwona. They had all been brought here, and nailed up as trophies.

"What is this place?" said Rej, his voice hoarse with shock.

"It's been here ever since they built the sewer system," said Mr. Okun. "When they rebuilt the sewers after the war, it became redundant. Nobody ever comes down here, because it doesn't appear on any of the official plans. It's safe, and secret. Just the place for a child to hide."

"And these heads?"

"If you are buried without your head, your soul can

never go to heaven. That's what he believes, anyway. He has deprived all of these people of their place in paradise. It's part of their punishment."

Rej shone the flashlight down to the floor. It was ankle-deep in gray, filthy water, and in the water there were scores of wet, grayish humps. At first neither he nor Sarah could understand what they were. Then they made out a white, childish face, its eyes as sightless as boiled cod's. Then they saw an arm, and another arm, and a foot.

"Oh, God," Sarah whispered. "They're all children. They're all dead children."

"He is a child himself," said Mr. Okun, with no passion in his voice whatsoever. "He likes to take children and play with them. Unfortunately he can't understand why they cry when he tries to take them back here. He doesn't know why they scream when he takes off their arms. It's sad, but what can you do? Every creature has to live after its own fashion."

"Is he here?" asked Sarah.

"Oh, he's here all right. Look. Look up . . . that niche in the roof, that's where he is."

Sarah looked up and saw a narrow, darkened crevice in between the vaulting. Just the kind of crevice in which a cockroach would secrete itself, damp and lightless and undisturbed.

"Do you want me to call him for you?" said Mr. Okun. "It would be a pleasure."

Sarah took a quick, shallow breath. "Rej, do you have that icon?" she whispered.

Rej felt in his pocket and nodded. "Don't worry about it. If it worked before, it's bound to work again."

Mr. Okun went half way down the concrete steps. He cupped his hands around his mouth and let out a high whooping sound, like a boy calling another boy out to play. He whooped two or three times, and then he stood silent.

At first there was no movement at all. But then Sarah

saw a black triangular shadow creeping out of the crevice. Then a bony hand, with spidery fingers. Gradually, a huge dark shape slid into sight caped in tattered, decayed velvet, and began to climb down from the ceiling by using the skulls as toeholds and fingerholds. Sarah watched it in dread and fascination as its fingers clawed in and out of eye sockets and gripped vacant jaws.

The shape reached the floor, and stood in the water, its cape floating amongst the dead, bobbing bodies of so many children.

"Did you ever see such a child?" said Mr. Okun, with dreadful pride. "Did you ever see such a creature? Born to slaughter, born to survive."

The shape came wading toward them. A few meters away, it stopped.

"These people wanted to find out where you lived," Mr. Okun told it, in a challenging voice. "These people want you to stop killing."

The shape stayed where it was, not stirring.

"These people want to bury you not just for years, not just for centuries, but forever. What do you say to that?"

There was a long silence, punctuated only by the sickening slopping of corpses in the shallow sewage. Then, with a terrible magnificence, the shape lifted its arm and threw back its hood.

Its face was ivory white, perfect as a miniature. Its head was large and lumpy, and covered in fine white filaments that looked more like mold than hair. It was a child, of sorts, and it was definitely human, but how it had managed to survive in these sewers and live for so long, Sarah couldn't imagine. It stood so still that if it hadn't been breathing, Sarah wouldn't have believed it to be real.

"They want to see the end of you," said Mr. Okun. "They want to take down your heads, and break down your home, and bury you so deep that nobody will ever find you again."

The child drew out the largest knife that Sarah had ever seen. It was more like a sword than a knife, except that it had a broad, curved blade. Without any more hesitation, it began to wade through the water toward, the steps.

"Sarah! Get back!" Rej shouted, and pushed her back toward the tunnel.

Mr. Okun pressed himself against the wall as the child mounted the steps and came toward them with its knife lifted.

Rej fired one shot. The child's cape flapped, but it kept on rushing up the steps.

"Stefan!" screamed Sarah. "Stefan, the icon!"

Rej pulled the icon out of his pocket and held it up. But the instant he did so, there was a deafening boom from inside the tunnel, and the left shoulder of Rej's coat exploded into a mixture of nylon, padding and blood. He spun around and fell heavily onto the floor. The icon bounced out of his hand, skipped across the concrete landing and dropped down into the sewage.

Just as the child reached the landing, one of Roman Zboinski's men appeared, a thickset man in a green suit, holding up a shotgun. Behind him came Zboinski himself, with his baling hook in his hand.

He saw Sarah first. She was up against the railings, one hand lifted to protect herself.

"You think you can put me in jail?" he snarled at her. "You think you can—"

He stopped. The child was standing only three meters away from him, its knife still lifted, its eyes as dead as asphalt. Zboinski looked it up and down, and then turned to his bodyguard. "What are you waiting for? Shoot him!"

But the bodyguard started shaking his head and backing away. "It's the devil. It's the Executioner. I'm not shooting the devil."

"Shoot the fucker!" screamed Zboinski. He snatched the shotgun and fired it, and the child's cape billowed and flapped. But it continued to drag itself forward, and its eyes never wavered, and neither did its knife. The bodyguard made a whimpering noise and ran away down the tunnel.

Zboinski lifted his hook. "Do you know what they call me?" he said to the child. "They call me the Hook, and you're going to find out why."

He advanced on the child, his hook waving from side to side, his mouth cracked into a triumphant grin. "Did you ever see a man with a hook through his nose?" he taunted. "Did you ever see a man with a hook in his ear? Lodge it deep enough, and you can swing him around the room."

He ducked to one side, and the hook tore through rotten fabric. It tore again, and again. Zboinski said, "Come on, you fucker, let's find your ribs!"

But then the knife flashed; so fast that Zboinski didn't even see it. He actually managed to say. "What?" before his head flew from his shoulders and dropped down into the water below. Blood pumped out of his severed neck in loops and ribbons and splattering question marks. His body rolled down the steps, its arms and legs uselessly flailing. His head floated for a moment, but then sewage poured into its open mouth, like an unwelcome helping of awful soup, and it bubbled once, and sank.

Sarah knelt down next to Rej. His face was ashen and he was shivering with shock, but his shoulder didn't seem to be bleeding too badly. "I'm all right," he coughed. "Run, while you've got the chance."

"You can run, too," she begged him, but he shook his head.

The child approached them quite slowly. It stood over them, staring at them. Sarah stared back at it, marveling at its beauty, paralyzed by the horror of it.

She thought for a moment that it was going to spare them; but she was her father's daughter, a Lewandowicz, and she knew that Mr. Okun had fed it and cared for it and given it a solemn duty of revenge. It lifted its bloodied knife, and she closed her eyes and waited for the blow.

It was then, walking at a pace that was almost leisurely, that Marek appeared.

"Are you there?" he said, his voice echoing in the tunnel. "Miss Leonard? Komisarz Rej? I followed your arrows!"

Sarah opened her eyes. "Marek! No!" she screamed. "The Executioner's here!"

Marek came running the last few meters. He saw Sarah and Rej and the Executioner, and he stood there, open-mouthed.

"Run!" Sarah told him.

But Marek stayed where he was, and reached inside his T-shirt, and lifted out the little silver cross that the waitress in the Welcome Bar had given him. Sarah looked at him in astonishment. "That won't work," she told him, her voice wavering. "For God's sake, that won't work."

"It was blessed by the Pope," said Marek. "It's the sign of God, and it was blessed by the Pope."

He approached the child, standing so near that the child could easily have cut off his head. He lifted the cross until it was only a few centimeters from the child's face. The child didn't move.

"Why don't you rest?" Marek told it. "Why don't you give yourself some peace? Don't you think you've lived long enough and killed enough people? This wasn't what your fathers wanted, was it, when they made you? They wanted you to protect people, not to murder them. It's time you stopped. It's time you put down that knife and rested."

"Don't you listen to him!" shouted Mr. Okun. "He's a deceiver! He's telling you lies!"

The child stared at the cross, unblinking.

Marek said, with increasing desperation, "It's over,

don't you understand? What you've been doing—killing people—that isn't God's work!"

The child slowly raised his knife and Sarah thought, *Oh, no, we were wrong about the holy relics; we were wrong about the icon. This creature has lived under the ground for hundreds and hundreds of years. It won't be deterred by anything.*

Marek took one step back, and then another, and the child came after him, its knife lifted higher and higher. Almost screaming, Mr. Okun called out, "You see! You won't stop him with that because you don't believe in it! His faith is total! His faith can *never* be shaken!"

Marek's hand began to waver. He glanced back at Sarah and Rej and his eyes were wide with fear. *Of course*, thought Sarah. *Father Xawery believed implicitly in the relic that he carried; and I believe in the Blessed Virgin Mary—but poor Marek doesn't really believe at all.*

She stood up, her heart pumping, and cried out, "*I believe!*"

But before she could take a step forward, she felt somebody pulling at her arm. It was Rej—his face white with shock, his shoulder bleeding, but with an extraordinary expression on his face, eyes staring, almost alight. "Stay here," he said, hoarsely.

He walked toward Marek until he was standing beside him. Marek looked at him nervously, but Rej kept his eyes on the child, with his upraised knife. He probably could have cut off both of their heads with a single blow, and he drew his arm back even further. But for some reason he hesitated.

Rej took the cross out of Marek's hand and held it up.

"*I believe,*" he said, with a note of triumph in his voice. "Until I saw you, I believed in nothing. I didn't believe in God and I didn't believe in the Holy Spirit.

But now I do, completely—and it's you—you've shown me that it's true!"

The child stayed where it was, frozen.

"I *believe*!" Rej shouted at it. "You've done what you were always supposed to do! You've carried the word of God! You've converted me!"

There was a long, stretched-out moment when Sarah was sure that the child was going to kill him in front of her eyes. Even Marek stepped back.

But then she heard a high, plaintive sound, a sound that echoed all around the vault, as if every skull that was nailed to the brickwork was crying in chorus. It was the child crying—crying for what it was, crying for what it had done. It was the eeriest, saddest, most unsettling sound that Sarah had ever heard in her life.

Rej stepped forward, and laid his hands on the child's black-caped shoulders.

"I forgive you," he said. "In the name of the Father, and of the Son, and of the Holy Ghost, I forgive you."

The knife stayed aloft, its blade gleaming. But already, something extraordinary was happening. Cracks were appearing on the child's face like the cracks in an old oil painting. Underneath his cape, his body started to sag, Sarah could hear crackling noises, like brittle bones breaking, or wing cases being crushed.

At the same time, she heard—she *felt*—a deep vibrato humming. It sounded like monks chanting, or thousands of insects in a summer field. It sounded like organs, and machinery, and engines rumbling. It began to swell, and to fill the vault from floor to ceiling, louder and louder, until the concrete landing began to vibrate under their feet and even the iron railings started to sing, like railway tracks when a locomotive is coming at speed.

The knife fell to the concrete floor with a dull ringing noise. The child's head dropped into his cape. Rej tried to hold him up, tried to support him, but his cape folded up, fold upon fold, layer upon layer. And the humming went on, until it was thunderous. The humming of soldiers, the bellowing of tanks, the thunder of bombing.

The child collapsed to the ground, but the noise went on and on, and Mr. Okun knelt on the steps with his hands clamped over his ears.

"Let's get out!" Rej shouted. "Let's just get the hell out!"

There was a crackling rumble, and a massive chunk of masonry dropped from the ceiling, and splashed into the sewage below. Then another piece fell, and another, and a whole row of brickwork dropped away, taking scores of skulls with it. The entire vault shook so violently that Sarah couldn't even stand up properly.

"Come on!" said Marek, and helped her toward the tunnel.

She turned once: to look at what remained of the child. There was nothing but a heap of decaying velvet, and curved, translucent pieces of bone and body-shell.

Mr. Okun came up the steps, his face rigid. "What have you done?" he screamed. *"What have you done?"*

He knelt beside the dead child and picked up pieces of velvet as if he hoped he could breathe life back into them. He turned to Sarah accusingly, and screamed, "You'll be punished for this! I swear it!"

At that moment, the vaulted ceiling cracked from one side to the other, and collapsed. Hundreds of tons of bricks and concrete buried the Executioner's trophies, and the Executioner itself, and Mr. Okun, too. The last that Sarah saw of him, a huge block of concrete was dropping onto his back.

"Come on!" Rej shouted at her "Before the whole damned sewer caves in!"

As they ran along the tunnel, they heard a final shattering rumble, and thick dust came billowing after them. Sarah and Marek took Rej between them, and together they made their way back up to the surface.

THE CHOSEN CHILD   401

Marek opened the manhole cover, and they climbed wearily up the ladder and into the hazy sunshine.

Ben was in Irena's office when she arrived, sitting on her desk and laughing; but when she walked in and put down her briefcase he stopped laughing, and stood up, and smiled, and coughed.

Her hair was still wet from the shower, and combed straight back, so that she looked like her father. She wore a plain gray tailored suit and a fresh primula-colored blouse.

"Well, well," said Ben. "I understand that congratulations are called for. You and Komisarz Rej have actually done the business."

"News travels fast," said Sarah.

Ben tapped the side of his nose. "Contacts, that's the secret. Contacts. Komisarz Jarczyk told me, as a matter of fact."

"I wanted to talk to you about contacts," said Sarah. "Why don't you come into my office?"

Ben heaved himself off Irena's desk and gave her a wink. "See you later," he said. "And don't be late."

He followed Sarah into her office and Sarah closed the door. "Did Jarczyk also tell you that Roman Zboinski is dead?"

Ben nodded. "Not a great loss to humanity," he said.

"A great loss to your bank balance, though."

"I really don't know what you're talking about."

"Oh, no? I'm talking about fraud, perpetrated through the Senate contingency account, that's what I'm talking about."

Ben innocently spread his arms. "Fraud? What fraud? You saw the statements."

"I saw the statements you gave me. But I also saw the real statements . . . the ones that Anton Dlubak printed out."

"The *real* statements?"

"Come on," said Sarah. "I'm not going to beat

around the bush. I have a copy of them and you could face criminal prosecution. You're certainly going to have to resign from Senate."

Ben gave her an amused, quizzical frown. "Do you know something, Sarah? I believe that all this Executioner business has really got to you."

"I have the printouts, Ben. You don't have any choice."

"All right, then. Let's see them, these printouts."

"Jarczyk has them at the moment. They had blood on them . . . they're putting them through forensic tests. Then I'll get them back."

"Jarczyk didn't mention any printouts to me."

Sarah had been opening her briefcase. She stopped, with the lid half raised. Ben came up to her desk and leaned over it, his face so close that she could smell the Binaca on his breath.

"Jarczyk didn't mention any printouts to me," he repeated, as if he were talking to a child. "In fact, Jarczyk specifically said that there were no printouts."

Sarah stared back at him, and at that moment she felt as if she had never hated another human being so much.

"You've done it again, haven't you?" she said. "Bribed, and bullied, just like you always do."

"Survival of the smartest, sweetheart." He kissed the tip of his finger, and tried to touch her on the lips with it, but she twisted her head away. He laughed, and then he said, "There wasn't anything else, was there?" and opened her office door.

"Oh," he added, before he left, "I don't know whether you're thinking of reconsidering your position, but I'm afraid that I've had to put in a very negative report on your labor-relations problems. You don't have to let me know directly; but if I were you, I would do it before New York does it to you first."

He left, leaving the door open. Sarah stood very still for a moment. Then she sat down. She couldn't have phoned Stefan, even if she had wanted to, because he was still in the hospital, having his shoulder dressed. In any case, there was nothing that Stefan could do about her career at Senate. He had been part of something very different.

She closed her briefcase, and snapped the locks shut.

When Marek came into the Welcome Bar, the waitress was wiping the tables and rearranging the cruets.

"Well!" she said. "I wondered how long you could manage to stay away!"

"I just came to give you this back," he said. He opened his hand, and there was the silver cross.

"Then this thing that you were involved in, it's over?"

"Yes," said Marek. "And that cross . . . well, I don't really know what happened, but it saved my life, I promise you. And other people's lives, too."

"My mother gave it to me, before she died. It was given to her at her confirmation. She always used to tell me that it was lucky."

"It wasn't just lucky," said Marek. "It was magical."

"Why don't you have a coffee?" said the waitress. "On the house; for old times' sake."

"All right," said Marek, and sat down. The waitress brought his coffee and sat down opposite. "My mother was in the Home Army, during the war. She helped with the wounded, and she helped to take messages. She always used to tell this story about how she was crawling along the sewers one day, and she got caught in a tangle of barbed wire. The more she struggled, the more tangled she was. She was down in that sewer for two days and two nights, and she thought she was going to die.

"She said she started to cry. And after a while, she heard somebody crawling toward her. It was another child, she said, but a very strange child with a face like the infant Jesus.

"She said it stared at her for a long time, and then it unwound the wire and pulled her free. She managed to crawl along to a manhole cover, and climb out. She never told anyone in the Home Army what had happened to her, because she thought it was all a dream . . . a mirage, you know, because she was so frightened and thirsty. She thought she had dreamed about the infant Jesus coming to rescue her, although she had probably managed to unwind the wire by herself.

"Whenever she told me that story, she always used to say, 'He had such a sad, beautiful face. He touched me as if he thought that I was wonderful, just for being so ordinary; and that there was nothing more he wanted in the world to be ordinary like me.' "

Unaccountably, Marek found that he had tears in his eyes. The waitress reached across and squeezed his hand. "You look exhausted. You should sleep."

Marek nodded, and cleared his throat. "I just want you to know something," he said. "That story your mother told you . . . that was true."

"Yes," said the waitress, as if she wasn't in the least surprised.

Marek finished his coffee. "Your mother," he said. "Is she still alive?"

"Oh, no, she died nearly twenty years ago. She's buried in the Municipal Cemetery. They gave her a birchwood cross, like the rest of the insurgents. Ewelina Lysiak."

"The same name as you."

The waitress stood up, took his cup, and unexpectedly bent over and kissed his cheek. "We will always be here to look after you," she said. "Always."

It was three weeks later when Sarah entered the Cathedral of St. John on Kanonia, in the Old Town.

It was mid-morning, and the cathedral was suffused with sunlight. She genuflected to the altar, and then made her way forward through the nave.

Rej was kneeling next to the center aisle, his hands clasped together. She came between the pews like a woman walking through a field of rye, and knelt down next to him.

"Nadkomisarz Dembek told me you were out of hospital," she said. "How are you feeling?"

"Fine. My shoulder's still stiff. They took thirty-six pellets out of it."

"I've come to tell you that I'm leaving . . . going back to America."

He looked at her for a long while without saying anything, and then he nodded.

"It was Ben," she said. "He made my position here completely untenable. It was either resign or face the sack."

"Don't you worry about Ben," said Rej. "He'll get what's coming to him, one of these days."

"I shall miss Warsaw," Sarah told him. "I was beginning to feel that this was where I belonged." She paused, and then she added, "I shall miss you too."

"Well . . . I won't be here for much longer. They're retiring me. I'm thinking of buying a small farm somewhere." He nodded toward the altar. "I'm just giving thanks that I'm still alive; and that I didn't go through the whole of my life not believing in anything but Lenin."

He smiled, and then he said, "I was just trying to think of a way of giving thanks for what happened. It seems heartless to call it 'the Executioner' . . . it wasn't an executioner at all. He wasn't even an 'it.'"

"He was a child," said Sarah. "A very strange child, yes, and a very terrible child, too. A child who was chosen to do something that no child should ever have been chosen to do."

Rej looked away. "I think, in Poland, that has happened to far too many of our children, don't you?"

Sarah waited for a moment. Then she touched his shoulder, and turned, and walked away.

18

The Senate International Hotel was opened the following October, seven weeks ahead of schedule and $3.5 million under budget.

Three days after the gala opening, part of the suspended ceiling in the conference area collapsed, killing five people and seriously injuring another twenty-seven. Engineers blamed the collapse on sub-standard concrete and reinforcing rods that were far thinner than the recommended gauge.

Among the dead was Ben Saunders, Senate's president of Eastern European development. A ninety-kilo section of concrete had pinned him to the floor, before a huge sheet of plate-glass had dropped eleven meters from the ceiling and cut off his head.